THINKWELL BOOKS

THE U
OF R

CW01475890

Mark Newies was .... Northumberland in 1969. After earning a Liberal Arts degree from Northumbria University, he began his career in publishing and financial services in London. In 2002, he shifted paths and retrained as a teacher, completing a PGCE and going on to teach History in Scotland and abroad. Mark is the youngest of two children, and his parents now live in Scotland. *The Unburdening of Ruben Miles* is his debut novel, and he is currently working on its sequel.

'"Being in the trenches made me a harder person", we read a third of the way through this book. Getting to know Ruben Miles, the 106-year-old wiz and human oddity, is both satisfying and disturbing. His tales recount dark episodes first-hand from the 20th century, but also love, loss and laughter. This is a book with style, glamour and gristle.'

Andrina Kelly

'The more Ruben Miles unburdens himself, the more his audience – and by extension the reader – is forced to bear the load. This is a very clever novel by a writer who has obviously researched the events of the past century in great detail in order to bring them to life through the eyes of one unique character. Like Ruben Miles: unforgettable.'

Mark Liam Piggott, author of *Fire Horses*

'"I think I can use a man like you", we hear throughout this novel by Mark Newies. Such a line hints at choice, excitement, blind will of sorts, but mostly the random events at the core of one's life. We can control only so much. Ruben Miles, through that giant brain of his, witnesses and does things which an ordinary man could not comprehend. He is central to so much - 20th century happenings both terrifying and redeeming – and yet we feel for him in a strange, ineffable way.'

Abigail Finch

'The Somme. The Blitz. Babe Ruth. Charlie Chaplin. The Spanish Civil War. New York in the jazz-infested 1920s. Writer Mark Newies takes us places. Very rarely sweet, sensible caverns. Mostly speakeasies, trenches and side streets courtesy of the rough exchanges between gangsters and showgirls. What this book represents though is life in its often incoherent jib.'

Andrew Routledge

'I fell into this book. Not because of its grasp of history, but because the characters Newies creates are lively and unbecoming. The author has that knack of bringing out great dialogue from the multitude of people he invents. Overall this is a fine debut novel from a burgeoning prospect.'

Sean Thomas

'*The Unburdening of Ruben Miles* is the tale of a man needing to document his life. Needing to release not the emotions within him, but the simple matter of his existence and how it is judged by others. It is a fantastic achievement by an author coming to the boil.'

Jessica F, album Peachy, *youtube.com/@JessicaFMusic*

MARK NEWIES

THE

UNBURDENING

OF

RUBEN

MILES

THINKWELL BOOKS

Edited by Kieran Devaney.

Second Editor & Proofreader - Jeff Weston.
Cover design by Alejandro Baigorri.
Interior formatting by Rachel Bostwick.
Published by Thinkwell Books, U.K.
First printing edition 2025.

For Helen,

my love and inspiration

"It is the mark of an inexperienced man
not to believe in luck."

– Joseph Conrad

TABLE OF CONTENTS

PROLOGUE

I t starts, as always, as a loose fragment of a dream. His subconscious mind selecting seemingly random memories. He stirs in his untidy sheets, the opening of the mental wormholes prompting physical movement. Even at his great age, he is active while he sleeps. He kicks his legs and clenches his teeth in a futile attempt to stop the inevitable journey. The process is immediate as the neurones in his dysfunctional brain settle on their target, selecting a memory reel like a mechanical jukebox. His eyes snap open and the images flood his entire being.

He can feel the prickling of the uniform on his dry skin. The taste of fear cloying at the back of his throat. The sounds of the last of the artillery barrage on the warm summer morning. He can feel the thump of his teenage heart in his chest. He can see the terror in the wide eyes of his friend, John Burgess, as he fidgets with his shaking hands stood next to him in the oddly pristine trench. Then the intrusive shrill of the sergeant's whistle leads to the grasping of splintered step ladders. July 1st 1916. Another day that Ruben Miles can recall in infinite detail. Just like *every* other day of his life since he was eleven years old. But then, on all those other days he does not put a gun to the forehead of his best friend and pull the trigger.

It was during the next war that they discovered the truth about his memory. American scientists with the help of the odd German psychiatrist who looked more like Lenin than Freud. Their intrusive experiments are the only events that he can't recall. Something that he regards as a small blessing. It's not that he views his phenomenal memory as a curse as such, but surely every man should be free to forget some of the things he has done.

Highly Superior Autobiographical Memory (HSAM) does not afford a man the ability to forget. Nor does it grant the opportunity to ignore. The stark visual replays of his life can come at any time of the day, awake or unconscious. Ruben Miles prefers them when they come   him when he is awake, it's less of a shock that way. He can prepare himself somehow. It seems to soften the blows a little. At night he is completely at their mercy.

The memories can also gang up on him, disparate days of his life in one visit, especially at night.

An hour later, bolt upright and conscious, he is no longer in uniform. At least not a khaki one. He is dressed in a sharp Italian suit the Babe had made for him by his favourite tailor as a birthday gift in 1928. He has a list of errands in his hand, scrawled by his famous boss in his surprisingly ebullient script. Little surprised Ruben Miles about his superstar employer, but the expensive stationery for a list of humdrum chores was one.

October 29th 1929, would go down in Depression folklore as Black Tuesday. For Ruben Miles, it started with a list of the Babe's culinary and other daily requests to satisfy his unquenchable appetites and ended with his American life turned upside down for good.

He can smell the delights of the Italian bakery that produced the Babe's favourite cannoli. His mind revisits the images like a black and white kaleidoscope. But it is the emotions that hit harder than the visions. They seem to grow roots to his very core. He again experiences the hope that his wife, Rita, would forgive him for the Babe's crassness and constant sexual innuendos, as if the events had just happened and were not seventy-seven years before. Is it any wonder he does not like discussing how he feels?

No penniless former big shots hurled themselves from the tall buildings on Wall Street. That myth didn't gain traction for about a month. But the sense of panic was profound. People ran in circles as if it were the most logical of responses. Others gawped at the headlines in the afternoon papers, as if they were reading some crazed science fiction.

Ruben Miles finished his chores amid the chaos and headed back to the Babe's place on West 88th Street. He can hear his own footsteps on the marble floor of the reception and the ping of the elevator when it reached the twenty-second floor. Outside the apartment, he wondered why it was so quiet inside. It was never quiet when the Babe was home. Then he opened the door and stepped inside.

He could never make it stop by just willing it. He learnt that a long time ago. You had to sit it out. Sometimes he got lucky and he would snap out of it and be back in the present. This was one of those mornings, and he was grateful.

BEGINNINGS

2006

Ruben Miles was preparing for the weekly visit of his great grandson, Luke. Outside his front door, he could hear the communal lounge room TV blaring out another banal quiz programme. Today was the show he hated most, the one where the contestants seemed to attribute mythical qualities to picking arbitrary boxes with random numbers printed inside.

'Jesus,' he said, the last time he witnessed several of the inmates watching transfixed, hanging on every word of the messianic presenter, 'you might as well believe in a God.' Ruben Miles most certainly did not believe in a God. But he did believe in luck, and he supposed that picking random boxes was as pure a form of that as was possible.

Besides the TV, he could also hear the sound of Albert Thompson's wheelchair coming down the corridor. He could tell it was Albert's because of the distinct reverberation the heavy wheels made. Ruben Miles still had excellent hearing. He was less pleased with this sensory good fortune at night when he struggled for peace and sleep. He could hear every groan, fart and prayer through the neighbouring walls.

Ruben Miles was as lean as a greyhound, and in his younger days could almost catch them. His athleticism had got him out of, as well as *into*, plenty of morally dubious escapades. He stood about five foot nine in his stocking feet, although he was well over six feet in his prime. He has a full head of thick grey hair, matching stubble and ears that had grown to the size of tea saucers. He was dressed this late winter afternoon in what he referred to as his 'smart outfit'. But as he often reflected when he looked into the full-size mirror attached to his bathroom door by the last, vainer, inmate, it was all relative as he only had three different outfits.

Ruben Miles thought about what stories he could tell Luke today. He only had one rule: never tell him anything *factual* about his life, either personal or professional. He didn't want that family of his causing any more problems.

The boy had first started to visit as a means of getting out of school-inflicted cross country running, on the pretext of some worthy local community service. Luke hated sport more than he hated school. The unlikely pair had bonded over their mutual dislike of most of their extended shared family.

Their discussions had evolved an unusual, although set, pattern. Luke would ask his elderly relative about what it was like to live through certain times and events. Before each visit, Luke would come up with a random topic for them to discuss. After all, he reasoned, not everyone has access to an eyewitness for the entire twentieth century, albeit one who had spent the better part of the last decade swearing at Noel Edmonds in the TV lounge of The Apple Orchard Community for the Elderly.

After his first ever visit, Luke had sat on the bus back to Jesmond and marvelled at the fact that Ruben Miles must have started receiving his state pension in 1964. This meant his great grandfather had been officially old for forty-two years! How could a boy of sixteen get his head around that?

Ruben Miles always knew when Luke had arrived in reception, because of the predictable increase in noise. Residents with no regular young visitors, which accounted for over half of the cohort, would at first gawk at Luke and then bark seemingly random statements at him.

'I had cucumber yesterday.'

'The dimmer switch in my bedroom is broken.'

Luke's personal favourite from his last visit was the truly genre-defying:

'I can't find my thing and it smells funny.'

Ruben Miles always tried to save Luke from excessive discomfort by walking the twenty or so yards to the reception area. He walked at the pace of a man of seventy. As he arrived, he saw that Luke was surrounded by several bewildered inmates, some of whom were claiming Luke as their own visitor. A rather sad event that happened on most visits.

'Come on now, folks, let the boy be. He is here to see me, you daft old coots.'

This was Ruben Miles at his most respectful and conciliatory.

'Hello Ruben,' Luke replied as he manoeuvred his way out from the scrum of disconcerting pensioners.

'Come on now, folks, you don't want to miss any of Noel Edmonds.'

As they walked out of the communal lounge, Luke could not help but reflect that, for a man who claimed to despise Noel Edmonds, he sure as hell knew what time his programme started.

'Do you know any really smart kids at your school that are good at writing?'

Luke and Ruben Miles were sitting in the little cafe area of The Apple Orchard Community for the Elderly. They were drinking weak tea and eating digestive biscuits that were, at the very least, of questionable provenance.

Luke was not used to the old man asking him questions about his life. Most of their conversations pursued a predictable routine, one in which Ruben Miles clearly did not divulge any personal information, but instead was quite happy to discuss the random historical questions that Luke effortlessly conjured up about the twentieth century.

'The girl next door to me is ridiculously clever and must be a great writer. She told me the other day that she actually *loves* writing history essays.'

'So, are you two friends or...?'

'Friends, we're just friends.'

Luke Miles felt the now trademark reddening of his cheeks when he even thought about JoJo Bartlett. He was getting another beamer.

Ever since puberty kicked in when he was twelve, Luke Miles had been prone to what other kids in his school called 'beamers'. This was when Luke's entire face would go traffic light red, usually because of the mere mention of sex, or a girl that he liked. Infuriatingly, the more he tried to stop it, the redder he got.

The first time it happened was all because of Miss Watson, his Year Eight English teacher. It was an early summer day, not long before the school holidays, and the northeast basked in temperatures of nearly twenty degrees. Being a native north easterner, Miss Watson was therefore celebrating this rare event in a short summer dress and pink flip-flops. As a rule, young people are not very good at guessing adult ages and Luke Miles was no different. In his mind, Miss Watson was about twenty-five and was the first female that made him think about the differences between boys and girls. She had an ample chest and a flirtatious manner. If Luke Miles had known she was thirty-six, would it have made any difference?

Miss Watson had a habit of leaning back on her desk as she stood during chalk and talk lessons. She became quite animated in her educational meanderings, usually in the field of historical fiction. A combination of The Battle of Hastings, the little dress and a lack of concentration, meant that Luke Miles and Bruce Ferris, a fat kid who always smelled vaguely of fish, got a very good look up Miss Watson's dress.

Unfortunately for Luke Miles, his longstanding middle school nemesis, Marcia Taylor, had followed him into secondary school and was sat on the adjacent row and had taken in the full scene of Miss Watson's glory and the reaction of Luke Miles.

'Luke, stop looking up Miss's skirt, you perv.' Marcia Taylor said these damaging words very loudly to a quiet class.

Luke had struggled with his beamers ever since.

'You could meet her if you like, she asks about you all the time.'

Luke's great grandfather began to smile. He had one of those smiles that seem to take over his entire face. He flashed Luke another good look at his unfeasibly healthy teeth. Luke thought his great grandfather had better teeth than he did. Luke felt that this was definitely because his mad parents insisted on taking him to Dr Dacre, the alcoholic dentist that had taken four of Luke's teeth out by mistake when he was ten, and did not recommend a brace, thus ensuring that he was very self-conscious about his slightly bucked front teeth.

'And she isn't your girlfriend?'

'No, she is just a friend that happens to be a girl. This happens in the twenty-first century.'

Luke had never been snippy with his great grandfather before. He thought his latest beamer deserved some kind of response.

'I see,' said Ruben Miles.

They sat in silence for a few minutes, Luke pretending to enjoy his tea.

'I would be delighted to meet your... friend. Why does she want to meet an old duffer like me?'

'I have been telling her about our conversations, she is well into history. In fact, she was hoping you might be able to help her with a project of hers that she is doing on the suffragettes.'

'I knew a suffragette called Emily,' he said eventually.

'Emily Davison?'

Luke found that he could actually remember some school stuff if he did not try to.

'No, not that lunatic! The one I knew was called Emily Bainbridge. She was quite a girl...'

'Hang on, hang on. Can't you wait until JoJo comes? She really wants to hear about the suffragettes.'

Luke Miles did not appear to notice that this was the first time the old man had *ever* been prepared to share a personal anecdote about his own life.

And so, the two generations of Miles's, from parts of the family tree that would require an exceptionally large piece of paper, agreed to wait for the girl next door to grace them both with her presence.

JoJo Bartlett was, to the outside world, a confident, intelligent and happy seventeen-year-old from northern Britain. She appeared to thrive in a competitive school environment and had an unusually positive view of not just her parents, but her wider family. She appeared to be sensible and well adjusted.

However, JoJo Bartlett knew that she was living in complete denial. She had known this for as long as she could remember. She was just very good at hiding her true self from everyone that knew her. She had more phobias than she could remember. She even had a phobia about not remembering all her phobias. She had an irrational fear for most occasions, and more than one for many occasions. She shared none of this with anyone, even her seemingly close friends at the school that she pretended to love, but barely tolerated.

She even had her parents fooled. Jane and Sam Bartlett thought their daughter was as 'normal' as was possible for a teenager in the twenty-first century. Yes, she spent excessive time alone in her bedroom and had appalling taste in music (loud and crashy) and sometimes the fashion sense of a blind Ukrainian nun, but she was also happy(!), hardworking and respectful of others at all times. If the truth be told, Mr and Mrs Bartlett were a touch smug about their only child. If they were being even more truthful, they would have admitted that they loved hearing from their many friends of the recent catastrophes that their selfish children had inflicted upon them. No other family's debacle was too messy for the Bartletts to feel slightly superior about.

JoJo did not know what to make of Luke Miles. But JoJo did not know what she was to make of most things. They had started talking about a year ago, even though they had been neighbours for nearly four years. She seemed to recall that he was outside his house, washing the family car rather ineptly with a bucket and sponge. She had never really thought about him before and they had never really spoken. But there was something so admirably incompetent about the way he was tackling what was clearly a designated chore that demanded comment.

'Great job,' she found herself saying, as the boy looked himself up and down in the car window. He appeared to have more soapsuds on his head than were on the car.

'I offer a thorough and professional service.'

'Is it compulsory to be soapier than the car?'

This seemed to throw him for a second, but he eventually smiled and said,

'So, the girl next door... she speaks.'

Over the course of the next twelve months, they had graduated to hanging out with each other, usually in Luke's bizarrely clean bedroom and very occasionally in JoJo's equally sanitised version.

JoJo was intrigued by Luke's visits to see his elderly relative. She could not fathom the fact that he was well over a hundred years old and, not only was he relatively fit and well, but according to Luke, he was totally lucid and capable of talking about the past in great detail, although mysteriously never about his own personal life. These conversations were the beginning of her desire to meet the old man. Luke gave his great grandfather a glowing review.

'He's very interesting and tells me stuff that I would never have known about, like sheep rustling in Northumberland during the 1930s…'

JoJo was on the verge of asking Luke if she could come with him to meet his great grandfather, but then unexpectedly Luke ambushed her by asking about her boyfriend. She fled the scene like a horrified drunk driver. There were some conversations that she really did not want to have with Luke anytime soon.

Luke did get around to inviting JoJo to meet his great grandfather at their very next interaction, and she had been delighted to accept the invitation. She was intrigued about the old man generally, but also wanted to hear his firsthand account of a suffragette of his actual personal acquaintance. She had been so excited that she did not get even the slightest bit frustrated with Luke Miles when he did his usual, semi-coherent rant about the hatefulness of old people on the bus to Jesmond. Luke really hated old people. At least the ones he was not related to and who did not give him money for his birthday.

'They wear beige like all the time and they smell.'

He may be repetitive, but JoJo did have to concede that Luke was both a) usually pretty funny and b) had a point about most old people.

The Apple Orchard Community for the Elderly was a short

walk from the bus stop halfway down Osbourne Road. The only thing that slowed them down was having to weave between the seemingly ubiquitous university students with posh southern accents who seemed to parade up and down Osbourne Road as if they owned the place. In fact, it was their *parents* who owned a considerable amount of the place.

'Jesus,' offered JoJo as she listened to the incessant braying of the students.

But before she could expand further, they had arrived at The Apple Orchard Community for the Elderly.

'Wow! You didn't tell me that your old relative must be rich.'

Luke Miles conceded that it was certainly quite a posh and impressive building.

The reception area consolidated her first impression. It made her wonder whether Luke was visiting the old man to get his money.

After they had signed in with the well-groomed receptionist, Luke pointed the way towards his great grandfather's apartment and they headed off down the nearby corridor.

And then Ruben Miles appeared, seemingly from thin air. One of his trademark skills.

'Hello Luke, and this must be...?'

'JoJo,' replied Luke Miles, shaking his great grandfather's hand. This was how they greeted each other and said goodbye, after one half aborted hug that neither had any desire to repeat. The Miles lineage was not known for being tactile.

'Nice to meet you, Mr Miles.'

'Call me Ruben, please.'

They made their way to the community lounge area *without* a TV. This plan ensured they were on their own, even if they would have to endure the almost painful bamboo furniture. Luke volunteered to go and get the hot beverages from the overpriced café, leaving JoJo alone with Ruben Miles for approximately five minutes. It was enough time for the old man to make his unusual pitch.

'So, you're the girlfriend he keeps going on about.'

'Actually, we are just friends, I have a boyfriend, though, but he is not Luke.' JoJo Bartlett had absolutely no idea why she just shared this combustible information with an elderly stranger.

'Ah, does Luke know that?'

'Actually no, so I would appreciate it if you didn't tell him. I have been meaning to have that conversation with him for a while.'

Ruben Miles seemed to reflect on this for a second.

'What do I get out of that arrangement?'

'What?'

'Well, you get to avoid an embarrassing situation with my great grandson, but I appear not to benefit in any way. I have always believed that the best type of arrangements are win-win situations.'

He gave her one of his trademark smiles and she was indeed dazzled by how good his teeth were.

'We have just met and you want me to bribe you with something, so you won't say anything to Luke about my boyfriend?'

'Bribe is an ugly word, JoJo. I prefer 'incentivise'. You need to be quick, he will be back in a few minutes.'

'What exactly do you have in mind?'

'I have led an interesting life. Some would say very interesting. I am beginning to feel more tired these days and I get the feeling I may be finally on the way out. I would like to tell my life story before I pop my clogs.'

'And you want to tell it to me? Why not Luke?'

'You're not family. I do not want to tell my family. I have my reasons.'

'But you've only just met me.'

'You think I should ask one of the demented old fools in here? I don't get the chance to meet many new people these days. Luke tells me you are a keen historian, a good writer and very bright. That's good enough for me.'

JoJo was as open to flattery as most people are.

'So how would we do it? If I agree to this, I mean.'

Ruben Miles handed JoJo an envelope.

'There's a hundred pounds in there, you will need plenty of notebooks and maybe a little tape recorder. You can come and visit any day. I'm not going anywhere. I think we would need to start as soon as possible. There is a lot to say. I will pay you for your time of course, shall we say ten pounds an hour?'

The fact that his offer had been pre-planned before her arrival confused JoJo momentarily, but she was nothing if not quick-thinking.

'Believe me, you will want to hear what I have to say. It would make some book. You could make a small fortune.'

'I think fifteen pounds an hour would be more acceptable.'

JoJo had heard her father say a thousand times that you should never, ever, accept the first offer you were given.

Ruben Miles looked at her with a little more respect.

Luke Miles then returned, holding three cups precariously.

'We have a deal,' said the old man.

'What deal?' asked Luke.

'I have agreed to employ your friend here with my project. I want to tell her my life story.'

Luke set the cups down on the coffee table and wondered whether he should be pleased with recent events.

'There is one condition though,' the old man continued. 'You need to promise not to discuss my story with Luke, or God forbid any of the other members of the family, until after my... demise.'

They spent the next twenty minutes of the visit making small talk about the unusual habits of some of the residents, not to mention the staff. Ruben Miles was able to describe their actions and movements with almost clinical precision. JoJo was thinking over the odd proposal from Ruben Miles. It did sound like it might be interesting, and she could feel the envelope and the money in her pocket.

Then the old man changed tack quickly.

'OK, so I seem to recall you wanted to know about the suffragette I knew when I was a kid. Well, not really a kid, I was about Luke's age.'

And so, the old man talked about Emily Bainbridge for the first time in over eighty years.

EMILY BAINBRIDGE

1914

'I met Emily Bainbridge about the time I had to leave the Royal Grammar School, a few months before the Great War started. I remember the suffragettes marching through Newcastle with their Flags flying. I remember they were making a fuss that day because Lloyd George was visiting. I don't think he was Prime Minister then, but he was still a big nob. Thousands of people turned up just to see him. I was there but I saw nothing, I was too far away.'

Emily had got arrested that day for throwing stones at Lloyd George as he disembarked at the Central Station. She was jailed for three months. The rich women she was with who threw the *first* stone got a caution. Ruben Miles had tried to ingratiate himself by pointing out this disparity when he next saw Emily, but to no avail.

'Did you meet any of the famous ones?' JoJo asked.

'You know that the nutter that threw herself at the King's horse during the derby is buried in Morpeth? She was from Longhorsley, you know...'

'Yes, our teacher mentioned that about Emily Davison. Apparently, she was not trying to kill herself. They reckon now that she was trying to pin a suffragette scarf to the king's horse to gain publicity.... Did you know her?'

'No, she was a lot older than the suffragette I knew. I remember her funeral though; they brought the coffin up from London on the train. The Emily I knew was far more interesting and just as brave, or stupid, depending on your viewpoint.

'I met Emily Bainbridge when I was fifteen, she was a year older. I was working part-time as a clerk at Armstrong, Whitworth and Co at Elswick; it's where they built all the big ships. The company was founded by Lord Armstrong in the mid Nineteenth Century, that's the same bloke who built Cragside and most of the University... he went to the RGS as well by the way.'

JoJo was instantly amazed by the seemingly total recall of

Ruben Miles. He spoke clearly and with an even, pleasant tone. If she shut her eyes, she would have thought that he was not much older than her parents.

'He even donated Jesmond Dene to the city. Emily was the daughter of a Bainbridge, although I can't remember which one. Bainbridge's was the John Lewis of its day; in fact, I think they took it over in the 1950s. So she came from money and went to a private school in Yorkshire, unusual for girls back then.'

'How did you first meet?'

'At the races. It was Northumberland Plate Day, 1913. I remember I backed the winner... Mynora, 6-1. She was a striking looking girl, Emily, and quick as a whip. She spilt my tea as we watched the horses in the parade ring and we got to talking. She was glad of the distraction; she was someone who did not see eye to eye with her family. Her father threatened to disown her when she joined the suffragettes.'

Ruben Miles paused as Mrs Maynard, the manager of The Apple Orchard Community for the Elderly, came into the family visiting room and offered them a complimentary plate of biscuits. Luke took the plate with thanks and Mrs Maynard left. Luke noted that his great grandfather always stopped mid-conversation when any member of staff came in. This also went for other inmates.

'We started courting after that. I remember we went to the Hoppings the week after we met. It was held at the racecourse then, not on the town moor. I can still smell the toffee apples. Emily wore a blue check dress; it was a lovely early summer evening and we kissed on the tram on the way back to the city.'

JoJo was pleased that she knew that the Hoppings was the huge traveling fun fair that came to the town moor every June. Clearly, the travellers had been coming for a long time.

'She was a total hothead of course, always flying off the handle. We rowed a lot, but we usually made up pretty quickly. I'm not too sure how she first started with the Suffragettes, but she did seem pretty tight with Audrey Brown, whose mother was quite high up in the local movement, I think. Anyway, she looked much older than sixteen and used to go on all the marches and demonstrations, she got arrested the first time for swearing at a copper on Grey Street. I think the second time was for chaining herself to the railings in front of the law courts.'

Ruben Miles smiled as he thought of Emily and her passion. It had been many years since he had thought about her. He realised that he did not smile as much as he used to, but then again, when you are as close to rotting in the ground as he thought he must be, there was not that much to smile about.

'They put her in jail for two months when she hit old Lloyd George with a stone outside the central station. I didn't see it, but apparently she hit him right on the forehead, came up like a golf ball! It took three coppers to restrain her. She did her time at Morpeth jail, funny enough. She went on hunger strike on the first day and, mind, Emily did not have any spare weight to lose. They force fed her after a fortnight. She said the pain was indescribable. She said if childbirth was worse, then she was not going to have any kids.'

Emily Bainbridge had been the first love of Ruben Miles. Albeit a slightly scary and unpredictable first love. Although they only courted for three months, it was enough time to place a small bruise on what was going to turn out to be the very resilient heart of Ruben Miles. It was the first time that he realised that you could not always get what you wanted and that you could not always get people to do what was right for them, no matter how hard you tried.

When she was released from Morpeth jail in the early summer of 1914, she was weak and even more bloody-minded than before she lobbed the stone at Lloyd George. Ruben Miles had cautioned her about her role in the movement, foretold her that events could be her undoing. Although she appeared to listen and would give Ruben Miles a large smile and a squeeze of the hand, she simply told him that he worried too much and that she would be fine. Besides, she would say, we will have the vote soon and that will be that.

Emily Bainbridge took the suffragettes motto 'Deeds not Words' very seriously. She fell out with the older suffragists in a matter of hours, as she felt that writing letters and getting petitions signed was a waste of time. After all, she reasoned at the first meeting she attended, had those tactics not just been ignored for fifty years? Emily felt she was a suffragette at least in spirit before the Pankhursts broke away to form their more militant group. Despite her youth, her fellow campaigners took Emily Bainbridge very seriously. They admired her intellect, reason and passion. Before long, she was one of the campaign coordinators, suggesting and planning acts of civil disobedience. She was one of four young women who slashed pictures in the City's Laing gallery. As we have discovered, she served time in jail for assaulting Lloyd George with an offensive pebble and had suffered the pain and indignity of being force fed. It was the memories of this humiliation that were to drive her further in her campaign.

Emily Bainbridge took a dim view of both religion and the people foolish enough to swallow its mumbo jumbo. So, when Mary Stuart, the treasurer of the local office, spent ten minutes at a weekly campaign meeting haranguing the Church of England clergy for not backing the campaign for women's suffrage and equality more fervently, Emily spied an opportunity. What better way to outline the cowardice of organised religion than by setting fire to churches? It had not been an easy sell. Although outraged by the church's lack of official support, many in the Newcastle branch of the Women's Social and Political Union (WSPU) were God-fearing Christians, or at least the next best thing: hypocrites.

Compromise was not an easy bedfellow for Emily Bainbridge. However, after several hours of repetitive and increasingly screechy debate, a resolution of sorts was agreed. There was to be a campaign of arson on churches, but these acts must take place at least forty miles away from the parish of Newcastle-upon-Tyne. The logic of this plan was minimal, the reality being that several of the committee did not want to be robbed of a regular, comfortable place of worship. After all, was there anywhere better to catch up on all the local gossip than at church on a Sunday morning? Although disappointed by the transparent self-interest of some of the committee, Emily Bainbridge was at least gratified that she could unleash some of her unbridled outrage in the direction of the almighty.

Ruben Miles was not impressed with the plan when he was

informed of Emily's intentions over cod and chips in Tynemouth on a bustling, breezy Sunday afternoon in July 1914.

But Emily refused to engage in any discussions on the tactics or actions of the campaign. She would tell him what they were doing, but not enter into further discussion.

You do not need too much of a clever plan to set fire to churches. Some petrol and a box of matches cover all the bases.

Why Emily selected a rural church in the East Lothian countryside a few miles outside of North Berwick, and a very long way from anywhere meaningful, has never really been explained. The fact that Whitekirk was in Scotland, and therefore had precisely nothing to do with the Church of England and its recent criticisms of the suffragette movement also seems baffling. Emily never got the chance to explain her reasoning.

Emily had assured Ruben Miles that the plan was not to get caught. She had seen enough of the penal system and its treatment of political prisoners for any lifetime. The force feeding had mentally, if not physically, scarred Emily Bainbridge and had hardened her resolve for the campaign to become more explosive. So once the deed was done, she was to flee and then use the local press to take responsibility for, and give justification for, her actions.

Despite looking as if they would be difficult to burn, churches, it seemed to Emily Bainbridge, were very compliant. She had made her plans. She was able to walk into the church with her basket of required goods on her arm. She had been able to ascertain that the church was deserted pretty much every day but Sunday. The rector of Whitekirk lived off site, and besides, was more often than not marinated in pale sherry by early afternoon, so clearly was not going to cause Emily any issues. She doused the spartan wooden pews with petrol; she also threw newspaper around the pulpit. She retreated to the main entrance of the church, took a quick look outside at the silent countryside and struck a handful of matches.

'So, she burnt the church down?' JoJo said when Ruben Miles stopped talking.

'Not entirely, and she was never able to take credit for her actions, at least if credit is the right word. I never saw Emily again as she simply disappeared, vanishing off the face of the earth. There were a lot of rumours of course, even some alleged sightings.'

'Did you ever find out what happened to her?'

'Some years later I heard that her father had followed her to the church, he had been on her case for weeks. He had a doctor with him. After she had set fire to the church, and I have no idea why he waited for her to set fire to the church. He captured Emily and he and the doctor took her away. They had her committed to an asylum up in the Highlands. It was quite easy back then, especially if you wanted to get rid of a disappointing wife or, in this case, a scandalous daughter.'

'That's terrible, I mean I know she set fire to a church but was anyone injured?'

'No and the church was not seriously damaged.'

'So, what happened to Emily eventually, do you know?

The old man's face darkened.

'The doctors gave her a lobotomy, so I was told. Do you know what that is?'

'No.'

'It's a brain operation of a very crude type, it turns the person into a vegetable. They can barely dress themselves, never mind speak.'

The old man had tears in his eyes as he spoke.

'The punchline is that the suffragette's whole campaign was called off several weeks later with the outbreak of war. If I had just talked her out of this one act, this one stupid act, then she could have lived out the rest of her life with all her faculties. It took me many years to realise that just one decision can have unfathomable consequences. For Emily, that decision to burn down a church in southern Scotland was the last meaningful decision she ever got to make.'

JoJo and Luke both looked a little stunned. Luke had been

silent throughout the story.

'Is this all true?' he said finally.

'Of course it's bloody true! Why would I make up such a story?'

Luke looked suitably chastened.

The old man turned to JoJo.

'Now you can see why I don't want to tell my story to a relative.'

JoJo was transfixed. She was unusually emotionally intelligent and knew when she was being lied to. She got no sense of this from Ruben Miles.

'I would love to hear your life story,' she said. 'If this story is anything to go by.'

'Believe me, JoJo, the story of poor Emily Bainbridge is only a tiny part of my story. That is the only reason why I was allowing Luke to be here to hear it. The rest is strictly for non-family only. Do you promise to honour that?'

She readily agreed. Luke, for his part, was apparently neither offended nor disappointed to be excluded from the project.

'But I can still visit you, right?'

'Of course! Your visits are the thing I look forward to most. I just don't want you to think badly of me and hearing my story might do that.'

'That sounds ominous. Have you done some bad things?'

JoJo loved a bit of true crime.

'There will be plenty of time for you to judge me on the things I have done, JoJo. Can we start as soon as possible? I'm not getting any younger.'

'I can come back tomorrow.'

'Great, we will start with my childhood, and particularly my parents. Like most people, I think my parents at least partially explain who I am and how my story unfolds.'

The following day, JoJo arrived punctually at ten in the morning and Ruben Miles talked about his childhood and his parents to another human being for the very first time.

ROOTS AND BRANCHES

1899

The father of Ruben Miles was an often predictable but mostly talentless man. However, he was a man blessed with good fortune and had the rare quality of not upsetting people, whatever his shortcomings. These traits had served him well. They landed him a fine and undeserved wife. Mary Montgomery could have married her pick of the local landed gentry. Instead, and ultimately only to spite her aged and wholly prejudiced father, she had decided on the ambitious and handsome young Jacob Miles. Ultimately, her dubious decision-making landed Jacob Miles the honour of becoming Mayor of Morpeth in the fine county of Northumberland in February 1899. Jacob Miles was not an overly numerate man, but was it a coincidence that his only son was born exactly nine months to the day he was sworn into his mayoral robes? He thought not.

For a man who had spent the previous six years of marriage quietly bemoaning his lack of progeny, the birth of Ruben Miles did not elicit much of an excited response from his father. Indeed, on those rare occasions when Ruben Miles thought all the way back to his early childhood, he could conjure little more of his father than an image of him sat at the dining room table after a substantial repast, stroking a fat cat he called Tiddles and simultaneously breaking wind and belching. Even at the age of seven, Ruben Miles was grateful that his chores did not include responsibility for the family washing.

If his early memories of his father were meagre and unsatisfying, his mother promoted more substantial recollections. For reasons that took Ruben Miles a long time to unravel and even longer to understand, his mother seemed to be completely ambivalent at the presence of her only child. She seemed neither to love nor loathe him. As she was a social, extroverted and controversial local presence when outside the Miles family home, her near catatonic demeanour inside its well decorated walls was a source of great confusion to the young Ruben Miles.

He was born in the local cottage hospital, during a ferocious early winter storm in late November 1899. Mary Miles had insisted on not giving birth at home, quite a rarity in the late Victorian era. The day's newspapers were full of the Boer's siege of Ladysmith in Natal. He was christened Ruben Henry Miles; Henry, after his mother's father and Ruben because his father had once met a man called Ruben in Berwick-upon-Tweed. The man was a sailor from some obscure part of the Austro-Hungarian Empire and Jacob Miles had admired both the name and the man for their rather mystical qualities. That and the ferocious handjob he bequeathed in the toilets of a local hostelry.

He was a child that did not merely suffer from colic but seemed to positively rejoice in it. Whether this was a cause, or a symptom of his mother's ambivalence is unsolvable. With no siblings or maternal affection to rely on for entertainment, the young Ruben Miles immersed himself, like so many only children, in a world of spectacular imagination.

While the fledgling Ruben Miles conjured Arthurian knights and Zulu hordes to his bedroom ramparts, Jacob Miles went about his business of accruing money via a variety of semi-legal means. As a mayor of a prosperous rural market town, he was able to personally benefit in a variety of worthwhile and low risk schemes and corrupt practices. Sheer good fortune was a recurring theme for Jacob Miles, and the easy corruptibility of the local constabulary was impressive, even by the standards of the day. Indeed, Morpeth had prided itself on being the last borough in the whole of the northeast to form a constabulary, and although The County and Borough Police Act was passed in 1856 and forced all local authorities to create a local police force, the town's attitude to policing remained lax at best. The townsfolk of Morpeth, like the rest of Victorian England, were much attached to their laissez-faire and self-help ideologies.

As Mayor of the town, Jacob Miles was entitled to a small share of the regular and thriving cattle market. He had enough common sense to share a portion of this with Neville Ashton, the senior police officer for the town and borough. This act of apparent largesse had allowed a multitude of other small backhanders and questionable practices to flourish. This made Jacob Miles a relatively wealthy man for one born of average middle-class stock. As a child, Ruben Miles could detect a certain grudging respect for his father from neighbours. They respected his luck, if nothing else. He may not have been talented, but Jacob Miles was far from being a stupid man, and this. coupled with his undoubted good fortune, allowed him and his family to flourish.

This manifested itself most significantly for Ruben Miles when his father decided, at the time of his eighth birthday, to send him to the Royal Grammar School in Newcastle-upon-Tyne. Founded in the mid Sixteenth Century, and one of the best schools in all of the north, this afforded the young master Ruben with a potential education unlike any provided for the local children who stubbornly refused to acknowledge him when he played outside. As he started the school as a day pupil only, it meant a slightly tiresome commute from the family home in Newgate Street in Morpeth, via the local railway station into the grand Central Station in Newcastle and then on, by the surprisingly efficient and speedy tram service that opened in 1901, to Eskdale Terrace in Jesmond. His mother accompanied him on the journey for the first week. He could still recall the harsh prickle of the coarse material of his trousers on his little legs, nearly one hundred years after their effect. His mother barely acknowledged his presence during the hour-long journey, instead spending the time politely chatting with other passengers and to Ruben Miles's young eyes, a suspiciously long time talking with the young train conductor Mr North. There was something about the nature of their whispered conversation that troubled Ruben Miles, without him being able to ascertain why.

He took to the academic side of the RGS immediately. He was instantly both impressed and cowed by the stern, viciously intelligent teachers. He devoured all the subjects with equal passion and, whilst not exactly becoming a pet of the masters, for no such animal existed, he was certainly treated with a mild form of benevolence which was about as far as the teaching faculty would allow for the times. Even the other students seemed to tolerate his presence, and Ruben Miles did not have any scarring memories of bullying or humiliation so common among other students from independent schools he met later in life. By the time he was eleven years old, Ruben Miles had become a fully-fledged week boarder and led a relatively uncomplicated existence. He thrived at school, at least academically, and at weekends came home to an unloving, or at best dysfunctional, family.

Ruben Miles's mother was certainly not as careful as she should have been. Although she was born in 1869, she was more of a 1969 type of girl. She was a nymphomaniac before anyone in Morpeth even knew the term. She had been aged thirty for little over a week when her only child was born. A little old for a first-time mother when Queen Victoria was still the ruler of all she stubbornly surveyed. Mary herself was amazed that she had carried the child to term. She had felt sure that the three painful and wholly unhygienic backstreet abortions she had procured in the mean streets of the west end of Newcastle would have made her infertile. She was therefore surprised, as well as reluctantly grateful, for her only child's birth. She was a very pragmatic woman and the increasing rumours of her lively social diary were beginning to be difficult to keep from the ears of Jacob Miles. Thus, she deduced that giving her tiresome husband the child he seemed to crave was the best course of action. She liked fucking her many lovers, but she certainly did not want to be taken care of by any of them. Mary Miles, it is fair to say, liked the rougher approach to lovemaking and found her numerous partners among the lower of the social order. She was particularly fond of farm labourers, especially if they could barely speak and were lax with their daily ablutions.

Mary Miles had been confident that Jacob Miles had been the father of the boy. She spent the dullest, longest and most frustrating three months of her life making love only to her husband. She had been relieved when she became pregnant and, a rarity in those days, partook in no alcoholic beverages throughout her term. The birth had been an ordeal that she had not fully prepared for, and she was in labour for nearly twenty-four hours. When the nurse from the cottage hospital offered the as yet unnamed Ruben Miles up for maternal inspection, Mary

Miles waved them both off with exhausted disdain. She might have given Jacob Miles a son, but she was already convinced that she wanted as little to do with him as possible.

Mary allowed the boy to be called Ruben even though she disliked the unusual and foreign sounding name; her husband had been most insistent.

'It is a majestic name,' he had said by way of his only explanation.

The child cried incessantly from the moment he was born until, as far as Mary Miles could recall, he was about five years old. At that point and quite suddenly, he stopped as if he simply had run out of tears. By then, Mary Miles had long since come to the conclusion, as she had always suspected she would, that motherhood was not only a bore, but rather got in the way of one's other interests. It is why she employed local girl, Celia Wood, as a twenty-four hour live in housekeeper and nanny.

As soon as Celia was in place, Mary Miles resumed her extracurricular activities with some haste and aplomb. However, her lack of care was her downfall. Jacob Miles had long since known of his wife's appetites and habits from early in their marriage. But as he had his own illicit secrets to keep, he had been more than content to look the other way. However, he was not prepared to countenance with being made to look both a cuckold *and* a fool.

Mary Miles should have had more sense than to be caught in flagrante delicto, especially by three women and an eleven-year-old girl, who happened to be the cousin of her chosen partner for the day. The fallout was too much to keep from both neighbours and her husband. Jacob Miles played the role of shocked and outraged husband well; in fact he had composed such a response many years ago when he astutely realised that his wife's behaviour had an ultimately inevitable outcome. He ranted and screamed his way through a rehearsed monologue of the betrayed and bereft. Mary Miles watched her husband's behaviour with sceptical eyes; she had never seen such passion from him before, not ever. She correctly questioned its legitimacy, though only internally. It was at this juncture that he struck out at her once, catching her hard on the right cheek with an animated slap. It did not hurt, but it was at that precise moment that Mary Miles decided to get rid of her husband. She was nothing if not decisive.

For his part, Jacob Miles was satisfied. He felt that he had pitched his level of outrage just right. He was also gratified that his wife seemed to know little of his own, although less frequent, unsavoury secrets. Although he would never claim to know his wife or her thoughts well, he felt certain that she would have fought fire with fire if she had been privy to *his* indiscretions. He was of the view that his offer of reconciliation, made immediately after his solitary slap, as long as she mended her ways, was believable. His only displeasure was that the boy had come back from school a little early and had undoubtedly heard some of the commotion and the act of violence.

It took less than a week for Mary Miles to come up with a plan. As she had no desire to end up at the end of a hangman's rope, she deliberated slowly and carefully. Because of the local gossip, and despite the lackadaisical approach of the local constabulary to even the most serious cases, Mary decided that an obvious accident was the only sure way of avoiding all or at least most reasonable suspicion. Like most men of early middle age, Jacob Miles was a man of meticulous routine and Mary drew up a scheme that could take the fullest advantage of those facts.

Ruben Miles was given a scarf for his twelfth birthday by his mother. It was the only time that he recalled her buying him a personally chosen gift. He loved the bold green colours and the impressive tartan of the clan MacArthur. He even enjoyed its excessive size. They had bought it together on a fine autumn Saturday morning, in Rutherford's, the splendid department store newly opened on Morpeth High Street. Neither he, nor anyone else in the Miles family, had any connection with the clan MacArthur, but Ruben Miles loved the colour, design and feel of his scarf. It was not until he was much older that he realised that the reason he was so attached to the scarf was that it was the solitary token of affection he received from his aloof mother.

He wore the scarf boldly every day on his way to and from school. Now that he was experienced at the route, and because his mother had no desire to accompany him, he travelled alone. He was thus wearing the scarf on the day he walked in on his mother and father having a huge fight. Ruben Miles could not hear what the argument was about. He just recalled he was a little frightened after he saw his father lash out at his mother and that he ran off to his room. He had never seen them quarrel before.

The next morning, being a Saturday, meant Ruben Miles was at home. His father was nowhere to be seen, not unusual for any day, but especially at the weekend. His mother was sitting in the parlour, sipping tea when he entered the room. She smiled at him as he came in; he remembered that because of its rarity. She wanted to talk to him about something important.

When he thought of those days, Ruben Miles remembered the attention and genuine care that his mother showed to him. She had told him not to worry about what he had seen. The fight was much less serious than it looked. His father had not meant to hit her and he was a good man. He was not to listen to anything the neighbours might be saying. Mary Miles spent nearly two weeks reassuring her son that all was well. During this period, Ruben Miles often heard his father in the house but never saw him. But he was at least comforted by the familiarity of the sounds. From his morning bathing to his last cigarette of the day. He always enjoyed the latter in the back garden, down the parlour steps, every night, rain or shine. Jacob Miles could be tracked almost to the second.

For his part, Jacob Miles was pleased with the way things were settling down after what he chose to call the 'unpleasant episode.' His wife, although reserved and formal with him as normal, had acquiesced to his need for a recantation of her past behaviour and a vow of marital normality and courtesy. Indeed, two weeks after the slap, he felt that life was returning to some kind of parity. His income streams were flowing, his alcohol consumption was manageable and he had met a discreet young man locally; all were fine reasons for Jacob Miles to be cheerful.

Jacob Miles was an alcoholic, although of the functioning kind. Every day he managed to work his way slowly through the equivalent of half a bottle of whiskey. A fair proportion of this was consumed in the Black Bull Hotel on Bridge Street, between eight and 10pm. He varied only his choice of poison. This ensured that by the time he returned home at approximately half past ten, after he had taken an unsteady walk along the River Wansbeck to the family home on Newgate Street, he was more than pleasantly 'refreshed'. He took the back-river route because he had always loved the sound of running water, it reminded him of his youth, when he would be tucked up in bed listening to the sound of his mother filling a bath with buckets of lukewarm water next door. This longer route did offer another potential obstacle in the form of the stepping stones that forded the river and needed to be crossed to get home. He had never fallen in, though he had drunkenly made the crossing hundreds of times. He was oddly proud of this record and would tell himself that if he was able to cross the stepping stones, then he was not really drunk.

On the night of Wednesday 27th June 1911, out of kilter with his usual routine, he was late to leave the Black Bull. He had unwittingly become involved in a game of five card stud poker with some of the bar regulars. This meant that, although he was over half an hour past his normal leaving time, he was heading out with much heavier pockets than when he arrived. In Jacob Miles's experience, the more a man wants to gamble, the less accomplished he is at it. His good fortune and a thimble or two more of the fine brandy he was quaffing these days, meant he attempted a whistle as he meandered his way along the river route. Up in the distance, too far to be seen, even in the moonlit early summer night, a small shadow stood behind a tall ash tree, just two short strides from the stepping stones. In their hands, they held a green tartan scarf.

Ruben Miles was woken by his mother the next morning with a cup of tea, a unique experience. She sat primly on the edge of the bed and proffered forward his favoured hot and sweet tea. He was still half asleep when she said,

'There has been a terrible accident. Last night your father tripped, hit his head and fell into the river. He is dead.'

Ruben Miles did not know what he should say, so he said nothing. Instead, he took a big gulp of his tea and burned his mouth so badly that he had to spit the hot liquid all over his mother. To her credit, she did not bat an eyelid. She simply took out a handkerchief that she carried always and patted herself down.

'Let's not make a big fuss now, son, you're not a kid anymore.'

That was as much compassion as he was granted.

'And Celia has gone away for a few days to Scotland, her mother is poorly again. So, if you want breakfast you will need to help yourself.'

Celia had been in the house all of Ruben Miles's life. He was much closer to her than either of his parents. She was the one who fed him, washed his clothes and looked after him when he was poorly. She was also the only one who ever showed him any affection. She would often give him a hug when he was upset, as long as his parents were not around, as they both strongly disapproved of any action that could be deemed as 'spoiling the boy.'

'Is she coming back?'

'Of course, we could not cope without her. We will need her even more now that your father is gone.'

'Poor father,' Ruben Miles said.

'Drunken old fool,' replied his mother.

His mother then got up from the bed and walked the short distance to the bedroom door. She then pulled the door open and began to leave, only to pause, turn and say very quietly, 'If anyone asks you, Ruben, perhaps a policeman, I think it would be much better if you did not mention the fight your father and I had last week. I would not want anyone to think your father was a bad man. Is that understood?'

'Yes, mother,' said Ruben Miles, and he began to think about what he could cobble together for his breakfast.

An hour later, as he was eating a rather stale ham sandwich, Ruben Miles could hear his mother whispering in the hallway to an unidentified person. Ruben Miles did not know why he did not tell his mother what he saw and knew. His mother had assured him that financially they would be well taken care of, as his father was quite wealthy and this seemed to be a far more pertinent issue than what he had witnessed. Ruben Miles was also very aware of the fact that his deceased father had not improved his daily life one iota, so what was there to miss?

As Mary Miles had a damning list of extra-curricular activities, the good folk of Morpeth had plenty of questions about the watery demise of their less than venerated town Mayor. It would seem that conspiracy theories are not just a modern phenomenon.

The local constabulary were as lazy as they were incurious. A habitual drunk, found face down in the River Wansbeck, next to the notoriously unpredictable stepping stones, did not require a visit to 221B Baker Street for prolonged discussions. Even if he was the town mayor.

However, the local populace were a good deal more animated. For a start, the town was abuzz with talk about the sums of money wagered and lost in the pub poker game. Several witnesses told everyone they could that an unsteady Jacob Miles left the Black Bull with over five pounds in winnings, a substantial sum in those days.

The police said Jacob Miles possessed only a set of house keys and a purple bump on his forehead, in keeping with hitting one's head off a stone, when he was found face down in two feet of water the morning after his demise. The local newspaper, *The Morpeth Herald*, claimed on its front page that there was no evidence of foul play, but its failure to mention the poker winnings meant few bought the flow of their argument. The editor had taken the view that, as the only witnesses to the card game were the town's ne'er-do-wells and villains, the population could do without the besmirching of the good name of the town because of the unseemly demise of its corrupt head official. The fact that said editor, Michael Forsyth, had been on the receiving end of a monthly retainer from the good mayor to prevent 'unfortunate' stories of local malpractice and corruption was surely coincidental.

The local gossip told a different and more diverse picture. The cold and unpopular Mary Miles playing a significant role in most of the less kind interpretations. This was *before* the townsfolk got wind of the not inconsiderable life insurance policy.

'What do you think happened to your father?'

JoJo Bartlett had a dark chocolate digestive halfway to her lips when Ruben Miles said something that halted prematurely its planned destination. They were alone in the uncomfortable communal sitting room of The Apple Orchard Community for the Elderly, the sound of a buzzing floor cleaner in the adjacent hallway the only disturbance. For reasons that Ruben Miles could not articulate, he felt his private quarters were *not* the appropriate place for his first session with JoJo.

'Oh, I saw what happened clearly, I just did not tell anyone.'

'You saw the accident that killed your father?'

'It was no accident. I even saw who killed him, and with my bloody scarf!'

JoJo gave up on the biscuit.

'You saw your father get strangled? With a scarf? Your scarf?'

'It might have been dark, but there was a full moon and I could see quite clearly. My eyes have always been good, even at night. They still are, mostly. But he wasn't strangled. It was quite clever really. She knew what his route would be, knew he would be pissed as a fart and that he would not see the scarf at ankle height.'

'She? Your mother killed your father... with a scarf?'

'It wasn't my mother. I would have given my mother up, I think.'

The old man thought about this comment for a moment and then changed his mind.

'Actually, I don't think I would have. I would have been an orphan and sent to the new orphanage on Pottery Bank, not anyone's notion of a positive development in 1911.'

JoJo digested this thoughtfully. She really did love a bit of true crime.

'It must have been a girlfriend or the nanny. Maybe your nanny *was* his girlfriend.'

Ruben Miles's face betrayed the fact that this set of circumstances had never occurred to him before.

'Is that possible?'

'That is something that I have never given much thought to before, but considering the one conversation I had with Celia many years later, it's not plausible.'

'What do you mean?'

'I thought Celia might be in love with my *mother*, not my father. She almost told me as much, years later.'

The old man certainly seemed to come from an interesting family.

There was no gossip about Celia the nanny, despite the fact that she disappeared up to Scotland for a month the very night of the murder, at least according to Mary Miles. Instead, the fingers were pointed in one predictable direction. Unpopularity is a dangerous commodity in any small town. For her part, Mary Miles seemed as thick skinned as they come. The fact that she had an alibi constructed with the assistance of the local vicar and a dozen upstanding local middle-class women may have been enough to convince the Morpeth constabulary about her innocence, if not the near pitchfork-toting locals. Her one question was: who had told them about the life insurance policy? She thought that had been only known to herself and her unfortunate late husband. He had been most convivial on the subject when she had raised the issue the previous spring.

'What did you see?'

JoJo had turned on the tape recorder and checked that the little red light was on.

'My father walked into the intended trap singing that he was Henry the Eighth. The scarf, *my* scarf, was tied between trees adjacent to the footpath, sending him sprawling forward toward the water, as was its intention. He hit his forehead on a protruding stone with a sickening crack and went face down in the water.'

'Did you not think to help him?'

'I don't think so, it all happened quite quickly, but then Celia came out from behind the big sycamore she had been hiding behind. She checked that no-one was about. I was safely hidden away behind a garden wall by this point and then very calmly she walked toward my father and, as he showed small signs of movement, held him firmly by the back of his head in the water and pressed down until he completely stopped moving.'

'Goodness, she actually drowned your father.'

'I then saw her take some things out of his jacket pocket, but I could not see what, and then very nonchalantly strode off into the night in the direction of our house.'

'Not your average viewing for a twelve-year-old.'

'I should hope not.'

'You must have told your mother?'

'I nearly did several times, but it never came out. I suppose I was a bit in love with Celia. I may have only been twelve but that is old enough to…'

'Quite,' said JoJo and that seemed to stop the old man from saying whatever else he was just about to confess.

'Besides, the next morning my mother spoke to me and when she told me that my father had died, she made it very clear to me that we were much better off without him, in every conceivable way. And that although we should show everyone how sad we were, we should not be asking any *awkward* questions or giving what she called *controversial* opinions on what may have happened.

'So, you didn't let on?'

'No and I know this makes me look very bad, but I did not like my father much and when I got over the shock of what I saw,

I thought that actually it was not the end of the world.'

'I see,' said JoJo, although she was well aware that she did not.

'Why did Celia do it, do you think?

'I think my mother got her to do it. She seemed to have a very strong hold on Celia, something as a kid I did not understand or question.'

The gossip amongst the townsfolk certainly concurred with that conclusion. Even after the local vicar gave a sermon on the dangers of spreading false accusations, from the pulpit of the Methodist Church on Howard Road, three days after the event. Reverend Easton was most vociferous in his remarks. Mary Miles had been at a meeting of the local suffragists that he himself had attended on the night of the accident, as he referred to it on multiple occasions. The meeting did not break up until after midnight. Jacob Miles was seen leaving the pub, by multiple witnesses, a little after ten. It was less than a ten-minute walk from the meeting hall. Thus, there was no way that, *'Mrs Miles could have had anything to do with the tragic accident that befell Mayor Miles on that night.'*

The disappointment of the majority of the congregation was palpable.

'Is it not enough that Mrs Miles is now a widow, having to bring up a son on her own, she now has also to suffer the outrageous and dangerous rumour-mongering of half the town?'

Amongst the murmuring that this provoked among the pews, a lone voiced asked, 'What about the life insurance policy?'

Vicar Easton eyed the whole congregation despairingly, having not identified the speaker.

'Mrs Miles had over a dozen witnesses of the highest calibre, myself included. There is no evidence of foul play, the police have said as much. Any insurance policy is irrelevant, and thankfully a blessing for the bereaved.'

Despite Vicar Easton's best intentions, his intervention merely sent the haters down another false cul-de-sac. Rumours about Mary Miles's many infidelities had reached a critical mass that meant there were several suspects that clearly had motives to murder Jacob Miles, either for their own benefit, or much more likely, for the benefit of Mary Miles. All roads seemed to lead back to the existence of a life insurance policy.

'But I don't get it,' offered JoJo.

She and the old man were taking their empty mugs back to the canteen. They were both sticklers for tidying away after themselves.

'He was found with a bruise on his head and was face down dead in the water. Surely, the assumption must have been that he tripped and fell. You said multiple witnesses said he was drunk.'

'The police never had a doubt about that. It was just as you say, a drunken accident. They never even questioned anyone. But that didn't stop the gossip.'

'How did your mother deal with that?'

'It merely hardened her dislike of people, especially British people. Which might explain some of her later leanings.'

'What do you mean?'

'There will plenty of time for that. One of the things that you will need to get used to is my strict adherence to chronology. Unless absolutely necessary, I want to tell my story from beginning to end. If I start getting ahead of myself I will possibly leave things out. Besides, it's how my memory remembers as much as it does. It is difficult to explain, but my memory is like a long and winding road. It needs to be followed step by step, in one continuous direction of traffic.'

It was some of the men of the town that made themselves scarce in the days that followed. Mary Miles's partiality for the lower end of the social spectrum meant that the local farms were shorter staffed than normal after the death of Jacob Miles. Most just went walkabout for a couple of weeks, mostly on sheep farms to the north and west of the town. They were too dumb to a man to understand that their disappearing acts did two things. Firstly, they confirmed the suspicions of many that they must have danced with the town she-devil and secondly, one of them at least must have been a murderer, despite the protestations of the local police and clergy that no foul play was suspected.

Mary Miles was brazen and, without the security of a crowd, most of the gossipers did not have the front to say anything directly to her face, the direct ancestors of the keyboard warriors of a later century. Not for the first time, Ruben Miles was glad that he did not attend a local school. He even asked his mother if he could board full-time at the RGS for the following term. However, Mary Miles said that she needed a man about the house now, and this may have been the first and last time that she paid him any sort of compliment.

For her part, Celia the nanny returned after a month. She told Ruben Miles that she had been tending her ailing mother who had sadly passed away. He accepted the long hug that she gave him and, in return, he never uttered a word to her about what he witnessed on the moonlit night. His mother seemed very relieved to have Celia back in the house, and the two reverted to the former ease of their working relationship, even if they did seem to have more whispered conversations than they used to have in front of Ruben Miles.

'It took a couple of months for people to move on. I had no relationship with my mother before my father died and that certainly did not change afterwards. People move on eventually and find someone, or more typically something else, to blame for their own shitty lives.'

JoJo was finding it difficult to empathise with Ruben Miles. She was not particularly close with her mother, but she still thought she would tell people if she witnessed her being murdered, even if it was by someone she liked. But even this thought did not help her. What if her dad did it? She was much closer to him. Would she keep quiet too? But then she realised that she was hypothesising about a hugely improbable scenario. The old man was looking at her in an unusual way.

'Are you OK? I seemed to lose you for a minute or two there.'

'Sorry, I sometimes get lost in my own thoughts.'

'You were thinking whether you would have done as I did.'

'I suppose I was.'

'JoJo, in my long experience, it is very difficult to second guess yourself in any, how shall we say, unusual circumstances. So, it's probably wise not to spend time thinking about what you would do in hypothetical situations.'

'It's a pretty amazing story though. Actually, witnessing your father's murder, by your beloved nanny, using your scarf, when you were just twelve years old.'

'I still have the scarf. It is the only thing from my childhood that I kept.'

He went to his rooms to retrieve it. JoJo marvelled at how a very old person could walk with such sprightliness. On his return, he handed the scarf to her.

'Well, it makes more sense seeing it. It's enormous! Why did you keep it?'

'I just did. It's the only thing from my childhood that I have. I've saved a lot of things from the other chapters of my life, but I have nothing else to show from my hometown and my younger self.'

JoJo was surprised by how much she enjoyed listening to Ruben Miles. Their initial session flew by as she recorded his every word on the tape recorder and handwrote some additional notes. She was very organised and thorough. She was already of the view that her rather impulsive decision to start the biographical process had been a good one. And that was before she remembered the payments. Ruben Miles handed her a small envelope at the end of the session and they agreed to reconvene the following afternoon to discuss his role in the Great War.

FOREIGN FIELDS – PART ONE

1916

'**R**eady?'

Ruben Miles was sitting in the rose garden of The Apple Orchard Community for the Elderly on the wooden bench festooned with the least amount of bird shit.

JoJo Bartlett sat at the other end of the bench, notebook and pen in hand, tape recorder at the ready, wondering why there were so many rose bushes but no apple trees at The Apple Orchard Retirement Community.

'I was sixteen when I joined up. It was the 12th of December 1915. I went to the recruiting office on the Quayside. I joined the 23rd Battalion of the Northumberland Fusiliers, it was full of dockers and workers from the Armstrong works. Good lads to a man, despite the fact that we were part of the Tyneside Scottish Brigade. There weren't many Jocks, mainly just Geordies who liked to drink and fight, usually in that order.'

'Hang on, let me put my tape recorder on if you are going to give so much detail. Can you say that again?'

Ruben Miles obliged and surprised JoJo by seemingly repeating himself word for word without any changes.

'You have good recall. Is your memory always this good?'

'Pretty good. I remember the details of the important stuff, if that's what you mean.'

He was not going to tell her about his condition yet.

'I had to lie about my age as eighteen was the minimum, not that the recruiting sergeant minded though. He let one lad in who could not have been more than fifteen. Poor bugger died on the first day of the Somme, bullet through his left eye, not five feet from where I was standing.'

JoJo tried hard not to think how much a bullet in the eye would hurt. She failed.

'That sounds awful,' she heard herself say.

'Not really, at least it was quick. I saw worse and heard about a lot worse. Men split in two by shrapnel shells. Decapitation was quite common, and I even heard of a crucifixion at Passchendaele, but they covered that up.'

'A crucifixion?'

'A Canadian lad, an officer. Apparently, the Germans did it because he interfered with prisoners.'

'Interfered?'

'You know what I mean, sexually interfered.'

'I see,' said JoJo, but again she rather wished she didn't.

'Anyway, my story of The Great War really starts when we got to France in the spring of 1916....'

'Hang-on. So, nothing happened of interest to you between the ages of twelve and sixteen?'

'Did anything happen to you at those ages?'

'I suppose not.'

'I went to school, sat some exams, I even passed a few. I told you about Emily, she was the only interesting thing that happened to me then. I suppose she was the reason that I signed up.'

'The suffragette that burned the church down?'

'That's right, poor Emily never got to be an old lady.'

The spring of 1916 in northern France was warm and wet, a most unusual combination in that part of the world. Ruben Miles and tens of thousands of his fellow countrymen found themselves bivouacked in the lush, flat and green countryside. By the end of May, even the lowliest of ex farmhands or dockers knew that a 'big push' was on its way. The French army were still experiencing the horrors of Verdun and the tactical necessity of easing their burden was going to fall on the riff raff of the old country and mindlessly cheerful colonials from across the globe. Ruben Miles was a member of Kitchener's Army. One of so many who had volunteered since the slaughter started in July 1914.

The British forces that would fight in the Somme Valley in the summer and autumn of 1916 were largely volunteers. Most of the regular army had perished or were no longer fit for the frontlines. Even the territorials had mostly been used up. Kitchener's army had answered the call to arms and had been through months of basic training. Ruben Miles spent nearly three months cold and wet in the Scottish Borders near Melrose for his training. He and his fellow recruits learned the basics of soldiering. They spent hours on drilling exercises, cleaning and learning to fire weapons and most importantly blindly following orders. Or 'accepting military discipline' as the portly battalion sergeant informed Ruben Miles at regular intervals.

Basic training seemed like a lifetime ago to most of the soldiers stationed near Albert in the Somme Valley, mid-1916. Most were still enthralled with the wonders of a foreign country, foreign beer and of course foreign women. Not that Ruben Miles and his fellow Tynesiders saw much of the latter. Most of them talked a good game though.

Most of the boys had received little or no formal education. Ruben Miles decided quickly to hide his educational past, for reasons he never really articulated, even to himself. He did not want to be an officer, but one of the enlisted men. Besides, he said to himself, no one likes a smartarse, especially a young smartarse. So, from the day he enlisted to the day he was ushered out of the side door of the British Army at the end of the Great War, Ruben Miles kept his intellect and education to himself. It seemed to him later that this was very much in keeping with the conduct of the British Army on the Western Front 1914 to 1918.

Ruben Miles bonded easily and quickly with the men of his battalion. In particular, he gravitated toward a couple of brothers from Felton, the Burgess brothers, John and George. Although brothers and with only eighteen months between them, John and George Burgess were radically different, both physically and in nature. John was the tall, thin, quite serious one and George was the more rotund and with a quick-fire humour. Despite their differences, the brothers were very close and together formed a strong unit. Ruben Miles was bunked next to the brothers and the three men soon formed a close-knit group. Although they got along well with everyone, the three young men spent all their time together.

John Burgess was one of life's worriers. There was very little that could not bring out his pessimistic nature. Being at close proximity to death and destruction certainly did not ease his burden.

'Of course, I'm going to be killed, it's a case of when not if. I'm also bound to get a bad one, you know like the sergeant always talks about.'

Ruben Miles did know what John was talking about. Sergeant Lawson was known for his gory tales of impalement, lost limbs and internal organs being on the outside.

'It's being so positive that keeps our John going,' said his brother George, lighting one of the sixty cigarettes he smoked in a day. He was grateful that Ruben Miles gave him his ration.

'And you will live to be a hundred, I suppose?'

'Well, I won't waste every day I have left worrying about it. You're worse than the others. All they do is talk about bullets with their name on them.' George pointed at the other men in the battalion nearby cleaning their rifles.

The men did spend a lot of time talking about their mortality and the variety of ways of achieving it in a hurry. Ruben Miles wondered if this was just the men of his battalion. After the war, on the few occasions he spoke with veterans of the Western Front, they all confirmed that the topic of conversation was indeed universal among the men that fought in the trenches.

'So why did you join up, John?' Ruben Miles asked a question he had been wondering for a while.

'To look after him.' John motioned toward his brother. 'I promised our mam that I would always look after him when she was ill.'

'We've had this argument so many times, Ruben. She didn't know there was going to be a big war and she would not have wanted you to join up just to look after me. Besides, I am not the one that needs looking after.'

'A promise is a promise. I told her I would keep an eye on you and here I am.'

It was late June 1916, and none of the boys were under any illusions about what was coming soon. None of the Battalion had experience of 'going over the top'. But they knew how to assemble and clean a rifle, they knew how to pack a kitbag, they knew how to march, and they had learned to follow orders unquestioningly. What else did they need?

'Morton says it's on for next week.'

'This would be the same Morton who said it would be three weeks ago?'

'I think we should have an agreement; I've been thinking about it a lot.'

'What sort of agreement, John?' asked Ruben Miles.

'An agreement to do the right thing in certain circumstances… you know what I'm talking about.'

'Actually, brother, I don't have a fucking clue what you are on about.'

But Ruben Miles did.

'I think John means that we should agree to help one another if we end up in a certain state…'

George still looked puzzled.

'Jesus, George, your brother wants us to agree to finish each other off if we're in a bad way.'

'Is that right, John? Is that what you mean?' George Burgess looked truly horrified.

His brother nodded solemnly.

'Makes sense to me, George, I don't want to end up a cripple, or worse. Did you not hear about that bloke from Byker who lost half his face and survived? I mean who would want to live like that?'

It took another twenty minutes to finally get through to George Burgess. Eventually, they shook hands and promised to finish each other off if it came to it. Then they went to the mess and ate a disappointing steak and kidney pie, presumably because it contained neither kidney nor steak.

Morton had to be right eventually. Three days later, the battalion received their instructions and battle plan for Saturday 1st July 1916.

The Tyneside Scottish were part of the 34th division and they were positioned at La Boisselle, south centrally placed on the Somme front, which stretched over fifteen miles across. As well as a week-long artillery bombardment to hopefully destroy the German frontline positions, several mines had been dug deep beneath the German fortifications, the largest of these was adjacent to the Tyneside Scottish's position near La Boisselle.

Ruben Miles and the Burgess brothers, along with the rest of the 34th division, were to attack the Albert–Bapaume road, aided by the blowing of the Lochnagar mine on the outskirts of the village of La Boisselle. Each man carried over thirty KGs of equipment. All the men were ordered to walk toward the enemy positions; there was no need to run as the enemy would all have been destroyed by the artillery bombardment or the Lochnagar mine.

Zero hour was 7.30 a.m. The mine was detonated at 7.28 a.m., entrapping some of the frontline German soldiers, but only temporarily. The Tynesiders had over a mile of open ground to traverse to reach the German positions.

The soldiers of the 34th division, like their comrades elsewhere on the line, did not have their heads full of battle plans and objectives, they left all that to the officers. Instead, they complained about the weight on their back and concerned themselves with how many of the German frontline remained intact. They were right to be concerned.

Ruben Miles and the Burgess brothers stood amongst their peers in the second line reserve trench which was to be their jump off point. Even those who had not smoked before the war smoked heartily now. Only Ruben Miles had refused the traditional tot of alcohol. Many had heaved their dry guts onto their boots. Some whispered prayers. Others shook involuntarily. The NCOs and officers walked up and down the lines of men, babbling words of encouragement. Not many listened.

'Remember to stay close,' George Burgess said, lighting another cigarette from the stub of his last.

'And remember our agreement,' his brother said quickly.

Then there was the piercing shrill of a whistle.

'We will have to call it a day now, I have to meet my mum at six. I can come back tomorrow though?'

JoJo Bartlett had been fully engaged with Ruben Miles's descriptions of his experiences in France in 1916. She wished she hadn't agreed to pick her mum up from work.

'But we're just getting to the big stuff...'

'I'm sorry but I have to go. I can do tomorrow at the same time, OK?'

'I suppose I can wait one more day to tell someone what happened. After all, I have waited all these years.'

'You mean you've never told anyone about your war experiences?'

'JoJo, I have not told anyone about any of what I am going to tell you. That is the whole point. I have kept my whole life to myself. Now, as I near the final curtain I have surprised myself by wanting to get it all out there... despite how it might make me look.'

'I am looking forward to hearing it all and don't worry, I won't judge you harshly if you had to kill people. War is a horrible business. I learnt that in Key Stage 3 with Mr Fowler.'

'I think you should wait until you have heard all I have to say before reaching a judgment. At this stage, you have no idea about what I'm going to say.'

JoJo felt the first pang of hesitation on the process she had embarked upon. It was not going to be the last.

Later that evening, JoJo was surprised to hear her mum call her from downstairs to say that Luke Miles was at the front door. After their last interaction, she thought it might be a while before she saw Luke again.

'Fancy a walk to the Dene? I'm so bored revising.'

'Yeah alright, I'm sick of being cooped up in my bedroom. What have you been revising anyway?'

'I've been pretending to revise Physics. I have discovered I'm very good at pretend revision.'

'Hold that thought, I need to get my keys, won't be a sec.'

Her forecast on how long it took her to return was questionable.

'Ready?' she said, eventually.

Luke Miles merely rolled his eyes.

They walked along the banks of the Ouseburn in Jesmond Dene. Around them were the usual eclectic mix of young families, dog walkers and teenagers drinking cans of cider.

'I need a definition of 'pretend revising', I think.'

They had been walking in silence for a minute or two and JoJo was concerned that at any moment Luke was going to bring up the recent, controversial story of her new boyfriend. She was right.

Luke always took most questions too seriously, especially from JoJo, who, he reluctantly conceded to himself, he was always in a position of trying to impress. In addition, he did find her a bit on the brainy side and did not want to come over as some kind of retard. Luke reminded himself that it was semi-OK to think of the word retard, but it was never OK to say the word out loud, unless of course you were on your own and there was no way anyone else could hear you. Luke often had these sorts of mental conversations with himself. He assumed everyone did.

'Pretend revising is when you convince everyone, meaning parents, friends etc, even yourself, that you are properly revising when you are really doing nothing. Thus, you will earn all the rewards, such as meals, computers etc, without having to do the boring stuff.'

'So, you're not actually revising?'

'Of course not, that is the beauty and simplicity of pretend revision.'

'So, if you're not actually revising, what are you doing? Presumably on your computer and stuff.'

'I have gotten pretty good at just staring blankly into space.'

'Is that not boring? I mean I would rather revise than stare into space. Actually, I quite like revising.'

'Well, sometimes I move the textbooks around on my desk, or even draw up another exam timetable. I like making exam timetables.'

'Luke, why don't you just revise? I mean, you say you want to go to university. Surely you will have to revise at some point, so you may as well start now before it's not too late.'

'But it's so boring.'

'And staring blankly into space is what, exciting?'

They walked in silence for a minute, watching the annoying yappy little dogs chasing after the bigger, less yappy dogs.

'So, what do you see in him then? You know, apart from the car and everything…?'

Luke had held off asking for as long as he thought was possible. He had managed fifteen minutes, which was considerably longer than he had anticipated.

JoJo sighed a little too loudly.

'Luke, he is just another friend, OK? I mean you have more than just me as friends, right?'

JoJo knew that this approach was not going to work.

'As a rule, I don't normally get off with my friends.'

JoJo was silent as she sought a suitable response. She realised that she did not have one. So instead, she kissed Luke Miles flush on the lips.

That should shut him up for a bit, she thought. She was right.

The following day, JoJo headed back to The Apple Orchard Community for the Elderly to visit Ruben Miles and continue his World War One memories. She found herself keenly anticipating what she was going to hear, as if she was turning the pages of a much-loved book. She had spent a restless night after the 'incident' with Luke. She found she could deal with her actions more calmly if she referred to the kiss as an 'incident'. In bed, despite not being able to sleep, she had managed to distract her over-active mind with thoughts about what direction Ruben Miles's story would go in. She felt uneasy as she recalled some of what Ruben Miles had said to her before she left. But then she remembered the 'incident' and her cheeks flushed red once again.

'What were you thinking?' she said out loud.

Nobody answered.

She spent the morning pretending to revise. This had not been her plan, but as she sat at her desk, she found that she could only keep focus on the topic in hand for a few minutes before she was thinking about her boyfriend whom she thought she liked a lot, plus Luke Miles and the 'incident'. None of which helped with the revision of Neo-Marxist views on the role of education.

Luke had sent a text message, but she could not bring herself to read it.

Jamie had also sent a message, but she had not read that either.

Is life always going to be this complicated? she thought, as she gave up on revision and went to get ready to go and see Ruben Miles.

Ruben Miles had had a restless night too. He spent at least two hours wrestling with whether to continue with the project or not. Why bother telling his life story now after all these years? Had he not spent four years writing it all down? And yet he knew that he was going to continue telling JoJo Bartlett about what he did in World War One and what he then went on to do over the next decades and across various continents.

'Absurd,' he said, staring at the beige ceiling and listening to the hearty snores of his near neighbours. Then he started thinking about the events of the summer of 1916 and the Burgess brothers. Sleep did not come easy. Ruben Miles wondered why, after so many years of apparently lacking any, he had seemed not only to be growing a recognisable conscience, but also an unease about many of his actions. Eventually, he literally gave himself a shake and said,

'Oh well, I'll be dead soon.'

And on that cheery note, he eventually dropped off to sleep.

FOREIGN FIELDS – PART TWO

They walked as per their orders, although Ruben Miles clearly remembered the feeling of helplessness and an inner desire to run as fast as he could. Only the direction would have changed. He could still picture the colour of the sky and the smell of the discharged artillery shells. The taste of dry dust and fear cloying at the back of his throat. His memory *could* be a real curse.

Because the Tynesiders had jumped off from a reserve trench position, they had over half a mile of open ground to cover before they reached No Man's Land. They were to make their way to the south of La Boisselle, to advance up the marvellously misnamed Sausage Valley. Sniping machine gun fire came murderous and fast as they began to advance past the British frontlines. Ruben Miles could hear the impact of bullets as it hit turf or flesh, two very distinct sounds.

Miraculously, Ruben Miles and the Burgess brothers made it unscathed on the long and perilous route to the German frontline positions. Others had not been nearly as fortunate. Many had fallen, most never to rise again. The shell holes and craters of No Man's Land were littered with the Tyneside Scottish, at the end of this day they would have suffered greater casualty and mortality figures than any other regiment across the whole Somme offensive, over six thousand in all. The first of July 1916 was the worst day the British Army has ever suffered, it was disproportionately worse for many families in the east end of Newcastle-upon-Tyne and surrounding areas.

To their surprise, the German frontline was deserted as Ruben Miles and the Burgess brothers clambered into the relative safety of the impressive German trench. Almost immediately the soldiers recognised how superior the German built defences were compared to their British counterparts. Everything manufactured was of a superior quality and there was so much more of everything. However, their thoughts on their surroundings did not take precedence for long.

'Right, you lot, we have to advance on the next enemy

position.'

Sergeant Taylor did the shouting, he appeared to be the only NCO that had made it. There was not a single officer. One can sympathise with the 'lions led by donkeys' overview of the British Army on the Western Front, as long as you remember that most of the junior and middling donkeys died too.

'There aren't enough of us, Sergeant Taylor, there are less than thirty of us.'

'We have to advance. Those are our orders.'

'Can we wait a few more minutes for some others to make it?'

Sergeant Taylor was one of the popular NCOs as he was decent and friendly and was not officious like so many others.

'That seems like a good idea,' he said, as he walked up and down the trench, counting heads.

Ten minutes later, at approximately 0800 hours, exactly fifty men began the journey to the next British objective of the day, the second line of German trenches near Contalmaison. Sergeant Taylor was reluctantly in charge and led the way through the communication trench.

After nearly four hundred metres, Sergeant Taylor brought the group to a halt and, using hand signals, told the men to silently clamber out of the trench on each side, fan out and advance on their stomachs for the last five hundred metres to their second objective of the day. The second line near Contalmaison was on slightly higher ground then the frontline. This had been why the German machine gun fire had been even more effective than normal, as they had been able to pin down and slaughter the huge majority of the Tynesiders that advanced that morning before they got anywhere near the first line. The Germans had evacuated the frontline at the cessation of the week-long British bombardment that pre-empted the attack. They had two machine gun positions, and this may have led to their complacency, as they assumed that no British troops had made it to the old frontline position. In addition, because of the gradient of the slope, existing barbed wire defences and machine gun positions, it was very difficult to see soldiers advancing on their stomachs just a few hundred metres away. German ineptitude and complacency were a very rare commodity on the Western Front in July 1916 and doubtless would not last long.

For Ruben Miles and the Burgess brothers, they could not understand why no one was shooting at them. All the enemy fire was still concentrated down behind them on the second and third wave of the Tynesiders' continued assault. It seemed that a brief window of opportunity had presented itself to Sergeant Taylor and his forty-nine men.

Unusually, Ruben Miles remembered little precise detail about the frontal assault on the German 2nd line position. Violence is the one event that clouds his recall. He *did* remember shooting and yelling a lot. He remembered the sounds of hand-to-hand combat and the cries of pain. He remembered the unnerving kick of adrenaline, like swallowing a dozen double espressos. He remembered kicking a German soldier in the face as he lay dying from bayonet wounds to the chest. He remembered looking down at a badly wounded John Burgess, his brother George crouched beside him.

John Burgess had been shot in the stomach at close quarters. His brother George had watched it happen. Everything appeared to happen in slow motion after the impact. John was conscious and still lucid, despite already losing a lot of blood. He was in shock and so thankfully the pain had not kicked in yet. It would come soon enough.

The perpetrator was one of the last Germans to be overpowered and killed. The Tynesiders had achieved their second objective of the day before eleven hundred hours. Indeed, before the day was done, they would capture nearly four kilometres of German positions, the biggest single success across the entire Somme theatre.

For Ruben Miles and the Burgess brothers this was of scant consolation. John Burgess was dying, the look in his eyes was telling. The bullet had ripped through his large intestine, stomach and spleen.

'Remember our agreement,' John said quietly to his brother.

'Don't talk like that, you're going to make it.'

'We both know that's not true,' John managed, before searing pain stopped him from saying more.

After a moment, George Burgess stood up and looked at Ruben Miles beseechingly.

'Can you help John, Ruben?'

Ruben Miles took a few moments to assess his options. He could either do nothing or allow his friend to die an agonising, probably painfully slow death. Or he could put the muzzle of his rifle to John Burgess's forehead and pull the trigger.

He made his mind up.

'I need you to find Sergeant Taylor for me George, do you hear?'

'In a minute, Ruben, I need to…'

But the words caught in his throat and never came out. Instead, he lay down next to his brother and held him in his arms. John Burgess was still conscious and was now moaning loudly in pain. His brother wiped the sweat from his brow with his handkerchief and spoke into his brother's ear.

'I have to go and get Sergeant Taylor now, John, do you understand? I have to leave you now with Ruben…'

'Thank you, George,' his brother managed, barely audible.

'Goodbye, John.'

'Look after our mother when you get home.'

They held each other for a few moments.

George Burgess kissed his brother on the cheek and then walked away from him for the last time. He strode away with purpose, pretending to look for Sergeant Taylor. He did not flinch when he heard the gunshot, nor did he turn back. He would remember his brother the way he wanted to.

A couple of minutes later, Ruben Miles appeared at his elbow.

'Thank you, Ruben,' said George Burgess. They never spoke of it again.

INFAMY

'You killed your own friend?'

JoJo Bartlett surprised herself by interrupting. She had never done that before when he was speaking.

She pressed pause on the mini tape recorder in her hand.

'That is one interpretation. I prefer to say that I committed an act of kindness.'

They were sitting in the garden as it was a mild, bright day and Ruben Miles liked to be outside of the rather stuffy conditions inside The Apple Orchard Retirement Community whenever he could.

'You put your gun to his head and shot him. You killed him.'

'He was dying and in pain. Is it any different to putting a sparrow out of its misery after it has flown into your sitting room window?'

'Of course it's different, he was your friend. I mean, he could have survived.'

'Not with the injuries he had. A twenty-first century surgeon could not have saved him. Believe me, JoJo, all I did was put him out of his misery. Poor John Burgess.'

JoJo was finding his use of her name odd to listen to. It sounded different coming from someone so old.

'I haven't told you the worst part yet.'

'What could be worse than shooting your friend in the head?'

Ruben Miles paused for a moment, as if deciding whether to say more. He decided against it. He reasoned that if he said out loud what he was thinking, JoJo may decide to call a premature end to the memoir recording sessions.

'Nothing, there was no worse part, you were right. Killing my friend, albeit out of compassion to end his suffering, was the worst part.'

JoJo Bartlett was savvy enough to know the old man had

changed his mind. She could see there was something else there, hidden behind his pale blue eyes. She quickly calculated that her chances of pushing him there and then and finding out what he was now hiding were slim. She was right. JoJo decided merely to make a note of what had happened in her notebook.

She wrote, 'Said there was a worse part than killing his friend... but then would not tell me what. Remember to come back to this at a good time.' She highlighted the words in yellow and drew a big asterisk beside the words.

'So, what happened next?' she asked and pressed the record button on the tape recorder.

George Burgess and Ruben Miles spent the next several hours fighting off German counter attacks as they attempted to regain their lost positions. Their fifty strong group dwindled as the shadows lengthened in the late afternoon sunshine. They managed to hold the Germans off three times before sundown. By then they had lost Sergeant Taylor and there were only twelve soldiers left standing. There was no chance of reinforcements arriving, the men had been unwilling spectators on the slaughter of their fellow Tynesiders; wave after wave of futile attacks had been launched behind them during the long summer day, as no changes were made to the original Battle plan. Flexibility and initiative were not traits that were encouraged in Haig's army.

It was George Burgess who did the talking as the remaining troops listened on wearily and solemnly.

'The way I see it, we have an obvious choice. We can either all die here in this stinking Hun trench, or we can surrender and maybe live to see another day.'

It was an accurate assessment of their plight, as retreating was not an option. There was no dissent. Within a few moments the men agreed to surrender, and a white flag was hastily assembled from used handkerchiefs. Ruben Miles was given the dubious honour of waving his rifle with the accompanying home-made flag. While Harry Burns, an annoying joiner from Heaton, used what little German he had practised before the battle started.

'Wir geben auf! Wir geben auf!'

The Germans responded quickly, and very promptly the remaining men were disarmed and walked towards the rear German trenches under heavy guard. Ruben Miles remembered clearly thinking that they would be shot as they walked. But to his surprise and immense relief, he and his fellow men found their captors to be of fair mind. In truth, despite the casualties that the small band of Tynesiders had inflicted, the Germans felt mostly sympathy for the dozen that lived to surrender. After all, the Germans had massacred so many of their fellow countrymen from the safety of their machine gun nests. It would be many months before the men would realise just how bad a day the 1st of July 1916 had been for the Tynesiders and the whole British Army on the Somme front.

Of more immediate concern to Ruben Miles, George Burgess and the remaining men, was what was going to happen to them now? The immediate answer was a lengthy march deep into German held territory that went on until nearly midnight. Eventually, utterly spent, the men were told to stop, and they were bivouacked in what appeared to be a temporary holding pen with no more than a couple of hundred other British servicemen. But sleep came out of necessity before even the most rudimentary questions could be asked of their fellow prisoners.

The following morning, the men were given some very stale bread and water for breakfast. Ruben and George managed to strike up a workable conversation with one of the Germans guarding the prisoners. Ruben Miles could not believe that a German soldier could speak such passable English.

'You will be treated OK, but there is little food for you. The commander does not want to waste our resources on prisoners who will be moved on in a couple of days. You will all go to Döberitz I think, the large camp near Berlin. It will be tough, but you should all live, unlike so many.'

Their fellow prisoners had been less effusive and positive about their situation. A guy from a Lancashire regiment called Smith had told them that he and a few of his comrades had been here for nearly two weeks on meagre rations and had been told nothing about their immediate future.

'Our sergeant keeps telling us that we will never get out of this place.'

Fortunately for all concerned, the Lancashire sergeant was as reliable as a politician's word.

The very next day, over two hundred British troops from a wide variety of regions and regiments were herded into foul smelling trucks that then trundled their way out of the makeshift prison camp and headed east toward Germany. But the trucks only went a short distance from the camp, barely five miles, and then stopped. Once more the soldiers were corralled into a formation, this time single file. And then they walked. Then they walked some more.

'It took over three weeks to get there and we walked every step.'

Ruben Miles could almost feel the blisters back on his feet. He had lost nearly all the skin on the balls of his two feet during the march. But he was one of the lucky ones, plenty did not make the journey, instead collapsing and being left where they fell, despite the protestations of their comrades. It is difficult to argue with a loaded gun.

'Surely that goes against the Geneva Convention?'

JoJo was pleased that she had remembered something of value from the Citizenship course she had had to endure with Miss Hardy in Year Nine. Miss Hardy was so dull that even the nice kids hated her.

'That was much later I think, maybe the thirties. We had nothing and no one to look after our rights then.'

JoJo made a note to check later when she got home. She discovered the Geneva Convention was not signed until 1929.

'Can we wrap it up there for today, Ruben? I need to get going.'

After a lot of persuasion, JoJo had finally agreed to call him 'Ruben' rather than Mr Miles.

'I have started dreaming again. For the first time in years.

Every time we have a session, that night the events all come back to me in vivid dreams. It's like I am watching a film of my life. Extraordinary. When can you come again?'

'Tomorrow if that's OK? I want to try and get a lot done before I have to start revising more for my mock exams.'

'So, I will pick up from arriving at the German prison camp in late July 1916. JoJo?'

'What is it, Ruben?'

'There is an awful lot more to my life than the Great War, you know? We have hardly started. I am just beginning to realise how much there is to tell and how long it is going to take to tell you it all. Is that OK? Will you see this through to the end?'

'Of course.'

'It's funny. For the last several years I had begun to get impatient with death. He seemed to be taking far too long a time getting around to me. Now I am worried that he is going to come and take me away before I have had a chance to tell all my story.'

'I'm sure we have time. You look like a man thirty years younger than you are. Besides, I'm enjoying hearing about your life and want to get it all down for posterity. Don't disappoint me now.'

She smiled warmly at the old man.

'Don't judge me too harshly,' he said.

She was surprised by how little she did.

To add to JoJo Bartlett's conflicting thoughts, as she walked along her home street a little over an hour later, she saw Luke Miles sitting in a deckchair in his front garden. He was trying to get a little sun on his very pasty looking skin. He was reading a magazine, wearing a pork pie hat and devouring a Fruit Pastille ice lolly. It was not a good look.

'Hey,' he said, over the rim of his John Lennon sunglasses.

'Are you thirtysomething and from New York?'

Luke Miles looked confused by the question.

'If you are not a thirtysomething from New York, then 'hey'' is not an acceptable form of greeting. Especially for a teenager from Northern Britain in the twenty-first century. Have you been watching *Friends* again?'

It was an accusation not a question.

Watching *Friends* was a guilty pleasure Luke had recently shared with JoJo, much to her great hilarity. She thought the show was beyond lame. I mean, people actually having friends they want to spend time with.

'There is a fair on at the Quayside tonight. Would you like to go?'

Luke Miles was surprised that he had managed to ask the question in a laid-back manner. He was even more surprised when JoJo replied.

'Yeah, that might be fun. But let me do some work first. Shall we go about eight. I think I can get the car tonight.'

Luke Miles decided not to over-analyse this response. He had decided again that he was not going to spend most of his time finding meaning in every JoJo utterance. He managed to keep this up for nearly twenty minutes. A new record.

For her part, JoJo was herself confused. When Luke had asked her to the fair, there was no part of her that even considered saying no or coming up with an excuse. What did that mean? Rather than try and answer that question, she decided to read Thomas Hardy's *Far from the Madding Crowd*. JoJo thought this was a fair trade as both pastimes were equally frustrating and ultimately pointless.

Three hours later, and JoJo and Luke had arrived at the Quayside for the fair. It had taken an increasingly stressed JoJo fifteen minutes to find a parking space within a reasonable walking distance from the Quayside. Two stalls, an alarming roll back on a slight incline and a near miss with a red Peugeot later, Luke Miles got out of the car with a little more speed than was necessary, a fact not gone unnoticed by JoJo Bartlett.

'What?' she demanded.

Luke Miles pretended not to hear; he had often experienced his father doing this when his mother was annoyed. She was always annoyed, it just varied by degrees.

'What is wrong with my driving?'

It did not work for Luke's dad either.

'Nothing, what makes you say that? I'm just keen to get to the fair.'

JoJo merely rolled her eyes.

'I want to establish some ground rules for tonight. I will not go on any ride that looks scary or that is operated by someone who looks like they are waiting to evolve opposable thumbs. In addition, saying 'aw go on' will not alter my decision-making processes. There will also be no mention or even passing hint of what we will now refer to as 'the incident'.'

Luke Miles had a fleeting moment while he questioned why he liked JoJo Bartlett.

'The incident?'

'You know what I am referring to, and we will not be discussing it tonight or any time soon.'

So, Luke pretended that he knew what on earth she was talking about.

Fifteen minutes later, as JoJo deftly but noticeably refused to let Luke Miles take her hand, he began to realise what 'the incident' may have been.

He still had an excellent time. The dodgems and the Waltzer had been his favourites, but that was really because he was able to scrunch up close to JoJo.

JoJo had also had a good time, at least until she saw Jamie Taylor emerge across the blinking eye bridge from the Baltic side of the Tyne with his arm draped around a tall, unknown brunette. She looked to be about twenty-five. Jamie had not been looking in JoJo's direction and she was sure that he had not seen her. She felt a sense of palpable unease rise in her stomach. But was it anger or relief? JoJo Bartlett had no actual clue.

MRS HAZEL WHARTON

Mrs Hazel Wharton had been at The Apple Orchard Community for the Elderly for nearly two years. After her husband Brian died, she had decided to sell up the three-bedroom semi in Jesmond that had been the family home for all but one of their forty-seven years of marriage. It had been hard to leave. The house had beautiful views over the nearby Dene and most of the marriage memories she had were relatively happy ones, or at least not unhappy ones. As long as she did not think about the kids, especially *him*.

At least the financial side of leaving the house had been beneficial. The Wharton's had bought the house in the late sixties for just over £2,500. She sold it for £360,000 less than a month after Brian had been cremated. The scale of the profit had been one of her motivations. She did not want to leave any inheritance to any of her three children (especially him, God forbid). As a youthful, sprightly and to the best of her knowledge healthy seventy-two-year-old, she hoped she had many years left to spend her money on the annual fees of The Apple Orchard Community for the Elderly.

Mrs Hazel Wharton was not a sophisticated legal mind, and had she been aware that she could simply have had a will written to ensure that her children were disinherited, she may not have sold the house in the first place. Nevertheless, after taking a little while to settle in, Mrs Hazel Wharton felt happy and comfortable in the retirement community. True, she was younger than most of the residents, but she had made some friends and had been delighted that there were so many relatively young and healthy inhabitants. There were plenty of activities to keep her entertained, with regular outings and trips that also reduced the amount that sat in her TSB current account. All she had to do was stay away from the senile, the angry and the spectacularly mean. Which, by her rough calculation, totalled about 50% of the inhabitants of The Apple Orchard Community for the Elderly.

Mrs Hazel Wharton had never given Ruben Miles much of a thought. To her, he was just the apparently remarkably old man who did not look anything like how old he was, who lived along the corridor from her apartment. Initially, she had not been even remotely curious about him or his life. Then she noticed his regular meetings with the pretty girl who seemed to be recording their conversations. She thought this was both odd and a little interesting.

Though it was rather out of character, she decided to initiate contact with Ruben Miles. She slipped in behind him at the dinner buffet queue on a Tuesday evening. Tuesday night was a seafood-themed night. Dinner started at 5.30 p.m. and finished at 7.00 p.m., although all the inhabitants were sat down by six at the latest. Mrs Hazel Wharton was not an experimental eater; indeed, she was beyond conservative in her menu selections. Tuesday night meant prawn cocktail to start and haddock and chips for mains. The dessert was more of a lottery.

'Good evening, Mr Miles. How are you this evening?'

Mrs Hazel Wharton flashed her most expressive smile, one that she usually saved for cute pets and babies.

'I am well, thank you,' stammered Ruben Miles in reply. He had simply no idea what the woman's name was, although he felt fairly confident that she lived on the same ground floor corridor as him.

'Mrs Hazel Wharton, I don't think we have formally been introduced,' she said, offering forth her right hand, which, after a slight pause, Ruben Miles grasped firmly but not overly so.

'Nice to meet you,' they said in unison.

THE FIXER

Being a prisoner of war in World War One was every bit as miserable and boring as it sounds. It was so dull it is never mentioned in the school textbooks and the worthy documentaries filled with academic historians spouting either traditional or revisionist interpretations either in ill-fitting suits or dowdy frocks. There are good reasons it is so under reported, very little of note happened. Just thousands of cold, miserable and underfed men, counting off days as slow as a long weekend at the dullest of in-laws, the ones that don't even drink. Ruben Miles would have thought he was in purgatory, but he had neither read the Bible nor believed in God.

The biggest issue for the prisoners, besides a permanently growling stomach, was the diarrhoea and other nasty bugs that seemed to be the only things that prospered in the camp. Ruben Miles and George Burgess were not exempt; indeed, by Ruben Miles's reckoning, George Burgess had been ill to some degree or other, for the whole 647 days they had existed in the camp since they arrived. And existed was the correct terminology. Ruben Miles had chosen to largely ignore those nearly thirty months of captivity that he endured before his release in November 1918, but what he found impossible to overlook was the sense of dread about how long and how mind-numbing each single day was. That and the smell. He could wake in the middle of the night decades later and feel it irritating his nostrils. It was worse than the trenches. Who would have thought that possible?

They were playing cards. One of the few almost agreeable ways to pass the time, at least if you did not gamble like George and Ruben. Both had seen men commit murder with bare hands after losing cigarette rations in games of crooked three card brag. Whilst the prisoners were never given enough to eat, there were always some cigarettes, go figure.

'Have you met the American yet?'

It was October 1918, and the camp had accumulated a handful of the American doughboys who were in the process of finishing off the Germans.

'Not properly, although I heard him talking to that twat Price yesterday. It didn't seem to take him long to realise exactly what kind of a man Price is.'

'Have you heard what he calls himself, the American?' George Burgess winced in terrible pain as the cancer slowly eating his insides contracted in his stomach.

Ruben Miles pretended not to notice and shook his head, throwing down another losing hand.

'The Fixer. He actually refers to himself as 'the Fixer'. What the fuck is that about?'

And so, the Fixer entered the life and times of Ruben Miles. No other person would play such a monumental role in his life, not his numerous wives, uncaring mother or long dead father.

He was born Arthur Jamieson, in Cork in 1898. The youngest of a family of six children that emigrated to America when he was two years old. His father was a drunk who liked to use his fists to communicate. His mother was a saint. At least that is what the Fixer would tell people if they asked. The Jamiesons settled in Chicago and lived amongst their fellow Irish immigrants on the South Side of the City, on 107th and Western. His father worked in a giant meatpacking plant, a factory with over 2,000 employees. Arthur remembered his father smelling of cheap booze and raw meat all the time.

The young Arthur Jamieson was an unduly perceptive boy with knowing eyes and discerning ears. He missed nothing in his neighbourhood. By the time he was twelve years old he could tell you the weaknesses of every adult in his street. Arthur Jamieson would spend a lifetime gathering information on people and he put a good deal of it to use for personal gain.

Like most kids in his neighbourhood, Arthur Jamieson ran with a gang who fought with their fists and stole with their fingers. He ended up in reform school where he met some other 'interesting' people. For Arthur Jamieson, you were either a person of interest or you were a nobody. By the time he was nineteen, a fed-up city magistrate gave the young man a choice. He could either do some real time in Bridewell prison or join up and fight for Uncle Sam. Reform school had taught the young Arthur Jamieson that he might be better off taking his chances in France.

'My name is Ruben Miles.'

The American looked Ruben Miles straight in the eyes.

'They call me the Fixer.'

Ruben Miles thought this was funny, but the expression on the American's face told him that laughter was not a suitable option. The American had a presence beyond his years. He had a look in his eyes that seemed to bore into your very soul.

'Are you going to let that friend of yours die a slow and painful death or are you going to do something about it?'

'I don't know what you mean.'

'Oh, I think you do, buddy. I think you know exactly what I mean. I have been watching you, it's all in the eyes. A man's eyes tell me all I need to know about a man. I am not talking about women, you understand, they are an entirely different proposition altogether.'

Arthur Jamieson a.k.a. the Fixer may well have been only twenty at the time, but he already had an almost ageless manner to him and a face that was neither young nor old, just consistent. Ruben Miles had never met anyone with such presence. He did not merely fill the room, but the entire landscape.

'I can help you if you want. That's what I do. I fix things.'

'Can you get me a gun? I know that he is suffering, but I need a gun. I could not put my hands on him, I just couldn't do that.'

'That would be difficult, I could arrange something from the medical store that would do the trick, for a fee, you understand.'

'I don't have anything to give.'

The American gave this some thought for a minute.

'Well, the way I figure it, this war is nearly through. I can't see the Germans lasting more than another month or so. I could use a man of your talents back home. How about you come and help me out for a while back in the States as a way of paying me back for my help?'

'What kind of help? What do you do?'

'I've told you. I fix things for certain people.'

'What would you want me to do?'

'I'm sure we could come up with something to suit your talents.'

Ruben Miles was intrigued by the American and the prospect of spending some time in the new world. Two days later, Ruben Miles had been given a bottle of strychnine by the mysterious American. He knew that George was dying, you could actually smell death if you have been around it enough times. How George was managing to conceal most of his pain without the benefit of any medicine was a Herculean effort.

And so, Ruben Miles administered the fatal poison that killed his second Burgess brother of the war, ending his suffering and fulfilling the promise he made to both brothers.

Once again, he felt little. Just like the Fixer could see with his ice cool eyes.

'Why are you telling me these things?'

JoJo Bartlett paused the tape recorder and put her pad and pen on the coffee table in front of her.

'I told you. I want there to be a record of my life, what I have done.'

'I hope you're going to start telling me about charity work or inventing some lifesaving gadget, because at the moment this is making for pretty grim hearing. I accept what you say about both brothers, that they were dying. But I don't seem to get any regret from you or relief or frankly any other emotion about these acts.'

'I made a vow with the Burgess brothers. They were suffering, and I stopped that. Is that not a good deed?'

'Can killing another human being ever be a good deed?'

This seemed to make Ruben Miles think.

'Can we come back to that question at a later date? I think we need some more context.'

'Well, it will have to wait because I have an... appointment.'

'Would this be with your boyfriend perhaps?'

'I'm really not sure,' she replied, and genuinely meant it.

Luke Miles, meanwhile, had been reflecting on his own dilemma and it had nothing to do with the GCSE revision that lay undone on his desk. If one more teacher tried to lecture him about the fundamental importance of having good GCSEs if you wanted to avoid a shit life, he was going to either hit them with a stick or alternatively do and say nothing but internally whinge about it. The success of his night out with JoJo at the Quayside fair had done nothing to dampen his enthusiasm or indeed his ardour. Indeed, it was his ardour that was consistently the problem. It never seemed far from view and seldom far from thought. However, he was determined to avoid the use of visual stimulus, he held a dim view of the use of the internet for such requirements.

'Demeaning, corrupting and shit.'

He had begun to dread having the house to himself for any period of time as it led to temptations that, as a normal teenager, occurred freakishly often.

Fortunately, Luke's machinations on the subject were interrupted by an incoming text message from JoJo suggesting they get together for a drink that evening. At nearly seventeen, Luke Miles was at the age when going to the pub was still an adventure of Lara Croft proportions. Going to the pub at JoJo Bartlett's request took it to epic space travel proportions.

JoJo Bartlett was oblivious to the excitement that her rather humdrum request had bequeathed to Luke Miles. Instead, she was preparing to meet up with Jamie Taylor, her boyfriend of two months standing, who now draped his arms around sexy twentysomething women when he wasn't with JoJo, apparently.

She still had not worked through how she felt about Jamie or indeed Luke. She did notice that she was quicker to anger at her parents' overwhelming niceness these days, not that she showed any outward signs of such feelings. JoJo's parents were always oblivious to what was going through her mind, which she viewed as a very good thing, based on some of the more recent thoughts that had been recurring regularly, especially when she was on her own.

She met Jamie at Nando's in Eldon Square at his request. He had actually used the phrase 'cheeky Nando's' in his message. Was he being ironic? Or was he merely just a bit chavvy? Life is so confusing, mused JoJo, giving Jamie a half-hearted wave as she entered the restaurant and saw him ensconced at a table by the large frontal window so they would be on display to the passing shoppers. This despite the fact that there were several more private tables nearby.

Jamie got up and awkwardly kissed her on the cheek as she arrived at the table. JoJo found herself rubbing at her cheek as if she had just been assaulted by an elderly uncle.

'You look great,' he said.

'Thanks,' was all that JoJo had.

JoJo had belatedly begun to appreciate just how much Jamie talked about himself. She was surprised that she had not seemed to notice this when they first got together. Or was it that he did not just talk about himself then? She wasn't sure what the answer to that was. She was thinking about this when Jamie was giving her a rather verbose review of his recent man-of-the-match performance for his local Sunday football team. Apparently, he had 'two assists'. JoJo assumed that this meant that he must have helped a couple of the opposition players up after they had fallen over and hurt themselves. However, she did not ask for confirmation as, frankly, she could not have cared less. As far as JoJo was concerned there should be a law against anyone over the age of fourteen being allowed to play with any shape of ball.

'Did you enjoy the fair at the Quayside last Thursday?' she said quietly, when he eventually stopped talking about how great he was.

She watched his face first form a frown and then colour slightly.

'Yeah, I did. Did you see me there? I was with Amanda... my cousin.'

He was either a liar or he had a very odd relationship with his cousin, JoJo thought.

'Your cousin Amanda? You've never mentioned her before.

How old is she?'

'Twenty-three. I'm sure I have. Amanda and I have always been close.'

'It certainly looked that way when I saw you with your arms all over her.'

'Did you think I was with some other girl? Is that why you have been pissed off with me lately and either not replying or sending short messages?'

'She did not look like a cousin to me, Jamie.'

'But she is. Do you want to meet her or something? Will that make you believe me? She lives in London, she's a student down there so that would be difficult.'

'You're going to hate me, but I have to go, I have an appointment that I can't shift.'

'But we haven't even ordered?'

'I'm not hungry, besides I can't stand Nando's. I told you that the first time we went out.'

This made Jamie look a little crestfallen. She suddenly felt a twinge of feeling for him that surprised herself.

'Oh right, sorry, I forgot about that. Are you breaking up with me?'

'I'm not sure what I want to do. Can you give me a little time to work out how I feel?'

'She is my cousin, JoJo, I swear.'

'I believe you,' she said, although she didn't and could not fathom why she said so.

'Are you going off to meet him?'

'Who do you mean?'

'That next-door neighbour that is always hanging around.'

'Well, he does live next door, so technically yes, he is always hanging around where I live don't you think?'

'You didn't answer my question.'

'No, I am not going off to meet Luke, although I might see him later, if I have your permission?'

This came out slightly more aggressively than she had

intended.

'I'm meeting an older man, but I don't think you need to worry about it too much as he is one hundred and six years old. That being said, he seems to quite like killing people so perhaps you might not want to piss me off, as I think he quite likes me.'

Before a clearly dazed Jamie could reply, JoJo skipped out from behind the table and headed out the nearby entrance.

'I will message you when I've thought about things, OK?'

She was out the door so quickly she never heard Jamie's reply.

HOMECOMING

'**I** went home to Morpeth after I got back to Britain. It was a week before Christmas.'

'But that is over a month after the war finished. Why did it take so long?'

'Most of us were not in a very good way by then, so they thought we should be looked after for bit in a Red Cross hospital in France before they sent us back across the Channel. I got quite a shock when I got home. My mother had shacked up with a new gadgie, and a black one at that!'

JoJo was pleased that she had spontaneously decided to go and see Ruben Miles without an agreed meeting time, he seemed on fine form. She realised that she enjoyed listening to his stories, but she had the vaguest feeling that the old man might either be lying, or at the very least he may have a questionable relationship with the truth.

'You're not a racist, Ruben, surely?'

'No, but I would imagine you won't find many people over eighty who aren't at least a little racist. You have to put it into the context of the time. David Lloyd-George, Winston Churchill, even Abraham Lincoln in his day. All great men to some degree, but all complete racists as I am afraid befits their times.'

JoJo could see his point, but she still did not care to agree with him.

'All I am saying is that there were hardly any blacks in the whole of London back then, never mind bloody Morpeth. He was an American, big as a brick shithouse, he was a prize-fighter. He used to take on all comers, even the gypsies.'

JoJo quite enjoyed the fact that Ruben Miles was beginning to be a little less formal when they talked now. She did not know what a 'brick shithouse' was, but it conjured up a feeling of strength.

'Let's just say that I caught him and my mother a little by surprise when I opened the back door with the spare key we kept under the plant pot in the backyard.'

Ruben Miles's mother had a slightly less sanguine view at the time of being caught in flagrante for the third time in her energetic life.

'He said he was a descendent of Bill Richmond, but I think that was just wishful thinking.'

'How did he end up in Morpeth? It's not exactly a throbbing metropolis now, never mind 1919.'

'I never got a satisfactory answer about why he was in Morpeth, but I'll get onto why he was in the north in a moment... But then again, I don't think my mother liked him for his conversational skills. His understanding and use of his mother tongue were quite basic.'

'Was your mother relieved to have you home safe?'

This produced a derisive snort from Ruben Miles.

'My mother never showed or expressed a single emotion on my return from the Great War. I don't think she even asked me about the trenches or being a prisoner of war once. You see, for reasons that I never appreciated, my mother was, how do you say it? Indifferent, yes, she was indifferent to my entire existence.'

'That must have been hard.'

'To be honest, it was like that when I was a kid. I was well used to it by the time I got back from the war. Besides, I did not stick around for too long after I got back, and I certainly did not spend any time speculating on the nature of my relationship with my mother.'

'You are on very good form today, Ruben. I don't think you've been this animated before.'

'Thanks for noticing. I do appear to have been in a good mood this week.'

He was very aware of why he was in such good form, but he chose not to mention Mrs Hazel Wharton. At least not yet. There would be time for that later.

Like many of his brothers in arms, Ruben Miles found the readjustment to civvy street a tough one. He was one of several veterans of the Western Front that returned to Morpeth, apparently relatively unscathed, at least physically. No missing limbs to tell their own story. But at night, as he struggled adjusting to a warm comfortable bed to sleep in, his dreams were full of death and trenches, smells and explosions, confinement and boredom and of course the Burgess brothers. Unlike some, Ruben Miles did not seek out the company and solace of fellow travellers. Indeed, he made a tangible effort to avoid conversations with the other returning soldiers, as he had no desire to talk about any of it. Instead, he faced the daily night terrors on his own.

He spent the waking hours trying to avoid his mother and Mr Richmond's impersonation of besotted teenagers.

'Do you want to make some easy money?' asked his mother's lover as he completed endless press ups in the back yard, pausing only to alternate between left and right-handed versions. Ruben Miles had been watching for several minutes and the man had not broken the slightest of sweats. Based on the longevity of the headboard banging sessions emanating from his mother's room, the big man had only just begun.

'I guess that can never be a bad thing. What did you have in mind?'

'I've fixed me a fight with the king of the Gypsies. I want you to put some bets on. We can't lose.'

Ruben Miles was old enough to recognise one of the truest of falsehoods when he heard it.

'He's from Darlington, and he has agreed to fight me on the Quayside in Newcastle. Two hundred to the winner, jack shit to the loser. My sort of contest.'

'Are we betting to win or to lose?'

Big Sam stopped his exercising and looked at Ruben Miles with some amusement. Big Sam got his nickname because he was large and from the USA. Ruben Miles assumed that it probably wasn't Oscar Wilde that had given Big Sam his moniker.

'I have never been beaten in nearly thirty fights.'

'That doesn't answer my question.'

Ruben Miles thought he might have to draw Big Sam a

picture.

'Are you going to deliberately lose to make a lot of money? What are the odds on the gypsy?'

'Two to one I reckon, most folks in this country know all about my fighting.'

Ruben Miles waited a few minutes, but no realisation came to the big man's face.

'So, if we make a lot of bets on the gypsy and you deliberately lose, we can earn a lot more than two hundred pounds, right?'

'But the loser gets nothing.'

Ruben Miles realised that this might take some time.

Louis Welch had been the King of the Gypsies for several years, defeating all comers on a monthly basis. He was as big as his American opponent and twice as ugly, his face a trophy to years of brutal, bare-knuckle contests, some lasting twenty rounds before his opponents were finally beaten unconscious. He could not spell rules, never mind Queensberry. But then again, he could not read or write at all. He had agreed to fight Big Sam on Saturday 20th February 1919, in a ring made of empty fish boxes adjacent to where the Tyne Bridge would be built on the northern side of the river several years later.

Despite his record, Louis Welch was indeed an underdog going into the fight. This was because in the last four years, Big Sam had roundly defeated all the other bare-knuckle boxing champs of the age in eagerly anticipated and well attended bouts in wartime London. Illegal bookmaking had financed the bouts and fuelled antisemitism, as many of the biggest bookies were Jewish. In fact, one of the reasons Big Sam had headed to the wilds of the north in the first place was to try and make it on his own, without more help from his 'friends'. At least that is what he told himself. In reality, he was in hiding from one or two dangerous faces. In particular, a certain Charles 'Derby' Sabini, who had overseen and pocketed most of the proceeds of Big Sam's UK fighting successes. A ruthless gangster and main controller of racecourse bookmaking in most of England, Sabini played a pivotal role in illegal boxing matches. He was not one to be seen to lose face, never mind hard cash.

Ruben Miles knew nothing of this. He was spending his time helping Big Sam get ready for the fight. He spent hours every day throwing a medicine ball at his chest and abdomen. He never flinched once. He also went out running with him every morning at six. Ruben Miles was always wide-awake way by then.

'I have a question,' said Ruben Miles, placing the medicine ball at his feet. 'Why are you training so hard when you are going to throw the fight?'

Big Sam looked a little in pain, like he had a big splinter stuck under the nail of his big toe. He always adopted this expression when he was confused. It got a lot of practice.

'I have my pride. I don't want to get whupped too easy. I'm gonna make him work for his win.'

'So, as well as lose you are going to let him fight you? How many rounds are you going to fight for?'

'Ten, maybe more.'

'Ah, so you actually like getting hit in the face. You enjoy the pain, right?'

'I certainly don't seem to mind it,' was all that Big Sam was prepared to admit.

'That makes a lot of sense. We don't want people to think you have thrown the fight, do we?'

'But I am throwing the fight.'

'Yes, Big Sam, I know that.'

Ruben Miles's mother was not in on the fix. She hated everything to do with Big Sam's fighting and therefore was deliberately kept out of the loop. Ruben Miles was surprised by how quickly and easily he gained Big Sam's trust. But Mrs Miles was suspicious and perceptive, and she knew that her lover and prodigal son were up to something. As she watched them bonding over the training, she figured that whatever it was she would be best keeping her nose out of things. She would come to regret that view later.

The day of the fight was cold and damp. A gluttonous mist hung low on the Tyne. The fight was not scheduled to start until eight in the evening. The makeshift ring was lit by gas lamps atop the fish boxes, producing a unique, pungent aroma. Newcastle's Central Station had been welcoming a cross section of the country's betting and criminal communities for several days. The local police had been paid off and kept at a discreet distance. Nearly a thousand men watched the fight. There were few if any women. There was no undercard. The punters, gamblers and bookmakers were there for only one reason.

Ruben Miles had spent several days giving several local Morpeth men money to bet on the outcome of the fight with as many people as would accept the offer. There were plenty of illegal bookmakers up from London who seemed prepared to take some decent stakes. Including Charles 'Derby' Sabini. Ruben Miles was smart enough to bet some of the money on Big Sam, one-way traffic would have screamed of a fix, no matter how careful he thought he was being. All told, he figured that they would clear nearly five hundred pounds for losing the fight. A huge sum of money in 1919.

Big Sam had surprised Ruben Miles with a question a week before the contest.

'I know I'm as dumb as a big box of rocks, but what I can't figure is would we not make just as much money with me winning and betting on me?'

'It's complicated. But trust me, it's much better this way. Don't worry, you can win the rematch, and we'll make even more money on that.'

That seemed to satisfy Big Sam. At least he never asked another question about it, he just seemed to trust what his new young friend told him.

Ruben Miles may have taken part on the worst day the British Army had ever experienced, witnessing personally literally hundreds of deaths, but oddly there was something even more unsettling about witnessing a bare-knuckle fight by two experienced, skilled and ferocious pugilists. Years later, whenever he watched Hollywood films of cowboys brawling in saloons, he would realise how unrealistic these scenes were. They never correctly captured the sound of knuckles crunching into faces. There was almost a beauty to the violence watched by Ruben Miles on that numbing Tyneside winter evening.

He may not have been much of a thinker, but Big Sam could certainly fight. He could take a punch that would down a horse, grin and keep on coming forward. Louis Welch was King of the Gypsies for good reason. His huge hands took turns to aim at Big Sam's face and kidneys. He seemed content to use his own face to block Big Sam's incessant jabs. It was obvious to Ruben Miles, even after a couple of rounds, that both men were addicted to the pain.

Grown men screamed and shouted like annoying children being denied more ice cream. The smell of alcohol, cheap tobacco and rancid flatulence hung in the air like a grim miasma. Scuffles broke out among the gypsies, seemingly fighting amongst themselves for no reason other than desire. The noises of the crowd echoing under the arches of the nearby railway bridge.

Ruben Miles was in Big Sam's corner and had a much better view than he wanted. Although not following the Marquis of Queensbury rules, the fighters took a breather on little wooden stools every so often, by un-verbal agreement, usually just a nod of the head.

After about half an hour, both men were beginning to tire, obvious by their lack of movement. Both men had battle wounds, Big Sam had a large cut over his right eye and a broken cheekbone. Louis Welch's left eye was almost closed, he had two broken ribs and a dislocated knuckle.

'I don't think I want to wait too much longer,' Big Sam said, coating Ruben Miles's ear with a hint of spittle.

Ruben Miles agreed. Judging by the animation and arguments coming out of Welch's corner, there may not be many rounds to go.

Unfortunately, Big Sam's dive was about as convincing as Sonny Liston's in 1964 against the disbelieving Cassius Clay. Louis Welch was just as indignant.

'Get up, ya black bastard, I never touched you,' he roared, audible even over the frenzy of the crowd.

For a moment it looked as though Big Sam had realised his error and was going to get back on his feet to have another go of making it look convincing. Sadly, if this was his thought, he soon changed his mind and slumped from a half crouching position onto his back.

Ruben Miles groaned audibly. The referee seemed confused, the 'winner' bemused, and the loser was ineptly feigning unconsciousness. The crowd went berserk. Within moments, there were mass brawls between rival supporters. It took Sabini and his entourage to restore some sort of order to the ring area. Some bookmakers paid out on winning bets, most did not, claiming a fix. Their viewpoints determined by whichever lost them the least money.

Ruben Miles managed to get Big Sam to his feet and made a pretence of attending to his facial wounds as if this were the reason for his sudden loss.

'You could have waited until he hit you in the face at least!'

'Why is everyone so mad? It was a good fight, wasn't it?'

'Because everyone knows you took a dive, you could not have made it look any worse.'

It was then that Big Sam saw Sabini striding toward him with a couple of grim-faced goons at his sides. Big Sam took off without another word, running as fast as weary legs could muster. The goons took off in pursuit, Sabini came face to face with Ruben Miles.

'That nigger is my nigger. Do you hear me, boy?'

Without further embellishment Sabini produced a cosh from his deep coat pockets and caught Ruben Miles flush on the jaw. He was unconscious before he hit the ground.

'I don't understand, what did he mean?' JoJo Bartlett paused the recording on her tape recorder and put down her pen and paper. She was very much a belt and braces type of girl.

'Sabini owned Big Sam, apparently. He won him in a card game. You see, Sam had run away from Sabini and his crew, which is why he ended up in Morpeth, of all places, to try and get as far away from their clutches as possible. But thinking was not Sam's forte, and he had not figured on Sabini finding out about the fight with the gypsy all the way up in Newcastle. That was a pretty big mistake that cost the fella his life.'

'So Sabini and his men killed Big Sam?'

'Well, evidence was never presented in a court of law and nobody actually witnessed what happened. But Big Sam was found floating facedown in the Tyne the next morning, his corpse nearly got as far as Tynemouth. Let's put it this way, I am no lawyer, but I think the circumstantial evidence alone is proof enough. We may not know how, or have seen who did the stabbing, but I think who gave the order is pretty clear.'

'Sabini.'

'The biggest gangster of the time, and he was for the next decade or more, so I heard. I was out of the country so I would not know.'

'So, what happened to you after you were knocked out?'

'I got a helping hand from a familiar face. Or I suppose I should more accurately say, faces.'

Ruben Miles paused as if to collect his thoughts. JoJo Bartlett thought she saw him lick his lips.

'I don't know which face surprised me the most, all these years later. I have never been as surprised as I was that night, as those two faces helped me to my feet. The first face was that of my mother. I had never seen her look concerned for me before. As she helped me to my feet she even asked if I was going to be OK.'

'I didn't see that coming, your mother has not exactly featured high on the maternal stakes so far in your story.'

'And the second face was the Fixer...'

'The American from the prisoner of war camp?'

'The very same.'

'But how did he even know where you were? You have not mentioned him at all in this part of the story?'

'That is because I had not seen the Fixer since the night in the camp in Germany that I ended poor George Burgess's suffering.'

'So, he just appeared out of nowhere, with your mother, to save you from Sabini's thugs?'

'So it seemed to me at the time. Mind you, I had just been smashed in the face with a cosh by a notorious London gangster, so maybe I was not functioning at full capacity.'

'What happened next?'

'They got me out of there pretty damn quickly, and by the following evening I was on a steamer out of Liverpool, heading for New York with the Fixer. I would not set foot in Europe for over ten years...'

'So, this was when exactly?'

'February 1919. I certainly picked a pretty interesting decade to give Uncle Sam a try. I suppose it seemed the sensible thing at the time to do, what with Big Sam, Sabini and his thugs. It was only much later that I found out that this had been the Fixer's plan all along.'

'Is this the end of this chapter? If so, there must be some mistake...'

'How so?'

'You haven't killed anyone in this chapter.'

Ruben Miles gave a gruff laugh.

'I might make up for that next time.'

There was a hint of a sparkle in those grey-blue eyes.

GO WEST

The afternoon after the premature demise of Big Sam, Ruben Miles left the shores of his home country, destined not to return for over a decade. The Fixer had secured a pair of passages to the new world, New York to be precise. However, the Fixer, as befits his country of origin, was not an egalitarian. Thus, Ruben Miles found himself ensconced in steerage, whilst the Fixer had secured more prestigious, expansive and expensive accommodation. The Fixer was unrepentant.

'I may have saved your life, but I am not going to pay more than you are worth,' he said, as he informed Ruben Miles of the practicalities of their Atlantic crossing.

They were about to board RMS Olympic. The Olympic was the sister ship of the legendary Titanic, but a good deal more fortunate. She enjoyed a lengthy and remarkable career, including impressive service in the Great War. Indeed, the Fixer and Ruben Miles were to be on board on her first journey since her post-War refit, caused at least in part by her ramming and sinking of a German U-boat on May 12th 1918. She was not nicknamed Old Reliable for nothing.

It was not that Ruben Miles was ungrateful to the Fixer. He could easily comprehend that Sabini and his crew may well have wanted additional compensation for the fixing of the fight. The demise of Big Sam was very fresh in the mind of Ruben Miles. However, he had many questions that the Fixer seemed unwilling to answer. How had he known where he was? Why was it his business? Was he involved with the Sabinis? What did he want from him? Ruben Miles managed to piece together some of the answers to these questions many years later. As for the Fixer, he was a closed book. Only one statement was regularly forthcoming from the lips of the man.

'I think I can use a man like you, Ruben Miles.'

It was a mantra that Ruben Miles would hear from the American throughout the Roaring Twenties as their lives became seemingly destined to coalesce. As for the here and now, Ruben Miles was pleased that he had managed to avoid seeing his mother before he fled, that would have been an uncomfortable exchange, as he already felt as least partly responsible for the demise of Big Sam.

'I think it might be best if we arrange to meet on disembarkation. It is not easy for the classes to mix without a degree of unpleasantness for at least one of the parties. This should keep you in beer and food.'

The Fixer handed over the equivalent of a month's wages for a skilled worker.

'We can call it an advance on your earnings, which of course we will discuss on our arrival. I will look after you, Ruben Miles. I think I can use a man like you.'

Ruben Miles eyed the money in his hands.

'I don't drink alcohol. I have never touched a drop. I saw it kill my own father.'

'Well in that case you're going to the right place as the Volstead Act became law in the good old US of A a few weeks past. Giving some discernible gentlemen, like me, what can only be described as a business opportunity.'

'What is that?'

'The Volstead Act is the ultimate folly of the God-botherers and Do-gooders. The Volstead Act has banned the sale and manufacture of alcohol in all the States. You might as well have banned lions from eating zebras, it isn't gonna happen. Still, as I said, men like myself see it as a damn fine opportunity, as people will still want a drink and will pay a good price to get one.'

'So, you want me to help you sell illegal booze.'

'I have spent the last three weeks, when not saving the skin of an old comrade in arms, travelling the length of the west coast of Scotland and buying up some of the best Malt Whiskey the world has to offer. And as we speak, my right-hand man, Archie Knox, is setting off from Glasgow with my first shipment. He will bring it ashore in Canada and bring it over the border by truck. But the role I have earmarked for you is a little more specialised to a man of your undoubted talents.

'And when do I get to know any details?'

'All in good time, Ruben Miles, all in good time.'

Ruben Miles was becoming accustomed to the Fixer's habit of repeating both the content and his name with most utterances. It was not the most unusual of his habits, not by a long chalk.

The Olympic's crossing was a good deal less eventful than her sister ship. Five days after it left Liverpool, Ruben Miles got his first view of the new world, the Statue of Liberty perched on Liberty Island. He was nineteen years old and the land of the free would be his home for the foreseeable.

'That must have been so exciting!' JoJo Bartlett exclaimed as Ruben Miles rubbed at his tired eyes. He had been talking for over two hours and his voice was beginning to falter.

'I think that's enough for today. Anyway, it is a good place to stop.'

'Can you remember how you felt on seeing the famous statue?'

'I remember thinking that it needed a good clean.'

Emotion was not Ruben Miles's forte.

'Ha! I don't believe that. You must have felt something. I mean, you were so far from home.'

'After France, everywhere felt far from home, even home. I'm tired, do you mind if I go and lie down?'

'Of course not, I will come back on Tuesday. Is that OK?'

'I'm not planning on going anywhere.'

This was becoming their little ritual.

This was the first time that JoJo had seen Ruben Miles look anything like his age. His back was stooped, and he shuffled out of his chair with much caution. He turned to face JoJo before he reached the doorway.

'Mrs Hazel Wharton seems to be wearing me out.'

And with those words, he grinned and disappeared around the corner.

MEMORIES

Mrs Hazel Wharton was one of the more mobile inmates of The Apple Orchard Retirement Community. The residents of the complex referred to themselves as the 'inmates', just because this annoyed Mr Matthews, the pompous and corpulent Assistant Manager of The Apple Orchard Retirement Community, so much. This mobility meant that Mrs Hazel Wharton was in great demand by the less capable members of the community. At first, she was quite happy to run small errands for others when she went out and about, either in Jesmond or Gosforth. However, as demand increased and with her ingrained inability to say no, she found herself being forced to accept small payments by her fellow residents. She was uncomfortable with the concept of making a profit from performing small neighbourly tasks, but her fellow inmates were most insistent. Miserable Mr Garvey had been most forthright.

'Any pound I gave you is one less for those bloody ingrates to squabble over at my funeral.'

Mrs Hazel Wharton gave a nervous little laugh as she accepted his three pound coins and a small envelope.

'Just give this envelope to the man behind the counter and wait until he has checked it and given you a return copy. Remember? Just like last week. I hope you bring me as much luck.'

Mr Garvey's Yankee had paid over three hundred pounds the week before. Not bad for a two pound stake.

Mrs Hazel Wharton added Mr Garvey's instructions to her written notes on her notepad. Despite being one of the youngest inmates, she did not possess a mobile phone. She had quite a busy morning ahead. She thought she should check in on Ruben Miles before she left as he had looked so tired the previous evening. She needn't have worried. As in most of his adult life, a good night's sleep was all Ruben Miles required to recharge his batteries, even his one hundred and six-year-old batteries.

Her knock on his door was greeted with a booming answer.

'Come in!'

As she entered, Mrs Hazel Wharton was greeted by the sight of a clearly rejuvenated Ruben Miles busily tidying his living room. For a fleeting moment, Mrs Hazel Wharton wondered whether the big secret that Ruben Miles clearly carried around with himself, was that he was on drugs. She literally gave her head a shake.

'Good morning, Mrs Hazel Wharton! How are you on this fine day?'

'Never mind 'Mrs Hazel Wharton', I have told you that Hazel will more than suffice. What are you up to? You were exhausted last night. I sometimes wonder what you and that young girl do all those hours you spend together.'

Mrs Hazel Wharton was genuinely amazed that she recognised feelings of jealousy regarding the secret meetings between JoJo Bartlett and Ruben Miles. She still had not been introduced.

'I have told you already, she is recording the story of my life and, believe me, there is quite a lot to tell. We have barely started, I have only just arrived in America and that was on the 29th of January 1920, a Tuesday, I recall. A lovely day, blue sky and winter sunshine, although a bitter breeze came off the Hudson…'

Mrs Hazel Wharton eyed him suspiciously.

'Why Ruben, you could not possibly remember that much detail about something that happened so many years ago. After all, I can barely remember what I did last Tuesday.'

'Last Tuesday? That was the day you stubbed your toe in the garden and swore for the first time in years, do you not remember telling me that? You had salmon for dinner, and you thought it was overcooked. You wore your light blue dress with your pearl necklace. You beat me at scrabble by twenty-six points after dinner, the triple word score using the word zero was the winning move.'

Mrs Hazel Wharton stood open-mouthed. They had begun a habit of playing one game of scrabble after dinner every evening, they had been playing for over a month.

'How do you do that? What's the trick? How can you

remember so much detail? I am sure you must be mistaken. I think I wore my grey dress last Tuesday.'

'No, that was Wednesday. Do you not remember you spilled a little orange juice on it at lunch?'

'Ruben Miles, are you making fun of an old lady?'

'Well, firstly you are not an old lady, you are more than thirty years younger than me. Which, when you think about it, does that not make me a cradle snatcher?!'

'I'm serious, Ruben, how can you do that?'

'I just can. I remember pretty much everything. At least everything that happens to me on any given day. I can go all the way back. That is not strictly true. I can't remember very much before my eleventh birthday. But every day since then I have a good handle on.'

'Every day?'

'Every day. Well apart from a period in hospital during the Second World War. Try me, pick any date from 1920 to the present day and I will tell you what I did that day.'

'You're making fun of me! Stop it right now!'

'Hazel, I am not making fun of you. I really can remember everything. I view it as a sort of gift, I always have. Seriously, pick a date.'

She could tell he was sincere by the look on his face. Either that or he was an impressive actor.

'16th March 1952.'

'OK, so that was a Sunday. Now Sundays in Britain in the 1950s were pretty slow, do you remember?'

'I picked my tenth birthday; it was a Sunday. How do you do that so fast?'

'I've told you, Hazel, I can remember every day. I was living in London at the time, my art-deco pad in Balham. I did a lot of travelling back then and I had to pack for a trip to Washington the next day. It was a wet and windy day and that was the day I discovered that I had a hole in my left shoe when I stepped in a puddle outside Covent Garden underground station. I had gone to the market to buy some flowers for a girl I was seeing at the time, Edna Morton. I had bacon and eggs for tea.'

Ruben Miles neglected to mention that he was married at the time.

Mrs Hazel Wharton wanted to believe Ruben Miles. She just did not know whether she could.

'I need to be able to trust you, Ruben, you know what that means to me after everything I have told you. Things that I have not shared with anyone before.'

'You can trust me, Hazel, I am telling you the truth. I really can remember every day of my life since I was eleven years old. They have a special name for it. It's called hyperthymesia. It's a very rare condition. They reckon there may only be about one hundred people on earth who have it at any one time. I have never told anyone about it before. I've always kept it a secret. For some reason, I have wanted to tell you since we first became friends.'

'Hyper...'

'...thymesia. It is a proper condition. You can look it up on the internet.'

'And you really can remember every day since you were eleven?'

'Every day, except that short time in the war. Would you like to try another?'

Mrs Hazel Wharton tried to think of some famous days. She was not very good with dates, but she remembered a few.

'What about the 22nd November 1963? Or is that too easy? After all, they say everyone remembers where they were that day?'

'Too easy,' he said quietly. 'Try something harder.'

'OK, what about the 3rd November 1978?'

Ruben Miles effortlessly was able to conjure the day in question to the front of his mind. He was always happy not to think about the other day, he still felt he perhaps could have done something about *that*.

'That was a Friday and I went to see *The Boys from Brazil* at the Odeon in Newcastle. It was a film about Nazis hiding in South

America after the war. I enjoyed the film, although I did not think it was very historically accurate. I went with a girl called Polly, we went for dinner at La Toscana, a nice Italian restaurant next to the football ground. I had the veal, Polly had pasta pomodoro. The owner, Salvatore, gave us a complimentary brandy as we had to wait half an hour for our table to be ready.'

'I thought you didn't drink alcohol. I remember you telling me that.'

'Polly had mine.'

Mrs Hazel Wharton decided to let that pass without comment, she had already tried and failed to elicit any information about any of Ruben Miles's previous relationships.

'This sounds more like a curse than a blessing to me. Believe me, there are plenty of days that I am very happy I do not remember in much, if any, detail.'

During their brief, if already intense, friendship, Mrs Hazel Wharton had made numerous, often cryptic, references to unhappy aspects of her younger life. Ruben Miles was generally astounded to discover that he had a definite desire to learn more about whatever it was that Mrs Hazel Wharton did not wish to remember. He had never felt this emotion before. He would have remembered.

HISTORICAL INTERPRETATIONS - PART ONE

Mrs Bartlett

'I've never liked that boy,' Mrs Bartlett said as she sat with her daughter in the new conservatory, newly completed two weeks ago. The room had the fresh paint smell and the view of the back garden out of the new patio windows was still not old. So what if they were in dispute with the builders who were trying to charge them nearly two thousand pounds more than the original quote? It was most certainly worth it. But then Mrs Bartlett would say that, as she had badgered her husband for two years to get the thing built.

Mrs Bartlett had always viewed her relationship with her only daughter as positive. They had always got along well. Although recently she was beginning to wonder if they only *appeared* to get along. After all, over dinner last week she had been astounded to hear that JoJo was calling herself a 'Labour supporter'. She had been too stunned to challenge her on this frankly ludicrous development.

'Mothers never like teenage boys, isn't that a scientific fact? Luke's nice, you would like him if you got to know him. He's funny and he's not a Labour supporter.'

This teenage passive aggressive statement was very un-JoJo, who usually portrayed the chip off the old block routine with some aplomb.

Mrs Bartlett let the Labour supporter comment pass without commentary.

'I trust you, of course, sweetheart, you have always had nice friends and such good judgment. I never worry about you doing anything silly or wrong. Unlike some parents who must spend their entire time wondering what their kids are going to do next.'

'Actually, Luke is coming over soon. I'm going to help him with his Maths revision. It is not his strong suit.'

'That is very thoughtful of you, darling.'

And with those words, JoJo headed upstairs to give her room another quick tidy.

An hour or so later, Mrs Bartlett could hear the soothing monotone of a Maths monologue drifting from JoJo's bedroom via the open windows, as it was another surprisingly warm late spring evening. They had been revising for about forty-five minutes.

'I suppose I should make an effort, even if his parents are who they are. I will make them a nice coffee to help keep them going.'

Mrs Bartlett often spoke her thoughts out loud when she was on her own, increasing in frequency after she opened the nightly bar at 6 p.m. sharp.

She made the coffee and added the chocolate biscuits to the tray. She remembered that part vividly. The next thing she recalled was being helped off JoJo's bedroom floor by her daughter and that boy. She remembered absolutely nothing else. She simply refused to do so.

HISTORICAL INTERPRETATIONS - PART TWO

JoJo Bartlett

Jojo Bartlett was studying A level History. She was enjoying it even more than the GCSE course she had aced with an A* the previous summer. Her teacher was Mr Ryan, the sort of teacher that students remembered fondly in later years because he was good, he cared, and he had a sense of humour. How many teachers tick all those boxes?

Jojo had enjoyed the subjects at GCSE, most notably Nazi Germany and the causes of the Second World War. However, the A level course was opening her eyes academically. Jojo was discovering that historians had many different perspectives on the same event. There was no unfettered 'truth', just different opinions on the causes or consequences of events. Sometimes they even disagreed about what happened. For someone who was already attracted to conspiracy theories, this was a welcome development. Jojo remembered with clarity that, in the hour before Luke came over to study for his GCSE Maths (as Jojo knew without her input he was not going to pass), she had been exploring the different historical perspectives on the Cuban Missile Crisis. She had been appalled to learn that the world could have been destroyed by nuclear war decades before she was born. She had not warmed to Khrushchev or Kennedy. She was already blaming both men for the crisis and wondering whether female leaders would have come so close to blowing up the entire world. She was also enjoying the gender topic in her Sociology course.

Jojo had not recently examined her feelings too closely regarding Luke Miles. They seemed to vary widely. She had rather confusedly reached the recent conclusion that he was quite good looking. She already knew that he made her laugh.

And now she found herself appraising his bum positively. All slightly scary developments. That and the fact that, at least technically, she still had a boyfriend, albeit one whose messages she was avoiding. On the other hand, Luke was in the year below her at school (although admittedly not the same school, thank Christ), and until twelve months ago she used to refer to Luke as the 'slightly creepy boy next door'. And although she did not really care about her friends, she did acknowledge that she may have cared what they said. For some reason, she cared more about what they would say behind her back, rather than to her face. Her friends, like most seventeen-year-old girls, thought that dating anyone under the age of nineteen was seriously lame. I mean come on, fourteen-year-old girls date sixteen-year-old boys. Everyone knows that, right?

JoJo had been mulling this though as she heard the front doorbell ring and her mother shout for her to get it as it was 'that odd boy from next door'. JoJo smiled. It was good to know that a mother's disapproval still counted for something.

They started to revise in her bedroom. Luke's attention span was not great. When he studied on his own, he could maybe go ten minutes without checking his phone or picking his nose. Revising with JoJo meant he could stretch this to at least twenty minutes.

She could almost see his eyes glaze over as she struggled to explain rudimentary trigonometry. The events after that were much less clear in JoJo Bartlett's mind. It was almost as if her brain had deliberately clouded her memories to make full retrieval impossible. At least she hoped so. She remembered that they were kissing, although she was very unclear how this started. She seemed to vaguely recall that she was enjoying it. She remembered a new sensation, new but not unpleasant. Then she remembered the door swinging open, her mother standing in the doorway with a tray in her hands. Then there was the sound of her mother screaming and the crash as the tin tray and the mugs hit the wooden floor of her bedroom.

HISTORICAL INTERPRETATIONS - PART THREE

Luke Miles

L uke Miles had his own unique take on the *catastrophe*, as he and JoJo would both come to call it. They were unfortunately clearly burned into his brain. He just hoped that they would not last forever. He also hoped that Mrs Bartlett did not remember the events for the rest of her days.

The day had started normally enough. He had been bored at school but cheered by the prospect of going around to JoJo's in the early evening, as she had offered to help him with his Maths revision. Luke Miles hated Maths. Indeed, he was more than suspicious of anyone who did not.

He bolted down his tea of *pasta surprise*. He was amazed that his mother could still call it that after all these years. Indeed, the only funny line he had ever heard his father say was last month after the Year Ten parents evening and he looked at his wife and said, 'Are you sure that this is not called pasta fucking predictable?'

Luke's father was not known for his jokes and he seldom swore. Luke surmised that the Year Ten parents evening must have been an even bigger car crash than previous ones. Parents tended not to like Luke's father. He made them feel that they were the ones being told off.

He arrived at JoJo's just after half seven and tried his best to concentrate on the trigonometry, but he barely lasted twenty minutes before JoJo's personal attributes and the proximity of her bed became too much of a distraction. JoJo took revision very seriously and often used words that he barely understood. Much to his surprise and excitement, when he moved closer to her, she moved closer to him and within a few shocking seconds he found that they were kissing. He remembered wondering if he was doing it right as his experience in this area was limited. Fifteen minutes with Stacey Barnes at Rory Jamieson's fifteenth birthday party was pretty much the sum total of his experiences. That had not gone well. He tried to put those memories out of his mind. And he almost never thought about teeth braces again.

He also remembered wondering if he was comparing favourably with her boyfriend who was older and had a car. Luke Miles did not appreciate that comparing performance was something he was going to have to get a lot more used to as he got older. Although he had lost a real sense of time, Luke Miles felt that his recall of chronology was accurate. At some stage, items of clothing were loosened and subsequently lowered. He even recalled a not unpleasant draught from the open bedroom window. Now, strictly speaking, the activity taking place was one that he was well versed in, indeed he had accumulated nearly five years of pretty consistent practice. But there was most certainly a twist in that afternoon's proceedings. He remembered all these thoughts and even saying quietly out loud, 'Well, it certainly feels different.'

It was then that there was a knock and, simultaneously, the blue wooden door, with a poster of Kurt Cobain on the back, opened with a slight creak, as was its habit. He could smell the mugs of milky coffee before they hit the floor, he saw the plate of chocolate hobnobs decimated amongst the mugs. He could hear Mrs Bartlett's shriek of horror and surprise. Oh, and he saw Mrs Bartlett's eyes staring at his engorged penis as her daughter adeptly wanked him off.

THE BABE

For Ruben Miles, to paraphrase an inarticulate Welsh footballer, America was like a foreign country. There was literally nothing about New York that resembled home. The huge building works all over Manhattan Island. The skyscraper era in full swing and on such a daunting scale that no European could empathise. For every completed building, there seemed to be at least three more under construction. The majesty of the Brooklyn Bridge or the impressive Woolworth building were two of his early favourites. Ruben Miles followed the development of the Manhattan skyline keenly throughout the Twenties. That is, when he was not looking after George Herman Ruth, Jr. But we will get to that shortly.

The Fixer was true to his word and had a job in mind for Ruben Miles and what he called 'your special skills' (although he never, even once, attempted to explain to Ruben Miles what he thought these skills were). Ruben Miles was very surprised that the job had nothing, at least directly, to do with the illegal sale and distribution of alcohol. He had assumed after their conversation before their Atlantic crossing on board the Olympic that the Fixer wanted him to commit criminal acts on the Fixer's behalf. In reality, his new role was much more difficult than that. He was to entertain, contain and protect at all costs, a man of unique talent, unreliability and with all-consuming appetites. The Babe. He became Ruben Miles's life for nearly ten years.

'I don't suppose you will have heard of Babe Ruth?'

Ruben Miles was trying to get comfortable on the garden furniture of The Apple Orchard Retirement Community, fidgeting with the oversized cushions. JoJo Bartlett sat opposite him, preparing for the next instalment of the life of Ruben Miles and, frankly, glad of the distraction from thinking about the *catastrophe*. She had so far managed to avoid her mother for two whole days, but it was becoming increasingly difficult.

'I have actually, wasn't he a baseball player? Mr Ryan

mentioned him in class when we did the Roaring Twenties.'

Ruben Miles allowed himself a chuckle.

'To call Babe Ruth a baseball player may be one of the biggest and most misleading understatements of all time. The man was not just the biggest star in all of America for over fifteen years, he also happened to be a force of nature. I should know, as it was my job to contain him.'

Ruben Miles, despite all that the Babe put him through, always smiled when he thought about him. Which was often.

'Of course, coming from England, I had barely heard of baseball, let alone Babe Ruth. I think it is fair to say that my life would have been a lot easier and certainly safer if I had not taken on the Fixer's offer to be Babe Ruth's babysitter. Not that he sold it to me on those terms you understand, he made it out to be an easy job. I will let you decide…'

Ruben Miles was introduced to the man he was to look after at the Ansonia Hotel, on the Upper West Side, sitting pretty between West 73rd and West 74th streets. It was early February 1920 and the Babe was preparing for the upcoming spring training in Jacksonville, Florida. He had just completed his hugely controversial move from the Boston Red Sox. He was preparing for training in a way that was to become very familiar to Ruben Miles. The Babe called it 'The Three Bs Diet: booze, burgers and broads'. Ruben Miles would live in the Ansonia Hotel, two doors down from the Babe on the Twelfth floor for the next nine years. Two doors down *was* important.

'Hey Ruben, do you want a burger?' These were the first words the Babe directed at Ruben Miles. He must have gone on to repeat the question a thousand times. Not that Ruben Miles ever accepted the offer. He was not quite a vegetarian, but he was very fussy about meat and certainly did not eat New York hamburgers.

Despite their very different appetites, the two men had an instant rapport, which despite everything that one man can put another through, survived virtually intact until Ruben Miles was forced into making himself scarce after the events of the spring of 1931; fleeing the land that had been home for over a decade. But we will get to that later.

After just a couple of days of acclimatising to one another, Ruben Miles was to accompany the Babe and the rest of the Yankees to Florida. Spring training, although the destination changed regularly, became something that Ruben Miles would look forward to in subsequent years, not for its ease, you understand, it was just that managing the Babe was always easier outside of New York. There were simply less people that he had pissed off, offended, cuckolded or who simply wanted him dead.

It was at Rose Field, on the south side of Jacksonville, Florida, that Ruben Miles witnessed first-hand what the Babe was about to achieve in the 1920 season, namely fifty-four home runs. Being an Englishman, Ruben Miles initially lacked knowledge and enthusiasm for baseball, but even he could see that the Babe sure could hit a baseball. There was good reason why he was called the Sultan of Swat.

But it was also on that trip that Ruben Miles first learnt of the Babe's other great love: women. In the first week of training alone, the Babe slept with twelve women. Or if he did not sleep with them, then he certainly shared quality time alone in his room with them, accompanied by various energetic noises that echoed through the too thin walls. Ruben Miles was a quick learner; at the following year's training camp he made sure that his room was not adjacent to the Babe's. Two doors down *was* important.

The women came in all colours, sizes and styles. The Babe was very far from prejudiced, or it must be said, particularly discerning. Ruben Miles's job was not one of procurement, he would have found that distasteful, and besides it was unnecessary. The women came to the Babe. He did not need to go looking for them. No, his job was to conceal the evidence of his philandering from his wife, Helen, the Yankee management, the media and most importantly of all, angry partners or husbands. It was a tough task, and when he also had to monitor and restrict the Babe's eating and drinking, Ruben Miles had very few days off. In actual fact, he had very few hours off.

'I could tell you a million stories about the Babe, in fact we could probably make a whole book out of just the time I spent with him. But we don't have the time. As you will see, we have a lot of other stuff to get through. I could tell you the story of how he lost $3,000 dollars in a single night playing Snap. I could tell you the story about the night he spent sleeping with all twelve whores in a cat house in Missouri and ate an eighteen-egg omelette for breakfast...'

JoJo Bartlett's cheeks flushed at this stage. She was not normally shy about sex talk, but that was before the *catastrophe*.

'I'm not shocking you, am I?'

'No, you're good.'

'I could tell you of the dozens of brawls with outraged boyfriends and husbands that I had to fight. I could describe every car crash that he walked away from, and he crashed a car every other week. I could describe in detail every charitable donation or activity he was involved with. I could even tell you about the time he upset Al Capone. Only the Babe could get away with upsetting Al Capone. Hell, I could spend a month just describing a fraction of his sporting achievements. But as this story is about me, I'm going to tell you about the biggest impact the Babe had on my life and my deeds. I'm going to tell you about how I had to kill two men in cold blood to protect the Babe.'

JoJo Bartlett gagged on her glass of water. She had really timed that drink poorly.

'You weren't kidding about killing more people?'

'That's right. I had to, or the Babe would have been finished.'

'I mean I know you killed those two brothers in the War, the Burgess brothers. But they were mercy killings. You are actually telling me that you deliberately murdered two men to protect Babe Ruth from harm?'

'No, I am telling you that I had to kill those two men, or the Babe would have been finished. He probably would have been killed, and in 1927 I am not sure the American people could have lived with the downfall of the Babe.'

'So, you're saying this was like a public service and not just plain murder?'

'I think we can live without the sarcasm. But that is why I want to tell you my story. Not all my actions and crimes were bad. Some of my crimes were based on good intentions, I want you to see that. Maybe some of my other actions are less easily defended.'

'You mean there is worse than killing two men in cold blood?'

JoJo Bartlett's head was spinning, and she could feel the quickening of her heart against her shirt.

'Let's put it this way, I have never lost a minute's sleep thinking about those two far-from-gentle men. They lived a dangerous life and had ended more than their fair share.'

'They were killers too?'

'Gangsters, and pretty mean ones at that. No, they have never caused me any regret, which sadly cannot be said of some later events that I was directly involved in.'

This was a lot to process for JoJo Bartlett. She had experienced a twinge of moral disquiet when Ruben Miles talked of wartime mercy killings. Now he was telling her he murdered gangsters and that later there was going to be even more criminal tales?

'I think I need to take a break. Can we call it a day?'

'Of course, will you come back tomorrow as planned?'

'Yes,' she said quickly, but in truth she was far from sure. The very old man and his wish for a record of his life had just got a whole lot more complicated and much more serious.

THE APPLE ORCHARD
RETIREMENT COMMUNITY
FOR THE BEWILDERED

Mrs Hazel Wharton was the youngest and Ruben Miles was the oldest inmate of The Apple Orchard Retirement Community. Ron Hargreaves was quite possibly the funniest. He was one of those old people who could still make anyone laugh and, rather predictably, it was he that had scrubbed out 'elderly' from the home's signage hanging in the rear garden and wrote in perfect font and calligraphy, 'bewildered'. What was more pertinent was that none of the staff had seemed to notice, or if they did, they must have felt it was an official change in the name. Either way, it had been over two weeks since the vandalism and nobody had lost any remission.

Ruben Miles was clearly a little troubled. Mrs Hazel Wharton could see that by the way he played with his dinner. He was not trying to eat the spaghetti Bolognese, he was simply wrapping it around and around the spoon that he had specifically asked for. He had never understood the British using a knife and a fork to eat pasta. He learnt that in America a long time ago.

'Stop playing with your food and tell me what is bothering you.'

Mrs Hazel Wharton did not know where her sudden bluntness had come from. She had never, through her entire marriage, talked to her husband in such bold terms.

'I'm sorry I'm not much company tonight. I think I upset JoJo today and I'm not sure she will continue with what we're doing.'

In the last couple of weeks, Ruben Miles had told Mrs Hazel Wharton a little of what he was doing with JoJo Bartlett. Not that he had given her any details, you understand. He wanted to be much closer to Mrs Hazel Wharton before he would even think about mentioning any of his stories to her.

'Why was she upset? What had you told her?'

'We were talking about my life in New York in the 1920s and

maybe she was a little surprised by the direction we went in.'

'You say she is a really clever and mature girl. I am sure she can deal with whatever stories you had to tell her. I mean, how upsetting can they be?'

'You are probably right. Let's change the subject. You haven't told me much of your family life. Why don't you tell me a little bit about your family?'

'That is a difficult subject for me, Ruben. I'm not sure I'm ready to tell you about that yet.'

'I understand, Hazel, but rest assured I want you to know that you can trust me. I do not judge people for what they do in their lives. Me, of all people, should not judge others on what they have done.'

'Oh my, Ruben, just what have you done in your life?'

'Like you, I am not ready to talk about that with you just now. But like you, I have a very sure feeling that I will do before I die.'

'Don't talk that way!'

'Mrs Hazel Wharton, I am one-hundred and six years old, the one thing in life that you can be sure of, is that I cannot go on living indefinitely, even if I do feel physically and mentally the same now as when I was eighty. And no, I can't explain that either.'

'So, you are not ready to talk to me about your life, but you will tell that young girl. Tell her things that you say have already upset her?'

'I just needed to tell someone before I die and I thought that a young, clever stranger was the best way. But now I am not so sure. I may have to rethink that.'

LUKE, I AM YOUR GREAT GRANDFATHER

Ruben Miles was not the only one experiencing a rethink. JoJo Bartlett had at least found something to take her mind off the *catastrophe*. The revelation, although yet unexplained, that Ruben Miles was capable of cold-blooded murderer, was proving difficult to digest and evaluate. She was not even sure if she would go back to see him the next day, as was scheduled. She was not even sure she could go back at all. And yet. And yet there was something about this old man and his already weird and unsettling life that she wanted to uncover. She felt strongly that there was a reason that he wanted to tell his life story. She just had no concept of what that might be. And she liked recording his stories and she had many questions for him. The main one being: how come he had such a good memory? Plus, she was sure he would help a little with her A level History course.

'I mean, at this rate, he is probably going to tell me that he killed Hitler and caused the Cuban Missile Crisis.'

She said this to herself as she hid quietly in her bedroom and cringed every time she heard maternal movement from downstairs.

What she wanted to do was talk to Luke about his great grandfather and his stories. Then it occurred to her quite strongly, much more strongly than it had before, that the old man might not just be exaggerating, but making the whole thing up. Instead of a life story, she thought, is he getting me to write some novel that he never got around to writing?

Ruben Miles had made it clear from the first interaction that he did not want Luke to hear his story. That was the first complication. The second was that after the catastrophe she was not sure that she could be in the same room as Luke Miles, never mind have a meaningful conversation.

'Life is overrated,' she said, as she looked in the mirror.

Then her phone vibrated, and she saw that she had a new message from her 'boyfriend'

Oh fuck, she thought, I had completely forgotten about him.

Luke Miles, on the other hand, was not experiencing any kind of rethink about anything. He still thought revising was shit, that his parents were quite simply the dullest people on the planet, that there should be a law against *Deal or No Deal* being allowed on the TV and that the *catastrophe* was actually one of the most memorable moments of his entire sixteen-year-old life. OK, it could have ended better for sure. But the bit leading up to it, well that was certainly right on the money.

He was sure that he wanted to spend more time with JoJo. But he was also very painfully aware that in the two days and seventeen hours since they had last been together, he had sent her three messages and, as of right now, she had not responded to any of them.

So, it is fair to say that when she messaged him just after he had finished his frozen pizza that he had undercooked for tea, his joy was uncontained. The message did not answer any of the thirteen questions that he had asked her. Instead, it simply said, 'Can you go for a walk? I have to get out of this place!'

He knew that he should play it cool and not reply straight away. He waited three whole minutes.

JoJo Bartlett had at least managed to make one decision.

She had blocked her boyfriend's number from her phone. Well, ex-boyfriend would be the correct nomenclature now. It seemed that the rules on breakups had moved even further from politeness. Now, you did not even get a brief message to say that you had been dumped. You were digitally erased.

Feeling a little buoyed by her decisive decision-making, JoJo crept out of the family home as quietly as possible. Alas, she was neither quiet enough nor lucky enough. She literally bumped into her mother as she almost reached the connecting door to the garage (she had incorrectly surmised that this was the least likely place to cross paths with her mother).

The pair locked eyes momentarily.

'I am going out for a walk, bye!' JoJo managed, although it did come out a little high pitched and manic.

'But darling, we need to talk. We have not spoken since...'

But JoJo had made the door and was through it and away before Mrs Bartlett had finished her sentence.

Mrs Bartlett was disappointed to realise just how relieved she was. I mean really, what was she going to say to her daughter after *the event* as she referred to it. She had been shocked that her temporary amnesia about the event had lasted only a few hours. Mrs Bartlett gave her head a slight shake. She then wondered whether quarter to six was too early to open the bar for the evening.

HERE COMES THE TRAMP - PART ONE

JoJo Bartlett kept her arranged appointment with Ruben Miles the following morning. She felt that she had to find out at least the next part of his story. Her evening walk with Luke had, of course, resolved little, if anything. She still liked him, and he did make her laugh with ease, but she was far from sure whether she wanted to have another experience like the *catastrophe.*

Ruben Miles was very relieved to see her as she entered The Apple Orchard Retirement Community with her usual indifference to her surroundings the following day. He had spent most of the previous, near sleepless, night pondering on alternative plans if JoJo pulled the plug on helping him with his memoirs. He had thought about some of his own attempted memoirs and knew that he did not do his story the justice it deserved.

This ensured that Ruben Miles offered her his biggest smile and a packet of Maltesers, JoJo's clear confectionary favourite, when she settled down beside him in the far corner of the rear garden.

'I thought you wouldn't come back.'

These words surprised Ruben Miles even as he spoke, as he had previously determined to make light of her appearance, should she arrive.

'I very nearly didn't. But we are going to have to change things if you want me to continue with your story.'

'In what ways?'

'First, you have to swear on your family's life that you are telling me the truth at all times.'

'Done, although as you know, except for Luke, I have very little time or need of my family.'

'And secondly, I want to be able to tell Luke what you have

told me should I choose to and maybe bring him with me sometimes when I come and see you.'

'I can hardly stop you telling Luke anything, can I?'

This was of course true, but JoJo Bartlett had such an uncomplicated and pure relationship with the truth that it had simply not occurred to her to tell Luke anything after previously promising Ruben Miles that she would not.

'And he can come if I want him too?'

'If that is what it takes for you to finish my story, then yes, but it might complicate things a little later. You do know that we have barely started? Are you sure you have the time to spare?'

JoJo Bartlett had never started anything that she had not completed to the best of her ability and she had no intention of changing that now.

'Of course. So, you have and are always going to tell me the complete truth...'

'And nothing but the truth, yes.'

'I mean, I am sure that you will misremember things naturally, I mean my mother does not remember where she has put her glasses down and she is only forty-two, so I am sure that a hundred-and-six-year-old man will get a few facts, dates or events wrong from the 1920s or whatnot.'

'Well actually JoJo, in the spirit of telling the full truth, there is something about my memory that perhaps I should have told you about earlier. Have you heard of hyperthymesia?'

'No.'

'Well, it is a very rare condition. I mean exceptionally rare. I think there are only about a hundred or so people on the entire planet that have it.'

'And you are one of them? How do you spell it?' JoJo said, knowing she could research it on her computer when she got home.

He spelled the word out for her.

'It means that I can remember in detail, the events of every day of my life, well, from the age of eleven anyways.'

'You're fricking joking, right?'

'No, I'm not, have we not just agreed that I must tell you the truth at all times? This is a pretty important thing for you to understand don't you think?'

'You can literally remember every day of your life?'

'Pretty much. When I was younger, I thought everyone could. It was only much later when I worked for various governments that I realised how rare a condition it is.'

'Various governments?! Why do I already not like the sound of that?'

'Can we leave that until later? I do find chronological order to be the most logical way to proceed.'

'Right, tell me what happened to you on the nineteenth of January 1946.'

Ruben Miles wondered if there was another way to demonstrate his memory without the need for the same, predictable parlour game. He thought not.

'I was staying near Hanover in Germany. It was a Saturday. I went for a walk in a local park in the morning. I had bread and sausages for lunch. I got caught out in a snowstorm in the early evening, I was pissed off as it was not forecast on the radio.'

He had neglected to mention that he spent this period of 1946 working for British intelligence on the de-Nazification process in postwar West Germany. He spent most of that month interviewing staff from the death camp at Treblinka. *That* was a sobering experience.

'Ok, twenty ninth of November 1974.'

'A cold Friday in London. I had fish and chips for tea. I had a heated argument with my next-door neighbour about Ted Heath, he was a real moron.'

'Ted Heath or the neighbour?'

The old man smiled.

'Both. I could say much more if more significant events occurred. For example, let me tell you about the summer of 1927. I have already started telling you about the Babe. But you also need to know about Charlie. Have you heard of Charlie Chaplin?'

JoJo shook her head as she got ready to start recording.

Ruben Miles was genuinely shocked that someone so famous in 1927 could not even have been heard of by a very intelligent young woman in the early 21st Century. How was that possible?

'He was the biggest film star of the time. Probably the only person as famous as the Babe in 1927. I suppose that's why their two stories had to merge at some point, it was inevitable I suppose.'

JoJo made a mental note to google Charlie Chaplin later.

'Charlie shared the Babe's proclivities. By that I mean he was a womaniser too. Actually, young women would be a better description for Charlie. I mean his first two wives were sixteen years old.'

'His first two wives were younger than me? Did that not cause scandal?'

'Not as much as you would think. I suppose things were different back then. Although 1927 was not Charlie's best year. He had a very messy divorce from his wife, Lita, and in all truth, he had a bit of a nervous breakdown. Even the film he made that year, *The Circus*, was not one of his best. I never really met the man, but I saw him for the first time in the flesh in August 1927. I was at an event organised by the Fixer. It was at a party on the Upper East Side for some Wall Street hotshot. He had managed to get the Fixer to invite Babe Ruth and Charlie Chaplin to the same party. There was literally nothing that the Fixer could not arrange, if the price was right. I was there to look after the Babe, of course.'

But the two icons of an era were not the only noteworthy attendees of the banker's party. Marie and Rosa Lombardi were the seventeen-year-old twin daughters of one Stefano Lombardi. Lombardi was a regular hitman for Giuseppe 'Joe the Boss' Masseria, who in 1927 was one of the two most powerful mafiosos in all New York City. The girls had secured invites to the party because of their stunning beauty. It's a shame no one thought to ask who their father was.

'I suppose it was a little comical at first, the two great stars and notorious skirt chasers both going for the twins at the same party. But it really summed up both guys, they could have agreed to get one each, but that was not the way the Babe and Charlie thought or operated. They each wanted both of the twins.'

JoJo fidgeted a little in her seating position. It seemed that more and more of the old man's stories appeared to have what her mother annoyingly referred to as 'adult themes'.

'Do I presume that the rest of this tale is about sex and murder?'

'Simplistically I suppose, but I would have thought revenge or at least attempted revenge would be the main theme. Can I continue?'

Marie and Rosa Lombardi were not virgins, not by some considerable distance. They were thirteen when they realised just what it was that most Italian men were interested in. They were fourteen when they decided to see whether it was something they liked. It was. By sixteen, the twins had been discreet enough to keep a reputation, and indiscreet enough to keep demand for their charms exceptionally high. They became adept at playing the young innocent when around the wealthy and famous, which by the summer of 1927 was becoming a regular feature of their social lives.

Charlie Chaplin was instantly smitten. They were plum in the middle of his dubious Venn diagram of sexual attraction. Sixteen-years-old, seemingly pure, and yet with an undertow of possible debauchery. He could barely keep his eyes in his head. The problem for Chaplin was that, without his oversized clown shoes, cane and undersized hat, he was almost unrecognisable from his onscreen persona. Which is why his entourage followed him everywhere (infamously even into the toilet), to loudly proclaim his eminent arrival at any formal or social gathering. Buster Keaton cracked that he should have his own theme tune like the President, and it could be played whenever he walked into a room to announce his attendance. Here comes the Tramp.

The Lombardi twins knew who he was. They also knew about his tastes. They were keen to get to know the great Charlie Chaplin. But then the Babe made his entrance.

When JoJo Bartlett first googled Babe Ruth and started to watch the footage of him available on YouTube she thought she may have been watching a spoof sitcom about a sportsman who was a huge celebrity and star by mistake. Watch how he runs around the bases. He looks like an ungainly fat man. He was an ungainly fat man. But black and white YouTube footage does not give context. Nor can it illustrate the sheer presence of the man. The Babe had an aura as well as immense talent, and in 1920s New York it went everywhere with him like the cheap cologne he still preferred to liberally wear, no matter how many girlfriends tried to get him to apply something more tasteful and expensive.

Within minutes of his arrival, the Babe was sat in a crown-like chair in the middle of the main room of the party, beer in one hand, huge scotch in the other. A Cuban cigar firmly clenched in his mouth and a large plate of hot dogs on a little table sat directly in front of him. The Lombardi twins, one on each knee. Ruben Miles stood, as he usually did, just out of camera shot on the Babe's right-hand side, looking at the crowd for potential trouble.

Charlie Chaplin was not used to playing second fiddle to anyone, but even he privately knew that in 1920s New York, there was really only ever going to be one winner. Charlie Chaplin was not a nice man. He even said so himself. He was a jealous and bitter man, racked with fears of inadequacy, dating from his impoverished childhood in London. He always wanted to beat everyone at any game, whoever they were. And so, a little while later as Chaplin and his entourage decided to head off to a new venue, a friend of the host had clearly seen the look in Chaplin's eyes as he surveyed the scene of the Babe and the Lombardi twins and could not help himself.

'They sure are beautiful aren't they, Mr Chaplin? But they should come with a health warning if you ask me...'

Chaplin eyed the man unpleasantly.

'What do you mean by a health warning?'

'They are Lombardi's girls. He is understandably very protective of them. It is said that he has already personally castrated two guys from Brooklyn who became, how shall we say, over friendly with the twins.'

Charlie Chaplin winced and instinctively cupped his balls gingerly, as all men do when hearing the word castrated said out loud.

'Who is this guy Lombardi?'

'Masseria's personal hit man.'

Chaplin knew who Masseria was, he had even seen him once in one of the city's swankiest restaurants. Surrounded by some of the scariest looking men Chaplin had ever seen. And Chaplin had once been to Cardiff.

'Are you saying that Mr Lombardi would be most displeased to see his lovely, innocent young daughters bouncing on the knees of the great Babe Ruth?'

'I'm not sure about that, Charlie. But he sure will be pissed if he finds out that they spent the best part of tonight bouncing up and down on the Babe's most overused organ, and I am not talking about the great man's heart.'

Chaplin, despite his profession, was not one for profanity and smut. However, even he could not resist a malicious little cackle.

'And do you think Mr Lombardi may indeed find out about any potential tryst?'

'I have a friend who works for Mr Lombardi.'

And that is how easy it was. Charlie Chaplin was a man who did not like being ignored. The minute the Lombardi twins caught sight of the Babe he knew that tonight was not going to be his night. The friend of the host wanted little in return, just a guest appearance at a party he was throwing for his wife later in the year. Chaplin thought it a price worth paying in the event of their little scheme paying dividends. The deal was simple and quickly arranged. If proof of any encounter between the Lombardi twins and the Babe could be conveyed to Stefano Lombardi, events might take an interesting course.

'What a hateful man!' exclaimed JoJo Bartlett.

'I never formally met Chaplin. Indeed, that night was, I think, the only time I shared a room with him. But the tales of his unpleasantness were quite common. Luckily for the Babe, he had the Fixer and me to take care of him.'

For the Babe *had* indulged in his most favoured vice on that sultry Manhattan night. The twins had not only been prepared to share the great man; it had been their suggestion. They had been so engrossed in what they were doing that none of them heard the man behind the gold embossed drapes or heard his fidgeting with his camera equipment. Although it is fair to say that the flash and noise of the camera doing its work did get their attention. But in the time it took all three participants to fully comprehend what had just happened to them and its potential consequences, the cameraman had flown the scene, hurriedly taking his heavy equipment with him.

The Babe was not a worrier, in fact his only comment as he watched the twins hurriedly dressing and babbling to each other about the dangers of their father finding out about the events of the evening was typically self-absorbed.

'I think that sudden flash has given me indigestion.'

Of course, nothing to do with twelve hot dogs, a gallon of beer and a quart of bourbon.

The Babe did not even think to ask who their father was. He was not the sort to cry over spilt milk.

Ruben Miles was in his now customary position of being two doors down from the Babe. He neglected to tell JoJo Bartlett that the main reason for his slightly slow response to the kerfuffle was that he himself had been entertaining that evening, albeit just one young lady.

'There was no trace of the guy. It was as if he had disappeared.'

'So, what happened next?'

'Nothing for a couple of days. Then one afternoon, when I was waiting for the Babe to finish training, the Fixer shows up looking very un-Fixer like. I mean he actually looked worried.'

The Fixer did indeed look concerned. He had lost a little of his aura of complete confidence. He did not even seem as smartly dressed as normal. These were all signs to be anxious about.

'You have a problem, Ruben Miles, but I am sure a man of your skills can handle it.'

Some things at least did remain the same.

'I have a problem. Does that not mean we have a problem?'

The Fixer chose to ignore this comment.

'Our boy has been, shall we say, lacking in discretion and

respect. He has also been guilty of a rather unfortunate choice of… companions. I don't suppose you have heard of Stefano Lombardi?'

Ruben Miles confirmed he had not.

'Very heavy mobster, not the sort you want to be pissed at you, never mind get caught on camera fucking his two sixteen-year-old princesses…'

'Oh fuck.'

'Indeed. Don't worry, I have a plan for how you can sort this.'

'Don't you mean how *we* can sort this?'

Again, there was no response from the Fixer, there was no such thing as collective responsibility with the Fixer.

But the Babe did not want to literally pay up to cover up his actions. In fact, he was most adamant.

'I did not force those girls to do anything they did not want to do, believe me.'

'I'm sure that's true, Babe, but I don't think that is the point. Mr Lombardi is a man to be respected, feared even. He has definitive proof that you…'

'Yeah, I know what proof he has. I was there when the camera went off, remember?'

Like a lot of successful and therefore spoilt men, the Babe was not good at being told what to do. Or rather, more pertinently, what not to do. It was why every time the Yankees put more stuff in his contracts about moral behaviour, in his mind the clauses meant he had to perform even more immorally.

'And it's not as if you could even marry both.'

The Babe's long running divorce from his first wife Helen was only weeks old. As they were having this conversation, Ruben Miles had no idea that within a month the Babe would have married his long-term mistress, Claire Merritt. You would have thought he would have been more motivated to clear up this particular mess.

'The Fixer thinks he might take the money if we say the right things. It's our best shot.'

'But $5,000 is a hell of a lot of my money, Ruben.'

'But you will make plenty more. You have another renegotiation coming up, right?'

Ultimately, the Babe was convinced. The Fixer arranged for Ruben Miles to meet Stefano Lombardi to offer him the $5,000 apology. Hopefully it would be enough. Lombardi had wanted the Babe to be at the meet. The Fixer agreed to it, but omitted to tell Ruben Miles. This ensured that when Ruben Miles arrived at the arranged meeting point (the Chinatown entrance to the Brooklyn Bridge on Jay Street) at ten o'clock on a humid Friday night alone, the meeting with Lombardi and his sidekick, a six foot six guerrilla called Mikey 'the Ox' Martino got off to a poor start. It did not improve with time.

'Where the fuck is the Babe?' Lombardi said, by way of an introduction. 'The fucking Fixer told me he would be here!'

Ruben Miles instinctively opened both his palms in a defensive and conciliatory gesture.

'I don't know anything about that. I was just told to be here and give you this.'

Ruben Miles proffered the envelope with the money inside.

'The Babe is so sorry, Mr Lombardi. He meant no disrespect. He had no idea that the twins were your daughters, or he would never have...'

But Lombardi finished the sentence for Ruben Miles.

'Fucked them both, together?'

'Please accept this as an apology, Mr Lombardi.'

He tried handing over the envelope for a second time. This time Lombardi took it and handed it to Martino.

'Count it,' he said.

This was done under an available streetlight.

'It's all here,' declared Martino.

'The Babe is truly sorry, Mr Lombardi. He says if you ever want tickets to a ball game...'

Ball game may have been an unfortunate choice of words. Either way, Ruben Miles did not get the reply he was expecting.

Mikey 'the Ox' Martino pulled a gun from his jacket pocket and pistol-whipped Ruben Miles flush on the nose. He went down like a dropped bag of horse shit.

Lombardi then bent over the prone Ruben Miles and kicked him hard in the guts.

'Apology not accepted. And you tell the Babe that unless he wants me to come and find him and chop his dick off and shove it up his ass, he needs to meet me in person to apologise. And you can also tell the Fixer that I am not impressed. Fucking ball game tickets…'

With that, Lombardi and Martino left Ruben Miles to his kicking-induced retching. It was about fifteen minutes before he was able to get up and head home, with a streaming broken nose as a souvenir of his night.

A SMALL FAVOUR

Mrs Hazel Wharton was a woman with a very clear idea of what she wanted. She was even clearer on what she didn't want. Thus, having set her sights on Ruben Miles, the only male who could get any meaningful conversation or interaction out of her at The Apple Orchard Retirement Community, she feigned deafness or ignorance toward any other possible interactions. This did not endear her to the males that still gamely dreamt of elderly romance. They were even less pleased when she politely but firmly declined to complete the sundry outdoor tasks that she had, until she became acquainted with Ruben Miles, been happy to do. This of course also resulted in Ruben Miles being less popular, if indeed that were possible. Blame had to be apportioned somewhere and it was against every fibre of these gentlemen's beings to blame a sweet, petite grey-haired woman for anything. Ruben Miles had even noticed some of the frosty looks he was now getting when he sat with Mrs Hazel Wharton.

'Can I ask you something?' She said this as she poured them both a glass of sparkling water. Mrs Hazel Wharton thought that sparkling water was the height of sophistication. Ruben Miles thought it was a glass of water ruined.

She did not wait for him to reply.

'What I don't understand is why a man like you, who is still remarkably mobile, does not want to get out into the fresh air a bit more? What keeps you in your rooms all the time?'

Ruben Miles's first response was *not* to mention his recent outdoor visit to Derwentside with JoJo Bartlett, as he had the real feeling that he would regret it if he did.

'I have absolutely nothing against going outside more, Hazel. I suppose I had just got into the habit of staying in. I mean, at my age and having lived in these parts off and on for fifty years or so, there is probably little new to see...'

'Nonsense. Come on, let's go for an adventure. Besides, I have a small favour to ask you. I also have something to show you, it's going to help with our adventures.'

Fifteen minutes later, and despite the warm weather, Ruben Miles stood in the car park of The Apple Orchard Retirement Community with a cardigan and winter coat on. The one habit of the aging process that he shared with the rest of his cohort was the need for more clothing than seemed necessary. Mrs Hazel Wharton looked him up and down disapprovingly.

'Get that stupid coat off, it must be seventy degrees.'

She held out her hands until he reluctantly gave the coat up.

'Well, what do you think? I took some of your advice and spent some of my savings…'

She was pointing at possibly the smallest car Ruben Miles had ever seen. It was blue and looked as if it had been built as a toy for middle-sized children.

'It's called a Smart Car. What do you think?'

Ruben Miles thought that once again silence may be his best option.

Mrs Hazel Wharton gave him a look that told him that silence was not going to be tolerated.

'I like blue cars,' he finally and correctly settled on.

It was easier to get in than he expected. It only took twenty minutes. By the time he had removed the handbrake from his trouser pocket and the seat belt from his left ear, they were ready to go. But where?

'Where are we going?'

'The library in the city centre first. We have some research to do.'

'Research?'

'That's right. That little favour I was going to ask. Will you help me prove that my adopted son is a serial killer?'

This was going to need some explanation, even for a man who had led such an unusually full life.

'You're going to have to start from the beginning, I think.'

HERE COMES THE TRAMP - PART TWO

The Fixer was AWOL. Ruben Miles had never known exactly how to get in touch with him. The Fixer just appeared, usually when he was required. But not this time. This time Ruben Miles was on his own. He told the Babe that everything was sorted with Lombardi. Despite his crooked nose, the Babe bought Ruben Miles's words. But then the Babe was always capable of believing what he wanted to believe.

'Listen Babe, I am not able to come with you on the road trip this week. I have some family business I have to take care of.'

The Yankees were in the mid-west for a series of games that would keep the Babe out of New York for over two weeks.

'You're going to England?'

That sounded like a good lie.

'Yes, my mother's at death's door.'

The Babe was surprisingly relaxed about flying solo. After all, he was used to Ruben Miles looking out for him. He had been doing it for seven years.

'It's just a couple of weeks. I've arranged for Billy Docherty to cover for me for a few weeks. You like Billy, right?'

The Babe liked Billy Docherty.

'Sure, you take care of your mom, and I will be just fine with Billy for a few weeks.'

Billy Docherty was a reliable man. Ruben Miles had known him from various scrapes involving the Babe. He was sober, had a clear mind and fast fists, all of which were a necessity when you were looking after the *Bambino*.

The absence of the Fixer ensured that Ruben Miles had to come up with a plan on his own. He was certain of what it was he had to do. But unlike the Burgess brothers, the killing of Lombardi and his sidekick (for Ruben Miles correctly assumed that the two were seldom seen apart) would be no act of mercy. This would be murder without moral wriggle room. But as the Fixer had somehow determined in northern France in 1918, Ruben Miles was both a man without a God and very little in the way of moral consciousness. He was a pragmatist. Which meant that his mind was not grappling with the ethics of the plan, just the practicalities.

Ruben Miles knew that, on any given night, his targets would be at the Whiskey Curb, as the streets of Kenmare, Broom and Grand were called in the heart of Little Italy. They were the heart of Masseria's empire. They were no more than open-air booze markets and all within spitting distance of the NYPD headquarters. Mean streets full of gangsters and cops, not the best place to take out a couple of heavy wiseguys without being caught or killed.

But Ruben Miles's job was to protect the Babe and, as far as he could work out, the Babe was either ruined or dead if he did not take out Lombardi. That was as complicated as Ruben Miles's mind was.

The very night the Babe had safely left town with the Yankee entourage, Ruben Miles tucked a gun in his waistband and a knife in his right boot and headed for Little Italy. But that first night was a bust. He went to all the places that he knew Lombardi was seen at regularly. Nothing. Plenty of hoods, but not the ones Ruben Miles was looking for. He was smart enough to keep himself covered up, not ask questions and keep his powder dry. When the next three nights had similar results, he was beginning to lose patience.

But on the Friday night, he got lucky, which considering the streets were busier than they had been all week was a surprise to Ruben Miles. He was on the brink of calling things off early when he first heard and then saw the unmistakable figures of Lombardi and Martino deep in conversation with one of the stall holders.

He followed them discreetly through the crowded streets. The night air a powerful blend of booze, tobacco and piss, with a hint of horse manure for texture. There was much shouting and laughter that echoed loudly off the cramped rooftops, with the occasional scuffle or fist fight thrown in. The only women in attendance were there on business and there was seemingly no absence of punters. Ruben Miles followed them for two blocks before they stopped and entered a speakeasy, tucked away behind the façade of a firm of accountants. Ruben Miles decided to wait for them in a little dark alleyway adjacent to the back entrance of the club. He now began to realise that he had no real plan. Ruben Miles may not have believed in a lot, but the concept of luck was something he never dismissed. A mere forty minutes after they had arrived, the back entrance of the club creaked open and Ruben Miles saw a striking looking woman emerge. She was young, slender, auburn haired and incredibly beautiful. Ruben Miles edged closer into the shadows. Moments later a shorter, more rotund figure, dressed immaculately in a five-hundred-dollar suit came through the entrance speaking quietly to the woman. Lombardi.

Unbeknownst to Ruben Miles, the words that Lombardi said to the girl were to seal his fate.

'I can't wait, let's do it here in the alley. Mikey is guarding the door so no one can come out.'

Ruben Miles saw the opportunity play out before him. After a couple of minutes, Lombardi had his expensive pants around his ankles and the beautiful girl was making the appropriate noises, albeit with some restraint. The only thought that troubled Ruben Miles was the girl. He certainly did not want to hurt her, and he wanted to avoid her seeing his face, although his pulled down hat would have meant only partial observation. But then the girl tilted her head away from Ruben Miles. He took out the gun, slowly and silently reducing the distance between himself and the target. Neither noticed his approach, as they were too absorbed by their own actions. It was not like in the movies. Ruben Miles did not say anything smart or vindictive beforehand. He quickly placed the gun on Lombardi's left temple and pulled the trigger.

The girl screamed. Lombardi fell lifelessly to the floor.

'Run,' he told the girl firmly, and after a few seconds she did just that. Ruben Miles had barely got behind the back door of the club when it swung open for a second time that night, this time with much more purpose.

Mikey 'the Ox' Martino ran out to see his dead boss on the floor and the girl running off down the alley. He made the wrong assumption. He fired at the girl quickly, but missed and before he could get off a second shot, Ruben Miles put a bullet through the back and out the front of Martino's head.

The girl was quick, but no match for Ruben Miles. He had quickly calculated that she would now be the number one suspect in the double homicide. After all, there must have been countless witnesses in the club that saw Lombardi go out the back entrance with her. Some may even have known who she was. They would have heard the shots moments later and put two and two together to reach the ubiquitous wrong conclusion. Ruben Miles may have had no qualms about killing Lombardi and Martino, but he wanted no harm to come to the girl, despite her less than innocent-like appearance in the alleyway.

'I'm not going to hurt you!'

It had taken half a block for him to catch her. She struggled in his arms as they both recovered their breath.

'We have to get away from here. You will be safe at my place. Come on!'

'Get your hands off me!'

'Listen, if I wanted to harm you, I would have done it in the alley. I want to help you. I got you into this mess and I want to help you get out of it.'

The sound of running feet in the distance may have concentrated her mind. She had also quickly calculated how many people may have seen her leave via the back door with Lombardi. She also knew that as this had been the second time she had been with Lombardi in the club, there may have been some punters who even knew her name.

Twenty-five minutes later they were alone in Ruben Miles's rooms at the Babe's luxury pad on West 88th Street. With the Babe on a road trip with the rest of the entourage, they had the place to themselves.

He gave the girl a large scotch and lit her cigarette that she could not do herself because her hands were shaking so much. Now in the light he could see she looked about sixteen.

'I'm sorry that you got involved in this mess, but Lombardi was a bastard and I had to stop him ruining my friend's life.'

The girl's hands were shaking, but she managed to polish off the scotch in one quick pull. He poured her another.

'At least you're right about Lombardi. What's your name? Are you English or something?'

'I don't think we need to share any personal information. I am not sure that would help either one of us.'

The girl seemed to reflect on this for a few seconds.

'How attached to this city are you? You ever had some other place you wanted to go?'

'I'm a showgirl on Broadway, but I have the feeling that that particular opportunity may just have disappeared.'

'What's a Broadway showgirl doing with scum like Lombardi?'

'Clearly you have never been a nineteen-year-old girl trying to politely turn down the advances of a fresh mafia hood. He would not take no for an answer. Besides, he knows where I live, and I was worried he might do something to my sister Laura.'

Ruben Miles had to concede that this was true and that he was also hopeless at guessing people's ages.

The girl said that both her parents were dead. She had been brought up in Brooklyn by her older sister, Laura. She had a few friends but none that she would really miss. Her older sister took her in as there was no one else.

After her third scotch, which seemed to have as little effect on the girl as the previous two, she announced, 'I'm not going to be able to stay in the city, am I?'

'Too dangerous. I'm sorry, but you are going to have to leave town, at least for a year or so.'

'My sister certainly won't mind. I kind of get in the way. Besides, her husband's roaming hands were my biggest problem until you showed up.'

'I want to make sure you're safe and settled somewhere. I have money.'

'Well, I am an actress.'

And so, Ruben Miles agreed to take the girl to Hollywood.

She fell asleep fully clothed on the couch in the sitting room. Ruben Miles had a sleepless night, tossing and turning in his bed. They were at Penn Station just after ten the next morning. Just under three days later they arrived in Los Angeles. Ruben Miles set her up in a nice furnished apartment in West Hollywood, paying six months rent in cash up front. He also gave the girl nearly three hundred dollars in cash. He had raided the Babe's petty cash draw, usually reserved for hooker money.

'Just to get you started,' he said.

'Thanks,' she said and gave him an honest smile.

'Are you not even going to tell me your name?'

'I told you I don't think that is a good idea.'

'How does a decent guy like you end up killing people? For money?'

'That's a difficult question I'm not sure I can answer. But I didn't do it for money, just to protect someone.'

Ruben Miles neglected to say that he was paid very handsomely to look after this someone.

'My name is Ruby and thank you again for turning my life upside down, even if you did take care of Lombardi.'

She kissed him lightly on the cheek. He was on a train heading back east within an hour.

DOUBLE INDEMNITY

'And you never saw her again?'

'At least not in the flesh, no.'

Ruben Miles was rubbing his weary eyes; he could feel another post-unburdening headache coming on even quicker than normal. JoJo Bartlett had remained silent throughout, even during and after the description of the Lombardi and Martino murders.

'So, at least you have some good stuff to counterbalance the… less good.'

'I am not sure that killing Lombardi and Martino counts as less good. Rumour has it those two killed more than twenty between them.'

'And so that was it? You got away with it completely? And the girl… she just disappeared?'

'Not quite, but can we get to that tomorrow because my head is beginning to split?'

JoJo was meeting Luke Miles that evening for a drink. Their 'relationship' was proving to be more than a little ambiguous. However, she had at least decided on one aspect. She no longer felt it wise to bring Luke along to hear his great grandfather's story. She just felt it would complicate and possibly slow down the entire process. Besides, she could always give him the finished product to read, perhaps after the old man had died. After all, Ruben Miles had made his preference, keeping his family out of the memoir process.

'I have decided that GCSEs are a waste of my precious time,' Luke Miles announced as they sat in The Lonsdale, nursing a couple of pints of cider.

Luke Miles could be a little pompous for someone aged sixteen years and eight months. JoJo Bartlett found it quite amusing.

'Luke, you are sixteen. The average life span for a British male, even in the region that gave the world Greggs, is seventy-eight years old. Your GCSE exams therefore constitute two months out of a probable seven hundred and forty-four months that you are statistically likely to have left to live. That is conclusive proof that should you want a decent education and therefore statistically a better future and incidentally a longer life, then studying for your GCSEs is clearly not a waste of you precious time. Oh, and work out what that is as a percentage for revision.'

'I hate you when you are all logical and mathematical. Christ, you sound like my fricking parents.'

'As disappointing as it is for us teenagers to comprehend, sometimes, all be it rarely, our parents do have a meaningful contribution to make.'

'I refuse to accept my parents are right about anything. I mean, they wear beige clothes. How much more evidence do you need? I hate literally everything they say and do.'

JoJo Bartlett laughed; Luke's parents really did wear a lot of beige, sometimes in matching shades.

'I am getting on fine with my folks. My dad I never see as he is always at work, at least that's what he tells my mum he is doing. And my mum, well, we are both avoiding each other after the... *catastrophe*. So, that's kind of working out for both of us.'

This was the first time JoJo had acknowledged to Luke that the events of that almost fabled evening nearly two weeks ago had actually happened. He was beginning to think that he had imagined the whole thing. After all, it was the type of event he found himself imagining about, approximately, every ten minutes.

Luke Miles began to open his mouth, even though he was not sure where the upcoming sentence was going.

'Don't,' said JoJo Bartlett firmly. 'Just because I have acknowledged that it happened does not mean that I want to a) talk about it, or b) do something similar again. Give me a little time to process it. I mean, when I think about it, I see my mother's face. That can't be good, right?'

Luke chose not to share his contrary view. Mrs Bartlett had

featured in some of Luke Miles's more debatable thoughts.

'So, am I like, your boyfriend?'

He was aware of his desperation, only marginally too late.

'Are you going to revise properly for your GCSEs?'

Luke Miles failed momentarily to see the connection.

'I know a lot of teenage girls want to bring home the dropout that their parents will hate. God knows, you should see some of the losers my friends go out with. But I am not every teenage girl. You are far more capable than you make out, you are just incredibly lazy. Your GCSEs will be over in less than two months. The only time I will spend with you during this period is revision. Proper revision, in the study at your house with all of our clothes on.'

'And if I do that?'

'Then we can revisit your earlier question.'

It was only later that Luke Miles realised that JoJo Bartlett had made pretty much the same points that his parents made the last time they spoke about his lack of work ethic. Just with a very different method of incentivisation.

JoJo Bartlett decided that she needed a break from The Apple Orchard Retirement Community. She had surprised Ruben Miles by insisting on taking him out for some fresh air. She had driven them to one of the picnic areas in Derwentside, the other side of the River Tyne from The Apple Orchard Retirement Community. They were sitting at a new picnic table, watching the joggers and cyclists passing by whilst snacking on a packed lunch that was surprisingly tasty. Preparing food was not a noticeable strong point for JoJo Bartlett.

She was feeling a little guilty as she had not been to see Ruben Miles for five days, the longest gap since their project began. This was because she had been helping Luke Miles revise for his Maths GCSE exams, the first of which he was sitting that very morning. JoJo could not understand why she was so nervous as she never got nervous when she sat her own exams.

'You said that you never saw that girl again in the flesh. So, did you see a picture of her or something?'

'I was never one for going to the pictures. I suppose if I had, I would have realised earlier. It was August 12th 1965. I was living in London at the time. I had been involved in a bit of a misunderstanding and ended up with a broken foot. I had to keep my weight off it and so I spent a few weeks with a cast on, marooned on the sofa, bored out of my mind. I ended up watching a lot of TV, not something I ever did before or since. They were showing a selection of old films. It was called *Double Indemnity*. I recognised her straight away, even though the film had been made in 1944 apparently, seventeen years since I left her in Los Angeles.

'The girl was in the film?'

'Ruby was the star of the film, Barbara Stanwyck was her screen name. She may have been nearly twenty years older, but it was her. I am one hundred percent certain.'

'I think I've heard of her.'

Although she had not. But when she got home later, she googled Barbara Stanwyck and, sure enough, the actress Barbara Stanwyck had been a Broadway showgirl in 1927 when she was nineteen years old and her real name was Ruby.

'It was definitely her. As you know, I am not capable of forgetting much.'

They sat quietly for a while listening to the river running over the nearby sluice gates, Ruben Miles thinking about a girl he barely knew a lifetime ago and JoJo Bartlett wondering whether Luke Miles would remember even basic algebra.

'What happened after you got back from Los Angeles then? Did anyone suspect your involvement in the murders?'

JoJo had started recording again. The old man picked up the story from where he left off five days previously.

'The Fixer was in my rooms when I got back. Quite impressive, as he did not have a key.'

The Fixer did not need keys. He seemed to appear through walls like a fabled magician or ghost. Ruben Miles registered that he was not surprised to see him, although the Fixer had been noticeably absent when he could have done with some help and advice re the Lombardi business.

'You are in a good deal of trouble, Ruben Miles. However, I'm sure that a man of your skills and qualities should be able to resolve them. I take it the girl is safely in Los Angeles?'

'How could you possibly know…?'

But this was not an isolated example of the Fixer's legendary ability to know everything about everyone that mattered to him. The underworld and all its assorted hangers-on all knew of the peculiar talents of the man they referred to simply as the Fixer. Even the great Arnold Rothstein, who infamously bought the World Series in 1919, was eclipsed by the Fixer.

'Surely by now you must appreciate that there is nothing that escapes my notice, especially if it can be, how would you say, to my advantage to know. The girl will be quite safe, at least on that I can assure you. Masseria's men have been looking for her, of course. He has not taken kindly to the slaughter in the streets of his two best and most loyal goons. But the trail of the girl went dead at the end of the back alley. Clearly, she must have been helped. You seem to have done a good job.'

'I don't follow. If Masseria thinks the girl murdered Lombardi and Martino, why am I in such a fix?'

The Fixer gave Ruben Miles a look of bemused disappointment.

'You are in a fix, Ruben Miles, because the Fixer knows that it was you that killed Lombardi and Martino in that dirty back alley.'

Ruben Miles took a few moments to register what the Fixer was implying. But he still did not get it all.

'This is almost painful, Ruben Miles. You are in the position you are in because I know.'

'And you are going to give me up to Masseria?'

'Of course not. That would give me only a short-term benefit. I have a rather more long-term view about how recent circumstances could benefit me. Besides, I like you Ruben Miles, you are a man who possesses certain skills…'

'You're blackmailing me?'

'That is an ugly and unnecessary term. I would rather we agreed to an understanding between us.'

'An understanding of what?'

'An understanding that from time to time I may have some favours to ask of you. And as I have helped you from a stinking Kraut prison camp to a shitty alley in Little Italy, let's say that it will be in your best interests to help me achieve these favours.'

'So, you are blackmailing me.'

The idea of violence did not even enter Ruben Miles's mind. He had seen and heard enough to know that there was no man alive who could get the drop on the Fixer.

'You disappoint me, Ruben Miles. I have already helped you this very day by arranging for the only witness who saw you running out of the alley with the girl, after having watched you shoot Martino in the head, to move to Boston to help restart his family business in hat making. It might be also noted that this was a considerable additional expense. I am simply asking for you to acknowledge my help and to repay it at some point in the future.'

'Do I have a choice?'

'Men always have choices, but often not very good ones.'

'What if I don't agree?'

'I am sure Joe Masseria will be interested to hear from me…'

'He would have to find me first.'

'That would not be wise, Ruben Miles. You see that little girl in Los Angeles that you seem to have taken such a shine to? Who do you think is her landlord? Did you not question how you were able to get such a favourable deal in such a desirable area and so quickly?'

'She means nothing to me.'

'Maybe yes, maybe no. Either way, unless we agree on my proposal, let us just say that her career prospects will take a rather terminal backward step.'

Ruben Miles finally and unequivocally recognised his position.

'And if I agree to your proposal?'

'Then the girl will be safe to pursue her acting dreams. You do not need to look so glum, Ruben Miles. I assure you that being entwined in such an agreement with me is also to your advantage. I am sure there will be times in the future when you may need my help and I will not be found wanting. The Fixer is a most reliable friend.'

And so, Ruben Miles shook hands on the Fixer's 'arrangement'. Without fear of hyperbole, this simple act changed the future of not just Ruben Miles. He had now pledged to make himself available to the Fixer whenever he needed something fixed that he perceived to be perfect for the special skills of Ruben Miles.

MIDNIGHT IN THE GARDEN OF BEIGE AND EVIL

Luke's GCSE exams were dragging on for what seemed like an eternity and JoJo was rigorously sticking to her plan of only spending time with Luke to revise. Grudgingly, although he didn't share the thought with anyone, especially his parents, Luke accepted that the revision sessions were helping hugely. JoJo was patient with him and had also introduced him to revision methods that meant sometimes he could concentrate for nearly half an hour at a time. Unheard of.

His interactions with Ruben Miles had a completely new dynamic. Instead of talking about his past, the old man seemed rather more determined to quiz Luke on the here and now, with regular detours into serious crime, and most notably serial killers. For their last three meetings, Luke found himself discussing Ted Bundy, Fred West and a whole entourage of the mad and evil. Luke found revising for his Sociology exam the easiest. Almost a third of the course was on deviancy and therefore he could kid himself that the various well-thumbed almanacs he had devoured over the last four years on the world's most notorious serial killers was actually revision.

The old man seemed to be particularly interested in Ted Bundy, the seemingly charming and perfectly well-adjusted serial killer from 1970s America. This was the work of Mrs Hazel Wharton.

Two days before, Mrs Hazel Wharton had driven Ruben Miles to the city library. As she drove from The Apple Orchard Retirement Community, a tad erratically, she outlined the rough premise of her hypothesis. Namely, her adopted son, although seemingly successful and a well-respected member of society, was actually a serial killer of infamous proportions. Once parked at the library and ensconced in front of a computer that Mrs Hazel Wharton was surprisingly competent at using, she started googling Ted Bundy, Harold Shipman and other names that appear on lists of the most ghoulish crimes of modern times. She wanted to give Ruben Miles context, she said. He smiled as he recognised her employing one of his more over-used terms.

Ruben Miles was sceptical from the very beginning. That being said, he did find the information he read on the various subjects grimly interesting. Ruben Miles was a man well versed in the killing of others, but he had spent his life believing that, in almost all cases, he could justify his actions as self-preserving or morally the right thing to do. This was clearly a horse of a very different safari.

Ted Bundy seemed to be her 'favourite'. In fact, as far as Ruben Miles was concerned, he was the only example that she showed him of a seemingly well-adjusted individual committing many horrific crimes, which broadly supported her theory. And yet beneath the seemingly normal façade, Bundy had spent his lifetime raging at his mother for lying to him about both who his father was and, for most of his early life, convincing him that his grandparents were his real parents and his mother was merely his auntie. Mrs Hazel Wharton looked expectantly at Ruben Miles.

'Barry was our adopted son and he grew to hate me for not being his real mother and for not telling him that I knew who his real mother was. That was the one thing that my cousin made me promise when she gave him to us, that I would never tell her son who his real mother was. You must see the similarity?'

'And you agreed to that? Surely you can see that animosity about your mother's real identity does not turn everyone into a homicidal maniac.'

'I felt I had no choice. She said it was dealbreaker and we so wanted a baby of our own…'

'And you kept that promise?'

'To this day.'

Mrs Hazel Wharton began to sketch out more of her experiences with her adopted son. There were more tales of mutilated little animals and bullying of younger children. Many complaints from other parents and teachers about little Barry's actions and attitude. Then she told him the story of the missing little girl.

Lisa Pendleton lived three streets over from the Wharton family home. She was eleven years old when she went missing, seemingly disappearing off the face of the universe in the four minutes it should have taken her to walk from her grannie's to her home. It was early summertime and a warm, bright afternoon. The schools would be closing for the holidays in just over a week. In fact, Lisa should have been in school herself, but for a birthday treat. She had been given permission by her mum to stay off school and visit her grannie instead. The police put up posters, the local and then national media kept the story on the front pages for weeks. Nobody heard or saw a thing. There was a Crimewatch Special hosted by Jill Dando. The phrase, 'the police are baffled' became a staple in local conversations. There was not even a local random loner to blame, the usual fallback position for any confused constabulary.

Barry Wharton was thirteen at the time. His mother noticed no changes to his demeanour or any interest in the young girl's disappearance. And anyway, he was at school when the little girl went missing, right?

Barry Wharton should have been in PE, but Barry did not like PE and so when he discovered that the teacher, Mr Winters, was lackadaisical in his duties and responsibilities, he realised that as long as he was seen at the start line for the cross country run and an hour later turned up in the changing rooms looking tired and a bit sweaty, he could avoid the dreaded physical exercise. He had been doing this effortlessly for several weeks and, as he had none of his friends in his PE class, he had not shared his actions with anyone. He usually spent the time reading one of his crime books in the local woods.

Then the police found the body. It had been wrapped in a sheet and dumped in a ditch in those same woods, crudely covered over with branches and sticks, less than a mile from where the girl went missing. The poor girl had injuries that the police kept out of the media and public record. Everyone was so shocked that nobody seemed to ask the obvious question: why did it take over five weeks to find the body?

Mrs Hazel Wharton was as shocked as anyone. The whole community seemed to suffer collective trauma. The girl's poor family of course never got over it. How could you? Especially when the case was never solved. No one was even questioned twice, let alone charged. The Chief Constable eventually took early retirement because of the case.

'And you think Barry was responsible for the poor girl's murder?'

'I never thought so, at least not back then. I thought he was odd and a bit cruel, but then you could say that about so many kids, especially boys, and adopted boys at that. Also, he was at school at the time the girl disappeared. How could I have thought he was capable of...'

She heard her own voice catch.

'And then about ten years later, he was living down in London by then, he had just finished University, and he was home for a very rare visit. There was the Great North Run on the TV. Barry was saying how much he hated running and when he was at school, he had this great trick of how to avoid the cross country runs they had to do in PE. He said that he could hide for an hour in the woods...'

'That does not mean that he had anything to do with the murder. He was just a kid skipping PE.'

'Maybe, maybe not. But it means he potentially does not have an alibi for when Lisa was taken.'

'You have no way of knowing what dates he skipped classes. Besides, why would he have brought it up if he had something to hide? It doesn't make sense. I am sure Barry had nothing to do with that poor girl's murder.'

'But what about the others?'

'There are others?'

And then she told him about the list.

THE ROAD LESS TRAVELLED

JoJo had once again taken the old man out of the confines of The Apple Orchard Retirement Community. JoJo was not a very good driver. One of the positives of this was that, because she had to concentrate so hard on the mechanics of driving and the actions of others, her mind had no capacity to think of other issues.

'What about Cragside?' It was years since Ruben Mils had been to Cragside.

'Where is that again? How long would it take?'

'Near Rothbury, about an hour, I would think,' he said eyeing the speedometer hovering stubbornly around forty-five, on a dual carriageway.

'That sounds good, what is it?'

'A pretty amazing house that was built by an eminent Victorian. I like it even more as it predates me.'

Ruben Miles was aware that his mood always seemed to improve when he was with JoJo Bartlett. However, he was also still in possession of powers of perception and was aware that something was bothering her.

'I like the Victorians. They achieved a lot.'

'They were also arrogant vandals, that's what I like about them. A touch of Jekyll and Hyde.'

'What do you mean?'

'They knocked down a lot of old buildings to make way for their brave new world. In fact, it is difficult to think of more self-obsessed, arrogant so-and-sos as the English Victorians. Not all of them mind. Not Lord Armstrong of course, he was made of better stuff.'

'Is that whose house we're going to?'

'That's right, a fairly typical Victorian success story. Founded the University, gave Jesmond Dene to the City and also managed to make a fortune by selling ships, guns and munitions both at home and abroad. Plenty of money to be made out of 19th

century British foreign policy you know.'

JoJo had not really studied the Victorians or their foreign policies. If you were not a Tudor or a Stuart then the History curriculum tended to ignore you, seemingly loath to inform the current generation of the sins and moral flexibility of previous English ones.

'Could we go through Morpeth on the way?'

'Of course.'

'And I know what you are thinking.'

'What?'

'The daft old coot wants to see the place one more time before he dies.'

'I never and you aren't...'

'It's OK, funny really. I must have said goodbye to the place several times over the last thirty odd years. It just never seems to be the last time.'

'It will be one day. You're bound to get it right once.'

'This is true.'

Morpeth was a disappointment to Ruben Miles. The old, quiet market town of his youth was long gone. Now he just saw too many cars, too many people and too many gaudy shop and pub signs. Only the old clock tower remained remotely the same.

'Can we have a look at the river? Go straight on and then your next right.'

JoJo followed his instructions and parked the car on Abbey View, overlooking the stepping stones.

'Do you want to get out?'

'No, this is fine. You see that big sycamore tree? That's were my father fell over, banged his head and rolled into the river.'

'Where were you and Celia?'

'She was on the left near where that telegraph pole is, there used to be a big horse chestnut tree there, but a big storm brought it down in the early sixties I was told. I was over there.'

The old man pointed to the bushes near the stepping stones.

'It looked very different back then. I suppose this is where it all started. You can probably trace everything back to here. Perhaps everything I did, everything I became, can be traced back to the night of 27th June 1911. I was eleven. A very warm night, muggy. I couldn't sleep so I had come down to the river. I was going to cool down by putting my feet in. I reckon I might even have had a skinny dip. It was about eleven I think and he was walking across the stepping stones from the other side.'

Ruben Miles paused and pointed to the opposite bank of the Wansbeck.

'I could hear him coming before I saw him. He was singing one of the most popular tunes of the time... badly.'

At this point JoJo Bartlett was shocked as the old man burst into song. It was a popular music hall song by Harry Champion.

I'm 'Enery the Eighth, I am,
'Enery the Eighth I am, I am!
I got married to the widow next door,
She's been married seven times before
And everyone was an 'Enery
She wouldn't have a Willie nor a Sam
I'm her eighth old man named 'Enery
'Enery the Eighth, I am!

'Some people think it's a curse when they get a song stuck in their head. They want to try every song you've ever heard.'

JoJo was just pleased he had stopped singing. She often got embarrassed for other people.

'That must be awful.'

JoJo imagined having Coldplay songs stuck inside her head for decades and winced.

JoJo was scribbling notes down in case he said something she had not heard before, as she had not had time to set up the tape recorder.

'I have wondered if my life would have been different if my father hadn't been murdered. Would I have joined up in 1916? Probably not. And if I had not gone to war, I would never have met the Fixer.'

'Or the Burgess brothers.'

'Of course. The poor Burgess brothers. But the Fixer has

impacted me so much. Does one incident have the ability to change everything in a person's life?'

JoJo was seventeen years old, but a wise old soul. She knew exactly where the old man was coming from.

'It's impossible to know. If Celia had not drowned your father that night, would he have lived to be an old man or would your mother have killed him with a meat cleaver the following week? We cannot know what could have been from any action or event.'

'You sound like the first British intelligence man I got to know, in the run up to Hitler's war. Cavendish and his theory of randomness.'

'You worked for British intelligence during the war?'

'And beyond. But you know what a stickler I am for chronology. There is a lot to hear before we get to Cavendish and his science of the random.'

'That sounds fascinating.'

'More than New York, the Babe and the Fixer?'

'Well, no, that's amazing too. It's just... I didn't have you down as a spy.'

'Working for British intelligence does not necessarily make you a spy.'

'Do you really believe that Celia's actions made your life go in one unavoidable direction?'

'No, I think that one random action led to other random actions that led to other random actions, like exits on a motorway. We decide which way we go, it's just that past decisions influence the direction of travel. What if I told people that Celia had killed my father? What impact would that have had on my life or my mother's life.'

'I would advise not tormenting yourself like this.'

'It is easier said than done when you remember everything in such detail. Well, nearly everything.'

They watched some kids splashing each other by the stepping stones.

When he spoke like this, JoJo felt that it was unlikely that he was making it all up.

'I should have asked her why she did it.'

'Celia?'

'Yes, I suppose knowing why something happened is better than nothing. I mean, you're right. We can't know what impact one specific event can have on a lifetime, but at least knowing *why* something happened seems worthwhile to this old man.'

'Why do you think she did it?'

'For my mother, I think. Maybe they were lovers. They were certainly very close and Celia was certainly devoted to my mother. And based on hearsay, my mother was certainly broadminded in that particular area.'

'Why did you not tell anyone what you saw?'

'Those two key motivating factors, love and fear. I was in love with Celia. Well, I had a crush on her at the very least and I was definitely a bit scared of my mother back then. And as you will see later in my story, rather unpredictable. She certainly made one rather memorable reappearance in my later life.'

'But does that explain why you never told anyone later?

'Probably not, I just did not see what good would have come of it, for anyone. It's not as if it would have done my father any favours. Maybe I just wanted to please my mother, I don't think I ever pleased my mother.'

'I think I would have told someone, especially being so young.'

'Another point of randomness, any person will react differently to any given situation. Not to mention the historical context.'

'What do you mean?'

'Maybe I would have acted differently if it had been 1936 or 1963. Any time period has its own peculiarities, I am as well versed in that as most people, I would think. Youngsters in 1911 were their own individual group, of time and place.'

JoJo though she felt a headache coming on and her face said as much.

The old man smiled at her.

'Come on, it will take us another forty minutes to get to Cragside. I think I have scrambled your brains enough for one day.'

He took one final look at the river and the stepping stones, realising that this time, unlike all the others, *would* be the last time he was here.

GOODBYE TO ALL THAT

The Babe never did ask Ruben Miles what happened. When he returned from the Yankees road trip, he just resumed his routine of gluttony, boozing and fucking, with occasional hiatuses to hit effortless home runs at the stadium he effectively paid for. The House that Ruth Built. If the Babe knew what happened to Lombardi, he sure as hell never mentioned it. Besides, he had his hands full with the woman who would eventually become the second Mrs Ruth. The problem was he was still married to the callously treated first wife, Helen. She died in a mysterious house fire less than a year after eventually leaving the Babe and heading for rural Massachusetts. That had nothing to do with Ruben Miles. Although he could not for certain vouch for the Fixer.

Claire Merritt signalled the end for Ruben Miles and the Babe. She was all too aware of the primary function fulfilled by the Babe's entourage and Ruben Miles was the leader of that particular pack. Although loyal, the Babe allowed his men to be gradually removed over time. Claire was rich and headstrong and the Babe was so in love he could barely eat his second dinner. Symbolically, the final act occurred on Thursday 24th October 1929. The world would remember it for different reasons. They would call it Black Thursday. The day the stock market crashed on Wall Street.

It was an even darker day for Ruben Miles personally. Although he had nothing invested in the stock market – he was and would always be, a cash man – he felt he lost just the same as the colossal losers who lost literally everything they owned. He managed to lose both his job and his wife on the same day. Not the sort of double you want to bet on.

Ruben Miles met, courted and married his first wife in a whirlwind four weeks. From their first glance at each other, to the honeymoon, less than a calendar month passed. He would say that it was love at first sight. In truth, ever since he had helped Ruby flee New York for Hollywood, Ruben Miles had been, at the very least, in love with the idea of love. So, when he caught the attention of a gorgeous brunette with a fabulous figure whilst strolling down Broadway, he changed his habits of his young lifetime and approached the woman instantly. The realisation that she could have been Ruby's sister, if not twin, only occurred to Ruben Miles many years later. We all believe the fictions we tell ourselves.

Rita Seymour was from a wealthy Nantucket family who could almost trace their ancestry back to the Mayflower. We are talking serious old money. She was educated, opinionated and independent. She had been a Vassar gal and had recently graduated with a degree in English literature. She may have dressed a little like a flapper, but she neither drank nor smoked. The one vice she had was a permanent desire to antagonise her parents. And this was Ruben Miles's in.

Of course, his English accent was a fine accompaniment to his rather old-fashioned good looks. His educated Northumberland lilt really did make Rita Seymour go weak at the knees. In truth, it was the only reason that she did not leave him cold-shouldered on Broadway the afternoon they met. So caught up with one another were they, that it was over a week before they started discussing each other's backgrounds and current circumstances. Ruben Miles was cautious about his rather middle-class upbringing when Rita reluctantly mentioned her family.

When Rita first asked Ruben Miles what he did for a living, he replied that he was a personal assistant to someone 'quite famous'.

Rita Seymour did not even ask who it was.

The second time the topic came up was in bed after they had slept together for the first time. Ruben Miles had been very aware that he was not her first. They were visiting her family. She had snuck into his separate room a little after midnight, ecstatic that her parents could not have been more open with their hostility to Ruben Miles over the dinner table. Her father's eyes fizzed with rage the entire evening. Ruben Miles had no idea how desirable this made him to Rita Seymour.

'I suppose you should meet my American family now that I have met yours,' Ruben Miles said as they lay in the crumpled silken sheets.

'I am sorry about my parents. They're such snobs. Your American family? I thought your only family was back in England.'

'It is. My mother is my only family. But believe me, you can do without meeting her. I meant my employer, he is more like a brother to me, I have been looking after him for nearly ten years. He takes some looking after. Don't worry about your parents, I have never been very popular with parents.'

This was true.

'So, who is this quite famous employer of yours?'

'I work for Babe Ruth, that's who I look after.'

She looked at him a little blankly.

'Does he do some kind of sport?'

Ruben Miles could not believe it. He felt he may have just slept with the only person in America who did not know exactly who Babe Ruth was. He may not have recognised it himself, but it was another reason why he was beginning to fall quite hard for the charms of Miss Rita Seymour. Of course, he had no idea that she was lying.

Two weeks later, they got married in the city with just a hired witness to oversee the legal formalities. Ruben Miles had asked the Babe's permission for Rita to live with him in his rooms.

'Sure thing buddy. When do I get to meet the girl who thawed that cold, cold, English heart of yours?'

The Babe loved to tease Ruben Miles over his perceived English aloofness.

Ruben Miles had thought about telling Rita Seymour about the habits of the Babe but decided against it. She was a clever woman, he reasoned, and she would figure it out for herself.

As for Rita herself, she was so intoxicated with joy after being excommunicated from the entire Seymour clan for her unforgivable choice of husband, that she barely gives the Babe a thought.

They lived together in marital bliss for almost a whole month.

'It was the day the stock market crashed. You will have read about that, I suppose?'

Ruben Miles was sitting on a bench in the formal front gardens at Cragside, overlooking the pedestrian iron bridge. It had been over twenty years since he had visited. It had been many more years since he had spoken of Rita Seymour.

JoJo was captivated by the Victorian masterpiece; she had already decided to try and persuade Luke to come back on another visit this coming weekend. She needn't have worried; Luke Miles would have accompanied her to his own lynching.

'I have. Was it as bad as they say?'

'Worse, I would say. People went from being rich to having literally nothing in one day. Of course, worse was to come, the depression lasted until the war. But I did not get to see that. I am glad I did not see the true misery of the 1930s after the glory of the 1920s, it would have been too soul destroying, I think. I left the States in 1930.'

'But you had your own version of Black Thursday?'

The old man nodded.

'I had been out running some basic errands. I think I said I would be a couple of hours. It stretched to three or four because of all the crowds on the streets and all the mayhem. When I got back, I remember thinking how quiet everything was. There was usually always a lot of noise when the Babe was home. Anyway, when I went in, the three of them were waiting for me. My wife, the Babe and his fiancée.'

JoJo thought she could see where this might be going.

'It was she who did the talking.'

'Rita?'

'No. Claire, his fiancée.'

'What did she say?'

'There are some things I would like not to remember in my life. In fact, there are a lot of things now that I mention it. I have told you some already. But it's funny how my memory works, I don't just remember what she said, I can hear her saying it. Does that make any sense?'

JoJo nodded and yet it didn't.

'She said, 'Ruben Miles you have twenty minutes to pack your things and leave this house for good. You are fired as of this minute and on your way out, take your whore with you'.'

'My God, what happened?'

'What do you think happened? She caught the Babe doing what the Babe did every day. With my wife.'

JoJo took a few moments to digest this.

'Is this one of the reasons you don't like talking about real personal stuff?'

'Well, it's a pretty good reason don't you think?'

She did.

And just like that, Ruben Miles's near decade with the Babe was over.

Rita Seymour never so much as looked him in the eye again, but at least she did not deny it. The Babe had the good grace to at least look sheepish and said nothing as Ruben Miles quickly retrieved his few belongings and sizeable savings he had hidden under the floorboards of his bed. He was going to need that nearly ten thousand dollars now.

'Did you not say or do anything?'

JoJo Bartlett had seldom looked so indignant.

'What was the point? The Babe was just doing what the Babe did. I should know, I had lived with him for ten years and, to my regret, had watched him have hundreds of women. The Babe tried to sleep with every woman he met, it was just what he did and every day. For him not to try would have been unnatural, like a lawyer with a conscious or a German with a great sense of humour. I was naïve enough to think that my wife would say no. The one thing you could say about the Babe was that if a woman said 'No' he left it at that. He was never sore or insistent, he just moved on to the next woman. I guess she did not say 'No', which meant I had nothing to say to her either.'

'Did you ever hear from her again?'

'Once. I got a letter several years later, just before I headed for Spain. I had already remarried by then.'

The old man neglected to tell JoJo that he hadn't actually got around to divorcing his first wife. He figured the Atlantic Ocean was a good enough buffer.

'I assumed the Fixer gave her my whereabouts. She told me that I had a son named Jeramiah. I never wrote back. I could not see the point. Besides, I had my own problems at the time.'

This was quite a lot of new information to process.

'Did you ever meet your son?'

'No.'

The look in his eyes made JoJo baulk from any follow up questions.

'Did you see the Babe again?'

'No, and I sure as hell missed him more than I did her. Well, I suppose we did spend nearly a decade together.'

'Did you forgive him?'

Ruben Miles smiled involuntarily, which in itself was an answer.

'It would have been impossible not to forgive the Babe. He was not a normal man. I am not clever enough to put this into words, but the Babe was not a mere mortal. He was more like a life force. He lived his whole life on full throttle. He is one of only a handful of people that I truly wished I could see just one more time. And when you get to one hundred and six years old and you have hyperthymesia, that is an awful lot of people that you don't want to see again.'

'Did you leave America straight away?'

'No, I needed to clear my head, so I had what I think is now commonly called a gap year. More likely a kind of a breakdown. I travelled all around the country. I visited every state. Used up some of my savings. Why don't we talk about that next time? I think we should be getting me back home before Mrs Hazel Wharton has mobilised the police and military.'

'Who is Mrs Hazel Wharton?'

'That may be as hard a question as you have asked me today.'

THE ROAD TRIP

In early 1930, Ruben Miles traversed the length and breadth of the USA. He started in the northeast corner and worked his way clockwise in ever decreasing circles. He set foot in every one of the then forty-eight states. He even liked some of them.

He travelled by all means available at the time, from hiking to flying. He was mugged twice, although both times the assailants did not find the large stack of cash hidden in his crotch. Instead, they made off with the few measly dollars he kept in his pockets; dressing like a vagrant was as good a defence as any. He was arrested once (for vagrancy by an uptight, bald Sherriff in Wyoming) and even managed to fall off a freight train in Michigan. But he survived what he called his 'road trip'.

Ruben Miles did not know he was suffering from anxiety and aggravated depression when he left New York City after being thrown out by the Babe and his wife. The only decision he remembered making at the time was the one to get out of the city. He took a train to Philadelphia, leaving Penn Station in the dead of night. He did not have a plan or a coherent thought in his head.

He stayed five nights at the Bellevue-Stratford Hotel on Broad Street on the corner of Walnut. It was the fanciest hotel in town. He spent his time staring at the ceiling, prone on his bed. He did not speak to a soul for the duration, he ate no meals and water was his only sustenance. By the time he hauled himself vertical and took a puritanically cold shower just before leaving, he had lost nearly ten pounds in weight. He had to go and buy a belt to keep his pants up.

He was heading for Richmond, Virginia. He had bought a Ford Model A from a dealership in the south of Philly and pointed the vehicle further south. The dealer gave him a twenty-minute lesson on how to drive. He stopped off at Baltimore and liked it so much he stayed for a week. He then drove on to Richmond. And then drove straight out again. The Klan were in town. Ruben Miles watched the two hundred or so hooded members strolling down Main Street, with many of the townsfolk smiling and waving as they paraded down the street. Ruben Miles was somewhat enlightened in matters of race for a man born in Nineteenth Century England. Before he set out for the battlefields of Flanders, he had never so much as seen a non-white person in the flesh. But during his tenure as a member of the British Army, he saw literally thousands of Africans, Indians and others from he knew not where, serving on behalf of the British dominions. Just like their white equivalents, most did a pretty remarkable job in horrendous conditions. They filled combat as well as non-combat functions. Ruben Miles learnt that non-whites lived and died just like everyone else. From then on and for the rest of his days, Ruben Miles was without racial prejudice, at least none that he was conscious of.

This may explain why he did not spend too long in any of the notorious southern states. He spent less than a day in Alabama. Long enough to realise that such was the scale of unemployment, any stranger was a bad stranger. He left on a freight train. The Ford A had lasted less than a month before he ran it ruinously into a ditch in South Carolina. He was lucky to walk away with just a temporary limp.

Ruben Miles rode the rails for the next several months. He would act and dress like the rest of the poor deadbeats who spent endless months criss-crossing the beleaguered continent. Moving from town to town, state to state on the fallacy of a job just around the next bend. He could normally stand this for over a week. Then he would check into a good hotel, paying cash upfront to the usually extremely sceptical receptionist. He would spend most of the next day in a steaming hot bath.

'What were you doing this for?' JoJo Bartlett did not often interrupt Ruben Miles, but his narrative was becoming less and less focused.

They were sitting in the McDonalds on Northumberland Street. Ruben Miles had never been inside such a place and had been most insistent. He was pleasantly surprised by the quality of the coffee. He was a good deal more cynical and circumspect about his Egg McMuffin. He took a while to answer.

'My condition allows me to remember the events of any day very clearly. How I felt about what I was doing is sometimes more difficult. I do remember a feeling of loss, but more like a feeling of being permanently lost. I think we can assume I had what used to be called a nervous breakdown. What do they call them now?'

'A nervous breakdown. Although most people now just say stress and anxiety. One of the 21st Century's few real growth areas…'

'It was as if I wanted to blend into the background of my own life. Depression era, dust-bowl America was not the time and place to be feeling sorry for yourself, I can assure you. But at least I had money.'

'Did you visit the showgirl?'

'No. I never even thought about it. Or her. It is fair to say that I was not thinking clearly. I suppose travelling across states with deadbeats and other lost souls was where my mind was at.'

'How long did it take to feel a bit better?'

'I reckon about six or seven months. I certainly remember smiling at a sunrise in Wichita on August 3rd.'

JoJo laughed naturally as she thought he might have been joking. Apparently not.

'There were plenty of War veterans on the rails, some as mad as a mongoose. Often you would get woken up in the dead of night by some poor tortured soul barking at the moon.'

'When did you stop?'

'After Las Vegas.'

JoJo Bartlett obediently turned her Dictaphone back on.

Las Vegas in 1930 was a small, semi-legal town on the up. In July, President Hoover had signed the appropriation Bill for what was then called the Boulder Dam. The population of Las Vegas went from 5,000 to 25,000 almost overnight. It was a close call whether there were more construction workers looking for jobs or criminals on the make. Ruben Miles, as was his habit, seemed inextricably linked to the more disreputable of the newcomers.

Las Vegas *became* Las Vegas because of a depression era infrastructure project. The construction workers for what would become known as the Hoover Dam needed somewhere to spend their money. What better solution than gambling, whorehouses and speakeasies in the middle of a desert?

Ruben Miles took a room in a whorehouse that doubled

down as both a casino and a speakeasy. Only the latter was illegal in Nevada. Although Prohibition still had a few years to run, the far-sighted state of Nevada had legalised gambling seemingly, although actually coincidentally, with the construction of the Hoover Dam.

Ruben Miles may not have had the more common vices for the times, but he loved to gamble. He liked it even more when he could persuade a little flexibility into the local rules. Even though he had his fingers burnt over trying to fix a fight back in the UK that had forced him to flee the country and had been stiffed in a handful of crooked poker games in New York with the Babe, Ruben Miles was keen to sit down at one of the seemingly endless games of straight poker that occupied the main table of the saloon bar. As the police had almost no authority in primitive Vegas, the bootleggers did not have to go to any creative lengths to disguise what they were selling. It seemed that everyone was on the make and no one was playing to the rules. Not that there were many of those.

Ruben Miles bought himself some clean clothes and treated himself to a haircut and a hot shave at the barbers next door to his lodgings. He then spent two straight days watching the endless game unfold in the saloon bar. He saw plenty go bust, at least three fistfights and one particular antsy fella pull a gun when his two pair failed to hold up against a hopeful straight draw. No one seemed to bat an eyelid and the man reluctantly put his weapon away, mumbled an apology of sorts and then spent his last five dollars being entertained by the star attraction of the upstairs facilities. Ruben Miles took it all in.

Ruben Miles liked to gamble but he was no emotional hothead who thrived on the thrill of risk and the possibility of going broke in a gloriously implosive minute. He chose his stake carefully and never exceeded it. No amount of goading or trash talk could put him on tilt. He calculated how much he could potentially afford to lose and did not bet another nickel.

There were six seats at the oval shaped wooden table. Three of them had been occupied by the same men since Ruben Miles started watching. Minimal toilet and food breaks were the only pauses in the continuous game. The other three seats rotated at an unerringly similar rate. Either these three seats were pure bad luck, or the other players knew how to play straight poker. Or perhaps another factor was determining matters. Ruben Miles kept watching and wondering.

He tried to get some information as to who the regular winners at the table were. But neither the grumpy barman nor the sprinkling of other spectators wanted to furnish Ruben Miles with any workable knowledge. In fact, unlike the rest of the new town's inhabitants, they seemed far from friendly.

'I would quit asking your dumb questions, son,' said the more communicative of the locals gathered around the bar.

Ruben Miles simply smiled politely in response.

He watched another handful of newcomers to the game go bust before he himself took a chair. Poker was still a primitive game then. You got five cards dealt face down and you could change three cards, four if you had an ace. There was no bet or pot limits. The dealing was done by the house. The players paid five dollars per day to be dealt in, even if you lasted half an hour, you still had to pay your five dollars upfront. Clearly, the house was doing quite nicely out of the game before even a drink had been bought.

There was a small blind of ten cents and a big blind of twenty. This meant that if you bet little and rarely, you could spend many hours relatively cheaply looking for a hand to play. This was Ruben Mile's strategy. In the first two hours he played three hands. He won one of them. The other players paid him little mind and there was little table conversation.

Ruben Miles played for nearly forty-eight hours the first time. He came out dead even, which he viewed as some kind of vindication. He watched the moves and styles of the other players. He watched the weak and the reckless lose their stake and half their wits. But progress was slow and he was a man of limited patience. He realised he may need a plan B. He just did not know where to find one.

'I had decided that it was time to come home,' he told JoJo.

'I just wanted to take a little more insurance with me. The problem was I was not a great poker player, in fact I'm not even sure I was even an average one. I needed something that might give me an edge. Then I met a tall Missourian that went by the name of Titanic Thompson and what he taught me meant I returned to England with even more money in my pockets.'

TITANIC THOMPSON

I t was a couple of years after Titanic Thompson had given evidence at the trial of George McManus, the poker hustler charged with the murder of infamous New York crime boss Arnold Rothstein, the legend made famous for buying the World Series in 1919. Thompson had been playing in the poker game that led to Rothstein's murder. But then Titanic Thompson was no stranger to murder. His personal tally was already up to four by the time he crossed paths with Ruben Miles.

When giving evidence at McManus's trial, Thompson neglected to inform the court that he had been the person responsible for fixing the poker game that cost Rothstein over three hundred thousand dollars. Rothstein's decision to not make good this debt because of his certainty regarding the crookedness of the game was his final error of judgement that led directly to his shooting at Manhattan's Park Central Hotel in November 1928.

Ruben Miles may have not heard of Titanic Thompson, but then he was probably one of the few in Las Vegas that could boast such ignorance.

'It was Titanic Thompson that taught me that if people like to gamble, they were then likely to bet on just about anything, especially if it looked like a sure thing.'

'I take it Titanic was a nickname, how did he get it?'

'Well, some say that he disguised himself as a rich lady to get himself into one of the all too scarce lifeboats on the doomed ship in 1912. Although there was no mention of him in that film.'

JoJo had seen the film. She liked Leonardo DiCaprio.

The old man thought it best that he didn't mention the other legend that could have given the man the nickname.

'I saw him fleece men of their entire savings on a round of golf, the turn of a card or a toss of a coin. But it was his walnut throw that made the little boost to my going home fund.'

JoJo was intrigued.

'If something sounds too good to be true then run for the hills and don't look back. But there must be something ingrained in human nature that means a lot of folks can't see a scam when it's right in front of their noses. Pick a card, any card. Which cup is the coin under? They were the staples back in the day. I suppose the internet will be the next growth area for the scammers. Trust me, JoJo, never trust anything that sounds too good a thing. But Titanic Thompson was more than happy to take money from people who couldn't smell a rat, even if you set it on a plate right in front of them. The con he showed me was the nut throw.'

'A nut throw?'

'That's right. He would show the rube an empty walnut shell and bet him a princely sum that he could throw the nutshell over a very tall nearby building.'

'What's a rube?'

This made the old man smile.

'That's why he talked to me, when he heard my name was Ruben. A rube is American slang for a country yokel, a bit of a dimwit I suppose we would say. He thought my name was Rube as he didn't have the best of hearing on one side. He thought that was hilarious and let me watch him do the con.'

'So, he just picked someone at random?'

'No, that was the clever part really. He would take some time to observe the fellow in the casino. See if he had money, see if he had gumption. What he wanted was a fella with deep pockets, the burning desire to gamble and little sense. He had a fine nose for such men and in Las Vegas back in them days there was no shortage. I would imagine it would be much the same if we went there now from what I've heard. I have not been since September 1951. I saw the first show Frank Sinatra ever played in Las Vegas.'

Even JoJo had heard of Sinatra. Her dad still listened to his CDs, usually at Christmas when he had too much to drink.

'So, how could he throw a nutshell over a tall building, surely they are way too light?'

'Of course, that's why you need a rube. It is just a slight of hand trick. Show the rube an empty walnut shell, let him feel how light it is. Then make the bet, get a so-called neutral, in this case me, to hold the money. Then swap the nutshell for one you prepared earlier lined with lead.'

'Ah, that would do it!'

'It certainly did. That nutshell would fly over pretty much any tall building. Titanic could have been a baseball pitcher, he had one hell of a throw. He taught me how to throw too.'

'So, you stayed in Vegas and conned people with the nut throw, that's how you got more money to go home with.'

'No, the deal I made with Titanic was I had to go to a place as far away from Vegas as possible, where people still liked to gamble. I paid him a $100 tip for his nut trick, I must have made thirty or forty times that when I discovered Atlantic City.'

'Where's Atlantic City?'

'On the New Jersey coast, south of New York. It was perfect really, I stayed a couple of weeks, made my money and then headed for home via *The Mauritania,* ironic really as she was built on the Tyne at Swan Hunters.'

'And so, thanks to Titanic Thompson and a lot of suckers, you were able to come back with plenty of money.'

'That's right. I was a lucky man. Few in the 1930s had no concerns about money, but I was one of the rare few.'

'How did you feel when you got back to England?'

'Closest I ever felt to wanting to throw myself off a tall building. It was cold, wet and everyone had a miserable, sour-looking expression. It was like you owed everyone money.'

'You're not the biggest fan of our country or its people, are you?'

'It's not that. It's just that the contrast with the brave new world was so large. You go from a country where everyone is optimistic about the future to a place where people seem to just want to hide under a rock. But it was more than that, America was in technicolour, this country is just shades of grey. Mind you, I would have had a different view of the States if I had only been there in the 1930s.'

JoJo had never been to America. But she had studied the depression.

'And I suppose I was a little in mourning.'

'What for?'

'My life in America with the Babe in New York. It really was a magical time and a magical place.'

JoJo had not seen such a wistful expression on the old man's face.

'But I grew to love London, it just took a while.'

'Did you know anyone in London when you arrived?'

'Not a soul. It was not like now when people move around the country to live and work. The only people in London were Londoners and it was not like it is now. The last time I was in London I saw as many non-white faces as white faces. In 1931 there was not a single person who was not as white as you or I.'

JoJo squirmed uncomfortably in her chair. It sounded like the old man *was* a typical old racist after all. She braced herself for complaints that things were certainly better in the good old days. The old man read her expression wisely.

'I've told you I'm *not* like that. I saw brave boys of every which colour die in France. I'm just pointing out the place looked different in pretty much every way to how it looks now. Besides, I don't know how anyone can spend any time in America and not realise that skin colour is meaningless. Or at least it should be.'

'What do you mean?'

'Well, if you listen to some of the spiteful bigots in The Apple Orchard, they will tell you that white folks are better than the rest and more civilised too. A little too close to the Nazis for my liking. Answer me something, which country is the richest and most successful country on the planet?'

'America.'

'That's right, America. The only country on the planet built by immigration. Unless you were a native American or a slave, you were an immigrant or a descendant of immigrants. It seems to me that immigration can't be that bad a thing, not that you will get many people round here agreeing with me about that anytime soon.'

JoJo was pleased that the old man did not fit in with her stereotypical view of old people and their prejudices. She thought she heard her own mother say something overtly racist the previous week in *Sainsbury's*, but she had convinced herself that she must have misheard. Her own mother was not like that, surely?

'It was quite the change I can tell you. But at least London was a big city, if not on the scale of New York. I remember thinking, what if I had gone back to Northumberland?'

'I suppose the northeast would be a bit of a comedown after New York.'

And on that understatement, they decided to call it a day.

THE LIST

Mrs Hazel Wharton held the handwritten list in her unusually large hands. They were also nearly wrinkle free, something that she was rightly proud of. She was slightly grumpier than her usual demeanour, on account of Ruben Miles being late for their meeting by almost an hour. Mrs Hazel Wharton did not appreciate tardiness. But she also knew that being grouchy with Ruben Miles did not get her what she wanted. Unlike her husband, who was almost comically cowering of her mild mood swings, Ruben Miles appeared to be completely immune to emotional game-playing.

'How are you, Ruben? Did you have a good session with JoJo?' She positively beamed as she spoke, not even a hint of recrimination in her voice. She was a real trooper when she wanted to be.

They ordered sparkling water from the residents' café. Ruben Miles even pretended to enjoy it. Clearly, he was not immune from a little game playing himself.

'I see you have your list ready,' he said as they made sure they were sitting as far away from other residents as was possible.

Ruben Miles had already made up his mind that Mrs Hazel Wharton's son was not a serial killer. What was much more difficult to fathom was what he was able to do about her convictions and her damned list. The list consisted of several names of some of the young women who had seemingly vanished without trace in the UK over the last twenty-five years. She had also included the geographical locations of their last identified sighting. In addition, there was also information about any suspects at the time or subsequently. None of the missing women had been found and no one had been formally charged with any crime in relation to their vanishing.

'The internet is amazing. You would not believe how much information you can find, and so quickly.'

Mrs Hazel Wharton had surprised herself enormously with

both her comprehension of and appreciation of modern technology. She had never considered herself capable of either of those things previously.

'Hazel, I am convinced that your son is not a serial killer. I fear that you have taken your mutual antipathy and frankly... ran riot with wild imagination.'

Ruben Miles had rehearsed his forthright opening statement. Usually, when it came to Mrs Hazel Wharton he spoke in more conciliatory ways. Either his infatuation for her was diminishing, which he actually doubted, or he was simply trying to get her to see sense. Although he had taken the sensible and slightly disarming approach of calling her by her first name only. This was something that they normally bickered about good-naturedly.

Mrs Hazel Wharton seemed to weigh up this opening statement evenly.

'Bollocks,' she said.

This surprised them both in equal measure.

She handed him a copy of the list.

'We will start from the top,' she said.

'Number one, Helen Pearce, aged twenty-four, disappeared on a night out in Windsor on the 24th of September 1989. She was last seen leaving the nightclub Blazers. Barry spent a lot of time in Windsor in 1989. His best friend from university, a lad called Peter lived there. I spoke to him a year or so ago, he confirmed that he and Barry used to go to the club a lot, but he was very fuzzy on dates.'

'Circumstantial at best.'

'OK, number two, Sarah Farnish, aged twenty-six, disappeared in Cranbourne Park, Windsor, on the eighteenth of June 1990. Last seen having a row with her boyfriend, a bloke called Ryan James. The police questioned him for several days over a few weeks, he was never charged. The police concluded that she may have run off to Thailand to meet up with an ex-boyfriend. Peter said that Cranbourne Park was a place that Barry liked to go walking in...'

Ruben Miles chose to add nothing to this information. Mrs Hazel Wharton eyed him challengingly.

'Number three, Caroline Barnes, aged twenty-one, last seen leaving the beach at Weston-Super-Mare on the twenty-ninth of July 1992. Barry's ex-girlfriend Gill, her parents lived in Weston-Super-Mare, and they used to visit a lot in the summer of 1992 as Gill was a teacher and had the whole summer off. I have not been able to speak with Gill. We did not really get on the couple of times we met.'

Ruben Miles decided to let her continue without comment.

'Number four, Bethany Watts, aged nineteen, last seen exiting Mudchute DLR station on the fourteenth of April 1994. Barry lived in a flat in Docklands that year on his own after he split up with Gill. He lived in a flat near South Quay station, just two stops from Mudchute...'

'Number five, Gail Roberts, aged thirty-one, last seen leaving the Spar in Salcombe on the third of August 1995. Barry once told me his old schoolfriend Jon had a family holiday home in Salcombe. I spoke to Jon last month, he confirmed that Barry was among a group of six lads who stayed there in August 1995, he just could not be sure of the dates...'

Ruben Miles placed his hands on Mrs Hazel Wharton's prodigious hands.

'Why don't I just read through the rest of the list?' he said quietly. In a matter of minutes, he had gone from thinking his new friend was delusional about her son, to thinking that she may in fact be on to something. But what?

Ultimately, the list held a clear pattern, young women disappearing seemingly without trace, all in areas that Barry Wharton had an immediate or closely linked connection with. Ruben Miles was no lawyer, but he felt convinced that should this list be given to the police and, should they take it seriously and make even the most basic of checks, at the very least Mr Barry Wharton could expect a visit from the police for what could be a lengthy chat.

'And you are sure that you have these details, correct?' he finally said.

Mrs Hazel Wharton simply nodded.

'What are you going to do?'

'I was hoping you could help me,' she said.

Ruben Miles felt an immediate sense of foreboding.

COMRADE MILES

O**n his return to England in the spring of 1931, Ruben Miles found himself with a healthy bankroll thanks to his considerable savings, the generosity of the Babe and the skills learnt from Titanic Thompson. However, he had little in the way of aim and even less in purpose. He had been away from his homeland for well over a decade, but he was stunned by how little seemed to have changed. He had left the land of modernity, even in the midst of the depression, and stepped back to what felt Edwardian, almost Victorian London. The city was dark, grey and seemingly crumbling. It was about as far removed from California as it was possible to be.

He rented a little flat in Soho on Wardour street, next to a club that nearly thirty years later would become the legendary Marquee Club. He knew literally nobody. He was married within a month and, during the next five years, he had three children with his second wife, Eileen Bennett, a dancer he met in the strip club next door to his flat. When their first son was born, christened Arthur Edgar Miles in the autumn of 1932, they moved to Eileen's home manor of Bethnal Green, in the heart of the East End. Within twenty months, their daughter Rose Mary and youngest son Albert John had arrived. They just moved to a slightly bigger terraced house in the adjacent street, Vallance Road.

Ruben Miles got a job through his father-in-law, probably the only courteous gesture the man offered during their often fraught relationship. Eileen's father was, like so many Eastenders, a docker. Harry Bennett got Ruben Miles a job at the King George V and Royal Albert dock. He did nearly twelve back-breaking months, unloading the vast cargoes of the Empire before realising that being a union rep meant you could keep out of the worst of the cold in winter and do your back one huge favour. You even earned a little more money. Practicality rather than ideology had been the primary motivation.

'I became a family man. I worked a five and a half-day week, I came home every night for my tea and I bounced snotty nosed little kids on my knee.'

Ruben Miles was drinking coffee in Starbucks with JoJo Bartlett. He was not convinced on the merits of twenty-first century globalism. He was also trying to work out why his coffee tasted vaguely of cinnamon.

'Were you happy?'

'That's not a question you asked of yourself in the 1930s East End. I existed. We existed.'

'Well, did you love your wife and children? Surely, you could answer that question?'

'Eileen was a fine-looking woman. Arthur was not exactly planned, but Eileen loved being pregnant so much that she insisted on us having more children quickly.'

'You haven't answered my question.'

Ruben Miles looked reflective for a few moments.

'I was very fond of them, certainly. I'm not sure I totally understand the notion of love.'

This made JoJo think. Why would he lie to make himself look cold? If he was being honest about his feelings, then maybe he was being honest about his life.

'I think being in the trenches made me a harder person.'

'Not to mention a lack of maternal love.'

JoJo could not help herself. She thought his mother sounded hateful.

'*That* is something that I have never got to the bottom of. What did I do to her?'

JoJo felt guilty for bringing up something that had clearly never been resolved. She changed the subject. Her favoured technique was distraction.

'What was your family life like then?'

'Our lives were decent enough for those five years. We had enough to eat, I kept most of what I brought back from the States in the bank earning interest. Our house was the same as all the others on the street. We ate the same things and went to the same places as our neighbours, it never occurred to me to spend any of my savings on improving our lives. Anyway, there was very little to spend it on back then. Most of the neighbours spent most of their money in the local pub.

Ruben Miles was aware that he was being more than a little disingenuous here. He always knew that the money in the bank was his escape route, should he want one. And he knew at some point he would probably want one.

'So, did you become, you know, political when you joined the union?'

'Not at first. I knew nothing of politics. I had never given any thought to it, either here or in the States. I do remember some of the lads in the regiment were always banging on about socialism, not that I ever paid any attention. And then I met Pablo and Francisca.'

'When was that?'

'October 12th 1935. It was a Saturday. I had been dragged along to a football match. West Ham versus Newcastle. All the lads knew where I was from but I'm not sure how as I had never told them. They were all big West Ham fans. They were very happy as they thumped Newcastle 4-1 that day. We were in the Aldgate East Tavern afterwards. Normally I didn't go to pubs as I did not drink, but Rose and Albert were both very gripey and I was in no rush to go home.'

In the pub there was a group of loud and emotional young Spaniards. They were saluting one another with socialist songs and proclaiming that Francisco Largo Caballero was going to bring Republican, Socialist glory to Spain. And they drank a lot of beer. Through some chance encounter that bypassed Ruben Miles, the English football supporters and the Spanish socialists merged, something that can only happen with the addition of copious amounts of alcohol. Most of the Spanish spoke excellent, if highly accented English. Pablo and Francisca were from Valencia. They were so affectionate with one another that Ruben Miles assumed they were lovers. But about halfway through what turned into quite a long evening (Eileen threw Ruben Miles's tea at him when he eventually made it home at 11 p.m.), it became clear that they were in fact siblings. Ruben Miles was aware that he had been very happy to receive this news.

'I began to spend time with them socially. As I have told you,

I was not a drinker, so we would go to galleries and museums. After a while they started taking me to meetings or to Speakers' Corner at Hyde Park. I became political for the first time. I was an unusual ideologue. I was more against Fascism than I was for the left.

'After a little while, I found that I was spending more time with just Pablo and Francisca.'

'And you fell in love with the girl and left your family.'

Ruben Miles almost gagged on his blueberry muffin, causing a certain amount of amusement with the representative sample of coffee drinkers in a High Street franchise.

'Why did you say that? It's not like you to be so judgemental.'

'Well, your eyes have gone a little misty by just talking about her, and you have not really said anything yet.'

'I did not leave my family and I did not have a relationship with Francisca.'

But of course, the truth was far from that straightforward. There was a touch of Clinton explaining Lewinski about this statement.

Ruben Miles's domestic life had become compartmentalised into three very distinct aspects. By day, he served the members of his union in a variety of mundane and pedantic ways. In the early evenings, he took part in earnest political discussions and meetings with a plethora of disparate left-wing groups and tried to get Francisca to take him seriously. It had not taken long for Ruben Miles to grasp that if he was to have any chance of winning Francisca's heart, it would be via him achieving some form of political epiphany. It was a shame his antennae were not as accurate in other areas.

He returned home later in the evening, his wife quite unaware of the existence of even theoretical competition. Eileen Miles was quite imposing, if that was possible in a quietly spoken, pretty women in her late twenties in the mid 1930s. What she lacked in education she made up for in puritanical certainty. She was adamant that the Good Lord was keeping a watchful eye on her and her brood and she was equally convinced that her husband was one day going to be a good and a great man.

Unsurprisingly, she was wrong on both these counts, however it is debatable as to which was further from reality.

The epiphany Ruben Miles eventually and belatedly 'enjoyed' was far removed from the political one he had envisaged. In those terms, he was still struggling to differentiate and judge the rambling strands of radical rhetoric which were almost a daily norm. Instead, he was walking down Brick Lane after a tedious union meeting with his colleagues, when he saw a woman up ahead who even from behind, looked very like Francisca. Except that it could not be Francisca as this woman appeared to be holding hands with another woman.

Talk about putting your money on the wrong horse.

'She was a lesbian!' JoJo Bartlett blurted, still a tad too loudly for some, even in the first decade of the twenty-first century.

Ruben Miles simply nodded.

'You have to understand how unusual this was then. Women being open and intimate on the street was not the norm in 1936. People even spat at them, apparently.'

JoJo did not have the heart to tell him that things had not changed as much as they should have in the seventy-odd years since.

'I stood in a doorway and watched them kiss. I have rarely felt like such a fool. It made me feel worse than the discovery of my first wife and the Babe.'

'But I don't fully understand. Nothing had happened between you, right? There were no events or even a conversation between you.'

'That is true. But I genuinely felt that there was a great connection between us. It was not just lust. I was old enough and experienced enough to know that it was far more significant than that.'

JoJo Bartlett was of course neither of those two things, so this caused her to infuriatingly blush.

'It sounds like a platonic affair.'

The old man seemed to approve of the definition.

'I think it is fair to say that this platonic affair of ours had a pretty big impact on my life. Without it, there is no way I would have ended up fighting Franco and the Fascists in Spain for nearly twelve miserable months.'

JoJo had been studying the Spanish Civil War in her History classes. She found it quite confusing. Her only re-occurring thought was that Franco and the Fascists sounded like a 1950s rock and roll band. She chose not to share this view with Ruben Miles.

'I was hoping that you might be able to help me with my studies, I find the Spanish Civil War difficult to fully understand.'

Ruben Miles sighed.

'JoJo, even the soldiers who fought in that war would have great difficulty in explaining the damn thing. So many factions. At least it cured me of ideology. The Spanish Civil War taught me that all forms of ideology lead inevitably to division and ultimately bloodshed and wars. How are you going to find common ground with your fellow man if you view the world through one narrow political view?'

JoJo did not know what to say to *that*. It seemed to her like Ruben Miles had prepared that little speech in advance.

TRAGEDY

oJo loved the fact that hearing and talking about Ruben Miles's life, or at the very least the stories he told her about his life, made her own concerns fade away. At least for a couple of hours. They were once again off campus. Ruben Miles either loved being out and about or he really did not want to be in The Apple Orchard Retirement Community all day, every day. Either way, they found themselves at the Gibside estate, in the Derwent valley, a short dive southwest of the city centre. They were warmly ensconced in the National Trust café, one of JoJo's new favourite pastimes. She shared this secret with no one as she realised it made her sound at least fifty-three.

She savoured her skinny latte and blueberry muffin. Ruben Miles had a bowl of soup containing cruciferous vegetables and blue cheese, one of life's more curious combinations, and a National Trust staple.

'Francisca and her brother politicised me. I became a strong believer in the threat of popular nationalism. This from a man who had fought at the Somme, never really giving a thought for who and what I was fighting for. I suppose you could say I became retrospectively bitter about so many ordinary working-class men that had died for essentially a royal family dispute. I suppose that joining the union started the process, but without meeting Francisca and Pablo I would never have gone to Spain in early 1937 to fight fascism.'

'What did your wife say when you told her you were leaving her and the children to go and fight in a foreign war? She must have been livid.'

The old man's face became ashen. This was the tale that he really did not want to tell JoJo, but he felt he had to be honest about everything. Well, almost everything.

'There was another, tragic factor that led me to joining the International Brigades and fighting in Spain. I needed to get away from my life. My wife and youngest son were killed in a house fire on New Year's Eve, 1936. I was at a union meeting until late, when

I returned home there was very little of the house still standing. The next day I discovered that I had lost half of my family.'

'My God, I'm so sorry.'

'And people here in The Apple Orchard wonder why I do not believe in any God and go to their bloody prayer meetings. We never found out what caused the fire. It was the closest I ever came to becoming a drinker.'

'I don't believe in God either,' JoJo found herself saying, as if her previous statement needed to be clarified. 'What did you do?'

'Something I cannot fully rationalise to this day. I'm not sure you will understand what I did next. I ran home to my mother's house in Northumberland and deposited my two remaining children with her. I gave her some money and stole away in the middle of the night. I never saw those kids again.'

JoJo Bartlett did not know how to process this information. On the one hand she could not begin to understand his pain at the sudden loss of half of his family. But could that ever justify or even attempt to explain giving away his remaining children and never seeing them again?

The pair remained silent for several minutes.

'I am not looking for forgiveness or even understanding. I just want to tell you my story, there is a lot more to tell. But I have nothing more to say on abandoning my children, other than I thought they would be better off without me. I made sure they were looked after financially.'

This was deceitful. When his mother turfed them out after they finished a poor state education, he did not support them in any way.

'How old were you at this point?'

'I left for Spain on the 24th of February 1937, I was thirty-seven.'

JoJo realised quickly that she was not going to find out any more about the abandoning of his children. She did not know what shocked her most. The act itself or the fact that he told her. She decided they needed to move on.

'What about Francisca and her brother?'

'They took me to Spain. I would not have made the decision to go or even undertaken the journey without them.'

'Did you ever tell her how you felt?'

'No. I felt such guilt after the fire, as if my desire for Francisca had somehow caused the fire. Absurd I know, but despite being in love with Francisca, I loved my family too and I was grieving. But I think she knew on some level. I only discovered later that Pablo had assumed we were lovers, as she had hidden her preferences successfully from her brother. Surprising, when they were so close.'

Ruben Miles blinked hard several times, not to hold back tears, but to try and remove the pictures in his mind. One of the reoccurring curses of his condition was his ability not just to remember what happened, but to *see it* happen again, like a video playback. At that very moment he was speaking to JoJo, he could see himself tiptoeing out of his mother's home, his childhood home in Morpeth, after taking one last glance at his two remaining children, lying still in his old bedroom, asleep.

'What did your mother say when you brought the children to her?'

'I did not tell her I was planning to leave, I said we were staying for a short time.'

JoJo Bartlett involuntarily shuddered at this implication.

'You told her nothing of your plans?'

'I know it is hard to understand. But I don't think I had a plan as such. I went back to London and was off to Spain within two months.'

The old man seemed to be on a real roll with the understatements.

'And you never saw your kids again?'

She knew she shouldn't ask, but she could not stop herself.

'Never.'

JoJo wondered how anyone could be so cruel, not to mention incurious.

'Did you have any *proper* reasons?'

The old man just shook his head.

'Perhaps, we should just pick up the story from Spain then?'

ESCAPES

'I travelled with Pablo, Francisca and her girlfriend, Carmen. We took the night ferry from Victoria to Paris Gare du Nord. We splashed out and travelled first class, it transpired that Carmen's father was a wealthy landowner from Sevilla and he gave her an enviable allowance, even if he disapproved vehemently about the 'socialist nonsense' that she espoused. Still, at least we travelled in style to Paris because of her bourgeois ways.'

'It's not like you to sound a little bitter.'

'One is always bitter when one loses out in love, especially to some ditzy rich girl. I could tolerate Francisca's tendencies, but her taste was a bridge too far.'

It was evident that whenever Ruben Miles talked about Francisca, his heart grew a little darker and his words grew sourer. And this from a man who had just lost his wife and favourite child in an as yet unexplained house fire a mere two weeks before. JoJo had not seen this side of Ruben Miles before. It was far from pleasant.

'We arrived in Spain on the 17th of March 1937, after a boring and cold two-week trek across France and the Pyrenees, the day the Battle of Malaga started. But we weren't heading that far south. We met up with the brigade in Zaragoza. We were then taken by primitive trucks to the defence of the Madrid to Valencia Road, just to the south of Madrid, on the Jarama River. We took up defence positions in the trenches on the west bank of the river. The fascists held the high ground to the north. They wanted to take our positions to close up the road between Valencia and Madrid. You see, Franco had failed to take Madrid and he was trying to cut off her supplies from the Republican headquarters, which was in Valencia.'

JoJo found the Spanish Civil War nearly as confusing as the French Revolution. Too many protagonists and too many confusing ideologies. She hoped Ruben Miles was going to keep it brief and not attempt to explain the frankly baffling divisions and subplots that her A level teacher either did not understand himself or at the very least, failed to communicate effectively. Either he was not the teacher that she thought he was, or she was not the student she thought she was.

'So, the fascists are the nationalists?'

'That's right.'

She was aware that this was not showcasing her intellectual abilities to the full.

'They sent you to the frontlines straight away, without training?

She was a little happier with this contribution.

'All Great War veterans went straight to the frontline, I was put in the XV brigade, mostly British. A lot of the guys were very young and had no experience of combat. Remember, the fascists had much more military experience than us. I fought alongside some who could write an essay on the war but sure as hell could not contribute much to it, except to get in the way and then get themselves killed.'

'What about Pablo and Francisca?'

'That was the inevitable punchline. As soon as we got to Zaragoza we were split up. Pablo was sent to Barcelona, and Francisca went with him. I have no idea what happened to her girlfriend.'

'So, you found yourself in a foreign civil war without the people that you were trying to help.'

'I was fighting for a cause, not some people. At least at that point. Actually, fighting against a cause would be a better definition.'

'But you went to fight mainly because of Francisca, or have I got that totally wrong?'

Ruben Miles conceded that this may indeed have been his initial motivation.

'Were you not disillusioned right from the start?'

'No. It's not as if I had been duped into going or deliberately abandoned. However, the disappointments were not slow in revealing themselves.'

'How so?'

'The trenches were a nightmare. The rancid filth, the vermin and stench of human excrement. The only thing that had changed from France was that someone had turned the temperature up. It was OK in February, but by June it was unbearable.'

'It sounds dreadful.'

'The conditions were not the worst part. Unlike many of my peers, I had not needed alcohol or opium to rationalise all that had been done in God's name. Of course, not even alcohol would have stopped me from remembering too much about what I witnessed in France. The roaring Twenties in New York and the Babe were what stopped me reliving those events every day like most of the poor souls who came home. The sheer exuberance and innovation of New York made me realise both the good in mankind and new technology. Fear, hate and pessimism had been replaced by hope, peace and opportunity. That was how I was able to process my Great War memories to myself and justify my actions.'

'And Spain killed that?'

'Stone dead. On my first night back in the trenches in Spain I never slept a wink, I just watched, my mind on a permanent loop, the very worst of my French war experiences. I saw every sight as if I was front row at the cinema. So, my Spanish Civil War experience was fought not just in foul smelling trenches, but also in my head. It was as if I had never left the meadows of Beaumont-Hamel.'

'How long did you fight in the war?'

'Only a few months. Another opportunity presented itself, and by then I had had my fill of taking orders from idiots and watching young men die.'

'What sort of opportunity?'

'All in good time.'

'Did you see many young men die?'

'One hundred and fifty-seven in Spain. One night, just before I left, I counted them all up as a way of trying to fall asleep as I was not on duty. My way of counting sheep...'

JoJo could not think of anything to say to this.

'My memory took a snapshot of each of their faces as they died.'

She could not think of anything she wanted to say about this either.

'And of course, it was all in vain. Franco won and ruled Spain into the mid 1970s. In many ways, I found the events in Spain even sadder, and as equally futile as France a generation before. But I suppose I had changed. I was getting closer to forty when I left Spain. I think thoughts of my own mortality made the deaths in this war, although so many less numerically, more poignant somehow. Ironic, don't you think?'

'How do you mean?'

'Well, if I had known I would live to be well over a hundred-years-old, I don't think I would have been contemplating my own navel quite as much.'

Ruben Miles gave a little chuckle as he spoke.

'Did you kill more men during the time you were in Spain?'

'Some.'

JoJo was disappointed that she wanted to hear about them. All of them. She did not have to wait long.

SPANISH EYES

The man in charge was a fat waiter from Guadalest, not particularly inspiring from any perspective. As far as Ruben Miles could ascertain, he got the gig because he had the deepest growl of an accent. This attribute at least hinted at authority. There were few other recognisable qualifications. He had a body odour issue that brought both tears to the eyes and acid reflux to the throat. Of course, they all smelled in the trenches, so for Manuel Perez's distinct aroma to cause comment amongst all the men, it had to be truly memorable.

Ruben Miles, like many British recruits, spoke only a little Spanish. Ruben took most of his translation from Bernie Myers, a former warehouseman from Manchester. Although he did not trust Bernie, his Spanish certainly sounded authentic, which was more than the other alleged linguists could muster. It was therefore Bernie Myers in his nasal Mancunian accent that issued the orders from Manuel Perez. They rarely sounded good.

'He wants you to lead a patrol out tonight with four other men, he wants you to try and gauge their strength in numbers and weaponry. We are expecting a frontal assault.'

Bernie was picking the ever-present dirt out under his too long fingernails with a blunt knife. He was smoking a Ducados, the distinctive strong aroma from the black tobacco enveloping the speaker's head in a tiny circling cloud.

'He said you could take anyone, except him and me – as we went out last time. At least some of us are still democrats, comrade.'

Ruben Miles had no way of knowing the veracity of these remarks. But Bernie's smirk seemed a little too obvious.

'I think you are taking for granted my lack of understanding, comrade. Our rancid commander-in-chief made no reference to you in his remarks.'

Ruben Miles was adopting the frontal bluff he had seen the Fixer use with much success.

'Entiendo más de lo que piensas, comrade.'

Bernie Myers reflected on this momentarily, not knowing that it was a phrase parrot-learnt by Ruben Miles at the beginning of his Spanish adventure at the insistence of Francisca and Pablo.

I understand more than you think.

It had served him well so far.

'I am happy to come with you, comrade, don't forget the extra rations for volunteers.'

Myers was talking of the extra shots of the cheap Spanish brandy that went to those going on patrol, both before and after the mission.

Ruben Miles chose Hendricks and Jenkinson to join them for the raiding party. The two had arrived with Ruben Miles just two days prior, they had joined up together, two union men from the Birmingham canals. Ruben Miles felt at least a vague kinship with these men, until they spoke in their impenetrable Brummie brogue. Then they began to get on his nerves.

Ruben Miles had experienced two patrols into No Man's Land on the Western Front in the spring of 1916. In preparation for the Somme offensive, it was felt by the powers that be that soldiers should be at least aware of how it feels to be marooned from the sanctity of home defences and facing the enemy at bowel-clenchingly close quarters. Ruben Miles spent two seemingly endless nights lying in a shell hole, in a few inches of dirty rainwater, listening to Bavarians belching in their frontline trench thirty yards away. Whenever he reviewed those nights afterwards, it was not at the absurdity of it, or even the danger of it, but more the frustration that he had no idea where in France he was lying. Where was the nearest town? He could have died and not even known where he was. This seemed perverse in the extreme.

With this in mind and using Bernie Myers to translate, Ruben Miles made it his business for Manuel Perez to tell him exactly where in Spain he may well die.

'Moreta es la ciudad más cercana.'

'Moreta,' Bernie Myers said again needlessly.

It sounded as good a place as any.

The Nationalists were encamped in the hills to the north. The Republican chiefs were convinced a large-scale attack was imminent, as Franco's forces needed to break the supply lines between Madrid and Valencia. Therefore, across the three-mile front in the valley surrounding the town of Moreta, small raiding parties were being readied to try and gauge the extent of what lay ahead.

Ruben Miles made himself more popular by giving his share of the brandy to his comrades. Teetotallers are a rare breed in any war. They set off at one in the morning on an unusually cool, overcast night. The lack of moonlight meant a slow meander in the silence. It took them over an hour to traverse the already pockmarked terrain. Ruben Miles was surprised by the discipline and care of the men, even their footfall was muffled. All he could hear was the regular nasal breathing of Myers, the result of too many foul smelling Ducados.

The Nationalist soldiers, by contrast, were not so concerned about the noise they made. The men could be heard talking from nearly two hundred yards away. The Spanish are not renowned for their quietness, seemingly even in war. Unlike the Somme, there were no elaborate barbed wire defences requiring patience, skill and some cutters. The Nationalists were not expecting any guests. Most were not even carrying their weapons, which were instead propped up against the shallow walls of their trench.

Ruben Miles had given his instructions orally before they departed. He now signalled with his hands that the existing plans were good to go. Hendricks and Jenkinson just about managed to nod through their fear. It was a simple plan. They would find what was clearly the end flank of a position and wait a few minutes to hear if there were any walking patrols. Ruben Miles would go over first and would signal the others over as required. The target was one man, brought back alive for questioning.

Manuel Perez had a thing for night-time trench raids. Even when his superiors were less inclined, he regularly sent out sorties, worthwhile or not. The men under his command became bitter and resentful of other soldiers in companies which hardly ever undertook such raids, unless ordered. They rarely stayed bitter for long, as a good many of them never came back. And those that did quickly cottoned on to the fact that open insubordination would simply result in more invitations to get yourself killed. The men of the company never understood why he ordered so many raids, they never asked him directly. They figured he was just a *gilipollas*. A wanker.

Ruben Miles was himself reflecting on this accurate description as he readied himself for action. He may have been the only one sober enough to have a chance of success. Manuel Perez had been unusually generous with the pre-raid brandy allocation. But for all of his many failings, Ruben Miles also possessed an attachment to a vague concept of honour, and it was this attribute, silently instilled in him during his irregular parental socialisation, that made him lead from the front.

He silently told the others to sit tight. They were all happy to oblige. It took him less than a minute crawling on his front to reach the frontline trench. For a man of his Western Front experience, he could not believe the scarcity of frontline defences. Where was the barbed wire and sandbags? Where was the soldier's frontline discipline? He could see the smoke from their cigarettes ascending above their heads, he could hear but not understand their coarse and loud tales of made-up debauchery. He got closer still and now saw that they weren't just passing around a bottle, but multiple bottles.

Surprisingly, and with a grunt of physical effort, one of the Nationalist soldiers clambered over the front of the trench and stumbled a few yards forward. Ruben Miles waited, his hand on his unsheathed knife. His Great War issue revolver, 'borrowed' from a dead officer on the Somme, still tucked away.

'Ahhhhh,' the soldier exhaled and with it a great torrent of piss irrigated the slightly parched terrain.

Ruben Miles was so close he could see the man's slender penis. He was just contemplating making a move when another soldier noisily clambered out to join his now sated companion. This suggested a plan of sorts. He watched the two stumble back over the trench amid much noise from the other soldiers.

He had to wait nearly fifteen minutes for the next soldier to emerge. This one seemed even more unsteady on his feet than the others. He also appeared to be dressed as some form of junior officer. This guy needed more than a piss and so walked a little further out from the trench, passing less than ten yards from a prone Ruben Miles.

He waited until his pants were around his ankles and he could detect the sound of concerted effort. Ruben Miles emerged out of the dim night light with his revolver pointed at the soldier's head and his finger to his lips, a universal language of sorts.

'I will never forget the expression on his face,' Ruben Miles chuckled as he recalled the night. 'At least I let him finish!'

JoJo Bartlett found herself laughing despite herself.

'What did he do?'

'Well, at least he did not need to shit himself!'

This produced a far from ladylike snort from JoJo.

'We got him back to our positions within five minutes. He never made a sound.'

'So, mission accomplished. What happened next?'

A sudden darkness spread over the face of Ruben Miles.

'Then, I met the Russian.'

THE BUDGIE

For someone who did not drink alcohol, Ruben Miles was beginning to learn what a bad hangover felt like. It seemed that after every session with JoJo Bartlett, when he ventured deep into the recesses of his remarkable mind and excavated the events that unfolded around him, he felt like shit. His head pounded and he felt that he permanently needed the toilet. Not the best starting point for a serious and surreal conversation.

'You need to tell me about your son.'

'Actually, he isn't my *real* son. We sort of adopted him really. You see we did not think we could have children. I was never what you could call regular. Anyway, after we had been married for several years and pretty much given up even trying, who should arrive on our doorstep one night but my fifteen-year-old cousin Brenda from Carlisle. Apparently, she had hitchhiked all the way, which considering it was 1979 and with the Yorkshire Ripper being on the prowl and seemingly local after that tape recording that had been sent to the police... Well, you can imagine.'

Ruben Miles couldn't, but chose not to say so.

'She did not even know she was pregnant although I could tell straight away. She had a huge fight with her dad and had run away from home. She said that she had nowhere else to go.'

'So, you and your husband took her in?'

'That's right, although she made us promise not to tell her parents where she was.'

'Over the course of the next month a sort of plan came together. Brenda could get on with the rest of her life and we could have the child that we had so wanted.'

'A common enough family story, I suppose. Admittedly more common earlier in the century.'

'We called him Barry and told all the neighbours that we had been on the adoption waiting list for ages. We gave Brenda some money and she said she was going to London, we never heard from her ever again. She never even hinted who the father might be.'

'What about all the legal paperwork?'

'My husband dealt with that. He said it was not a problem. I suppose I was very naive.'

Mrs Hazel Wharton had never told a living soul the events that led up to her becoming a mother. Her husband had gone to his grave as the only person that knew the truth.

'He was a lovely baby. Not so much as a sniffle and slept all night right from the start. We were so happy.

'What happened? You said you were happy.'

'Brian and I were happy. We never had a cross word in forty-seven years. Mind you, not that Brian was much of a talker. But he was a good man. If I could turn the clock back, we would never have taken him in.'

'But surely you do not believe your adopted son is a murderer?'

'I did not say murderer, I said serial killer. There is a world of difference.'

They sat silently for a few moments as they finished their after-dinner coffee, both taking it weak with lots of milk.

'He was four or five when I began to notice little things. He had been such a good toddler, no terrible twos like so many. He started looking at me with a blank, empty expression, almost as if he did not recognise me. Then when he was eleven, one day I went out into the back garden, it was a hot summer day and I let him play in the back garden because there was no way he could get out. Anyway, for some reason I just stood and watched him, without him being able to see me. I could see that he was playing with something in his hands although I could not see exactly what it was, I thought it might have been a sparrow as there were so many nesting in the overhanging trees. Then he suddenly jumps up and throws something very hard at the side garage wall. Then he went over and started laughing hysterically.'

'Was it a bird?'

'Yes, his dad had got him a budgie for his birthday. He would not stop laughing. His dad loved that little thing.'

'That does not make him a serial killer, Hazel. Little boys are capable of nasty things.'

'It's not normal though, is it? Anyway, it got worse as he got older.'

Mrs Hazel Wharton had become obsessed with the concept of people being born evil. She had convinced herself from the day of the budgie killing, that he was a boy with evil in his heart. The smashed little body of Billy the budgie was evidence enough. She went to the local library and read psychology books on criminality and sociological books on deviant behaviour. She was relieved to see validation for her prejudices within the nature versus nurture debate. She scarcely noticed that although she remained clearly observant of Barry's young actions, she detached herself more and more from him. It was a house of no affection, but that made it far from unique. Especially in the northeast of England in the early 1980s.

'I had always wanted a family,' said Mrs Hazel Wharton before she bade Ruben Miles a troubled goodnight. It was a toss-up as to which of them slept worse.

THE RUSSIAN

Ruben Miles has only come across one individual in his very long life that shared the same level of imposing presence as the Fixer. The Russian. The two also shared some defining visual and other characteristics. They both had eyes that seemed to look into your very soul. Deep blue eyes that rarely seemed to blink. They both spoke slowly and often quietly but still with obvious authority. They both had prominent but not unattractive facial features. They both invariably got what they wanted. And they were both as cruel as they were devious.

Ruben Miles got his first look at the Russian moments after his small raiding party took their prisoner into the interrogation hut, an old farmer's shed requisitioned for the use of senior officers. It was five hundred metres behind the frontline.

Ruben Miles had seen inside enough public houses to notice that the prisoner was more than a little drunk. Ruben Miles could smell the brandy and stale bread emanating from the prisoner's chapped lips. He did not seem to understand his position. One look at the Russian as he strode confidently into the small space and the prisoner seemed to sober up very fast. He started off by apologising for Franco and calling him, 'Un hijo de puta.'

Ruben Miles wondered whether the Russian spoke Spanish, he guessed correctly that he did. He also guessed correctly that the questioning of Franco's genealogy was not going to do the prisoner any good whatsoever.

The rest of the raiding party were ushered out of the hut. It seemed that leading the successful raid had accorded Ruben Miles a privileged position and access to the interrogation. He later wished that it had not been thus. As well as the Russian, the gluttonous Manuel Perez had squeezed his cascading stomach and wince-inducing odour into the tiny space. The Russian did not seem to notice or at least did not seem to care. He gave the accompanying Bernie Myers no more than a passing glance.

'Me contaras todo.'

It was a calm beginning.

Bernie Myers looked like he was about to translate but Ruben Miles waved him off. He knew that todo meant 'everything', so he was able to surmise the rest.

The prisoner began babbling, speaking quicker than even the average Spaniard. Ruben Miles was able to identify a few words only and the key one seemed to be nada, which was repeated regularly.

Again, he motioned for Bernie to stay quiet. The little information he had gleaned from the prisoner's response and the clear agitation of Manuel Perez spoke volumes. The Russian remained passive, his face blank.

Then he kicked the prisoner between his legs with the speed of a cobra strike.

The prisoner spent the next several minutes writhing on the floor, clutching his violated body. Then he puked up the stale bread and copious brandy. By the time he had been hauled back to a standing position by Perez and Myers, he had begun to babble again. Albeit now requiring a degree of effort to get the words out.

The Russian put a finger to his lips, touching his nose. This was the second time in less than an hour that this almost ubiquitous sign language had been used on the soldier. He stumbled to a halt.

'Tu estas quedando sin vida camarada.'

Bernie Myers looked at Ruben Miles and whispered, 'He says that he is running out of lives. The prisoner says he knows nothing, that he only arrived here yesterday, and he is not an officer.'

The pistol Ruben Miles had relieved the prisoner of on capture did not fit this profile. He removed it from his back pocket and handed it to the Russian.

The Russian turned the weapon in his hands. As an expert gunsmith, he had quickly identified it as a top of the range Luger. The gun of the officer class in the Wehrmacht. In fact, Ruben Miles as an inexpert, had been able to come swiftly to the same conclusion. Some Nazi had given this gun to the prisoner to recognise his officer status. So much for the non-intervention pact.

The Russian pointed the gun at the prisoner's head.

'Necesitas hablar ahora.'

He spoke the words slowly. The prisoner blinked but said nothing right away.

'Nada, nada, no se nada,' he said eventually, his voice noticeably higher pitched with tension.

The Russian turned to Ruben Miles and spoke quietly in perfect, almost accent-free English.

'Take his shoes and socks off.'

Ruben Miles did as he was instructed. Watching the prisoners baffled face, there were drops of sweat coming from his eyebrows although the hut was not even warm.

'Necesitas hablar ahora.'

The prisoner either knew nothing or he was very committed to his cause. The Russian decided that it was time to find out. He blew off the big toe of the prisoner's right foot with his own pistol.

The shouts of pain seemed to bounce off the warped corrugated iron roof of the hut. Ruben Miles actually put his fingers in his ears to reduce the volume of them.

The Russian remained passive to any pleas of mercy.

'Necesitas hablar ahora.'

The look of terror on the prisoner's face was one Ruben Miles had not seen since the summer of 1916.

'Por favor.'

The Russian was an impatient man. It was one of his defining characteristics, along with his many prejudices. For example, he had come to dislike and distrust most Spaniards. This was not a combination to give solace to a man begging for his life, or to a man watching it unravel before his eyes.

Once again, the Russian turned to Ruben Miles and said, 'Take his trousers and pants off.'

Ruben Miles did as he was bid, with a creeping sense of unease. He may have seen plenty of violence, but a lot of it from a distance and he did not like the look of the twelve-inch blade that the Russian produced from his right boot. Even in the dim light of the hut, the blade of the knife glinted. He handed the

Luger back to Ruben Miles.

'A souvenir,' he said pleasantly.

He turned back to the prisoner, now naked from the waist down.

'Necesitas hablar ahora.'

This produced more pleading, but no information.

The Russian did not even look disappointed.

The Russian took the poor man's cock and balls in his left hand and with his right he used the very sharp knife.

A man with hyperthymesia remembers everything, but even a man with this rare condition remembers some things *much* more clearly than others. Ruben Miles can vividly recall the pattern of blood sprayed on the hut walls. He can hear the volume and pitch of the screams. He can recall the contents of the pool of sick that poor Bernie Myers had produced. He can see the look of complete disinterest on the face of the Russian.

'He knew nothing,' was all he said, in his perfect English. Then he walked slowly out of the hut.

The stricken man begged to be put out of his misery.

Ruben Miles obliged the poor Spaniard with his own Luger.

JoJo Bartlett looked *very* pale faced. She may not have much knowledge of male genitalia, but the concept of having them cut off with a sharp knife is something that crosses the gender empathy divide.

Seeing that JoJo needed to be distracted, Ruben Miles continued to talk.

Half an hour after Ruben Miles had felt compelled to end the suffering of another doomed man, he found himself alone in a room with the Russian.

'I have heard a lot about you, Ruben Miles. And today I see your compassion, what a very British characteristic. As you have witnessed, we Ukrainians are… less so.'

Don't be confused by a name, the man known as the Russian, was in fact a Ukrainian, by birth if not by loyalty. But then again, the Russian would prove to be loyal only to himself.

'You seem to have me at a disadvantage, sir, as I know

nothing of you.'

'Let us just say that we are on the same side and desire the same end.'

Ruben Miles doubted that right from the get-go.

Sergei Kovalenko was old enough to remember Moscow before the Bolsheviks took over after the revolution and yet more convincingly after the conclusion of the civil war. He was a dyed-in-the-wool Marxist, having even claimed to have read almost all of *Das Kapital*. He had arrived in Spain on the direct orders of Stalin to help man the barricades against the rise of Fascism on the Iberian Peninsula. He was given two hundred men and some assorted, poor-quality small artillery as well as small handguns and a box of unreliable World War One machine guns. Not what you would call one hundred percent commitment to the cause. Especially when Hitler was proving to be a very generous friend to Franco.

'I can't see them defeating Franco. The Nazis and Italians are helping them much more...'

The Russian seemed to stop himself from further explanation. Perhaps even a makeshift, tinpot office on the frontline of the Spanish civil war could still be heard by a drunk and paranoid Stalin in the Kremlin.

'A prisoner I interrogated yesterday was a lot more forthcoming. We are expecting a major offensive in the next few days. Franco thinks he can seize his supply line from Valencia to Madrid and win the war. I was hoping that today's prisoner could have told us exactly where and when this attack would come.'

'And what do you think, comrade?'

'I think I do not like being called comrade by a British man, who is not, I think, a real revolutionary socialist.'

Ruben Miles decided to ignore this questioning of his ideological purity, despite its accuracy.

'Forgive me, then how should I address you?'

'They call me the Russian here, that is as good a name as any, despite its inaccuracy.'

'Are you in charge here?'

'That is a difficult question to answer simply. Technically no, but perhaps theoretically... maybe. I certainly do not get given any orders by anyone.'

Ruben Miles thought that was easy to believe.

The attack came the next morning. The Republicans held their positions, but only just, and at great cost. Hundreds were killed on their section of the line alone, including Bernie Myers and Manuel Garcia. It was hand to hand and relentless. Ruben Miles actually could not count the men he had either killed or at least seriously wounded. He chose to share this with JoJo Bartlett.

'You mean you don't know how many you killed? There were that many?'

'I mean that everything was so manic that even my memory could not keep up with the carnage. That was the day that I came closest to death, I took a bayonet in the chest, another couple of inches and I would not have made middle, never mind great old age.'

Ruben Miles gave another one of his throaty chuckles and then lifted up his shirt and jumper to reveal a four-inch scar, just to the right of his heart. Did JoJo Bartlett have at last some form of corroborating evidence? It certainly looked like a scar that could have been inflicted by a 1930s bayonet. She had seen a World War One example on a school trip to Ypres when she was in Year Ten.

'What happened next?'

'Let's just say I had a sudden reappraisal of my commitment to the cause. Or to put it another way, I went AWOL.'

'You ran away?'

'Technically, as a volunteer, I was free to go. In practice, if they caught you, they shot you.'

'How did you manage to get away?'

'Two factors, the chaos after the slaughter of the battle and... the Russian.'

'How did he help you?'

'Money and transport, he gave me a motorcycle, not that I could ride the bloody thing very well, but at least it got me several miles away before I crashed into a ditch.'

'Your second transport accident of your life.'

'Correct. I'm glad you're paying attention, but this one hurt more than the car crash in the States. You see, I was already poorly stitched up after the bayonet wound, the crash into the ditch took out the stiches and gave me an added bonus of a dislocated shoulder.'

'That sounds bad. Before you go on, why did the Russian help you so much, what had you done to deserve such help?'

'He thought I had saved his life during the battle.'

'Did you?'

'Whether I did or didn't is almost irrelevant, he thought I had, and that's what mattered to him.'

'Why is it almost irrelevant and why don't you know? Did you not remember something?'

This drew a disapproving look from Ruben Miles.

'I have told you, in the chaos of battle not even someone with my condition is going to be able to process and therefore remember every detail of every manic event. The Russian said I saved his life and he wanted to thank me.'

'You don't sound convinced.'

'I wasn't, but why should I doubt him then? Why would he say I had if I hadn't?'

'Was that the last you saw of him?'

'No, we are sadly going to hear more from my interactions with the Russian. He popped up next in London in 1940.'

'During the Blitz?'

'Just before, but let's not get ahead of ourselves. After I fled the battlefield on the Russian's motorcycle, I suspected that I had not seen the last of him.'

'Why did you feel that?'

'What he said to me when he gave me the motorbike. And the way he looked at me when he said it. He said that in the future he may need my help and he hoped he could come knocking on my door if he needed it. He then said something that I found odd, he said he had friends all over the world.'

'But hadn't you already saved his life? How come you owed him more help?'

'That's pretty much how I felt, and it made me more uncomfortable about the fact that I could not remember saving his life. Anyway, he was most insistent and besides he gave me a decent roll of money, pesetas and dollars. The Russian might have furnished me with a way to escape, but without the old widow I am not sure I would have made it out of Spain. We should forget about the Russian for a while, but next time I will tell you about one of the best people I have run into in my life. She certainly saved mine.'

'Well, that would make for a refreshing change of direction. What with the Fixer and the Russian, to name just two, you seem to have been involved with a lot of the darker side of humanity?'

'I don't think I can dispute that. But the Spanish widow or Senora Maria Delores to give her full name, now she was a fruit from an altogether different tree.'

PRETTY PERSUASION

L uke Miles was not known for his soft skills. He thought *empathy* was a brand of incense sticks from JoJo's bedroom. His biology teacher at school, Miss Yates, had told the class during the Easter revision sessions that it was 'inevitable' that you would eventually become either your mother or father, in terms of both personality and appearance. It was at this precise moment that Luke Miles realised two of what he thought must be some of life's undoubted universal truths. 1) God either a) does not exist, or b) is a twat. 2) All old people are shit, especially your parents.

Luke Miles *was* angry that he had such shit parents. He was also angry that JoJo Bartlett kept telling him otherwise.

'They're not that bad. I mean, they let you come and go pretty much as you want. They give you some money and they seem to like me.'

'Well, my dad certainly likes you.'

This made them both feel a little uncomfortable.

It was JoJo who decided to change the subject. They were walking in Jesmond Dene, the only couple without either a screaming child or a boisterous dog. Most couples seemed to have both. None of them seemed to smile much, not even the dogs with a big stick in their salivating gobs.

Luke Miles was convinced that his ancient relative had had absolutely no exceptional or even mildly interesting adventures. In fact, like most teenagers, he felt old people had always been old. It was as if every person was born at a particular age and stayed that way for ever or at least until death. Wisely, he chose not to share this ignorant philosophy with JoJo.

'I think you are going to have to trust me, your elderly relative has been involved in some crazy shit. Either that or he is a first-class liar. I tend to think he is telling the truth as he never seems to get mixed up or make any mistakes. His memory is extraordinary.'

'Give me an example.'

'I can't. Remember, I promised him I would not tell you anything of his life. I can't break that promise.'

Luke Miles decided to go in the huff at this news. According to a recent survey, the fall-back position of eighty-nine percent of the British male population when they do not get their way.

'There is also his condition, I mean your great grandfather is a very rare human being, he has hyperthymesia. Sometimes called Highly Superior Autobiographical Memory or HSMA.'

'And you expect me to know what that means? I don't even know what a hypermarket is.'

'Hyperthymesia is an exceptionally rare condition, they reckon less than a hundred people worldwide have it. If you have it, you can remember every single day of your life... in detail.'

'Who reckons?'

'I looked it up on the internet and everything. It's a real thing, although only discovered pretty recently. So, I don't know how your relative says he was diagnosed with it many years ago. I need to ask him about that.'

Luke would never question the modern oracle that is the internet.

'And he says that he has it?'

'He told me about his condition after a few weeks of our sessions. I have tested him, picking dates and things, he always gets the checkable facts right, like specifically what day of the week it was. It is really, really weird. He is always right. It's like I said, if he is making this stuff up, he is very good at it.'

Luke Miles took a little time to reflect on this information.

'You do realise you have broken your promise and told me something of his life?'

JoJo Bartlett looked a little crestfallen.

'Shit,' she said.

'Don't worry, your secret is safe with me, but I want you to talk him into letting me join in what you do with him. I want to know everything.'

'That's going to be really difficult. I've already tried.'

'Well, as my father has bored me to death for years by saying, if at first you don't succeed...'

'Alright, alright, I will speak to him again, but I am not telling you anything unless he gives his permission. I promised.'

'But you already told me about the hyper-what's-its-name.'

'Hyperthymesia. Anyway, I think I am allowed to tell you that as it does not tell you anything about the many things he has seen and done. It is just his condition.'

JoJo was a little disturbed to find that as she said this, her mind reran a spool of images she had self-generated about some of Ruben Miles's more extreme deeds. *She* suddenly felt like she was watching an internal movie. She could almost hear a gangster soundtrack when Ruben Miles blew the two New York gangsters away. This was not a welcome development.

Luke and JoJo had to take evasive action on the narrow path to avoid a rampaging three-year-old boy and his treasured tree branch with dog shit on the end.

'Can you explain something to me?' she said when the indiscriminate human Tonka Toy had been at least partially pacified by a clearly haggard mother.

'Why do people have children? I mean, whenever I see parents with their young kids they seem at the very least knackered and harassed or at worst borderline depressed. I don't get it. I'm never going to have kids.'

Luke Miles was a pretty typical sixteen-year-old-boy. His concepts of fatherhood revolved entirely around the creation of children, not the rearing of them. In fact, he realised as he pondered JoJo's stringent views as to whether he even had a view on the subject.

'I suppose it can't be all bad, otherwise everyone would not have them, right?'

JoJo looked far from convinced and a little disappointed in Luke's offering.

'That's just nature's big con job. We learnt it in Biology with Miss Yates last year. Apparently, when parents have a child, they experience this complete hormone overload of love. It's the thing that stops parents from abandoning their offspring, like some animals do.'

Luke Miles must have been distracted when they did that in class.

'What, like some kind of natural drug?'

'Pretty much. Miss Yates said that without it, humans would not look after their children for so long. Mind you, she is a bit of a feminist, Miss Yates. She wears Doc Martens and might even be a lesbian.'

JoJo had a sudden revelation. Maybe this was what the old man was missing. Maybe his hyperthymesia got in the way of these hormones that made parents love their children. Or at least not abandon them. She wondered if there would be anything on the internet about *that.*

For his part, Luke Miles had been reviewing his own views on Miss Yates and they were far from positive. 'She made a big fuss about World Women's Day this year. We had to have an assembly,' Luke said miserably. It was twenty-five very long minutes that he knew he wouldn't get back.

'You can be a feminist and not a lesbian, you know.'

Luke Miles had little idea of just what JoJo was talking about. He thought for a horrible moment JoJo was going to ask him to define a feminist. He just about knew what a lesbian was, although he was unlikely to reveal his sources.

'I am seeing Ruben again tomorrow. We have reached another memorable part of his story. Mind you, there seems to be a lot of *them*. I will try to speak with him again before we start. But last time I brought up you coming along he was very strongly against it. I don't know what I can say that will make him change his mind.'

Luke Miles thought long and hard about this.

'Just tell him what an amazing boyfriend I am.'

Clearly, the long and hard had been a complete waste of everyone's time.

SENORA MARIA DELORES – PART ONE

R uben Miles remembers falling off the old Russian motorbike and pitching headfirst into a ditch. He never knew how close he had come to hitting a very old Holm Oak tree without a helmet. He did not remember landing at all.

He woke up on a lumpy sofa bed in a small room that smelled faintly of lavender. Little chinks of light could be seen in the small gaps of the external window shutters. They seemed to shimmer on the whitewashed walls. He could hear quiet singing from an adjacent room. He recognised the language but not the voice. After a few minutes he noticed that his chest wound had been freshly bandaged and more surprisingly, although heavily strapped, his left shoulder was very painful when he moved. He stopped moving. He drifted back to sleep.

When he awoke the second time, several hours later, the room was in total darkness and although he could not see, he knew where he was. Well, at least in terms of his previous memory, now seemingly intact, of waking up in a strange room on a lumpy old sofa bed, in a room that smelled of lavender and with an unknown person singing in Spanish in an adjacent room. Other than that, he knew nothing. He went back to sleep.

The third time he awoke, once more in daylight, this time with the shutters slightly open and with the sound of animated sparrows filling the little room, there was a woman, aged somewhere between forty and sixty, dressed in traditional Spanish widow's black and sitting on an uncomfortable looking wooden chair. She was smiling at him.

Ruben Miles made an instant and inexplicable decision to pretend that he was mute. He made gestures towards his neck and mouth. The woman responded by pouring a mug of cold water from a large jug at her feet. Ruben Miles gulped the contents straight back and proffered the cup back in the woman's direction, she filled it once more, still smiling.

He drank four cups before his thirst began to dissipate. Finally, the woman put the mug at her feet and said,

'Del lado de quien estas?'

She repeated herself again quite slowly.

Ruben Miles knew what she was asking of him. She was asking which side he was on in the war.

'Lo entiendes?'

Perhaps his Spanish was getting better. He did understand what she was asking, but at this stage he saw no possible benefit to be gained from telling her that information. She did not look like a fascist sympathiser, but she hardly fit the profile of a communist or anarchist either. Either way, she seemed to accept his lack of communication without irritation. She disappeared for several minutes and came back with what appeared to be more fresh bandages and strapping for his shoulder. She also appeared to be carrying a bottle of light brown liquid of unknown origin or content, but once she removed the rubber stopper, a pungent alcoholic aroma filled the room.

She redressed his chest wound. Ruben Miles could see no signs of infection as she worked and nor was there the sour smell of it. The shoulder was an altogether different situation. Once the strapping had been removed, with obvious care, he saw that his shoulder was dislocated. The woman spoke to him in Spanish again.

'Su hombre esta dislocado.'

That seemed pretty straightforward, as he could see that for himself.

'Necesito volver a ponerlo, bebe un poco de este.'

She tried to give him the bottle. He shook her off. But she was insistent. Much to his surprise he took the bottle and had a little sip.

'Mas, mas, dolera.'

Ruben Miles had spent enough days on the front lines of the Spanish Civil War to know exactly what dolera meant. It meant it was going to hurt.

He processed this information for a few seconds and then reached for the bottle and took a very large gulp. As he was teetotal, this was an unobvious and poor decision. As soon as he had stopped coughing and dry retching, the small, but surprisingly strong and mobile woman of indeterminate age, forcefully put Ruben Miles's shoulder back where it belonged.

It did indeed hurt.

By the time the women had strapped his replaced shoulder and brought him a little warm soup, Ruben Miles was beginning to feel a little bit better.

'Soy Maria Delores,' the woman said, pointing at her chest with a slender middle finger.

She smiled again at the silent Ruben Miles.

Ruben Miles found himself smiling back.

Senora Maria Delores was actually aged fifty-two when she took in the injured Ruben Miles in early 1938. Like many Spanish women she flowered early, turning the heads of the men in the village when she was only twelve. But by her late thirties, she looked like a woman at least fifteen years older. This, no doubt exacerbated by the premature death of her husband, Diego, struck down with tuberculosis in the autumn of 1932. His death left her alone and at best living a subsistence existence from the small copse of olive trees, medium sized allotment of vegetables and a small menagerie of goats, fowl and a pair of grumpy black Iberian pigs. She did not appear to have a great deal to smile about.

Over the course of the next two weeks, Ruben Miles made a good recovery. Senora Maria Delores washed and changed his bandages twice a day. His chest wound healed well, and his shoulder was back to normal, if a little ginger. He was displeased with himself that it took him almost a fortnight to realise that he should be paying back Senora Delores's kindness, hospitality and caring with some of the unearned pesetas that the Russian had donated to his escape. When he gave her a handful of the notes, her eyes widened in amazement. Ruben Miles had not been in Spain very long and his understanding of the value of the currency was flawed. He was offering her the amount of a worker's annual pay and in large denomination notes. For these two reasons Senora Dolores said,

'Eso es demasiado.'

So, he gave her less.

'Eso es demasiado.'

At the third attempt, Maria Delores put the money in her shawl pocket, turned on her heels, retrieved a wicker bag from what passed as the kitchen and headed out of the front door.

When she returned a little over an hour later, she seemed very quiet and subdued. She had been successful with the shopping, even managing to bag a brace of rabbits. Senora Maria Delores liked eating meat. She just did not like killing her own animals, not through squeamishness, but because the animals were the only daily interactions she could count on. Ruben Miles could smell the freshness of the citrus fruit, vegetables and bread that she unpacked with care on to the small round table in the sitting room.

She had reason to be quiet. At the market, she was accosted by two of the village's most notorious busybodies who unfortunately bumped into her after she had spent some of her money. The two old crows wanted, nay demanded, to know where she could possibly have got the money for all that she had bought. As a good woman of faith, Maria Delores was not one for lies and therefore, when pushed to produce a credible one, she failed. She fled the scene unconvincingly calling out that one of her goats was sick and she needed to get home to tend her.

Maria Delores knew there would be a knock on the door in the near future. She just did not know when, though she had her suspicions. In addition, as the village was close to the frontline, it was patronised by both sides. She could have the fascists at the door as easily as the Republicans. Although she did not care who's side the injured man was on, she had no time for political prejudices. She was acutely aware that those knocking at the door would very much want to know what side the strange mute man was on.

She tried to communicate this to Ruben Miles, but in her worry, she spoke that little bit quicker and he could only pick out some of the words. He made out Fascista and Republicano easily enough. But he suspected, incorrectly, that she was trying to find out what side he was on again. Then he remembered that puerta meant door. Two minutes later he was shoe-horned into a tiny space in the attic of the old house, barely big enough to house him, his shoulder screaming its displeasure.

But Maria Delores was right. There was going to be a knock on the door and she had guessed that it would be sooner rather than later. What she could not have known was that the colour of the shirts of whoever came a calling was irrelevant. Whoever they were, if they discovered Ruben Miles, he would be in a difficult situation.

As he tried to keep as quiet as he could in the attic and as Maria Delores tried to swiftly conceal any evidence of a house guest, Ruben Miles found himself with only one coherent and admittedly thoroughly odd thought.

'Anyone but the Russian.'

DO WE HAVE TO TALK?

L uke Miles's dad was not a man people enjoyed talking to. He was devoid of the merest trace of humour. At least the type that any young person would recognise. He also had issues with invading people's personal space. In addition, he was a secondary school Chemistry teacher. Overall, far from a winner in the charismatic lottery draw of life. His other defining trait was irritation. Especially toward a) young people, especially his students at school, and b) members of his own family.

Luke Miles therefore approached his father rarely and with caution.

'Why does all the family hate the old man?'

Physical if not linguistic caution.

Luke's father did not know what surprised him the most, his son initiating a conversation or the topic of the conversation. Either way, he did not rush to respond, making an impatient Luke ask a follow up question.

'I mean, what did he do to make you all hate him so much?'

'That's an unusual way to start a conversation.'

Luke's mother entered the room. She put her hands on her hips, her typical annoyed body language gesture and said, 'Your father hates the old man more than I hate vegetarians!'

This may have been the only time since he was a little kid that Luke laughed at something intentional his mother had said. He may not have agreed with his mother's bizarre and frankly irrational hatred of all things vegetarian, but at least she had something she got worked up about. Ordinarily she was fairly placid about everything. Her father had been a beef farmer in Somerset and he seemed to have ingrained in his only child's mind that it was mankind's primary function to farm, slaughter and consume animal's flesh and blood.

'First of all,' Luke's father said, 'Ruben Miles is not the most reliable of sources. You should hear some of the people he claims to have known. Some of the places he has been, events he has been involved in. Once he even told Uncle Richard that he knew, personally knew mind you, some of those involved in the Kennedy assassination!'

'He's never said any stuff like that to me.'

But then he remembered JoJo's project.

'But apparently he is writing his life story with JoJo.'

This information seemed to shock both parents.

'What?!'

'He's telling JoJo his life story and she is recording it and writing it down. She has not told me very much. Well, nothing really. But she has said that he claims to have been involved in a lot of bad things.'

'We should speak to JoJo's parents,' his parents said, in harmony for perhaps the only time in their marriage.

Luke and JoJo's parents did not socialise. In fact, they were barely on polite waving terms. Both sets of parents believed themselves to be in some way superior to their neighbours. However, without the need for objective evidence, as befits most lazy prejudices. The relatively recent friendship between their two youngest children had taken them a little by surprise. Firstly, Mrs Bartlett had to endure the *incident* and now the Miles's were literally knocking at their door. No wonder she thought the country was going to the dogs.

Ten minutes later, the reluctant foursome were sipping sherry in the Bartletts' sunroom, or conservatory as Mrs Bartlett seemed determined to call her cherished but rather prosaic extension.

They made some polite chitchat for as long as they could, almost five full minutes on the difficulty of finding a reliable plumber and whether the weather was going to last much longer.

Eventually, Mr Miles thought he could bear no more and made a break for it.

'We understand from Luke that JoJo has been visiting an elderly relation of ours, his name is Ruben Miles.'

'That's right, she mentioned it a few weeks ago.'

'He is over a hundred years old and he has lived in a posh old folk's home for the last fifteen years or so. And frankly, he is not the sort of person I would want my daughter to be listening to about anything. He is a born liar and, well, he has rather an unpleasant past.'

Mr Miles seemed to falter here a little and so Mrs Miles, sensing her time to shine, continued for him.

'He's not *just* a liar, but also a convicted criminal and a thoroughly terrible human being. We think that you should tell JoJo not to visit him, like we should have done with Luke.'

Mrs Miles's head prod in the direction of Mr Miles was another of her patented passive aggressive gestures.

'Oh my God!' said Mr Bartlett, 'How had I not put two and two together? He was convicted for some famous bank job in the early Seventies, right? I don't know why I hadn't realised that before.'

'It was 1978 actually,' Mr Miles offered.

If Luke's parents thought that this meant that the Bartletts would 'do the right thing' and stop their daughter visiting Ruben Miles, they did not know Mr Bartlett very well. This was because they did *not* know Mr Bartlett, their neighbour of twelve years, very well. As a defence lawyer and a classic, even by his own definition, 'happy clappy liberal', Mr Bartlett was a sucker for any potential miscarriage of justice and, if he remembered rightly (and he usually did), then Ruben Miles had always denied being on the London bank job that put him in various of HM prisons for most of the 1980s.

They managed to keep the conversation civil, if at least painfully transparent. The Bartletts (well, Mr Bartlett) had no intention of stopping his daughter from helping Ruben Miles write the story of his life. Indeed, it may even be a blessing as it may rekindle his daughter's now almost dormant interest in a law career, which to his admitted self-disappointment, he really wanted her to pursue.

'But he's a criminal!' Mr Miles insisted once again.

'That may be an unfortunate technicality. Regardless, I am sure that Luke will ensure that the old man does not misbehave with my daughter.'

And on such a misguided and practically incorrect assertion, the parental conversation ended. The one and so far, only prolonged social interaction of Luke and JoJo's parents. On the plus side, both parties thought their pre-existing prejudices had been totally vindicated.

Simultaneously, Luke Miles had received a text message from JoJo.

It read:

Why are your parents at my house? Are we living in a parallel universe? Meet me at the pub ASAP x

Luke was becoming oddly fond of some forms of obedience and conformity.

What Luke Miles could not possibly have anticipated was the long-standing family rumour that his parents never, ever, wanted to talk about. Namely, that they shared the *same* biological father. Luke's grandfather John Miles, another of Ruben Miles's abandoned progeny, had been a local philanderer of Boris Johnson proportions. According to gossip, he was not only Luke's paternal grandfather via conventional means, but due to a longstanding fling with a nearby neighbour, was also the father of Luke's mother via the cuckolding of her husband. It was John Miles himself who had started the rumour six months after Luke's parents had married.

Luke's parents dealt with the innuendo and rumours the only way that made sense to them, by completely ignoring them and moving out of the old neighbourhood. The fact that they shared no obvious physical or character traits seemed evidence enough that the rumour was just what it must be, an ugly, untrue rumour. And yet, they never talked about it, as they never really talked about anything meaningful. But of course it lurked in the tiny shallows of both their subconsciouses. How could it not? The fact that John Miles had moved south a week after initiating the rumour and cut off all contact with the entire extended family had certainly helped the ostrich approach to the story.

The only pre-emptive action they had taken was a solitary

visit from Luke's father to The Apple Orchard Retirement Community to see Ruben Miles. It had been a perfunctory meeting that neither man welcomed. The intention was clear from the outset.

'My son wants to visit you. He is intrigued about having a relative that has lived as long as you. My wife and I are very reluctant for you to meet him for the obvious reason.'

'The rumours started by that idiot father of yours.'

'That idiot would be your son.'

At least they agreed about one thing.

'I don't, as you know, normally want anything to do with the family. But I suppose old age must have mellowed me. What's the boy's name again?'

'Luke.'

'It goes without saying that I would not mention those rumours to Luke. Whatever you think of me, that is not my style.'

Luke's dad remained sceptical.

'Your relationship with the truth is a little sketchy, I would say.'

'Now it's your turn to be spreading dodgy rumours.'

The usual impasse.

'Your relationship with your father is not *my* fault.'

The topic that both men knew to be relevant to both their lives.

'Can we stick to why I'm here? My son is not normally very enthusiastic about anything. But he seems genuinely determined to make your acquaintance for reasons that are not all together clear, at least to us.'

The true motivation for Luke wanting to visit the old man was simple enough and quintessentially teenage. It was the one thing he could think of that was guaranteed to piss both his parents off equally. Genius.

'We have not told him about prison and we would ask you to not mention that either, we fail to see what good that will do.'

'As you are very aware, that is an episode that I never want to talk about. Ten years of my life down the toilet for no good reason.'

Another well-trodden disagreement. Ruben Miles was the only member of his family that thought he did not deserve a lengthy prison sentence.

Much to his surprise, Luke's father found himself believing that the old man would not mention the rumour or his prison sentence during any time spent with Luke. However, when he returned home his wife was quick to avail him for his mistake.

'Your grandfather is a grade A arsehole. You seem to be forgetting that and the fact that *he* was the one who fucked your father up completely by telling him that he was not his real father. Jesus! How did I ever marry into such a fucked-up family.'

'We agreed that we should let Luke meet him.'

'I fail to see how this can go well.'

'It wasn't me who told Luke about *him.*'

Luke's mother did at least concede that point. One evening two years ago after too much chardonnay during a rare family barbeque, it was Luke's mother that had told him about the very old man living in The Apple Orchard Retirement Community.

Luke's dad was buoyed by this silent admission of her guilt.

'He won't mention the rumour, he has no reason to.'

'And you trust him?'

Not a question he really wanted to answer.

DINERO

The knock on the door came just fifty minutes after Ruben Miles had been secreted to the hopeful sanctuary of the attic. He had heard them conversing quietly in the street. He could not ascertain their allegiance as the only words he could make out were neutral. It was more a bang than a knock. It even shook the dust on the beams in the attic.

'Ya voy, ya voy,' he heard the response from below.

They invited themselves inside.

If Ruben Miles's Spanish had been up to it, he would have heard the following conversation.

'We hear that you may have come into some money, Senora Delores, which is very interesting to us. How has this happened?

There were three men in the delegation and the oldest and tallest appeared to be the one in charge and he did the talking.

'I bought a few items at the market. It hardly makes me rich as a queen.'

'Our information is that you had a considerable sum of money at the market. Maybe many hundreds of pesetas, mostly in ten peseta notes. How did you come across such riches in these… difficult times?'

'If your information comes from those two interfering and gossiping old women, I would not trust its reliability.'

'Indeed, but we also spoke to the stallholders and one said they saw clearly a bunch of ten peseta notes in your hand.'

'They are mistaken. There have not been sums of money in this house like that since my dear husband was taken from me. I have no such notes. I will show you my purse.'

She took out a sad collection of coins from her little purse that was on the sitting room table.

'You see?'

The youngest and fattest of the men took the purse from Senora Delores's hand and checked for himself. There were no notes inside.

They were communists. She could probably have guessed this by their fixation on money. The village had changed hands twice in the last nine months. There was literally no family that had not lost at least one of their men. For some it was many more. Senora Delores had little time for Communists, but she did at least hate them a little less than the Fascists. Was it a good thing when you wanted neither side to win?

'You know where my loyalties lie, Senor Hernandez, why would I lie to you?'

The man seemed to reflect momentarily at this observation.

'Senora Delores, it is very difficult to see into the hearts of anyone in these dangerous times. Even a woman of good faith.'

Despite her interaction with the gossipmongers at the market earlier, she had up until now been free from suspicion and inquisition. She was angry with herself for letting the stallholders see the notes in her hand, they would be worthless to her now for years. How could she change them without causing more suspicion? She would have to squirrel them away until one day in the future when all the bloodshed and chaos would be over. She had buried them quickly in a tin can in the chickens coop, minutes before the investigators arrived. She was already trying to think of a more long-term hiding place.

'We are sorry for the intrusion, Senora Delores, but you won't mind if we take a little look around, seeing how we are already here?'

It said a lot about the war that this statement would make sense to any householder.

'Por supuesto.'

They poked around the small rooms and few possessions for a while, but the attic entrance was as secure as it was totally invisible. Not that it felt like that to the hiding Ruben Miles. He was fully aware deserters on either side were shot first and then nobody really bothered to ask any follow-up questions later.

They were polite and respectful as they left. All three men accepting Senora Delores's innocence and suspecting the accuracy of their informants. Not through any malevolence on their part, but rather their poor-quality eyeglasses. Besides, where would anyone get money like that around here, especially a poor, respectful widow?

Ruben Miles was released from his temporary jail after a further fifteen minutes, as Senora Delores found a hiding place that she was happier with for her money.

Over the course of the next few days, she taught him a lot of useful Spanish. He found he could even understand most of what she said. Both his wounds were nearly healed, and he knew he was going to have to make a move sooner rather than later. As if reading his thoughts, she led him into the enclosed and not overlooked area at the back of the house where the vegetables were grown, as it was south facing. She threw off an old rug to reveal the battered Russian motorcycle.

'No funciona.'

Then Ruben Miles surprised himself and shocked Senora Delores.

'Si, una persona, puede arreglarlo?'

She looked at him with astonishment and then, in her typical pragmatic style, thought about who might be able to help fix the motorcycle.

'Tal vez George,'

Ruben Miles was not a practical man, and fixing a motorcycle was out of the question. So, it looked as though, if George couldn't fix the thing, he was walking his way out of the Spanish Civil War.

But fix it George did. The next morning when he awoke late, Ruben Miles heard Senora Delores in conversation at the back of the house. When he emerged outside, he was surprised to see a boy of no more than fourteen crouched over the motorcycle with various tools in his small hands. The woman and the boy were smiling at him rather disconcertingly.

'Esta funcionando!'

Ruben Miles found himself grinning too.

The land at the back of the house was just big enough for Ruben Miles to both test the motorcycle and also try to learn to ride the bloody thing a bit better. He had a few wobbles and one fall which thankfully did not damage man nor machine. Once he finished, he joined Maria Delores and the boy over a cup of very strong and frankly strange coffee. Senora Delores thanked the boy profusely and gave him a few coins for his trouble, Ruben Miles was surprised that she did not give him one of the many ten peseta notes that he had given her.

After the boy had left, Senora Delores told Ruben Miles that the time had come for him to go. She did not attempt to spell out the reasons why she believed that there was possible urgency to the timing of his exit. She had been shaken by her recent inquisition and, although she bore no resentment toward the stranger, she had helped him and now he was fit and had a means of leaving.

'Esta noche,' she said.

Ruben Miles simply nodded.

If she had known that Ruben Miles had slipped George a ten peseta note on his way out as payment for his essential services, she would have told him to risk leaving in the daylight and as soon as possible. But it all depended on whether George had attempted to spend the gift, and in war time, rare note.

George may have been an adept fixer of machinery, but he was not a bright or savvy boy. The other boys in the village made fun of him behind his back for being a bit slow. So, he foresaw no reason to be shy about his newfound wealth. Senora Delores had said clearly that he must not mention the man whose motorcycle he fixed to anyone. Indeed, she promised him a few more coins if he kept quiet about him, but she never said anything about not spending money. The boy not comprehending that she was unaware of the more substantial gift.

He tried to use the note to buy fruit for his family at the market. The stallholder used words that George had rarely heard and certainly did not fully understand. By the third refusal, at the stall selling olives and sun-dried tomatoes, George had inadvertently caused something of a commotion. Ten minutes later he found himself talking to the three communists who had spoken to Senora Delores a few days prior about large denomination bank notes. George saw no reason not to show the men the note and, although he did not want to disobey Senora Delores, when they asked where he had got it from he did not think to lie as he knew he had not done anything wrong and he was sure that Senora Delores would understand that.

THE BARTLETTS

L ike all great men of moral conviction and ideological certainty, Mr Bartlett was more than capable of being a sanctimonious twat. His interactions with the next-door neighbours had filled up his hump of superiority. The politically challenged Miles household being the object of his ire.

'Did you say they read the Daily Mail? Christ, only the old, insane and the fucking police read that!'

Mrs Bartlett preferred not to comment, although she was wise enough never to bring said publication into the house. However, when she went for her monthly appointment to get her hair done in a posh and overpriced hotel hair salon in Gosforth, she had always enjoyed the paper's women's section. For no other reason than she liked reading the letters of wives who were as frustrated with their husbands' shortcomings as she was with hers.

'I cannot believe I did not twig about the old man sooner.'

Mr Bartlett was keen to return to one of his more familiar riffs.

'People who read that paper think that anyone even suspected of a crime should be shot. They hate all foreigners. I dread to think what *that* lot will do to this country if they ever dominate the political agenda again, like they did in the eighties. I mean, at least Blair is a decentish type of Tory.

The Prime Minister was another topic frequently aired in the Bartlett household. Usually in close proximity to the words traitor, smug, Tory and cunt. Sometimes he mixed up the order of the words just to try and keep it fresh. The fact that he had almost praised Blair, despite the Iraq debacle, illustrates how deep his loathing ran for the far right of the millennium Tory party and their beloved Daily Mail.

Mr Bartlett was a student politicised in the late 1980s. As he just missed out on his grades for Oxford, he took one of the usual runners-up spots at Durham University to read law. He spent as much time selling Socialist Worker in the city centre as he did getting pissed on cheap cider in the main Union bar. He had not realised that Durham would be full of southern private school students, the fully paid-up offspring of the privileged ruling elite. If anything politicised him more than Suzy Chalmers, the sexy, dark-haired girl from Yorkshire that talked him into joining the Socialist Workers Party in Freshers' week, it was the ubiquitous posh southern students that were everywhere in the tiny city.

He emerged from his student days with his ideological zeal still intact and a mild dose of the clap after an unfortunate boys' weekend trip to Amsterdam to celebrate graduation. And he was the one that did *not* go to the brothel.

Three years later, he was married to a pretty, middle-class, but slightly uptight dental nurse. His wife had insisted on a huge mortgage to relocate to the sunny uplands of Jesmond on the outskirts of Newcastle-upon-Tyne. Still, at least work offered some solace from the less than radical lifestyle. He made a name for himself as a competent and open-minded defence brief. This ensured that by the time he was thirty-two, he was doing financially well by representing some of the more well-known 'faces' of the northeast criminal fraternity.

The pretty uptight dental nurse was now a slightly less pretty uptight housewife. But as he reminded himself regularly, at least he had JoJo to show for his marriage. He had always been proud to be her father. She had been the ideal daughter for a man who had never really wanted or indeed embraced fatherhood. She was low maintenance. A self-soother who slept all through the night as a baby, was docile and agreeable as a toddler and frankly an idyllic pupil once she was packed off to the local primary in West Jesmond. It had not taken him long to embrace the benefits of modern capitalism. Like most ideologically pure Socialists, he was quite well-off.

Mr Bartlett had decided that he needed to fully engage with the Ruben Miles case. He had long since harboured a desire to write a true crime book and he sensed that this might be his best or even only opportunity to do so. He therefore spent a very worthwhile three hours surfing the internet on his trusty Apple Mac, reading the newspaper coverage, legend and conspiracy theories behind the 1978 London bank job that had put Ruben Miles away for ten years. It was interesting stuff. Even the merest whiff of a royal scandal.

When he had finished his research for the evening, he had his usual couple of aperitifs before he could face the paucity of his wife's culinary menu. Mr Bartlett had discovered that a pair of generous gin and tonics did wonders for Mrs Bartlett's coq au vin, not to mention shifting the emphasis from the dubious authenticity of her beef stroganoff. He was even beginning to enjoy the disappointed look she gave him each time he 'forgot' to offer to make his wife a drink.

'How are you getting on with Ruben Miles and his confessions then?'

It seemed a safe question to ask his daughter over the dinner table.

'It's been really interesting actually. He is quite the storyteller. Do you remember I told you that he has hyperthymesia? Well, it is either true or he is quite the most amazing bullshitter.'

JoJo was still at the age where she coloured slightly when she used some words in front of her parents, although it did seem to be getting less pronounced.

'So, if it is true and he is one hundred-and-six-years old, he must have some interesting stories to relate.'

'We are up to the Spanish Civil War. He enlisted and then went AWOL from an International Brigade. We started with his childhood and then the Great War. He took part on the first day of the Somme campaign and ended up a prisoner of war. Then he lived in New York as Babe Ruth's bodyguard…'

It was not that Mr Bartlett was a natural sceptic. As a socialist, his view of human nature was almost cheerfully optimistic. But as a defence brief who was used to the more creative aspect of the human psyche, he was at best a little cynical. But now he had a goal in mind, namely an interview with the old man about the London bank job, he sensed that further negativity as to the authenticity of the old man's tales should be filed for another occasion.

'That sounds amazing! Is he wanting you to try and get his story published?'

JoJo decided to let go the obvious insincerity of her father's opening words. She knew that he did not believe that Ruben Miles's stories were true. Somehow this gave more credence to the old man, or at the very least she wanted to believe him even more.

'Actually, he hasn't mentioned that, but it is a good idea, isn't it?'

JoJo was not sure why she had insinuated that the old man had *not* mentioned publication of his memoirs. He had made clear this goal at their first encounter.

Mr Bartlett nearly said yes. After all, historical fiction was a popular genre, but he eventually demurred.

Ultimately, JoJo agreed to ask Ruben Miles if his father could visit him and ask him questions about the London bank job. However, he laboured the point about being on 'his' side and how important it was to let the old man know that Mr Bartlett believed in his 'innocence.' Were all old people hypocrites, mused JoJo? He won't believe, without hearing supplementary evidence, any of the old man's other stories. But her dad believes without question that he was not guilty of a part in a bank robbery that put him in jail for ten years because it fits snugly into the small alcove of his personal biases.

At least she had a good handle on her father.

She did not have a Scooby Doo about her mother. Was that normal?

SENORA MARIA DELORES – PART TWO

Ruben Miles was in the outside toilet when they broke down the front door, his pants around his ankles. An upset stomach probably saving his life. If he had been in the main building of the house, he would have had no chance. As it was, he emerged swiftly into the back yard. The motorcycle was thirty yards away, propped against the wall via the back gate that led to the small road that led out of town. The keys were in his pocket, his right hand dropping swiftly to confirm. He heard shouting and the sound of furniture being overturned. He heard the sound of a hard slap and the distressed cries of Senora Maria Delores. He ran for the machine.

Despite his recent injuries, he covered the ground in mere seconds. But he fumbled as he drew the keys from his pocket and dropped them. He stooped to retrieve them and smacked the top of his head onto the right handlebar as he rose. He did not have time to share his outrage. The communists had made it to the back yard, the three men from the last visit. Curiously only one had drawn his weapon. Maria Delores pursued them, a large red blotch noticeable on her left cheek.

The motorcycle roared into life at the first attempt. George may have unwittingly brought the wolves to the door, but at least he had supplied the means of escape. Like many who fought in the Spanish Civil War, the communists had received minimal training, even with essentials such as firearms. The first shot hit the bark of a lemon tree four feet from where Ruben Miles was about to depart for the backyard gate. The second whistled past his right ear as he made it to the gate. It was locked.

He did not have time to search for a key. Quickly reviewing the gate, he noticed that it was far from secure. The soldiers were moving closer. He killed the engine and jumped off the bike, not breaking stride as he hurled his right shoulder toward the barrier. He misjudged how much force was required and he found himself forward rolling through the smashed gate. He heard more shots.

Ruben Miles scrambled to retrieve the motorcycle, but it was too late. The fittest of the soldiers stood pointing a revolver at his chest from several yards away.

He could of course remember exactly what he was thinking as the man shouted at him. What a waste.

He heard the shot and went down.

It took a few seconds for the realisation that he had not been hit and that either his knees had buckled at the moment of reckoning or it was an instinctive reaction. Looking up he saw that the tall communist was prone on the ground, motionless and silent. He saw Maria Delores with a tiny pistol in her hand and he registered the small smile that she gave in his direction. He then watched in horror as the fat communist who she moments earlier had shot in the leg, rose from the ground and with one huge swing, brought a metal bar down. The force and sound of the blow were sickening. At least she died instantly, her fragile skull smashed into unrecognisable pieces.

Ruben Miles jumped on the motorbike before the fat communist had time to react.

Moments later, as the Russian motorcycle flew down the stony path at the south side of town, Ruben Miles snatched a quick glance behind and saw an empty road. He slowed the bike a little and thought about going back. But he knew it was no use. He knew that the kindly widow who had cheerfully and selflessly nursed him back to health, was dead. Besides, apart from a knife in his boot, he was without a weapon. In his experience, a knife is of little use in a gun fight. To the best of his knowledge, he had not needed his life saving before. Although he did accept that when involved in hand-to-hand combat in either the trenches of northern France or central Spain, one could not be completely sure. The Fixer boasted to have saved him from Sabini's goons back in Newcastle after the fixed fight, but Ruben Miles had his doubts as to the reliability of the main witnesses, namely the Fixer and his mother. At least in this instance he was certain, without the intervention and bravery of Maria Delores he would now be dead or waiting to be executed for desertion at best.

It took him three days to get to San Sebastian and a ferry

back to England. He had been out of the country less than three months and yet it seemed much longer.

'Oh my God!' exclaimed JoJo.

Ruben Miles was crying.

He refused to grieve for the wife and child he lost in a housefire, but he could grieve for a brave and caring Spanish widow who saved his life and lost her own in the process.

Ruben Miles stopped crying and apologised.

'What for?'

'For getting all emotional, it never does anyone any good.'

'I think that crying over someone who obviously saved your life is more than understandable.'

THE DEVIL AND MR LOWES

L uke Miles did not have a complicated view of the world. He saw the world around him in simplistic terms. There was good and bad. That was pretty much it. Not a whole lot of wiggle room.

When JoJo first realised this, she felt relief that Luke was *not* hearing first-hand about his great grandfather's life. The moral vacuum that Ruben Miles had created for himself would not have sat well with Luke. She wondered how Luke had developed such an uncomplicated, childish view of the world. As a sociology student, JoJo already had reason to question his primary socialisation. Now she thought there might be some teachers to blame too.

She was right on the money.

When Luke was seven years old, he had been given a pictorial bible by one of the religious aunts who, at that stage at least, were still on friendly terms with his parents. It had stayed on his bedroom shelf untouched for several months. Then he caught the flu. He was very poorly for over a week and this remains the only time he can remember his mother being affectionate and truly maternal. She hardly left his side and even slept on a pull-out sofa in his bedroom. One evening as he lay in a semi-delusional state, his mother had decided that reading to him might put him back to sleep, albeit of a restless kind. Mrs Bartlett was not particularly religious. If asked, she would admit to having some general feeling that there must be something about one of these Gods worshipped by so many for so long. But if you drilled further down, she was more of an inherent sceptic. She simply pulled a book randomly from the pile. It was the pictorial bible.

She opened the book at an arbitrary section. She was not wanting to teach an RE class, just get her sickly child back to sleep. What Mrs Bartlett could not have known was that little Luke

Miles had been affected significantly by the local death of a six-year-old girl who had been run over by a speeding drunk the previous month. Talk of death had opened up Pandora's box for the young boy. What exactly was death? What happened afterwards? Some of the key questions for any seven-year-old. Some of the answers proffered by well-meaning adults had helped a little. The answers provided by Mr Lowes, the pugnacious and rotund ex-army headteacher of his primary school had palpably not.

Mr Lowes was of the generation that never really recovered from the frustration of missing out on World War Two active duty. He spent the rest of his life trying to get his own back. Consequently, he had embraced the Anglican church, The Conservative Party and Freemasonry. He then stirred in almost obsessive patriotism and added a flavouring of racial, class, regional and religious intolerance. He once conducted an entire assembly on the evils of unemployed immigrants in Liverpool to an audience of confused and rather frightened six-year-olds.

The young Luke Miles's world took an unfortunate step when Miss Jones, his kindly and popular Year Three teacher got unexpectantly pregnant. That was not the adjective Mr Lowes used when he heard the news. When he realised he would have to take over the teaching of the class due to financial shortcomings, he used even more colourful vocabulary.

Therefore, in short order, Luke Miles and his classmates found themselves seeing a lot of Mr Lowes. They went from seeing and listening to him for ten minutes at the start of the day, to spending all the long hours of the school week with him. Some of the students never fully recovered. Others were merely scarred.

The days that still nagged away at the subconscious mind of the teenage Luke Miles occurred that summer term. On the Monday the daily assembly was longer than normal. Twenty minutes is an eternity when you are seven years old and in a hot stuffy assembly hall, with the windows bizarrely shut and listening to a terrifying fat man pontificate on the evils of trade unions. The first period after assembly had been Maths. This was by far the easiest for the class to endure. There were far fewer political and theological rabbit holes for Mr Lowes to explore, taking the class mentally kicking and screaming with him.

The trouble began after morning break. Barely had the fizzy pop and assorted salted snacks been consumed and Year Three were into the white-knuckle ride that was RE with Mr Lowes. The man himself called it religious instruction. And he certainly had plenty of those.

Luke Miles did not remember any of the preamble. Not even what the original alleged topic had been. In reality it did not really matter what the topic was. Mr Lowes invariably steered the conversation toward whichever of his prejudices were festering within him the most on any given day. Then one of the students asked about poor Lucy Dewer. The local little girl who had died in a hit-and-run incident a few weeks previously. Lucy Dewer had not attended the school. She had gone to the *other* school as Mr Lowes referred to it. It was a Catholic school. A lot of the children had known Lucy Dewer and were friends with her and her older sister Daisy.

'Well, she will probably be in heaven,' began an unusually reticent Mr Lowes. His views on Catholicism were predictable and forthright but he managed to dial them in, at least a little.

'Although real heaven is for Protestants, I am sure that the Papes, I mean the Catholics, have their version too.'

The children fidgeted in their too-thick school trousers and skirts. Mr Lowes was against the wearing of shorts as they were not smart enough for any self-respecting Church of England Primary School.

'When you die you will either go to heaven if you have been a good boy or girl, or hell if you have been a bad boy or girl.'

Mr Lowes seemed proud of his explanation.

The class seemed to reflect on this unambiguous statement for a short while and then Michael Denton, the almost sitcom-esque, camp, class swot asked in his reedy voice, 'How do you get to hell and *who* decides that you should go there?'

'Good question, *Martin*. Well, firstly it is the Devil himself who comes for you. Lucifer, the fire-breathing anti-Christ will come and take your immortal soul to the bowels of hell. You will be tortured horribly for eternity. It will be Lucifer himself who decides whether you deserve to go to hell.'

Mr Lowes was further pleased with his extended explanation. Especially as he had never really got around to reading any of the Bible, not even the kids version piled high in each of his school's classrooms.

But *Michael* Denton had not finished *his* contribution. Besides, he was annoyed that Mr Lowes never got his name right. He had understood every word of Mr Lowes's explanation and sought clarification in language more suited to the rest of the class cohort.

'So, what you are saying, sir, is that the Devil is a real creature that can take you to hell when you die and you have to stay there forever being tortured?'

Mr Lowes nodded and then confirmed further with a simple,

'That's right, Martin. If you have been a bad boy or girl.'

Mr Lowes, in his academically restricted and prejudice-infected mind, had thought RE and the threat of Beelzebub was as good a way as any of trying to get the little buggers to behave themselves.

Luke Miles had a nightmare about being taken to hell by Satan that very evening. He was not a particularly clingy or needy child, so he managed to self-soothe. This was just as well as his mother was neither patient nor maternal, something that Luke Miles had instinctively grasped at a very young age.

Which is why it was even more memorable that his mother looked after him diligently when he had the flu the following winter. As he drifted in and out of delirium, he felt oddly comforted by her presence. However, he was struggling with the vivid but unfathomably manic dreams that seemed to repeat on a loop-cycle. Ultimately, the two entities merged.

When Mrs Miles opened the book randomly, she had a one in one hundred and seventy-five chance of producing the page that she did. The book had not been opened or read by anyone since it had been placed on the shelf.

If she had known just how delirious Luke was, she may not have attempted a biblical distraction.

The book was large, an oversized hardback book festooned

with huge pictures of dubious authenticity. On the front cover was a very WASP looking Jesus. On the back was a depiction of Noah and his unfeasible Ark.

However, on pages eighty-seven and eight-eight was the looming presence of Satan, resplendent with fire breathing, shiny hooves and a tail, clutching a trident with ominous demonic eyes. Lucifer was depicted dragging some evil wrongdoer to the very pit of hell at the bottom of the picture. To a young boy riddled with fever and already having a fear of death, this was a powerful vision. The incoherent ramblings of a dangerous Head Teacher. The tragic death of Lucy Dewer. The pictorial bible. They all combined to produce a childhood defining moment for Luke Miles. It shaped his simplistic view of the world as a place populated by just good and bad. He carried this fallacy well into adulthood.

PAYING DUES

'I went back to the village over thirty years later.'

The old man had insisted on taking JoJo to the cinema for reasons he did not really explain. They went by taxi, something that JoJo still found a little exotic. Her parents were too mean to pay for a taxi when you could wait half an hour at a bus stop in the pissing rain. Her father thought there was something mythically egalitarian about public transport.

They were going to see *The Da Vinci Code* at the Metro Centre Multiplex. JoJo hated the Metro Centre; it reminded her of America, and yet she had never been.

They bought soft drinks and popcorn and the unlikely pair got stared at by everyone that came into the auditorium. The old man insisted on sitting in the third row on the aisle.

He told her the epilogue to the story of Maria Delores before the Pearl and Dean adverts started.

The house looked pretty much how he remembered it. The only noticeable change to the external appearance of the property was an iron gate where the old wooden one had been. The gate he had crashed through to make his escape thirty years before. He memorised enough Spanish to explain to the small, middle-aged man who answered the door that he had been housed here during the War. The man said nothing, but gestured him inside.

He could easily have described the courtyard from his memory. The lemon tree was of course much bigger, but the damage caused by the bullet was still clearly evident. There was only one feature that had not existed back in 1937. A small, simple wooden cross, facing towards the house surrounded by bougainvillea.

It could have been for someone else, but it was not. Maria Delores's name was inscribed in small, neat engraving. Ruben Miles stood in front of it for several minutes lost in his thoughts.

Then he was distracted by the man clutching at his arm.

'You are the man with the motorbike.'

The man had spoken slowly in his native tongue and Ruben Miles understood his words.

He remembered enough Spanish to reply.

'Si, soy el hombre con el moto.'

The man had tears in his eyes.

'I am George,' he said.

Ruben Miles stayed for a cup of coffee and a piece of very sweet cake made with an unrecognisable fruit he had never tasted before.

Both men spoke very slowly but they still did not understand everything that they said to each other. George told him that the death of Maria Delores was his fault.

'Mi culpa,' he kept repeating and pointing out of the window at Maria Delores's grave.

Bur Ruben Miles did not understand the reasons for this admission at first, but then he heard the words,

'Le conté a los soldados sobre ti.'

George had told the soldiers about him. Ruben Miles remembered how the boy, although good with his hands, had seemed a little simple.

Ruben Miles dug further into the shallow trough of his Spanish and surprisingly managed to tell the man what he wanted to.

'Esta bien. No te culpes.'

He repeated the phrase until the man stopped crying.

It's OK. Do not blame yourself.

'She was some lady,' JoJo said.

'The kindest, noblest person I ever met,' replied the old man, blinking back fresh tears.

'How come George was living in her house?'

The old man looked puzzled. It had not occurred to him to ask.

'I am glad you finished off that story, but it's not like you to mix up the order of things. You said it was thirty years later that you went back to where you were during the civil war.'

'That's right. 1967 was another interesting year for me. Even with my memory, I did not want to forget to tell you about going back to Maria Delores's house. A lot was going on for me in 1967. That short trip to Spain was a bit of a necessary diversion, but more of that later.'

The adverts had finally finished and the film started.

JoJo enjoyed it. She liked Tom Hanks in just about anything.

The old man was less keen.

'Too far-fetched,' he said afterwards, with an admirably straight face.

LIGHT THE TOUCH PAPER

After his return from the Spanish Civil War, Ruben Miles settled once more in London. He had been back less than a month before he moved into a smart new apartment complex, Du Cane Court on the Balham High Road. Ruben Miles chose Du Cane court for its Art Deco design and modern appliances. The site boasted 677 separate units. It had 24-hour concierge, well-sculptured gardens and exclusive parking for residents. It was as close to New York modernity as he was going to get in south London. It was a popular location with musical hall stars and wealthy men with no apparent profession. Tommy Trinder moved into the apartment three doors down in 1939, a couple of months before the war started.

Ruben Miles had safely deposited the money he had brought back from America several years before. He had left it almost untouched during his marriage to Eileen and their three children. If she had known of his relative wealth, his wife would have realised she knew even less about her husband than she thought she did. On his return from Spain, it was almost as if Ruben Miles had only just remembered he had such funds. He was surprised to see that the nearly eighteen hundred pounds that he had first given to the National Provincial Bank's Soho branch, had grown by nearly another thousand pounds by the summer of 1937.

The large, modern two-bedroomed flat at Du Cane Court cost him a shade under thirteen hundred pounds, expensive at the time. The rather sceptical estate agent who had shown him around with more than a hint of annoyance, handed over the new keys with considerably more charm after the successful transfer of funds.

He had been in the flat less than a month when he heard his doorbell ring during his early evening routine. It was six p.m. He had just finished washing up his tea dishes and he was about to read the paper. He was actually enjoying the calm of his newfound routine and yet he was also beginning to wrestle with what he was going to do with himself. He still felt like a young man at forty and he looked like an even younger man.

There were two familiar faces at the front door when he answered and Ruben Miles would never have put the two men together, least of all at this front door.

'Are you not going to invite us in, Ruben Miles?' said the Fixer.

'I am sure that he is dying to hear what we have to say,' said the Russian.

The Fixer and the Russian sat on the plush armchairs Ruben Miles had recently purchased for his living room. The man himself sat awkwardly on the double sofa. He was not someone that had much of a relationship with anxiety, but he could feel a little trickle of sweat sliding down his spine and sticking to his thankfully dark blue shirt.

Ruben Miles did not know what he found more disconcerting. The fact that they knew where he lived or the fact that that the two men knew each other. His throat felt parched, so he told them he was going to get a glass of water from the kitchen. They followed him into the separate space to the left of the front door. It was a modern kitchen by British standards and yet had few of the features that he had become accustomed to when living with the Babe.

'I suspect you may have some questions for us, Ruben Miles,' said the Fixer.

'We will be happy to answer them,' said the Russian.

After downing a large glass of tepid water, Ruben Miles felt like he might be able to speak.

However, all that he could manage was a strangulated, 'How?'

'Do you mean how did we find you?' said the Russian.

'Or how do we know each other?' said the Fixer, gesturing toward the Russian.

'Why don't you start with those two answers and we will take it from there.'

Ruben Miles was pleased to have seemingly taken back

control of his vocal cords.

The Fixer and the Russian told Ruben Miles an unlikely tale of coincidences and good fortune, interwoven with ambiguous hints at working for their respective governments. Ruben Miles believed it was most likely all lies. They made no attempt to explain their knowledge of his whereabouts.

'And now that we have answered your questions, Ruben Miles, we can explain why we have come to see you.'

It was the Fixer that did most of the talking.

'You have a nice place here, Ruben Miles. Spacious, modern and away from the noise and prying eyes of the West End. We would like you to be friendly to some occasional house guests that we would like you to, if not entertain, then certainly be accommodating towards. You will find our governments most generous in terms of any expenses that you may incur.'

'Why are the Americans and the Russians working together? I may not know much about politics, but I know that circle does not square.'

'I do not want to ruin your day, Ruben Miles. But our respective governments have concluded that a war with Nazi Germany is inevitable. The only ambiguity is when. Hitler *will* invade the USSR as he foretold in that book he wrote, probably before the end of the decade. Roosevelt does not want a Nazi dominated Europe and so as unlikely as it may sound right now, we will ally with the Communists against the Nazis.'

'What sort of guests are you talking about? Spies? How long will they stay for?'

'Did I not tell you that Ruben Miles has many useful qualities, including a most pragmatic mind?'

The Russian smiled and nodded his agreement.

'We cannot give specifics, you must understand. But our guests may need to stay a week or two, occasionally more. We were of the view that a man of your political leanings would want to contribute to the defeat of fascism. Is that not the case, Ruben Miles?'

'I am not a Communist.'

'Of course not, but you volunteered to fight against fascism.

This suggests that your priorities about the future of Europe and your own country are clear. Do not think that Hitler will be satisfied with his *Lebensraum* in the east. Once that is secure, he will take the rest of Europe and Roosevelt will be helpless half a world away.'

'Do I have a choice?'

The two men merely shook their heads.

'We would also like you be a little more involved from time to time. With your language skills you could be a useful traveller for us.'

'I don't speak foreign languages. My Spanish is very poor.'

'We believe that you are a man that seems able to absorb new information very easily, Ruben Miles, and therefore new languages should not be an issue. We would like you to learn German and perhaps French. Your Spanish is of little consequence now, as Franco's victory is all but assured with Hitler and Mussolini's help. We will organise your training, we will send the right people here shortly.'

'At least tell me who I am working for. I mean one of your governments must be running whatever show you have planned?'

'You will work for us, Ruben Miles,' said the Russian, gesturing with his hand towards the Fixer.

The Fixer continued, 'I have always told you that you are a man of unique talents, Ruben Miles. You have the ability not to overthink situations. You just need to be trained in the correct manner. We will unblock all the potential you have. That will ultimately be our gift to you. We will show you just what we believe you are capable of.'

'And we also know that you have, how do you English say? A strong stomach!'

Of course, the memory of the Russian castrating the Spanish prisoner was never far from the front of Ruben Miles's mind. As was the habit the Fixer had of using what Ruben Miles deemed flattery to placate him. But somehow, declining the pair's 'offer' seemed unwise. At least he knew that he was not going to be bored. He figured that whatever he was about to become entangled in, for whatever purposes, the last thing that he would be was bored.

However, at least in the short term, he was incorrect. 1938 turned into the arctic start to 1939. Ruben Miles busied himself with his newfound sporting habits, namely cycling and swimming. In addition, he had begun to dabble in the stock market. He spent most mornings after breakfast browsing The Times for likely, albeit relatively conservative investments.

It was not that he forgotten the visit of the two mysterious men, as this was not actually possible. It was just that several weeks after their visit and request for his services, he felt perhaps they had found other men to do their bidding.

Then he received his first telegram. He was to expect a German tutor for two hours per day, beginning in three days' time. His name was Herr Weber. Perhaps his training, whatever that would be, was to begin.

FRIENDS REUNITED

Mr Bartlett had experienced many uncomfortable conversational exchanges during his career, usually, but not exclusively, in court. However, his first meeting with Ruben Miles seemed destined from the very get-go to also be his last.

When he had arrived at The Apple Orchard Retirement Community, the first thing that struck him was the smell. A vague aroma of boiled vegetables and liniment. It reminded him of childhood visits to his Great Uncle Thomas, a bachelor Korean War veteran who lived in Amble. Those visits also made him hate heavy trousers, stories about which old people had died recently and the wearing of new shoes. Sentiments that he never entirely grew out of.

The second thing that struck him, with quite some force, was how young Ruben Miles looked. Throughout his career he had interviewed many elderly people, but none of them were as remarkable as Ruben Miles in appearance. He could have passed for seventy-five easily and a very fit seventy-five-year-old at that. His face betrayed no evidence of his true age and he did not act or speak like a man who was well over a hundred either.

'You must understand I dislike lawyers. It is nothing personal…'

This had been the first thing Ruben Miles had offered after a cursory and overly firm handshake on arrival.

'I only hate the police more. If the people of this country knew how bloody corrupt their police force is, there would be riots on the streets.'

Whilst he might wholeheartedly agree with this attitude and he was quick to offer this information, Mr Bartlett was less sanguine about the consequences of such a revelation on the people. He, like all healthy liberal snobs, had less time for the 'people' than he did for the police. He held the working-class particularly in contempt. But then his constant exposure to the criminal, uneducated, state-dependent and downright lazy of this particular insipid species was always likely to prejudice even the most open of minds. As far as Mr Bartlett was concerned, the apathy and ignorance of the great British public was not something to be thankful for.

'I only agreed to meet with you for JoJo. She is a very nice young lady. You must be very proud.'

Mr Bartlett was wise enough to see a gift horse when he was offered one and so they spent the next ten minutes walking in the gardens discussing the many virtues of Mr Bartlett's daughter. It was a refreshing change from listening to Mrs Bartlett's increasingly hysterical commentary on the future that lay in wait for their daughter. According to Mrs Bartlett this would now involve a 'lower class husband', divorce, poorly behaved children and, God forbid, a semi-detached house.

'You are a blunt man, Ruben. May I call you Ruben?'

Ruben Miles nodded his acquiescence. They were now sat on a park bench type seat next to his favourite rose bushes.

'So, I will speak candidly. Did you do the bank job?'

'No.'

If Mr Bartlett was hoping for greater explanation, he was going to be disappointed.

'Why were you convicted then? What evidence did they have that linked you to the job?'

'Planted and faked, the lot of it. Fingerprints all over the crime scene and even on some of the bank notes. Two alleged eyewitnesses and a textbook cellmate confession, they did the works.'

Mr Bartlett took a moment to assimilate this information.

'Why?' he said simply.

This was clearly not the question Ruben Miles had been expecting.

'Let's just say there were interested parties that wanted me out of the way for a while.'

'Criminals?'

'That's one word to describe them. I can think of some others.'

The 1978 London bank job was one of those crimes that is big news at the time and ever since a lasting legend status has been conferred on it. Like The Great Train Robbery or the Brink's-Mat bullion robbery, people seemed genuinely interested in a heist committed nearly forty years before. What stood out about the London job was that only two of the five-man gang were ever convicted of the crime and almost none of the money was recovered. Ruben Miles was one of the two men convicted. The other, Johnny Denton, served nearly twice as long as Ruben Miles did.

'At least he planned the bloody thing,' was the only comment Ruben Miles had to say on that.

Johnny Denton was a big face in gangland London. His status grew with his association with the job. Not just because he helped plan and carry out the effective but simple robbery, but because he did not grass up his fellow robbers for a reduced sentence. This meant that three members of his firm were living it up on the Costa del Crime, while he was slumming it at Parkhurst and the rest. But that was only part of the story. He was reluctantly released on parole in 1995. Over the course of the next eighteen months, three ex-pats living within ten miles of Marbella were found dead in their own homes with their throats slit. The three men lived in expensive houses and drove flash cars, without any apparent profession. Johnny Denton had solid alibis for all three days. He was playing golf with ex-police officers.

Ruben Miles had a slightly different take on Johnny Denton.

'The bastard never gave evidence for my defence. Even though he knew I was not connected in any way with the job.'

'So, who were the dirty cops?'

'I tend to approach that topic from a different slant. Are there any straight members of the Flying Squad? Dixon was in charge of the case, but he was ably helped by Messrs Hutchison and O'Brien.'

This drew a facial twitch from Mr Bartlett. Detective Inspectors Hutchison and O'Brien were notorious for their flexible consciouses and surprisingly affluent lifestyles. They had been investigated for corruption on two high-profile occasions and both times had been exonerated. The second time leading to early retirement and swift exits to Florida and Cyprus, respectively. Dixon had managed to avoid any damaging claims, at least in public. But he too had been bundled unceremoniously into retirement at a rather suspicious fifty-four years of age. He had then written what can only be described as a self-serving autobiography in which he claimed to have single-handedly solved every case the Flying Squad had worked on for nearly twenty years and even claimed he knew where Lord Lucan was. There was however one glaring omission. The 1978 London bank job. It was like he forgot to mention it.

'Your chances of unravelling what happened are slim. Your chances of uncovering why are non-existent. If I were you, I would look for a different case to write a book about. Yes, JoJo did mention that you had your heart set on writing a book.'

Under most circumstances, Mr Bartlett would have agreed with the old man's diagnosis of his chances of writing a best-selling exposé on the legendary case. After all, several respectable and other types of journalists had tried and failed over the years. But Mr Bartlett held what he felt could be anything up to an ace up his sleeve. However, at least for the time being, he had concluded that he would not share this information with Ruben Miles. His wife was the niece of the aforementioned Detective Inspector Hutchison.

'I'm sure you are right. But I do have a little free time on my hands. So, if it is OK with you, I will see what I can dig up. I do have one or two contacts that may be helpful.'

'I suppose it will only be your own time you are wasting.'

And so, Ruben Miles agreed to a further meeting with JoJo's dad, which had looked most unlikely less than an hour before.

'Your father can be quite gently persuasive,' Ruben Miles told JoJo Bartlett two days after the meeting. They were walking around the base of the Angel of the North. Antony Gormley's sculpture had been up in Gateshead for several years. Ruben Miles had only seen it in the newspapers. He had been pleased when JoJo suggested they take it in on a clear but breezy day.

'Shall I pick up where we left off last time?'

'Of course. 1939 in London, wasn't it? You had just moved into the fancy new apartment and the Fixer and the Russian turned up at your new front door. I mean you could not make that shit up, right?'

After a few weeks, and to his complete surprise, Ruben Miles found that he was making excellent progress in learning German. The tutor, Herr Weber, had a clear and distinct process that involved conjugating verbs to such a laborious extent that Ruben Miles mastered the process in a few short sessions. After that, the entire learning process seemed to accelerate. Herr Weber was a short and avuncular man who seemed to collect curious personal ticks like coins in a swear jar. He had at least three facial twitches and trigger thumbs on both hands that sounded like a whip cracking. However, he appeared to be an ardent admirer of Hitler and insisted on describing the Nazi transformation of Germany under the Third Reich. Ruben Miles decided that engaging in political debate would be unhelpful and merely nodded when Herr Weber talked of the autobahns and the maintenance of law and order. Despite his political musings, Ruben Miles found it was impossible to dislike the curious but seemingly very competent man.

His rapid learning of German proved to be essential as he received his second telegram from the Fixer. The telegram was the ideal mode of communication for the Fixer, as he was appalled by unnecessary embellishments:

Herr Muller – 6th March at 6 p.m.

7 days

Ruben Miles did not need a code book to decipher those instructions. He also assumed that Herr Muller would speak little English and therefore his German would be tested.

At one minute to six on Monday 6th March there was a firm knock on the front door. Ruben Miles had spent the afternoon listening to the House of Commons debate on the radio about the need for greater defence spending. He was surprised to learn that he agreed with almost everything that Churchill had to say from the backbenches. Nearly forty-five minutes of unflinching criticism of the actions of the allies, especially Chamberlain and Daladier over the Munich Agreement and other errors of appeasement. Ruben Miles had not liked or indeed trusted Churchill since he learnt of his actions at Tonypandy, his old trade union colleagues obviously influencing his views. He was shocked by how much sense Churchill now made.

At the door was a tall fair man with tiny hands and an oversized almost rectangular head. He proffered his right hand to Ruben Miles and said in perfect English, albeit with a strong Bavarian accent,

'Ruben Miles? I am delighted to meet you. My friends have told me that you will be able to accommodate me here at your wonderful apartment for the next seven days.'

Ruben Miles shook his hand and ushered him inside.

Keen to make a favourable expression, although not entirely sure why this was necessary, Ruben Miles had been able to purchase some Weissbier from a German delicatessen in Holborn. The smile of gratitude from Herr Muller as he handed over the cold bottle and a glass almost made the two bus journeys worthwhile.

'Are you not joining me, Ruben Miles?'

Ruben Miles explained that he did not drink alcohol. Clearly, the Fixer had impressed on Herr Muller to address him in the same manner as he himself did. Ruben Miles asked if they could continue their conversation in German and Herr Muller consented. After a perfunctory dialogue consisting of polite conversation about the weather and the smog, Ruben Miles showed Herr Muller to his room for the week. It was the last time they physically interacted. The visitor came and went quietly and at very odd times of the day and night, he was heard but not seen. On his departure he left a spotless room, a thank you letter in German and a bizarre cactus in a little tin pot.

The foreign and universally odd visitors became a regular feature for Ruben Miles as 1939 turned more ominous as the months rolled by. Some kept exclusively to themselves, but one or two did attempt to engage with Ruben Miles. Although none revealed their occupation or why they needed to stay in a stranger's apartment in a foreign country. There were no political conversations and no mention of the seemingly inevitable drift toward war between Britain, France and Germany.

Ruben Miles received a robust retainer from the Fixer for his accommodation services and this, in addition to his healthy savings, meant he had no need for paid employment. However, Ruben Miles was not a feckless or lazy man and he wanted to occupy his mind as well as his time. Subsequently, he found himself applying for and succeeding in securing a position as a clerk in a merchant shipping office. He did not tell the office manager of his time as a trade union official on the docks, correctly surmising that this would have been a foolish admission. Mr Rawlinson, the office manager, viewed anyone to the left of Mussolini as a communist. Therefore, Ruben Miles concocted a contrived history of minor public school and five years in the Royal Navy before being invalided out with a perforated ear drum following an accident during naval manoeuvres. People were very trusting in those days and no paperwork was either scrutinised or even asked for. Which perhaps explains why confidence tricksters were a recognisable profession in the Britain of the 1930s.

He worked a standard nine to five day and rather enjoyed the regularity, if not the monotony, of the job. After two weeks, he began an affair with the only woman who worked in the office, a junior clerk fifteen years his junior. By now Ruben Miles had begun to lie about his age routinely, as people did not seem to want to believe his real age when he told them. She accepted without question that he was only a year or two older than her. That being said, Mary Saunders had also been economical with the truth when discussing her own position. She had seemingly forgotten that she was married with a four-year-old boy at home in Streatham. Not that this information would have meant a great deal to the morally accommodating Ruben Miles.

His foreign visitors persisted, and in truth he welcomed their presence, and they were always discreet when he was entertaining Mary, which was usually twice weekly, immediately after work. Mary's husband still assumed that she was attending her evening classes that she started six months before. Due to a slight diary mishap, Ruben Miles found himself answering the door to Herr Weber in his underpants, with a less than impressed Mary expressing her indignation at the interruption to proceedings in her rather shrill cockney tones.

'Have I got my dates or times wrong?' Herr Weber asked, in German as per their rules.

'Nein, der Fehler liegt bei mir.'

Poor Mary soon ascertained her true place in the pecking order as she was bundled without ceremony into her clothes and out of the front door, albeit with the money for a taxi to Streatham in her hand.

Herr Weber apologised for the interruption and then made a surprising statement.

'I have a message from your associates. They no longer wish to communicate via telegram. You are to expect your next guest tomorrow evening, he will be with you for two weeks.'

Ruben Miles knew better than to waste energy on follow-up questions about his incoming guest. However, he could not help himself from asking Herr Weber the following questions: 'Do you work for the Fixer? What do you know about my guests? Who are they and what are they doing in this country?'

He spat the questions out rapidly in perfect German, gaining a nod of respect from his tutor.

Perhaps surprisingly, Herr Weber gestured for Ruben Miles to sit and availed himself of a nearby armchair. He took out his pungent Turkish cigarettes and lit one without offering the pack to his student.

'You are making excellent progress with your German. You even have a convincing Berlin accent. I can understand your curiosity about my relationship with your associates, but I am sure that you realise that this is something of which I cannot speak. Similarly, it would be a strange man who did not want to know the dealings of people that you have made welcome in your fine home.'

'You must be able to tell me something useful?'

'Herr Muller, your first guest I believe. He is a scientist of some repute. I believe he escaped Nazi Germany in 1935. Your recently departed guest is another exiled from Hitler's mythical Fatherland, an engineer I believe.'

This hint of criticism of the previously feted Führer drew puzzlement.

'You have always been so complimentary about the Nazis and Hitler...'

'When you have had a cover story as long as I have Herr Miles, it becomes almost your true self. I left Germany the week before he became Chancellor, in January 1933. I could see which way the wind was blowing. I had met Hitler in Munich. I infiltrated their nasty but then small organisation in the spring of 1925, not long after he had been released after the Putsch in Munich. I was at close enough quarters to be left in no doubt about what they would do if they ever got into power in Germany. I got out before their suspicions about my real sympathises hardened.'

Ruben Miles found himself liking the little German a good deal more.

'I do not know for sure what your associates are up to as they would never confide in me, but I can hazard an educated guess. Your guests appear to be persons of some skill that have escaped the Third Reich and come to England. It may be that your associates have plans for the next stage of their careers that does not involve working with the English.'

'But why would the Fixer work with the Russian? Surely the Americans would be against their people working for Stalin?'

'Those are questions that I cannot answer. Who knows where any man's true loyalties are?'

They spent the next hour in extended conversation. Herr Weber probing both grammar and the correct conjugation of many rare verbs. At the end of the lesson, he shook Ruben Miles by the hand and said something unexpected as he left.

'I will try and find out more information about your guests if you wish? Or perhaps you would like me to talk to British intelligence. I have a contact there.'

Ruben Miles was not sure what to reply. He was intrigued by what he had got himself into, but very wary of the Fixer and more than a little jumpy about the Russian. But British intelligence?

'Yes, that might be an idea. But you will be discreet, Herr Weber, I think the last thing we would want is to upset our esteemed colleagues.'

'Of course, alternatively you could simply ask them what you are involved with. They may tell you the truth. It is in my own best interest not to displease our mutual associates. My association with them is much shorter than your own, but long enough to understand the need for caution.'

After a brief pause, he offered a final question of his own.

'Why do they want you to speak German when you have very little interaction with your guests?'

This may have been a good question, but how did Herr Weber know he had had such limited interaction? They had never previously discussed it. By the time Herr Weber had left, Ruben Miles felt like he was a little dizzy. He was not used to such abstract thinking and conjecture. Why was the odd little German, who came to him via the Fixer, volunteering to try and find out what the whole business was about? Where did *his* loyalties lie? And why was he asking questions that Ruben Miles had not thought to ask?

MR CAVENDISH

Ruben Miles was enjoying a post-swim coffee in a little Italian café adjacent to the Marshall Street swimming baths he attended daily, situated around the corner from Carnaby Street. He enjoyed watching the shop workers and seedy types bustling around the cramped, dirty streets. For someone who did not particularly like people, he certainly enjoyed observing them. He was thinking about his conversation with Herr Weber, as he had done quite incessantly since the exchange occurred the previous week.

He looked on as the pimps checked in with their employees, who all looked the same at the end of a shift... haggard. The pill pushers tapping their feet manically as they stood in their spots waiting for business, a result of consuming too much of their own produce. Every picture does indeed tell a story.

Ruben Miles then noticed a well-dressed man of average height striding purposefully towards the café, Times newspaper rolled up under one arm and an umbrella being used as a walking aid in his opposite hand. He wore a pin-striped suit and a rather incongruous white bow tie. He looked like he had taken a wrong turn from the city.

Surprisingly, the man walked straight up to Ruben Miles and introduced himself.

'Mr Miles? My name is Mr Cavendish, may I join you?'

The rather dandy looking man knew his name?

'Well, I was just leaving...'

Mr Cavendish looked at the full cup of coffee in front of Ruben Miles somewhat disappointedly.

'I think that you may benefit from a little conversation. Perhaps we could talk about your recent rather mysterious guests?'

'Do you know Herr Weber?'

'Mr Miles, you may discover that we are quite familiar with a number of your more interesting acquaintances.'

Ruben Miles nodded for the man to sit and waved over to the waitress, a busty redhead who had questionable personal hygiene and seemed to always have at least one stray curler in her mane at any one time; today it was two.

Mr Cavendish ordered an Earl Grey tea whilst surreptitiously holding his nose a little.

'Herr Weber mentioned that you may wish to ask a few questions about your recent guests, supplied by the gentleman who refers to himself as the Fixer.'

Ruben Miles took a moment to digest this information.

'And how do you know Herr Weber, never mind the Fixer?'

'Mr Miles, in my business and in this town, in these most interesting of times, it is essential that I, and my colleagues, know what a great many interesting chaps are up to.'

'Are you from British intelligence?'

'Let us concern ourselves with your main questions for just now, shall we?'

This seemed a reasonable enough proposition.

'Am I doing anything illegal by putting up these foreign men?'

'Legality is such a definitive concept, don't you think, Mr Miles?'

Mr Cavendish barely acknowledged the arrival of his tea; the waitress harrumphed her disapproval on departure.

'Herr Weber said they may be scientists. They certainly did not behave like any of the criminals I have come across.'

'It might be easier if I showed you some photographs, Mr Miles, and you can tell me whether any of them have been your recent guests.'

'Of course, that makes sense.'

Mr Cavendish extracted a pale envelope from his inside jacket pocket and his slender, elegant fingers gracefully removed a series of headshots. The first two that Ruben Miles was shown he did not recognise.

'No, I am certain that I have not had either of those at home.'

Mr Cavendish looked vaguely disappointed.

'What about this distinguished looking gentleman?'

Ruben Miles picked up the photograph that had been placed on the table before him.

'That is Mr Gruber, one of my more recent and more reclusive guests.'

Mr Cavendish did not seem either surprised or particularly interested in this news. Ruben Miles was shown five more photographs of which he identified two further recent guests.

'Your recent guests are scientists of various eastern European nationalities. Apart from their knowledge and skill set, they also share the misfortune of being Jewish. Not, you understand Mr Miles, that I am antisemitic myself. But I am sure you are aware that in other places there are very different views.'

Like many of his fellow countrymen, Ruben Miles had been both fascinated and disturbed by the portrayal of Nazi Germany in the press during the 1936 Berlin Olympic Games. He had not been alone in being greatly amused by the defeat of the Aryan master race by the black athlete, Jesse Owens.

'I would be grateful if you would keep a hold of these, Mr Miles.'

Mr Cavendish handed across two of the photographs that Ruben Miles had been unable to identify. He also produced a card with just his name and a telephone number.

'I would be most grateful if you would contact me if either of these two gentlemen are in residence.'

'So, what are these scientists doing here, Mr Cavendish?'

'You are making an assumption that all the men I have shown you are scientists, Mr Miles.'

'Are they not?'

'Let us just say that the men you have identified today are scientists.'

'And their purpose?'

'Has yet to be confirmed to us. But I think it is fair to say that we are interested in their possible activities and destinations.'

'Why should I let you know if I have these guests? I am sure the Fixer and the Russian might not look on my actions so favourably.'

'I can understand your caution in this area, Mr Miles, as your associates are indeed men to treat with appropriate prudence. If I told you that at this very moment those two gentlemen are being entertained by one of my colleagues at a fine restaurant, would that alleviate your concerns?'

'Are you saying that they work for you?'

Mr Cavendish looked like a disapproving teacher with an underachieving class.

'What I am saying, Mr Miles, is that to ensure that those fellows did not know about our little meeting, we arranged a little distraction for them at the same time.'

And with that, Mr Cavendish excused himself, informed Ruben Miles that he would stay in touch and spoke a few parting words.

'We would be most grateful if you called us if either of those men are with you in Balham.'

Mr Cavendish effortlessly blended into the now busy lunchtime streets and disappeared. Leaving behind a more than perplexed Ruben Miles.

OOH LA LA

Luke Miles had not been entirely straight with JoJo Bartlett about his interactions with Ruben Miles. Although he had no desire to hear the old man's elongated stories of his long life, he was very interested to understand how Ruben Miles had seemingly been proficient in relation to the opposite sex. As was evidenced by his several marriages and multiple offspring. Luke was also interested in the poisonous relationships that characterised the Miles extended family. At the very least, he thought it might help him explain his own rather torturous relationship with his parents and non-existent relationships with the wider family.

With these two central issues at the forefront of his thinking, Luke found himself at The Apple Orchard Retirement Community on a grey Tuesday afternoon, having already double-checked with JoJo that she had no visits planned with the old man that day.

'This is a welcome surprise, Luke. I got the impression from JoJo that you did not approve of our memoir writing.'

They were sat in the garden and, despite the relative warmth of the day, Ruben Miles was wearing three thick layers, including a heavy coat. His one obvious and recurring concession to old-age. Mrs Hazel Wharton would not have approved.

'I will leave that stuff to JoJo if that's OK? I wanted to talk to you about family stuff and other more personal things.'

The old man eyed his great-grandson with curiosity.

'So, you want to know how I managed to get married so many times?'

Luke did not expect to be outthought and second guessed by someone one hundred and six years old. He clearly looked a bit crestfallen as the old man gave one of his occasional chuckles.

'I might be old Luke, but I can remember every day of my life. I sure as hell can remember being seventeen and...'

The old man did not finish the sentence he was going to as it somehow did not feel appropriate, not a position he had often found himself in.

'You can't remember every day of your life, that's not even possible.'

'I have hyperthymesia, Luke. I took a test and everything.'

This was in fact not true. He *had* read an article about the test and had self-evaluated his responses to the questions – but he had never sat a formal investigation set by medical experts, at least to the best of his knowledge. Like most British people, Ruben Miles did not care too much for academic experts. They were too clever by half. Therefore, he had no intention of subjecting himself to their close personal scrutiny.

'I can remember the day you were born as if it was yesterday. August 15th 1990, it was a Wednesday. It rained hard in the morning, but the sun came out just after I had my lunch. I had a tuna salad and some brown bread, unfortunately the bread was a little stale. I had not heard from your father for years, but he rang me in the evening to tell me the news. I watched David Attenborough on the BBC in the evening.'

Luke Miles had to accept that the old man was convincing, but then so was David Blaine.

'Want to test me?'

'Not particularly.'

They sat in silence for a few moments, the pair of them eavesdropping on a rather odd tale being discussed on the adjacent table about a hamster, a plate of pasta and an annoying neighbour. It was *not* as interesting as it sounded.

'I am more interested in your actual life, not your stories...'

'Memories.'

'Tell me about your wives, I want to know why everyone in the family seems to hate each other. These things are much more real to me.'

For a man with hyperthymesia, Ruben Miles had never been keen to rake over the debris of his marriages and significant others. He was very aware that he did not come out with even much partial credit. However, he was starting to feel like he owed the boy something, although he could not explain why.

'Tell me about your first wife.'

Ruben Miles took a second to compose an introduction that did not include an immediate character assassination.

'Rita Seymour was her name. I met her strolling down Broadway on May 7th 1929. It was a Tuesday afternoon and unusually warm for the time of year. She was from a very wealthy family, not that I found that out for a while. In fact, now I'm sure that this was the reason that she even gave me a second glance that day.'

'What did she look like?'

Luke was a teenage boy after all.

'Tall, willowy and brunette. She was very much a roaring twenties girl, was our Rita. She looked like a movie star and sounded like a Harvard professor. A pretty overwhelming combination for a lad from Northumberland.'

'How old were you?'

'Thirty. She was three years younger, old not to be married in those days, especially when you consider what a catch she was. I had had a few girlfriends, but nothing too serious, except of the unrequited kind...'

'What do you mean?'

'I fell in love with a suffragette when I was your age. A bad combination. Let's put it this way, I wish when I was younger, I knew what I learned later. It would have made my life much easier. I also fell hard for what we would euphemistically call a strident feminist. And not, sadly, for the last time...'

Luke's GCSE History course covered just the usual suspects. The Nazis, Kaiser Wilhelm and Fidel Castro. The greatest hits of any century.

Ruben Miles read the room, one of his *other* fortes.

'Suffragettes were radical campaigners for votes for women back at the beginning of the twentieth century. They were militant and did crazy things. The girl I knew set fire to a kirk in Scotland... that's a church.'

'That's quite an effort just to vote.'

Spoken like a true child of the twenty-first century.

'Mind you, she was not the only time I fell hard for the wrong girl, but I guess we will get to that another time.'

'Back to your first wife then. How long where you together for?'

'Not long. We were married within four weeks of meeting, maybe that was the first problem. Although I thought we were pretty happy, I mean at least I was pretty happy.'

'What happened?'

Ruben Miles thought carefully about his use of language, *not* always one of his fortes.

'She became a little too friendly with my boss.'

Ruben Miles decided that he would not mention the Babe by name, after all Luke Miles was neither the sporty type, nor, judging by his below average historical knowledge, likely to know who the Babe was. Despite his betrayal, Ruben Miles still felt warmly about the Babe and found it vaguely depressing when people had not even heard of such a truly memorable man. He held no such warmth for Rita Seymour and when he heard via a mutual old New York acquaintance that she had died of a massive stroke at the age of just forty-six, he genuinely felt very little. He was aware that this did not make him look or sound good and so he withheld this information from his young relative.

'That must have been rough.'

Ruben Miles nodded his agreement.

'I suppose you could say I had a little bit of a breakdown afterward. I spent the next several months travelling around the whole country in a bit of a haze. What a waste of time!'

'So, what did you think you learned from your first marriage? What advice would you give?'

This made the old man trumpet his amusement so loudly that he offended the table next door, which had moved on to non-rodent related anecdotes.

'I suppose I learnt that you should always understand the reason why a woman might want to be with you. You also need to understand why that might not be good enough.'

'I don't follow.'

'Are you and JoJo an item yet?'

'Well we see quite a lot of each other and although we have not had a conversation on the exact nature of our relationship, some of our recent activities would suggest... yes.'

'Jesus, you sound just like your father, and that is not a compliment. What I meant was that Rita was with me because I was the last type of man her family would want her to associate with. Therefore, she was with me to get at her parents, not the most convincing of reasons. I mean most teenage girls go out with boys their parents will hate. It's almost a scientific phenomenon. Rita was a bit old to be behaving like a teenager and I was too inexperienced to know what the hell was going on until much later. I actually worked it all out during my mad journey around the country afterwards.'

'When did you begin to suspect?'

'When my boss's wife caught her husband shagging my wife over the kitchen table.'

The people at the table next door nearly choked on their cheese and pickle sandwiches. There are some things you do not expect a one hundred and six-year-old man to say.

'I suppose that is a pretty clear clue.'

Luke took a few minutes to digest this information and cross reference the findings with his present situation with JoJo. After all, what was the point of being a teenager if you could not be self-absorbed?

'Do you think...?'

'No. I think JoJo likes you because you make her laugh. She has mentioned that a couple of times. And presumably she likes the way you look.'

'So, to recap, your first wife married you to piss her family off, she didn't really love you and ultimately betrayed you by shagging your boss.'

Ruben Miles concurred that this was a more than adequate precis of his doomed first marriage.

THE MAN IN THE
PHOTOGRAPH

I t was nearly three months and four guests later when a man arrived at Ruben Miles's front door who keenly resembled one of the photographs handed over by Mr Cavendish at the little café in Soho. It was now the summer of 1939 and Europe stood closer to the abyss. Ruben Miles stood in his kitchen and wondered what to do next. Surprisingly, he had not predetermined what action to take should one of the men in the photographs arrive at his door and now that one had, he was going to have to make some sort of decision. To inform Mr Cavendish or not?

The man seemed broadly similar to the other guests. He was polite, introverted and gave off an aura of academia. Or was this merely Ruben Miles projecting these traits on to these men? He spoke in a clipped, northern German accent and looked vaguely Jewish. He declined the offer of tea or alcohol and spent all of the first night quietly in his tidy back room, not even tempted out by the offer of a light late supper.

In the sitting room, Ruben Miles found himself brooding on the reliability of Mr Cavendish and whoever the hell he worked for, not to mention the prospect of disappointing or God forbid angering, the Fixer and the Russian.

As often develops with people who live on their own, Ruben Miles talked to himself a lot. Whenever he was unsure of something, he would discuss the issue quietly out loud. He felt that this hastened and improved the decision-making process. Therefore, as the erudite German snored quietly in his room, Ruben Miles went through his options orally.

A half-hour later he had his decision.

The next morning, a little after nine, Ruben Miles rang the number Mr Cavendish had supplied him with on a little card. To his surprise, the very man answered the phone after just a moment.

'Cavendish.'

'Ah yes, good morning, Mr Cavendish, I do not know whether you may remember me, I am...'

'Mr Miles, good morning to you.'

This caused a second or two of mild incredulity.

'I am assuming that you have a house guest that may be of interest to us, Mr Miles?'

Mr Cavendish was a man who liked to move the conversation along whenever possible.

'Yes, that's right. The chap who arrived yesterday afternoon is a ringer for the man in the last photograph you gave me.'

'How long is he scheduled to stay?'

'Well, that is the odd thing. This time, unlike all the others, I wasn't informed...'

This seemed to give Mr Cavendish food for thought.

'I see, well perhaps we should act a little more swiftly than we would normally like to.'

Ruben Miles, of course, had no idea what this meant.

'Is he with you as we speak?'

'No, I heard him leave about half an hour ago, that is why I chose to call you now.'

'And you have no idea of his movements?'

'Actually, he left a note to say that he will be back by five this afternoon.'

'Splendid. I will have people over to you within the hour, Mr Miles, is that OK? I may even come myself, if I can swing it.'

Fifty-eight minutes later, three gentlemen, unaccompanied by Cavendish, presented themselves at Ruben Miles's front door. They neither showed nor were asked to present identification, which was just as well as they did not carry any. They asked to be taken to the guest's bedroom and then they politely asked Ruben Miles to leave them to it.

'Those are Mr Cavendish's orders, sir, he said he would be in touch shortly. He would have come himself, but he was unable to get out of a meeting.'

This was true. At the precise time this conversation was occurring, Mr Cavendish was in a stuffy room in Whitehall updating his superiors of recent developments in Balham.

The men were only in the room for twenty minutes and they made no sounds to give away any of their actions. As Ruben Miles was sipping a cup of camomile tea in his sitting room, the men were searching the room and discovering nothing of interest. They then took fingerprints and placed a rather rudimentary dictograph under the bed.

'Mr Cavendish said he would see you soon, sir,' said the tallest of the men as they departed.

Ruben Miles decided to carry on with his day as normal and headed off for his regular late morning swim in Soho. He had just finished twenty-five lengths, as was his custom, when a man in the adjacent lane removed his swimming cap and smiled broadly at Ruben Miles. It was Cavendish.

'Best exercise for you, you know.'

A somewhat superfluous introduction.

Quietly and quickly, they went to get changed and afterwards found a quiet table in the café next door and were served coffee by the regular brunette with the unruly head of hair.

Cavendish explained the situation and outlined the plan.

THE TRAGIC SECOND WIFE

The week after his initial visit to discuss the personal life of Ruben Miles, Luke Miles found himself back at The Apple Orchard Retirement Community. Like most sixteen-year-olds, Luke wished he could drive. But his seventeenth birthday was still several weeks away. Besides, just because his parents got his sister driving lessons for her seventeenth birthday present was no guarantee that there would be sibling equality. Experience had taught him that much.

He wanted to drive because of his dislike of public transport. Luke was too young to realise that it was other people he did not like, not buses. If he could drive, he would also not have to breathe in the disinfectant smell that pervaded every nook and cranny of The Apple Orchard Retirement Community, even the terrace and garden areas. He suggested a walk, but the old man demurred.

'Mrs Hazel Wharton has already had me out for my godforsaken daily constitutional.'

JoJo Bartlett had been the first person that Ruben Miles had shared the tragedy that befell his second wife and his favourite child on New Year's Eve 1936. Luke Miles was to be the second. Like so many of the few that shared his unusual condition, Ruben Miles often reflected on the curse of being able to remember too much. In the middle of a sleepless night, the images thrust themselves to the forefront of his troubled mind and would not let go. He could almost smell the burning house in his elderly nostrils.

'My second wife was called Eileen, an unusual contradiction of a women. When I met her, she was both an exotic dancer in a Soho strip club and a fervent Christian. I would have thought a rather unique combination.'

Luke Miles did not hear the second half of the unusual combination. He was still on exotic dancer. He was still surprised that his great grandfather was finally telling him about his personal life. Luke found it a little difficult to adjust to.

'She was a very forgiving woman, and it never bothered her that I was a committed unbeliever. Unlike my first wife, she was very close with her family. In fact, her family was pretty much the only thing I could fault her for. Her father was completely mad and twice as vicious. He blamed me for the accident. He actually tried to get the police to charge me with murder…'

Once again, Luke Miles had quite a lot to digest in a short time. He decided to ask the more mundane questions first. Exhibits A and B.

'How and when did you meet?'

'I popped into a dance club in Soho for a cold drink. Monday 27th April 1931, a wet but oddly warm day in London. I was in a good mood as I had won nearly a fiver on a horse that was tipped to me by my next-door neighbour, George. Poor beggar, he was dead before the end of the year. Ran over by a bus in Tooting. Eileen was the second dancer on and was the reason I stayed for another lemonade.'

'How long before you were married?'

'Less than a month again. I know there is beginning to emerge a clear pattern of undue haste, but it was not all down to me. Eileen told me on our third date that she knew I was the man that she was going to spend the rest of her life with. We got a place in the East End, Mile End. I got a job at the docks thanks to her mental father and we had three kids in just over five years. A fairly common and humdrum existence back then, I would say.'

'So, you settled down?'

'At least until the accident.'

This was another statement that was somewhat sparse on the honesty front. Ruben Miles had wandered from the righteous path of marriage a few times before his head was inappropriately turned by the Iberian charms of Francisca. However, Ruben Miles thought that these perfunctory and ultimately unsatisfying dalliances were not of sufficient merit to be mentioned. Or did he suddenly care about what a member of his family thought of him?

'What happened?'

'The police never discovered the cause of the fire. They even thought for a while it might have been arson. I blamed them damn candles that she insisted on having on in the bedroom. I

254 | Mark Newies

was devastated to lose my wife and one of my children and in truth I did not handle it at all well.'

It was difficult for Ruben Miles to answer the following, inevitable questions.

'What did you do?'

Ruben Miles told his young relative the truth.

'How could you do that?'

Ruben Miles made up what he thought was a plausible excuse.

'I think I had a sort of a breakdown, this time even worse than after my first marriage ended. I ran away and leaving the children with my mother seemed the only thing to do, at that time.'

Luke Miles could not think of the right thing or indeed anything to say about this subject for some minutes. The table adjacent had emptied and they sat in silence with just the sound of the light wind in the nearby trees.

'Whatever happened to the kids you gave away?'

'I genuinely have no idea. I never saw them again.'

At least he had the sense to look suitably ashamed. But even here he was incapable of going further, not mentioning the letters he received from his daughter years later that went unanswered. He spurned the reconciliation he did not deserve or desire.

Even a teenage boy could grasp that this behaviour was chilling at best and horrifically callous at worst. As it was, as the conversation was transpiring in The Apple Orchard Retirement Community, Arthur and Rose, the abandoned children from Ruben Miles's second, tragic marriage, lived less than ten minutes apart from each other in Leith, on the northern edge of Edinburgh. Arthur was a retired office clerk and Rose was a retired cook. It was therefore easy to confirm that being abandoned by Ruben Miles had done little for their social mobility. His mother had kicked them out unceremoniously when they reached sixteen. It would seem that Ruben Miles inherited his parental attributes from his formidable mother.

'Are you not even interested to know what happened to them?'

This was a tough question for Ruben Miles to face.

'Not really,' he answered truthfully. 'You see, I dealt with what I did by not thinking about it.'

'Does your condition not make that difficult?'

Another tricky question.

'Difficult, but not impossible. As I have no memories of them since I left them sleeping in my old back bedroom in Morpeth, their story ends there for me...'

But the vision of his last view of them, cuddled up in his childhood bed, was one that he relived more than he would ever admit, even to himself.

For his part, Luke Miles did not comprehend what he was getting out of this process, other than a vague sense of melancholy for people he would never know. He decided to change the subject.

'Is what you did the reason everyone in the family seems to hate you?'

A perfectly rational deduction.

'No, they don't even know about it. You and JoJo are the only people I have told about that. And I hope you will respect that by not telling them. No, they hate me for a variety of different reasons.'

Of course they do.

'Why does my dad hate you?'

Direct and to the point.

'Well, your Grandad John was the son that I had with my third wife, the boozer. Katy was her name. And before we divorced, she told me that I was not John's real father. That dubious accolade went to our next door neighbour, Nigel. I was angry and decided that I wanted to know for sure and so I had a paternity test done. Your grandad was ten at the time.'

'What happened?'

'I am not his real dad and the mistake I made was telling him.'

'When he was ten?'

A pathetic nod of the head.

'Jesus!'

Luke Miles found himself, for the first time, feeling something vaguely akin to empathy for his father and grandfather.

But he had not heard the worst of it yet, even if the old man had promised not to mention *that.*

THE SPECIALIST

'**I** I have the very person in mind,' explained Cavendish as he briefly outlined his plan for Ruben Miles's German houseguest. The plan was simple and as old as the hills.

'She is something of a specialist in this field. I am told that she has never failed to get the job done, so to speak.'

Ruben Miles found himself more than a little disappointed with the realities of pre-World War Two intelligence agencies. He had been expecting something a lot more *39 Steps*. As it was, the plan was more a twisted Mills & Boon.

'We know what the game is. Your associates are pinching scientists from Oxford and whisking them away to the good old US of A. What we don't know is what their pitch is and what exactly the nature of the work is they have been targeted to do. That is where the Specialist comes in, she will extract the truth from your guest.'

'What sort of scientists?'

'Physicists. You see all of these chaps got out of Germany pretty swiftly after the Nazis got in to power, most are Jewish after all. We gladly availed ourselves of such knowledge. They have been working on some projects that we helped put together for the last four or five years. Then, about the time when your old colleagues came knocking on your door, we started to lose a few of our more needed gentlemen.'

'But why would the Russian be helping the US?'

'He is an interesting fellow, your Russian. Dyed in the wool red by all accounts. But he views Hitler as the biggest single threat his country faces and is willing to side with the Yanks to stop him.'

'That sounds suspicious to me.'

'Yes, of course. We are going to have to see how this one plays out. Oh, by the way, you work for us now, Mr Miles. I could not have told you about what was going on otherwise.'

And so, Ruben Miles was recruited into British intelligence

in August 1939, a mere two weeks before the balloon was about to go up. They do say that timing is everything.

Carolyn de Villiers was the young woman known to British intelligence as the Specialist. A stunning and almost freakishly intelligent blonde with a double first from Oxford, she had been recruited whilst in her final year at St Hilda's where she studied both German and French. She had subsequently spent time in Paris and Berlin during 1936/7 and had developed a healthy cynicism toward any form of political ideology, left or right. Her political indifference made her a trusted and valued asset within the shadowy world of the 1930s Secret Intelligence Service. However, it was her other skillsets that meant she was of great use to the service.

Carolyn de Villiers had an aura of sexuality that was positively luminous. It was said that every time she walked into a room, she gave all the straight men within it an instant erection. But this startling attribute was only the beginning of the process. Through her unrivalled intellect and almost unfair levels of personal empathy, that she displayed towards every man she encountered, even the most admirable of alpha males were putty in her sensuous hands. Repressed German physicists were not exactly a challenge.

Ruben Miles was smitten before the end of the introductions. Cavendish was keen to highlight the key point.

'Miss de Villiers never becomes too friendly with fellow travellers, Mr Miles, so I would not waste too much time on that particular thought process.'

Carolyn de Villiers merely smiled politely and shook the outstretched hand of Ruben Miles. Even dressed as a humble housemaid could not camouflage her stunning figure.

'Have you informed the subject of the new employee?'

'Yes, I told him last night that a cleaner would be coming a couple of times a week. He did not seem particularly interested or concerned.'

Despite the counsel of Cavendish, as soon as he had departed after running through the expected timescales for the operation, Ruben Miles found himself optimistically chatting up the divine Miss de Villiers. She gave him a cool stare and declared with finality.

'Mr Miles...'

'Ruben, please...'

'As well as my strict policy of not becoming too friendly with colleagues, you really are not my type, sorry.'

'Well, you would have been offended if I hadn't tried.'

This was a line that she had heard on countless occasions. But there was something about Ruben Miles that gave her some food for thought.

'However, I think that my sister Eleanor would welcome the opportunity to meet a man such as yourself, Mr Miles. From what Cavendish has told me, you have some things in common.'

'Such as?'

'You both went to Spain to help the Republic. Unlike me, Eleanor does a bit of politics, from the socialist perspective. She volunteered as a nurse and I understand you saw action?'

Ruben Miles had not discussed his time in Spain with Cavendish on any occasion.

'She is also attracted to older men, and you must be, what, forty?'

She was and still is the only person that saw through the youthful veneer of Ruben Miles. Most people at that time would have had him down as late twenties, perhaps thirty at the most. Not Carolyn de Villiers.

Once he had recovered from this surprise, he found himself asking about her sister Eleanor.

'Well, we look quite alike. She is a couple of years younger and we both work for the government. She does something quite secretive in Buckinghamshire, at least that is what she tells me. But Eleanor can be prone to a little exaggeration.'

None of these revelations were in any way off-putting. The two new acquaintances agreed to defer any arrangements until after the Specialist had concluded her orders.

JoJo was not sure of what to make of the latest developments in the memoirs of Ruben Miles. Was being recruited by British intelligence in the run up to World War Two any more or less believable than any of the other stories he had shared so far?

Once again, the logical part of JoJo's mind was asking for some proof of the already amazing aspects of the old man's life. When he also kept telling her that 'we won't get to the really big stuff until much later', she found herself becoming more like her doubting father. She decided to share these thoughts on the subject with her father on a walk through Jesmond Dene that he had surprisingly asked her to join him for.

'I can't tell you if he is lying. But I think asking for some evidence to corroborate his claims is valid, especially if the thing gets published with your name on it.'

This was something that had not really occurred to JoJo.

'Published? How would it be published?'

'The old man must want it published, why else tell the story to you? And if he can persuade people that his stories are real then it already sounds like quite a book.'

They both reflected on these words as they swerved past a very large dog concluding a very large shit. The teenager allegedly looking after the animal thought that a) this was very amusing, and b) picking up the foul-smelling excrement was clearly somebody else's job.

'Do you think it's fiction? Is he dictating a story that he never got down to writing?'

'No, I am pretty sure some, if not all of it, might be true or at least contain as much truth and falsehoods as most memoirs. I mean, memoirs are not known for their factual accuracy, are they?'

'Have you asked for any proof? I mean not about anything specific that he may have said, but you said he fought on the Somme during World War One. Has he shown you any pictures or army documentation?'

'I never thought to ask. But if he wants to publish it, he will need to be able to back up some of the claims, surely? I suppose there is one thing that suggests that his stories may indeed be true. I mean he does not actually come out of most of his stories well. He talks about killing people and abandoning his children after the tragic death of his second wife in a house fire. If you were going to make stuff up, would it not be stuff that makes you look good or at the very least not a cold-hearted bastard?'

JoJo's father conceded that this was indeed a logical argument for there being some truth in the old man's words. Perhaps the real question was: how much?

JoJo brought up the potential publication of the memoirs at the very next session with the old man the following day.

'I have a story worth telling and having kept it all to myself for many, many years, I have finally decided that I want to share it. That is why we are doing this, remember.'

'I suppose that makes sense. This brings us to my other question. You will surely have to have some evidence to support your story, right? Like your army record or your secret service file.'

This brought quite a laugh from the old man.

'I am not sure they will have recorded some of the things they asked me to do.'

'OK, but you must have some things?'

'I have kept some stuff over the years. I am not entirely sure where it all is. A lot of stuff I put in storage when I decided to move into this place.'

Now that she thought about it, this was another aspect of the old man's life that JoJo felt needed explaining. Why was such a mentally and physically fit old man living in an old people's home for nearly fifteen years? She scribbled this thought down in her little book as she did not want to change the subject just yet.

'Could we maybe try and take a look?'

'Well, I suppose a publisher might want to see a few things. But a lot of stuff is going to have to be on trust, I'm afraid. Proof is not something that my employers were keen on keeping, especially when we get to the Cold War.'

JoJo felt a little more confident that the old man might have more than just his words to prove at least some of his claims. She was also pleased he was not upset by her questions. But even if he can prove that he served at the Somme, does that prove what he says happened? She thought she should save that particular rabbit hole for another day.

'Right, so what happened with your German house guest?'

The Specialist was well named. Her reputation was, if anything, not effusive enough. She first encountered the German scientist as he emerged from the guest bathroom, blinking through the steam of his absurdly hot showers. His skin was bright pink with the heat, contrasting with the large white towel that preserved his modesty. Herr Schneider had not had such a hot shower before. At the university and his modest lodgings, the water was never more than lukewarm and never plentiful. The modern fixtures of Du Cane Court had beguiled the scientist and he spent an inordinate amount of time in the bathroom.

For her part, Carolyn de Villiers made a believable, if overly attractive housemaid. She was dusting imaginary spider's webs from the hall ceiling (Ruben Miles was as fastidious with his cleaning regime as he was with his skincare) as she encountered the German scientist for the first time. Five minutes later, after a conversation that could only be described as one-sidedly coquettish, he managed to make it into his bedroom without having either a) a panic attack, or b) a heart attack. But it was a close-run thing.

Herr Schneider's familiarity with the fairer sex was almost nil. Apart from a spinster aunt and a slightly mad half cousin, his knowledge of feminine ways was zero. Neither of the aforementioned ladies prepared him for how to interact with Carolyn de Villiers. Despite wanting to see her and have her talk to him again, he could not force himself to leave the bedroom as his heart was indeed palpitating. Thirty minutes later and in fear of hyperventilating he went to the kitchen to get a drink of water.

Carolyn de Villiers was waiting in ambush.

When he thought about the events later, Herr Schneider could not recall everything that she had said. But his memory of what she did was a whole lot clearer. In fact, he could focus on little else. Over the next three days, Carolyn de Villiers, AKA the Specialist, made sure that Herr Schneider had ample interactions that he could mentally review at his leisure.

Cavendish was not surprised when the Specialist gave him an update on developments.

'I think he will be ready to talk now.'

Based on what he had heard, Cavendish wondered whether Herr Schneider would be able to manage a coherent sentence in his current state, but chose not to air this thought.

'Excellent, we think they may be looking to move him on in two weeks.'

'More than enough time then.'

Carolyn de Villiers was a rare breed. She was able to distance herself completely from her own actions. This, coupled with what can be sympathetically described as a 'healthy sexual appetite', allowed her specialism to evolve. She forswore personal attachments and simply went from one assignment to the next, as if it was the most mundane of occupations. Half of British intelligence had tried to get her into bed (the other half being either gay, confused or asexual), and not one had succeeded. She was a very focused young woman and was convinced that her country deserved such total commitment. She took her patriotism most earnestly.

Ruben Miles was among the many to be shot down in flames. But as his own views on such issues were equally liberal, he merely focused on the next possible opportunity, the sister Eleanor.

DARTH VADER AND THE ELEPHANT IN EVERY ROOM

Luke Miles found himself with an odd but now disconcertingly recurring feeling, a sincere desire to have a real conversation with his father. For most of his teenage years, their interactions were one-sided and usually paternal lamentations on his poor academic achievements. Luke would merely grunt as his father overused words such as disappointed, underperformance and immaturity.

After speaking with Ruben Miles about Luke's grandfather, Luke realised he *was* interested in who he was and where he came from. He also wanted to know why his family appeared to be so dysfunctional. He had even started to pay attention when JoJo talked about her Sociology classes on the family.

'Parents fuck their kids up,' was JoJo's rather succinct synopsis the last time they talked about it.

Luke's grandad had been just ten when Ruben Miles informed him that he was not his real father and from then on pretty much ignored him emotionally, even if, reluctantly, he continued to financially support him until adulthood. Unsurprisingly, this experience did not turn John Miles himself into a doting father. When his own family appeared in his late twenties, he failed to form any positive bond with either of his two sons. Luke's father, Paul, had a difficult relationship with his father from an early age and this deteriorated experientially in adulthood. And then came the rumour.

For his part, Luke had always assumed that his non-existent relationship with his father was due to his father's almost obsession with his annoyingly perfect sister. But perhaps it was Luke's gender, not his sister's perceived brilliance that was the primary factor regarding his position within the family. It appeared that, rather like the royal family, the Miles men did not get on too well with their sons, especially the first-born ones.

'I've been talking with the old man again. He told me about Grandad.'

Luke's dad appeared to register the information but offered no immediate response.

'I'm assuming you know that Ruben Miles says he is not your father's real dad?'

At least this got a non-verbal reply by a hint of a nod.

'Is this why everyone hates each other? I mean, I don't really get it. I understand why Grandad hates the old man, but I don't see why that has caused issues for the next generations.'

'It's complicated.'

'Is it? Or do Miles men simply not like their male offspring?'

'I don't dislike you Luke...'

This was perhaps as close as his dad had come to saying that he loved his son.

'We don't exactly get along, do we? And you hate your father with a passion, I've known that since forever.'

'It's complicated.'

And for now, this was as much as Luke could get out of his father. It then occurred to Luke that if he really wanted to get some truthful answers, he needed to do something that he did with even less regularity than speaking to his father: namely, speak with his mother.

Ever since the pictorial bible incident, Luke and his mother had tended to acknowledge each other, but without investing too much in the way of meaningful interaction. She told him when he did something that irritated her and he would reply that he didn't care. A teacher, like Luke's father, Mrs Miles had developed the ability of speaking down to everyone as if they were a rumbunctious pre-teen. This meant that she had cultivated no real friends and a mild drinking problem that she had managed to shield from her husband because of his almost pathological lack of perception and intuition, and from her son because of his total lack of interest.

She did like to cook, which was ironic as both her husband and children treated food as an irritating concept that had to be tolerated in the same manner as one tolerates regular bowel movements. She watched cookery programmes on the TV constantly. Her favourite being James Martin. She loved his 'I'm a well-off Yorkshireman' persona and his tasty but unpretentious food. It was unsurprising therefore that Luke found his mother in the kitchen with a new Nigella book propped up in front of her, shielding a rather generous glass of Sainsbury's finest Merlot. The kitchen counter was strewn with umpteen ingredients.

'Dad won't tell me why he hates Grandad.'

'We are having chicken shawarma for tea.'

Thus, their conversation began in a predictable fashion, each having a completely different agenda.

Part of Luke was impressed by his mother's ability to blank out her family's indifference to her culinary skill. However, another part of him wondered when she would realise that he never ate any of the things she produced, as he lived almost exclusively on cereals, cheese on toast, crisps and a narrow selection of inappropriate takeaways.

'Cowardice is one of your father's defining characteristics. That and flatulence.'

She took a rather restrained swig.

'Why won't he talk about it?'

'I refer the honourable gentleman to the answer I gave a short time ago.'

She was on her third glass.

Luke Miles did not understand the reference. He was as likely to have watched his parents have sex as he was Prime Minister's Questions.

'Your father hates his father because...'

Suddenly and without apparently obeying the laws of physics, Mr Miles was stood before them both.

'I hate my father because, on top of being a total arse, he also managed to have a couple of bastard children with a variety of my mother's friends and acquaintances.'

'A couple?' said Mrs Miles.

'All right, six.'

'Six? Jesus!'

Luke's mother was looking at her husband in a manner that Luke had not seen before, somewhere vaguely between fondness and respect. It appeared that truth was indeed a rare commodity.

'Are you going to tell him? I think it's time *we* faced the truth, never mind just telling our son.'

Luke's dad had belatedly reached the same conclusion.

'Unfortunately, my father was rather successful at covering some of this up. So, although we found out who some of our half brothers and sisters were, we did not know them all.'

Mr Miles was looking distinctly pale. He paused and picked up his wife's wine glass, perched beside a radiant Nigella. He threw the contents straight back.

There was clearly parental hope that Luke would be able to join the dots together himself, but this confidence was ill-founded.

Thus, forcing Mr Miles to take the long-hidden Miles family skeleton out of the cupboard and present it to his horrified son.

THE SISTERHOOD

JoJo Bartlett was quite taken with the Specialist. Ruben Miles was explaining how she effortlessly extracted the information required from the German scientist with a minimum of fuss and in near record time. She seemed, at least to JoJo, a real feminist. The fact that JoJo was currently doing Feminism in her Sociology class was probably a significant factor in this viewpoint. Her teacher, Mr Dawson, was OK. At least he was neutral and even broadly supportive. But the boys in the class were insufferable sexist shitheads. And yes, you could quote her on that.

There was something almost postmodern about Carolyn de Villiers.

'She ended up heading up one of the teams in Germany after the war. After that, Washington D.C. during the Eisenhower presidency, causing quite the stink.'

JoJo did not really get what this meant, but it certainly sounded interesting.

If she had asked, the old man would have told her that Carolyn de Villiers was said to have quite a hold over Mr President. Her usual hold, in fact. But as he did not know whether *that* rumour was true or not, he moved on without further comment.

'Cavendish told me what she found out from the scientist. Carolyn never told me a thing, nothing in all the time I spent with her and her sister that year.'

British intelligence had been right about the activities of the Fixer and the Russian. They had been efficiently collecting former German scientists, predominantly physicists, from Oxford and Cambridge universities. They were promised a lavish lifestyle in the States and all the chalk and blackboards they could ever need. But more than that, they sold them immortality. The ability not just to explain everything about the world, the universe and beyond, but also new technologies of science fiction proportions. They pitched multiple projects at their targets. Herr Schneider was one of the few that was swithering and that was, of course, because of Carolyn de Villiers.

'He asked her to marry him. They had only known each other ten days. He told her that he was going to refuse their offer unless she agreed to marry him and go with him to America.'

'What did she do?'

'Told him that she would marry him, but only in several months' time, after she had nursed her dying mother. He was to cross the Atlantic without her, begin his new work for the Yanks and she would follow. In the meantime, they could write to each other.'

'And he believed her?'

'Hook line and the proverbial sinker.'

Ruben Miles had an A4-sized box on his knee. JoJo had hardly noticed it.

'Would you like to see a picture of her?'

JoJo was surprised by how much she did.

The old man handed over the small photograph.

The picture was of two beautiful women, obviously related. If the picture had been in colour this would have been less clear, as one had golden, the other auburn, long hair.

'They are beautiful. Which one is she?'

'The one on the right, the other is her sister, Eleanor.'

The old man was tearing up again.

For the rest of the approaching war, Herr Schneider had secretly and diligently written to Carolyn de Villiers. In a code of her devising, he kept her and British intelligence up to speed on not just his own project but also those of some of his more trusting colleagues. It was heady stuff.

'You wanted to see some evidence of what I have been telling you.'

He handed her another picture, this one noticeably even

older. It was the only picture he had kept of himself and the Babe. The Babe was in his Yankee uniform clutching his *second* favourite bat. Ruben Miles was wide eyed and grinning.

'He had hit his record equalling Home Run that afternoon. That was a glorious day.'

JoJo was more interested in the twenty-something Ruben Miles.

'Not bad, but you weren't in the same league as the Specialist.'

'Well, it's a good job her sister did not share your views, Miss Bartlett.'

Ironically, they met for the first time on Sunday 3rd of September 1939. It was a beautiful late summer day and Ruben Miles had agreed to meet the De Villiers sisters in Regent's Park for a picnic. He had spent the morning, like most of the rest of the nation, listening to Prime Minister Neville Chamberlain on the wireless speaking from the cabinet room in 10 Downing Street and confirming that a 'state of war' now existed between Britain and Germany. That was a day that *everyone* could recall where they were when they heard the broadcast.

Even without the news, the park was a place of sunny foreboding. Sandbag bunkers and the frameworks for anti-aircraft guns were being noisily and hastily put in place. For reasons that were not initially clear to Ruben Miles, the Specialist had been most adamant that now her assignment in his Balham flat was completed and the German scientist securely and permanently manipulated, the coast was clear for her to introduce her sister Eleanor to Ruben Miles.

They may have shared the same absurdly high cheekbones, a BBC accent and a penchant for smelly French cheeses, but the sisters were essentially opposing characters. Carolyn was apolitical, her sister Eleanor had dabbled in radical left-wing politics in the mid 1930s. This had caused more than a few lengthy interviews before she was accepted into a new hush-hush government department being set up in a former stately home in Buckinghamshire, Bletchley Park. Carolyn's academic speciality had been languages, but Eleanor was a prodigious mathematician and it was her excellence at Cambridge that had ultimately led her to the Government's new setup in the Home Counties. She had set the time record for completing the cryptic crossword that had been one of the interview process staples.

Where Carolyn was calculating and perhaps even cold, her sister was genuine and empathetic, not skills usually associated with those mathematically inclined. Whilst Carolyn clearly embraced her sexual allure and hold over most men, by contrast Eleanor wore oversized clothes even on warm summer days in an attempt to camouflage her own body. For all of their differences, it was clear that the two were close and appeared to be very much in tune with each other's senses.

'Do you approve?'

The Specialist was pouring herself a gin fizz from a cocktail shaker she had plucked from the wicker hamper at her feet. She gave her sister a lukewarm bottle of stout. Both sisters did a double take when Ruben Miles explained that he was teetotal.

'Yes, I think I rather do,' replied Eleanor, leaving Ruben Miles none the wiser that they had been talking about him rather than the choice of beverages.

Eleanor de Villiers did have a thing for older, rather handsome men. The Specialist had known the first time that she clapped eyes on Ruben Miles that he would be her sister's type.

The talk, of course, turned to war and what the future may bring.

'I volunteered the last time.'

Ruben Miles explained his time in France as a teenager but left out his time as a prisoner in Germany. Nobody wanted to hear about that.

Eleanor hid her surprise that he was old enough to have fought on the Western Front.

'Will you be called up again?'

'Not when he's joined our lot,' replied the Specialist, who was genuinely puzzled why her clever sister could not seem to get her head around the importance of the line of business she was in.

Ruben Miles, for his part, could not take too seriously his recent attachment to British intelligence and said as much out loud.

'If Cavendish says you are in, then I am afraid you are very much in.'

It was an idyllic late summer afternoon and the park was crowded. The mood was oddly defiant, despite the second declaration of war within a generation. Ruben Miles and the sisters consumed hard boiled eggs and corned beef and mustard sandwiches. Eleanor seemed a tad merry after her pair of stouts, but the Specialist had made short shrift of the contents of the cocktail shaker, and with no apparent effect. Ruben Miles enjoyed spectating people consuming alcohol, although was never tempted to join in.

'She can't tell you what she does. Similar to us in a way I think, but a different department entirely. It must be a secret because even Cavendish would not tell me anything, and he always tell me what he knows.'

Ruben Miles had already noted that Cavendish was indeed somewhat talkative for someone of his profession and status.

'It is frightfully interesting,' offered Eleanor.

'Yes, but you say that about crosswords, sis.'

Eleanor replied with a playful kick in Carolyn's direction.

Ruben Miles was amazed to discover, as they packed away the picnic debris, that they had been in the park for nearly four hours and the shadows were beginning to lengthen. The conversation and bonhomie had been such that the afternoon had rather gotten away from them. As they made their way toward Regent's Park tube station, the three of them decided to make arrangements for the following weekend. However, by the end of the conversation, the Specialist had cried off, leaving just a date for two. How very convenient.

THE GENE POOL

'**S**o, just to be clear, what you are saying to me is that your mum and dad are brother and sister...'

Luke Miles had developed a slight facial twitch since he had been told the *rumour* by his parents. As JoJo spoke it had started spasming again. He did not know which phenomenon was more unnerving, the information or the reoccurring twitch.

'Half-brother and sister, they had different mothers.'

'And the same fucking father... literally. Wow!'

The pair had driven to Tynemouth beach to get Luke away from the family home for a few hours. It was a typical northeastern day. It was sunny, cool and very breezy. They plodded along the wet sand, occasionally sharing a moody look out over near black sea.

'Are they sure? I mean have paternity tests been done?'

This had not occurred to Luke Miles, who was still young enough to believe that most of what his parents said must be at least partially true. But his parents had merely said that his grandfather had told them the *rumour* was true. He would have to ask them. With a sense of doom he realised that he was going to have more conversations on this topic with his parents.

'I mean you're normal, or at least fairly normal. Surely, if your parents were related you would be a mental case or have webbed feet or something. You don't have webbed feet, do you?'

Luke clarified that this was indeed not the case.

'This isn't a joke, you know.'

'I'm being serious. I remember in Biology being told about the gene pool and the dangers of inter... relations.'

Luke felt a slight chill meander down his spine. Was he going to feel this weird for ever?

'I don't think it's true, you would have some ghastly genetic disorder if it was.'

These upbeat words would have carried more weight if she had not simultaneously looked Luke up and down as she said them, presumably searching for clues regarding genetic flaws.

Luke went home, locked his bedroom door and refused to listen to his parents arguing downstairs.

The following day JoJo spent with Ruben Miles. It was a scheduled meeting and the old man took off from exactly where he had left off two days earlier, without even a polite preamble or personal greeting.

'You became a spy?'

JoJo seemed a little sceptical, her occasional default position. She was beginning to wish that, one way or another, she had a definitive view on the validity of the old man's stories. This clearly rankled the old man, who could detect her undercurrents of cynicism. Ruben Miles was rummaging in his chest of drawers for another cardigan, he needed that third layer. This was the first time that they had held a session in his private quarters, as Ruben Miles rather grandly referred to them. JoJo was surprised by both the spaciousness and the lack of 'old people' smell that seemed to pervade all other parts of The Apple Orchard Retirement Community.

She was sat in a comfortable sofa chair, tape recorder on one knee, pad and paper on the other. JoJo had yet to decide whether she was old or newish school.

'Why are we in here today?'

'I can't stand the bloody wind, it goes right through me.'

He needed more layers, even indoors. He settled on another beige number.

'So, Cavendish just told you that you had joined British intelligence and you had no choice in the matter?'

Ruben Miles confirmed that this was a valid assessment.

'But you have to put things into context. The war, the stuff regarding the Fixer and the Specialist and besides, the shipping clerk job was pretty dull.'

He declined to mention the job's fringe benefit.

'It does sound a bit more exciting.'

Ruben Miles chose not to mention the other factor in his acquiescence. He had wanted to look good in the eyes of Eleanor de Villiers.

'Oh, by the way, Luke has just found out that his mum and dad are half-brother and sister.'

JoJo had not known how else to broach the latest salacious family development.

Ruben Miles sighed heavily and, with considerable effort and carefulness, lowered himself into an adjoining sofa seat.

'Did Luke's parents tell him this then?'

JoJo nodded.

The old man took his time trying to construct his next uttering. He seemed to be weighing up several possible approaches, his eyes darting around as if to spot the most righteous path.

'I think it's all bollocks,' he eventually offered.

'That's what I said! The only thing I don't get is, even if it were true, why would Luke's grandad tell his parents that they were half brother and sister? It doesn't make any sense!'

'Have you met him? I don't suppose you could have. Complete and utter fool. I am ashamed to be his father.'

'But I thought you said...'

'I lied.'

'You told a ten-year-old boy that you were not his father and yet you were?'

The familiar nod of the head.

Wow! JoJo thought, we have a new contender for the 'worst things the old man has ever done' prize.

'His mother was just as much to blame. She was a drunken nutter. Not my best decision.'

Despite his desire to leave a detailed chronology of his extraordinary life, Ruben Miles was, as we have already seen, much less verbose regarding his personal life and in particular his marriages. The 'drunken nutter' was clearly the pinnacle of this disinclination.

Katy Watson was certainly partial to the odd libation and she undoubtedly had issues with common sense and rationality. But these issues were all too common if you hailed from Newcastle-upon-Tyne in the austere post-war years. But, once again, we are getting ahead of ourselves and Ruben Miles, ever the stickler for process, was keen to return to the chronological narrative.

'Can we leave her until we need to? I mean, I did not meet her until the fifteenth of September 1959 and we have only just reached the spring of 1940. Suffice to say I think Luke's grandad talks a lot of shite and I for one have never bought the fact that his parents are half siblings. I mean just because people say something is true it doesn't actually make it so, right? Surely we've learnt that from bloody politicians.'

JoJo shared the old man's view with Luke over a McDonald's in the city centre. Luke was pleased the weather was half-decent as it made staying out of the family home for long hours slightly more achievable.

'It does beg the question as to why they have not had tests done.'

JoJo was attacking her fillet of fish with some relish as Luke looked at his rather forlorn-looking Big Mac with disapproval. It looked how he felt: deflated.

'I'm going to make them take tests. I need to know, or at least I think I need to know.'

And with that, he formulated what he thought was a coherent plan.

SLOW BEGINNINGS

Cavendish was trying to explain to Ruben Miles how things worked. There was an alarming lack of clarity, and he had the deft ability of answering any questions with one of his own. Ruben Miles had the feeling he was sparring with a ghost.

'Now we are officially at war, we need to keep tabs on some of our own people. You have a union background, Miles, don't you?'

Now that he appeared to be working for Cavendish, Ruben Miles had noted the loss of his title when spoken to.

Ruben Miles briefly explained his tenure in the Dockers union.

'Excellent. Well, we'll start you off with something small. We will fix you up with a job in a union with suspected communist sympathisers.'

'Isn't it Nazi sympathisers we should be bothered about right now?'

'We need to keep tabs on a lot of chaps these days, Miles. You did read about the Nazi-Soviet pact I presume?'

Like the rest of Europe and beyond, Ruben Miles had been horrified by the Molotov-Ribbentrop Pact signed less than two weeks before the declaration of war.

'So, what do I do?'

'Keep your eyes and ears open. Without being too obvious, mention your solidarity with Mother Russia and see what develops. You will have to give your job up at the shipping office and, if I were you, your mistress too. The husband is a very unstable individual, so I am told.'

Ruben Miles had never mentioned his employment. But he was more surprised that his service in the Spanish Civil War was not even questioned by Cavendish. Surely, they knew which side he had been on? However unconvincingly.

'Do I get paid?'

'Don't be ridiculous, Miles. Of course you get paid and a damned sight more than you got as a shipping clerk. But let us just say that you are in a kind of probation period. We will take a look at you and you can see how you take to it. You did a good job re the scientists. As far as we are aware, your chap the Fixer was none the wiser about the role and success of the Specialist. As I am sure you know, the target is now safely in the States and sending regular information, most of which we have been able to corroborate.'

The Specialist had indeed confirmed this to Ruben Miles at the recent picnic. Although he was less sure about the Fixer. His German tutor, Herr Weber, had suggested that it would not be long before the Fixer would be paying Balham a little visit. As usual, the odd but likeable little German was unnervingly accurate.

But that was for later.

Ruben Miles found himself as a union man again. Pretending to care about the workers, bitching about how hard he was working, whilst doing very little in the way of actual meaningful work. He rather enjoyed it. He even demoed successfully a mild south London accent. He had never liked how his rather posh Northumbrian lilt had been received, by Londoners in particular.

He turned up nothing of notable interest in his quest for the best part of four weeks. He was surprised that many of the men did not want to talk about politics at all. But then the Phoney War was an odd time all around, especially in London. In fact, the only interesting conversation he had with anyone was with a seemingly pro-Nazi government official who had come to inspect some of the safety standards of the shipbuilding yard Ruben Miles spent most of his time at.

'Mosley is the man for me. We should be fighting the fucking Russians, not the Germans.'

Ruben Miles feigned some sympathy with the shared view.

'You seem like a clever bloke. Tell me you're not one of these bloody socialists?'

He spat the last word out literally and figuratively.

'Have you heard Mosley speak? Great speaker. He tells it like it is. I was with 30,000 others at Earl's Court last summer, he was electrifying.'

In many ways it was a relief for Ruben Miles to relay the details of this conversation to Cavendish as it was the only remotely worthwhile information that he had accrued. The government safety standards chap, a man called Lyle did indeed seem worthy of Cavendish's attention.

'He may be a fifth columnist.'

Ruben Miles did not know what this meant but felt it was wise not to ask. He was used to Cavendish explaining most things he did not initially grasp.

'And you say he asked you along to a meeting, after you convinced him that you were sympathetic to Mosley?'

'That's right, although he was vague as to what the meeting was about or indeed who would be there.'

'And it's next week?'

Ruben Miles agreed to go to the meeting.

'It may well be of no interest. But it is worth an evening of our, or should I say, your time. After all, at some point someone is going to have to make a decision on what to do with Mr Mosley, although I doubt very much that man will be Chamberlain.'

Ruben Miles had, of course, heard of Oswald Mosley. He had been a prominent political figure for many years and the leader of the British Union of Fascists since 1932. His antisemitic and pro-Nazi views were not in any way a surprise, nor his arguments that Britain should make peace with Germany. He even sported the bizarre moustache and dodgy salute. Unsurprisingly, *The Daily Mail* was quite the fan. Disappointingly, so was *The Daily Mirror*.

The following morning, April 28th 1940, Herr Weber presented himself at Du Cane Court at exactly five p.m. for his German tutorial.

Ruben Miles was keen to discuss Oswald Mosley. Herr Weber, rather ominously, wanted to talk about the Fixer.

'Your acquaintance is not a man to be taken lightly, Mr Miles.'

'Ruben, please.'

Herr Weber did not seem keen to lessen the spoken formality between the men.

'Herr Weber, I am very aware of the capabilities of my acquaintances as you call them. Do you have any news that you would care to share?'

Herr Weber congratulated Ruben Miles on his German accent.

'You would fool any Nazi into thinking you were German born and bred. The Fixer was not entirely fooled by what occurred here, I think, despite what Cavendish may say. I am led to believe that there is a possibility that they knew all about the, how shall we say, changing loyalties of Herr Muller once he had made a certain young lady's acquaintance.'

'And he told you this?'

'He never tells me anything directly, but I have sources.'

'Who exactly do you work for Herr Weber?'

'We have been down this, how do you say, cul-de-sac before I think. Suffice to say you and I are on the same side, Mr Miles.'

'And the Fixer and the Russian?'

'To an extent, certainly. I believe that you may be due a visit from the Fixer. I think he has a proposal for you to utilise some of the fine German you have learned. I think he has earmarked a role in Switzerland for you.'

'Switzerland? And what will Cavendish and his lot make of that do you think?'

'I think it may be of some benefit to them if you take up the offer.'

Ruben Miles was once again feeling a good deal out of his depth. This was before Herr Muller said, 'Of course, a lot may depend on whether there is any mileage in that fifth column stuff they want you to look at.'

'What can you tell me about Oswald Mosley?'

'That Hitler was the guest of honour when he married that Mitford woman in 1936 in Berlin, at Goebbels's house no less. A committed Nazi, I would say. The issue to be discovered is whether he has been able to organise enough powerful and likeminded souls to be a significant threat. There are many shades in this debate. Lord Halifax, for example, he may not be a Nazi, but he is more than prepared to dance to their tune as he feels it could safeguard the Empire.'

'And Chamberlain?'

'A shell of a man at best. Munich did it for him. I'm not sure that he will be able to cling on to power much longer. Much will depend on whether anything ever happens in this strangest of wars.'

'I am going to a meeting of some sort, although I can't imagine it will be of any particular worth.'

'Indeed, I find it unlikely that they have invited a virtual stranger to a meeting detailing how Nazi sympathisers are preparing to aid an invasion when it comes. As surely it must. You will probably find that it is just a group of wealthy drunken antisemites, the usual Nazi supporters, and they will be of little meaningful consequence.'

The two men spent the remainder of the lesson practising obscure grammar and discussing Switzerland's neutrality. It was debatable as to which exercise was more tiresome.

THE PLANS

'It's not really a plan as such, is it?'

JoJo Bartlett was a young woman who did underwhelmed very well.

'I mean at least not a reasoned one with any chance of success.'

This was her form of soft-soaping.

'But if I have a sample of their blood I can get it tested, right?'

JoJo contended that at least this part of the plan stood up to some form of mild scrutiny.

'Would it not be easier to just ask them to take a test? I mean they must see why you would want to know, one way or the other.'

Luke Miles had thought about that possibility, but he concluded that it would be impossible without having some lengthy and jaw-droppingly harrowing conversation. He would probably even have to look at them. Whereas his plan took that almost completely out of the mix.

'How are you going to get them to cut themselves?'

'I have not quite finalised that part yet, but my dad is pretty clumsy.'

'And you are going to collect it, what, in a jar or something?'

Another part of the plan yet to be satisfactorily explained.

'I could look on the internet. I have heard of this new site called YouTube, it has little videos telling you how to do stuff...'

This was not what JoJo had heard about YouTube, but she decided to let that go.

They were sitting in JoJo's bedroom. This had not gone unnoticed by a scowling Mrs Bartlett, who knew perfectly well the intentions of outwardly polite teenage boys. And that was her view *before* the *catastrophe.* She could not rely on her husband for any moral support. He and JoJo now seemed to spend a little more time together every evening after dinner having what could only be described as in-depth conversations, invariably involving Ruben Miles and his memoirs as a recurring theme. Leaving Mrs Bartlett to fume in the kitchen, inhaling chardonnay over ice at an increased tempo.

Luke and JoJo had seemed to settle into the fact that they had become an item without actually having the conversation. Although they were now facing an issue of practicality. Quite a pressing issue.

'We could go away for a weekend?'

JoJo surprised herself with this statement. She had not previously been so open about what she wanted.

'I mean clearly your bedroom means being in the house with your folks and, understandably, given the current circumstances, that is not something you want to get involved with. Similarly, there is absolutely no frapping way we are having a repeat of the *catastrophe* here. My mother would have a stroke and I would have a nervous breakdown.'

'I'm skint and I just can't ask my parents for any money, sorry.'

JoJo was a saver. Unlike most of her peers, she had no real interest in shopping. She managed to pull off an acceptable look with a minimal wardrobe and would not buy a handbag or unnecessary pair of shoes even if her life depended on it. Consequently, she had accrued a decent savings account from her allowance, birthday and Christmas gifts and occasional babysitting duties with a selection of random neighbours.

'I have money,' she said simply.

They both were all too aware of the conversation they were really having and it was not regarding weekend accommodation. Luke could barely contain his excitement. In fact, he didn't, much to JoJo's silent enjoyment.

'Where could we go?'

'Well, we have the use of the car and it would be good to get out of town, I mean I have no desire to bump into anyone we know.'

Luke would have been fine with bumping into everyone he knew if he was spending a weekend at a hotel with JoJo, but chose wisely not to mention this view.

'Scotland?'

'Christ, we are not frapping eloping!'

'I know, but Edinburgh is supposed to be a great place and I've never been.'

JoJo conceded that she had enjoyed a school trip to Edinburgh a couple of years before.

'I didn't really want to drive too far, how far is Edinburgh?'

'Not sure, but Newcastle is practically in Scotland anyway, so it can't be that far.'

JoJo decided not to comment on this geographically-challenged contention. Especially from someone born and raised in the northeast. They looked it up on the internet on Luke's rather slow computer.

'It's nearly a hundred miles, Luke.'

'But it's just one road, look, it seems dead easy.'

JoJo spent a fruitless ten minutes trying to suggest other randomly chosen but closer venues.

'Durham?'

'Like Jesmond, full of spoilt southern private school wankers, according to my dad.'

'Berwick?'

'Too shit. I spent a week in a caravan there when I was a kid, it felt like a year.'

'Redcar?'

'You've clearly never been.'

They settled on Edinburgh. Luke could not believe that they had agreed to his destination of choice.

'Shall we try to book or just take potluck? I am assuming we are talking about next weekend?'

'Absolutely. I can't face trying to book anything on this heap of shit. It takes so long to do anything.'

Potluck it was then. As it was now August, this was a disappointingly naïve decision. As they would soon find out.

UNTIMELY ACTS

Eleanor de Villiers was by some distance the most intelligent woman that Ruben Miles had ever dated. Later in his life, he regretfully realised that only his American first wife offered even the merest of competition for this. Yet it was not her most notable feature. Eleanor de Villiers was a kind and open-hearted women. She saw the best in everyone and everything. No person that she met disliked her. Niceness is such an undervalued human commodity.

They hit it off straight away and after a few months were meeting most weekends in London. Whenever Eleanor de Villiers could get time off from her work, which she clearly loved, she would take the train into the capital and meet up with Ruben Miles. She told Ruben Miles what she did. She took the Official Secrets Act (1939) very seriously. Like her sister, patriotic duty was something she cherished.

The pair had not seen each other for three weeks when they met for high tea in the Ritz on Friday 10th May 1940. Ruben Miles was on a high, as Eleanor de Villiers had unexpectedly announced that she would be open to 'seeing' his apartment in Balham. He viewed this as an exciting development as their time together so far had been singularly lacking in sexual contact.

Although he had money, Ruben Miles was not always predisposed to spending it. His expenditure seemed to fluctuate without any evident pattern. He felt that tea at the Ritz would be very much to Eleanor de Villiers's liking and therefore a worthwhile expense. He was at least partially right.

She loved the food, but felt intimidated by the finery on display. She felt drab in her clothes and, for the first time ever, envious of how well dressed some of the female clientele appeared to be. They ate dainty cucumber sandwiches and drank Earl Grey tea. In the corner, a well-dressed and manicured middle-aged man played some mildly jaunty big band tunes on a grand piano, albeit quietly. One could still hear the clinking of glass and the chatter of the high-quality China cups.

As they were finishing their very English repast, a commotion outside the hotel entrance caught their attention. A newspaper boy was shouting about the Low Countries and France and an excitable crowd had gathered quickly around him. Ruben Miles excused himself from the table and ventured through the ornate entrance to the outside street. He elbowed his way through the growing throng and waved ostentatiously a sixpence in the newsboy's vision. This ensured he received the very next copy from the much-depleted pile at the boy's feet.

'Keep the change,' Ruben Miles said needlessly, for the boy had read his intentions instantly.

He unfurled the copy of the Evening News, digested the headlines and hurriedly read on. He returned to Eleanor de Villiers and handed her the paper.

'Well, we have been expecting it, or at least something like it?'

She seemed to be taking the news and reading the article very calmly.

Ruben Miles was less sanguine, but managed to offer the following commentary.

'It says that they are making extraordinary progress. Still, they said that last time and we stopped the buggers before Paris.'

The Phoney War was over and so were Ruben Miles's chances of entertaining Eleanor de Villiers at Du Cane Court, at least for the foreseeable future.

'I have to go back to work, sorry. We were told that if anything meaningful occurred when we were on leave that we had to return immediately. I think we can both agree that this constitutes something meaningful.'

They headed for Euston Station quickly and efficiently. There seemed a strange quietness to most of the streets. Despite the journey only taking five minutes from nearby Green Park station, Eleanor de Villiers wanted to walk to the station.

'I miss London,' she said, by way of explanation.

She took his hand as they walked north through the streets of Soho.

They could have had a meaningful conversation. They both

had developed feelings for each other. But their British reserve was a more powerful emotion. Instead, they silently watched the starlings perform their acrobatic and loud murmuration overhead.

Ruben Miles got to spend his evening, more ominously, with the Fixer, albeit without the Russian's brooding presence. He arrived unannounced. It was only the recent words of Herr Weber that meant Ruben Miles had been half expecting a visit for over a week. There was no small talk.

'France will fall in weeks. The stupid French never thought they would go around the Maginot Line. Can you imagine the arrogance and ignorance of a nation to be stiffed twice in exactly the same way?'

Surely one of the most expensive follies ever made.

They listened to the BBC news together on a new wireless. Chamberlain had gone. Forced to resign after a humbling vote of no confidence after the Norway debate in the chamber. He may have won the vote, but conclusively lost the argument as well as the good will of a nation.

With the backing of many Conservative MPs (even some who despised the man), senior Labour figures and a reluctant King George VI, Churchill had become Prime Minister.

'Quite a day,' offered Ruben Miles.

'At least Winston will talk a good fight, unlike that appeasing asshole, Halifax. He has American blood, after all. If I were you, I would be grateful for our German lessons, you are probably going to need to speak it very soon.'

Like most Britons, Ruben Miles felt that Churchill becoming the Prime Minister had been the obvious and right thing to do. Even if he had rarely agreed, trusted or even liked the man before. The fact that he had been railing from the sidelines about the threat of the Nazis for years had ultimately counted for something tangible.

'We were hoping you might have been able to go to Switzerland for us, but that's off now.'

Ruben Miles knew better than to ask who constituted 'we'.

'I gather from Muller that you are investigating fifth columnists for the British. I think that you and your colleagues might just have gotten a bit busier in that area. They should throw away the key on that son of a bitch Oswald.'

It was not an exaggeration to say that Ruben Miles had no clue who worked for whom. Or how he had been recruited into British intelligence. I mean it could not be that straightforward or amateurish, could it? His interactions with Muller and of course the Fixer made him feel that he was in a permanent snooker in which there was no geometric escape.

'I may be brave, but I'm not stupid. I am leaving for the States tomorrow.'

He declined to mention that half of the American Embassy staff were going on the same passage and with a heavily armed escort.

'I am not sure you guys have the wherewithal to hold out until Roosevelt can come to the rescue. The folks back home are not in any hurry to have their kids slaughtered in France… again.'

Ruben Miles had an odd view about the imminent invasion. Whilst most of his countrymen feared its inevitability, he doubted the plausibility of such an enterprise taken over water. Even taking into account the relatively short distance of the crossing, there was a reason that even Napoleon had never tried. However, like most of his thoughts, he kept this to himself.

'I will be back when it is possible and I will keep in touch, Ruben Miles. Men like you have a lot to offer in these troubled times. I was not surprised that Cavendish recruited you.'

Ruben Miles ignored the routine platitudes.

'What about your comrade?'

'Recalled to Moscow by Uncle Joe two weeks ago. Poor fucker did not know whether he was going to get a medal pinned on his chest or a bullet in the head when he got home. I believe that is the hallmark of Stalin's leadership technique. Unlimited power and drunken paranoia are not the most helpful of characteristics.'

Rueben Miles was gratified to have at least one continent between himself and the Russian. He still had occasional night tremors about that Spanish prisoner of war.

'I never did understand your relationship. How are you two on the same side of anything?'

'His ultimate boss and my bosses share the same view of Hitler. He has to be stopped and it might take a rather ungodly alliance to achieve that.'

He made it sound simple and of course plausible, but Rueben Miles was not buying what he was shovelling.

'We will work together in the future, Ruben Miles. I can assure you of that. As you are well aware, men like you will always be of value to men like me.'

'And that is why you have me at a disadvantage. I have no real idea of just what kind of man you are, or even what type of business you are ultimately involved with. I know you have no issue with breaking government laws and yet you claim that you work for the self-same government.'

'What's my name?'

Ruben Miles knew what he wanted to hear.

'The Fixer.'

'That's right, because I fix things. Let us say that I provide a service that links one world to another. Worlds who often do not even understand how mutually dependent they can be, in certain circumstances.'

'So, you do work for the US government?'

'That is one interpretation. Another would be that they work for me, or at least for my interests.'

'I don't understand.'

The Fixer headed for the front door, looking a little disappointed in Ruben Miles.

'When you worked for the Babe, who was the most powerful guy in America? I will give you a clue, it wasn't Calvin fucking Coolidge.'

By now he had reached the door and he paused as he held on to the handle.

'I'll give you another clue. He was a big fat wop who smoked Cuban cigars, banged teenagers two at a time and liked to hit people over the head with a baseball bat when they pissed him off.'

'Capone.'

'Of course Capone, genius. While you're thinking about that, I have another question for you to think about during my absence. How come you struck out with the Specialist and had to make do with her sister?'

And with that, the Fixer was gone. Unquestionably, he would be back.

BLITZKRIEG BOP

JoJo Bartlett had been fascinated by the story of the Blitz ever since she had watched *Goodnight Mr Tom* on TV as a ten year old. She had been impatiently waiting for Ruben Miles to get to events in London after September 1940.

'You did it in school?'

JoJo confirmed this was the case. Twice in fact. In primary school with Miss Gibson the Year Five teacher with a mild lisp and in Secondary in Year Eight with Mr Barber, a middle-aged bald man with chronic body odour. She always found it odd that she remembered teachers for their personal deficiencies.

'The Blitz spirit, yeah? Everyone pulling together to fight the enemy. Stiff upper lips and all in it together.'

'Something like that, yes.'

'Mostly rubbish, I'm afraid, at least from where I was standing.'

He could sense JoJo's disappointment.

'Don't get me wrong, there was plenty of that, of course. It's just there was also an awful lot of darker stuff too.'

'What do you mean?'

'Well, I bet your teachers didn't tell you about burglaries and robberies going through the roof and the rape and murder rates going off the Richter scale?'

JoJo's face told its own story.

'Didn't think so. Mind you, they are not the only ones to get it wrong. Most of the idiots who lived through it told a different tale ten years later. People look back with rose-tinted glasses about the past, just because they were younger themselves then. I've never understood that. Just because something was different years ago, does not make it better or worse. Just different.'

'So, tell me what it was really like?'

'Some good, a lot of bad and way too much death. Most of it just so random and unjust. That's what I remember when I think of the war and the Blitz in particular. Luck is the most underrated of life's essentials I would say.'

JoJo had never really thought about luck before.

Ruben Miles was touchy about the Blitz and with more than one good reason. He witnessed firsthand its randomness, its cruelty and occasionally even its benevolence. He figured that, like the men who came unscathed through the Somme or Passchendaele, London Blitz survivors all seemed to carry just a hint of survivor's guilt. They witnessed death and destruction. They all went in fear. They all said silent prayers of thanks when the bomb fell further down their street, on someone else's loved ones. And this was before the luck stakes were ramped up further with the tragically indiscriminate doodlebugs from June 1944.

'You also have to remember the context. The Blitz was supposed to be the prelude to the invasion. I am sure your teachers told you all about the brave boys of the RAF defeating the Luftwaffe and preventing the invasion?'

'Of course.'

'Well, at least that is mostly true. I mean it would not have been possible without the invention of radar, but there is no doubt the RAF boys did their bit. Mind you, I was never convinced Hitler's heart was ever in an invasion. I mean why did he stop bombing the RAF bases if he was going to invade?'

This was a question JoJo felt she couldn't answer.

'What do you remember of the Blitz?'

'JoJo, remember I can recall every long day of the Blitz, and the even longer nights.'

Ruben Miles's claims to have hyperthymesia were like an unspoken argument between lovers. JoJo oscillated between wanting to thrash it out once and for all or forget all about it, mostly at the same time.

'Even if I could not, I would have remembered the first night of the bombing, just like most folks. It was the night of another meeting I attended of the Nazi sympathisers. They had locked up Oswald after the fall of France, but there were still plenty of British men and women at large who wanted a Nazi invasion.'

Ruben Miles could not tell if JoJo was appalled or

disbelieving.

'I'm guessing that did not make the textbooks either.'

On the 7th of September 1940, the Luftwaffe turned their attention from the RAF airfields to London. Two thousand civilians were killed on the first night, many more were rendered homeless. For Ruben Miles, he had been attending a meeting of fifth columnists who had chosen the same evening seemingly by chance. The host was Sir Edmond Hawley-Banks, a retired merchant banker and fervent antisemite. At his palatial house on Grosvenor Square, he had invited a plethora of likeminded souls to enjoy ample refreshment and talk of treason. There was a retired army colonel, a Harley Street physician, a former crown court judge and selected landed gentry. A meeting of the great and the good.

Their amateurishness was even more breathtaking than that of British intelligence, who it was fair to say were woefully underprepared for the complexities and necessities of wartime espionage in 1940. Their Abwehr counterparts had been planting seasoned professionals in England since 1937 and had also collected a motley assortment of British citizens more than happy to side with the Führer.

Ruben Miles had been invited by Arthur Lyle, the civil servant with the loudmouth from the docks safety inspection. He had attended another meeting a few months before when, although he was expected, Oswald Mosley failed to attend and address, predominantly, his Blackshirts. He was interned a few short weeks later.

There was certainly no one with Mosley's oratory skills at Grosvenor Square, just a collection of half-drunk, upper-class racists. There was not a prole to be seen, apart from those employed to serve the drinks and hors d'oeuvres.

Lyle introduced Ruben Miles with the same introduction.

'He works on the docks and speaks fluent German.'

It was the latter piece of information that invariably got commented on.

His cover story was quite straightforward and involved at

least some general truths, interspersed with necessary deceits. He had served with distinction in the British Army during World War One. He had been converted to fascism and antisemitism during his time in a German prisoner of war camp and had gone on to fight in the Spanish Civil War, for Franco of course. The fifth columnists ate it all up eagerly with a spoon.

'Taught myself German to be ready, you know, when the inevitable happens.'

The one thing that was clear was how thick most of them were. Ruben Miles did not view himself as some intellectual force, but genuinely felt that if this was the best the fifth column could muster, then the Wehrmacht was going to have to do most of the hard yards themselves.

Sir Edmond Hawley-Banks was a case in point. Educated at Eton and Oxford, like a great many of the self-appointed ruling elite, he had gone on to increase his family fortune in the city. Mostly achieved by luck, knowing the right people and investing in South African gold and diamond mines.

'That's what I like about the Boers, they know how to keep the darkies down.'

Hawley-Banks was in his favoured position. He was consuming vintage champagne by the fireplace, monocle and cigar in situ, pontificating on the genetic inferiority of all non-white races. After the war he emigrated to Johannesburg and spent the last twenty years of his life rejoicing in the clarity and certainty of the apartheid regime; his attempted treason seemingly unpunished.

'You could be a handy chap for us, Jones.'

Ruben Miles wanted a cover name that he could not forget.

There were over twenty men at the meeting and none seemed remotely concerned about security, betrayal or the long arm of the law. Any mild cynicism they held toward Ruben Miles evaporated when he spoke in fluent German to the only other person in the group who could handle a very basic conversation.

Ruben Miles began to believe that British intelligence was amateurish and seemingly incompetent because they could afford to be. It was a view that changed considerably as the war dragged on.

The following day he travelled to Pimlico to brief Cavendish on the meeting. He took the bus and it took over an hour longer than usual as the streets were littered with debris, and an indignant clear-up operation had begun. Although the docks had been the main target, there was evidence of destruction throughout south London as the Clapham omnibus headed north for Vauxhall Bridge. The casualty figures were as yet unknown, but some of the houses on the Wandsworth Road spoke without ambiguity.

Cavendish seemed almost ebullient.

'We knew it was coming.'

They were in a small café in a back street near the Tate Gallery.

'Was there any mention of it by your new chums?'

Cavendish seemed to have an even lower opinion of the group than Ruben Miles.

'No, although when it started about six they all seemed to be in a hurry to seek shelter in the basement. Hawley-Banks seems very well prepared I must say, iron girder props and a fridge full of caviar, not to mention a wine cellar.'

'Are these serious people, Miles?'

'They may come across as spoilt fools, but there are one or two that seem a little more dangerous than that. They view the invasion as imminent and there was talk of contacting sleeper groups around the country.'

'Presumably for help with beach information and such for any attack. But surely without air superiority there can be no invasion?'

'I would certainly say so.'

'I suppose this bombing of the city could be a feint or even a one off, but that seems unlikely.'

'What are our sources saying?'

'That London is going to get more of the same.'

'They want me to go north with Lyle to make contact with a group in Northumberland, apparently the beaches there are most suitable for landing heavy artillery.'

'My God, you don't think they actually know anything?'

'No, nothing I have seen or heard tells me that they are much more than deluded fascists, but I don't think we can take that chance, do you? Besides, it's more names for the file, isn't it?'

Ruben Miles was heading back to his homeland, and for a reason he could never have imagined.

FAILED PLANS
AND ROAD TRIPS

I t was a close call as to which of the two plans was more inept. However, on balance, the notion of collecting blood samples from your parents by getting them to cut themselves was the winner. Luke Miles had certainly not improved his chequered intellectual reputation with this particular strategy. JoJo managed to hide her lack of surprise at the dismal failure of the ploy.

'You're going to have to talk to them, you know.'

They were on the A696 northbound heading toward the A68, having decided to take the more scenic route across the Scottish border and onwards to Edinburgh. The traffic was light, the weather warm and JoJo had put Band of Horses on the CD player. She had spent the evening before selecting six discs for the multi-changer that were least likely to get complaints from Luke Miles. So far, so good.

For his part, Luke Miles had no desire to conduct a post-mortem of his doomed plan, nor the correct assertion from JoJo Bartlett that he was going to have to have a conversation with his parents about whether there was any conclusive proof that they were blood relations or not. The ramifications of which were causing him sleepless nights.

Instead, he was savouring the thrill of expectation and nervousness that spending the first night with your first girlfriend produces. Of course, they had not directly discussed anything practical, nor had they booked a hotel room, but their plan to share a hotel room had been directly implied. What could possibly go wrong?

A hundred and fifty miles to the south, and Ruben Miles was beginning to get some of the feeling back in his legs. The cramp that was the result of his contortions to get into the low-slung passenger seat of the Smart Car. Ruben Miles would love to know what was so bloody smart about it.

Mrs Hazel Wharton was driving slightly erratically and often in the wrong gear. Ruben Miles knew better than to pass any comment. Besides, as he was accompanying her on her grim family research project, he had accumulated many brownie points and was not wanting to give any up so cheaply.

Ruben Miles had, by any stretch of anyone's imagination, lived a remarkable life. Among his many escapades, including personal involvement in some of the most historically important events of the twentieth century, but his current journey and prospective project took some getting his head around.

Mrs Hazel Wharton was adamant that her adopted son, Barry, was a serial killer responsible for the deaths of at least several missing person cases from the late 1980s and 1990s, including a young girl from near his childhood home. In her defence, Mrs Hazel Wharton also thought that the Royal Family were an important cultural influence on contemporary Britain.

In truth, she had produced some seemingly significant circumstantial evidence, most notably Barry Wharton's residential proximity to some of the disappearances. She had also done her best to portray Barry as having classic serial killer potential. There was the killing of the bird in the back garden, the general lack of empathy and even his failure to have any sort of relationship with his adopted father. For Mrs Hazel Wharton, this last piece of evidence may well be the one that troubled her the most.

Her husband Brian, by comparison, had been put on something of a pedestal by his wife during the course of their marriage. He was polite, hard-working, a good provider and he seemed completely disinterested in what Mrs Hazel Wharton defined as 'physical relations'. All of these traits were positives as far as Mrs Hazel Wharton was concerned.

During the course of their forty-five year marriage, her husband had never raised his voice to her, never mind a hand. Brian Wharton was pleasant if not overly chatty company. He never forgot her birthday or wedding anniversary. If Barry Wharton could not make peace with such a nice man, then clearly there was something very seriously wrong with *him*.

Mrs Hazel Wharton had just shared this synopsis with Ruben Miles for at least the fourth time.

'Where are we heading again? I know you have told me, but I can't remember.'

This was because he was not listening, rather than signs of memory failure.

Mrs Hazel Wharton shot him a quick, disapproving glance and nearly drove into the back of a braking white van ahead.

'Blackpool,' she said, when she had recovered her composure.

Of all of the grim family days out to Blackpool, this one might well be right up there. All they needed now was the ubiquitous stick of rock.

Things had taken a bleak turn in Edinburgh by early afternoon. Firstly, although it had been warm and sunny in Newcastle, JoJo Bartlett and Luke Miles arrived at the Scottish capital to be welcomed by a howling gale and horizontal torrential rain, the usual summer's fare in Edinburgh. As they traversed north through Meadowbank toward the city centre, Luke Miles began to notice the number of 'no vacancy' signs that illuminated the numerous bed and breakfast places that appeared on both sides of every street. However, he was not overly concerned. Surely there would be plenty of hotel rooms available in the city centre? He knew Scottish people were tight and assumed that they were all too cheap to stay in more central expensive accommodation. In reality, of course, there were no available rooms. They were full of shit comedians from Grantham and deluded mime artists from Croydon.

They arrived at a decently reviewed Travel Lodge on Waterloo Place. After taking half an hour to park the car in a nearby multi-storey car park and scratching the paint on the driver side door on the way out of the car, it was fair to say that JoJo Bartlett's enthusiasm for the whole 'weekend away in Edinburgh' thing with her boyfriend was losing some of its lustre. This was before the receptionist laughed in their faces when they asked for a hotel room, informing the incredulous receptionist with the revelation that no, they had not booked a room in advance.

'Surely not all the hotels are full?'

'You do know the festival is on, right?'

'What festival?' the teenagers said, simultaneously.

Cue more employee hilarity.

Three hotels later, and with the employee snigger count ever increasing, JoJo and Luke began to realise that they would be lucky to find a stable at this rate. It was not as if they could just explore the delights of the city on foot and find somewhere outside of town to stay later. The weather made any outdoor sightseeing a fool's errand. Both had dressed for summer, weather forecasts and hotel booking websites had been equally ignored.

They decided to make a run for the McDonald's on St Andrew's Street. It was much further along Princess Street than it looked on the dishevelled map they had liberated from their unsuccessful visit to a Premier Inn. By the time they had sat down they were soaked to the skin, miserable and feeling as sexy as a eunuch in an ice bath.

Not even their McFlurries could lighten their moods.

'So far, I would have to describe this trip as a partial success.'

JoJo gave a huge sneeze in response.

An hour later, things had taken a turn for the worse. They were on a guided tour of Mary King's Close, the underground labyrinth of streets below the Royal Mile. The guide was dressed up as an eighteenth-century whore and nothing pushed JoJo Bartlett's buttons more than the Disneyfication of history. Luke hardly assisted matters by openly trying to look down the young women's lacy shirt.

'At least we're out of the rain.'

The guide then made the mistake of asking if anyone had any questions.

JoJo Bartlett harnessed all her newfound reserves of burgeoning sociological feminism and indignant demand for historical accuracy in one demanding question.

The other tour guests even heckled her. The guide for her part just ignored the question and Luke Miles walked off, uttering that he had come away for the weekend with his girlfriend by mistake.

In Blackpool, Ruben Miles and Mrs Hazel Wharton had successfully checked into The Carousel Hotel, a small three star rated place on the New Promenade; twin beds, naturally. Mrs Hazel Wharton need not have concerned herself with the practicalities of the accommodation. Although Ruben Miles considered himself a ladies' man, he accepted that since he hit ninety there had been a noticeable diminishing of returns.

As they arrived at six-thirty in the early evening, it was way past their regular dinner time. This seemed to cloud both of their decision-making processes. Twenty minutes later, they were huddled on a seat on the promenade, unable to see the grey sea because of the ugly new casino on the seafront. Between them, they shared a below average haddock supper with what purported to be mushy peas. Like a lot of fast food, it delivered a lot less than anticipated.

'And the plan is?'

Ruben Miles was keen to change the topic of conversation from Mrs Hazel Wharton's musings on how long it had been since the chip shop had changed its oil in the fat fryers.

'We will finish this and have an early night.'

'I was thinking more about tomorrow's schedule.'

'I want to go to speak to the detective who handled the case, he's retired now, of course, and possibly try and interview a relative or two.'

Ruben Miles was genuinely surprised that there was a coherent plan.

HOMEWARD BOUND

Ruben Miles took the sleeper train from Kings Cross, sharing a compartment with the rather loathsome Lyle. It was the seventh night of the Blitz and Londoners were already beginning to wonder how much of this they could take. The total blackout made for an even longer and duller journey. In the tiny compartment, Ruben Miles could hear Lyle imbibe a sizeable flask of scotch. It was at times such as these that he never questioned his commitment to sobriety.

Ruben Miles had been given no formal training by British intelligence. Cavendish had offered a few general and rather unhelpful pieces of groundless and vague advice as he was about to go undercover with self-confessed fifth columnists. He finished with the truly insipid, 'Keep your wits about you'.

Lyle was on his own piece of official government business. He was heading north to check standards, procedures and precautions at the huge Clydebank docks. The less official order he had received from Hawley-Banks was to hand Ruben Miles over to a waiting contact on platform nine of the central station in Newcastle. He would then complete his onward journey to Glasgow as required.

Ruben Miles had tried without success to get Lyle to enlighten him about the purpose and likely outcome of the trip.

Lyle, for his part, was clearly beginning to regret bringing Ruben Miles into the treacherous fold. It had become clear even after a few relatively short meetings, that he was viewed in a more positive light than long-term fascists like himself. Indeed, there were the beginnings of a grudge. Ruben Miles was not concerned. He was well aware that he tended to attract some level of general animosity from most men that he met, without ever thinking to wonder why.

Ruben Miles spent most of the long night thinking about his mother and the children he abandoned with her before he had headed for the conflict in Spain. It was only four years ago, but it felt much longer. Despite his memory, he had been successful at keeping these images to a minimum in the intervening period. However, he had a permanent, irremovable visual file depicting his tucked up kids in his childhood bed as he sneaked brazenly out the back parlour door. Sometimes it concerned him how little guilt he felt. But not often.

Despite his paucity of introspection, the darkness of the night, the relentless sound of Lyle snoring and the almost hypnotic rhythm of the tracks seemed to put Ruben Miles into a kind of half sleep, with memories of his childhood and more looping in his mind like a broken projector. Lyle woke him with an aggressive shake as the train trundled into Newcastle. Although not yet sunrise, the blackness of the night had melted almost completely away.

His contact was a man of few words and an almost impenetrable Geordie accent. He said merely, 'We've booked you a room at the Royal Station Hotel. We don't pay expenses. After all, we're not fucking communists.'

The man laughed gruffly at his own comment.

'I will be back at eleven to take you to the meeting. I will wait outside.'

And with that he was gone, leaving Ruben Miles to push through the revolving doors into a still plush, though clearly Victorian, lobby.

After a tepid bath and a shave, Ruben Miles felt marginally better and managed a light but adequate breakfast in the hotel facilities before going outside to wait for his contact to reappear. He was late but offered neither an apology nor any form of greeting. Instead, he gestured for Ruben Miles to get into the cramped passenger seat of a black Austin 7.

It was a pleasant change to be driving through a city without any bomb damage, but within a few minutes they had headed north out of Gosforth for open countryside. He quickly got his bearings and realised they were heading in a north easterly direction towards the coast. He could actually smell the sea through the slightly open window on the driver's side, a cigarette wedged in his otherwise firmly closed lips.

However, they were not heading directly for the coast. Instead, and much to Ruben Miles's surprise, the car drove through his birthplace, Morpeth, and then on northwards toward the small village of Longhirst. As the car pulled up inside the gates of Longhirst Hall, a John Dobson-designed building dating from the early 1820s, Ruben Miles was almost tasting his teenage years spent in the family home less than a few miles from where he now disembarked from the car. His head was swimming with so many images, and few of them welcome. He was unable to stem the flow. It gave him his usual headache. But he managed to brush these disconcerting visions temporarily to one side as a tall, heavily built man descended the stone steps from the entrance to the hall and offered forth his large right hand. His left arm lay limply at his side, the result of a severed tendon received at the Battle of Mons.

'Nathan Jones? I am Sir Roger Benedict. We are so glad you could join us. We have heard good things about you.'

Benedict did not mention that he was a baronet and second cousin to Elizabeth Bowes-Lyons, the wife of King George VI.

'Nice to meet you, sir.'

'Well, come in man, we are just getting started.'

He was ushered into a grand drawing room with a huge marble fireplace as its focal point. There were three Regency red Chesterfield sofas placed in an almost-arc around the fire. Ruben Miles was ushered toward one of the several accompanying single seat pieces and sat down.

'We were just discussing the anti-tank defences at Druridge Bay. I think our mutual friend has the photographs.'

Benedict gestured toward a still attractive woman, seemingly in her early sixties, who was sitting to his right. She had several photographs in her hand and a look of bemused anxiety on her face.

She was Ruben Miles's mother.

MOTHER DEAREST

Ruben Miles had no recollection of his mother holding any, never mind extreme, political views. He could not recall a single political conversation from his childhood. You could describe both of his parents as having unconventional views, but more in a moral and sexual context, rather than political. He recognised her of course immediately and, like her only child, she looked much younger than her years and had hardly gained a wrinkle since their last encounter. Ruben Miles wondered for a second if she was going to give him up on the spot, but she recovered her facial expression swiftly and hardly missed a beat before she declared, 'I was able to take these pictures in good light and with relative ease. I have a feeling that the local authorities think that the threat of invasion may be exaggerated.'

This brought murmurs of agreement from the several other 'all male' members of the group.

Benedict spoke next.

'The beaches on our coastline are among the widest and easiest to deploy significant troops on in the entire country. In addition, we know that the sands are well suited to supporting the unloading of heavy artillery and tanks.'

Ruben Miles was now sure that his mother would not give him away. He was also sure that these fifth columnists may be more of a threat than he and Cavendish had previously envisaged. Benedict was particularly impressive and clearly more intelligent than the various crackpots he had encountered in London.

'We believe that our communication lines have been temporarily compromised and the Abwehr chaps think that this information is too important to take a chance with. Therefore, this evening they are going to surface a U-boat off Holy Island and you, Mr Jones, are going to row out to meet it and hand over the photographs and other data we have accrued.'

This led to more murmuring. This time of incredulity.

'Because I speak German?'

'Partially yes, but also because they asked for the 'new chap' to be the delivery boy.'

Ruben Miles hoped that his poker experience meant that he had managed to give nothing away in his facial demeanour, but inside he was reeling. First his mother reappears in the most unlikely of circumstances and now the Abwehr appear to know of his existence. What next?

Next turned out to be a formal three course lunch in which he was seated between his mother and Sir Roger Benedict.

'I can always tell a veteran, where were you?'

'The Somme.'

'Bad show. I got this at Mons.'

He motioned with his head toward his left arm.

'I do find it slightly ironic that so many of our people fought in the bloody trenches against the Germans. What turned you?'

At least it was to the point. Cavendish had insisted that Ruben Miles go for excessive antisemitism as opposed to any other reason for his pro-Nazi cover story.

He told a rather elaborate tale of personal misfortune at the hands of international Jewry. Ruben Miles thought it rather clumsy and overlong, but Benedict seemed to accept it all unquestioningly.

'I agree, this war is about race, not nationality. If only that bloody drunken fool Churchill could see that.'

Almost all the fifth columnists that Ruben Miles had met were white supremacists. It was their unifying ideology. He feigned enthusiasm.

'I couldn't agree more.'

Throughout this interaction Ruben Miles's mother had been engaged in quiet conversation with a man on her right, who happened to be a policeman from Haddington in East Lothian. He had brought data about the beaches further to the north in Scotland. But now she turned towards her son and said, 'Mr Jones, you do look familiar to me, are you certain we haven't met before?'

'I think that is very unlikely. Are you in London much?'

'Never. I can't stand the place.'

'Well, I hadn't left London for some years until yesterday.'

They continued the charade for the rest of the meal. Once again, Ruben Miles could not quite believe the ludicrously cavalier approach that these conspirators had for security. Moreover, some of the group did not even wait for the servers to depart the room before launching into another scathing attack on Churchill, the inevitability of a successful invasion or of course the scourge that was the Jewish and other inferior races. Ruben Miles had heard it all before, but at least this time it was semi-articulate.

At length, as Sir Benedict went off in search of a post-prandial beverage, Ruben Miles found himself alone with his mother by the French windows overlooking the excessive formal gardens to the south of the building.

'I would never have had you down as a Nazi sympathiser.'

'I could say the same.'

Although Ruben Miles could see how some of her parental methods could be used as evidence against her.

'Are you going to do it? I didn't think you looked too keen.'

'Of course, we have to make sure that they have all of the data that you have collected.'

His mother eyed him with suspicion.

'I don't recall you having any in the way of strong political convictions.'

'Again, I could say the same.'

They stood in awkward silence for a few moments.

'I assume the name change is for a good reason, or is it just so your own children can't track you down?'

She was always capable of a powerful opening thrust. But at least it explained the name change.

'The Reds are still after me after my actions in Spain, it was the sensible thing to do.'

Sometimes a lie is easier if it contains a fragment of truth.

However, he was spared further questioning by the returning Sir Benedict, working hand firmly grasping a large tumbler of Laphroaig.

'Right, Jones, all set for tonight? I will get someone to fetch your belongings from the hotel. I take it you are travelling light?'

'Yes, that's fine.'

'We will need to set off by about eight, it's at least an hour's run, even in the Bentley.'

Two hours later, Ruben Miles was reflecting on a lifetime lacking in meaningful interaction with his own mother. This fact had seemed to please her as much as it did him. His relationship with his mother had always been strained and distant. As a child he was largely ignored, receiving only affection from the housemaid, Celia. As he grew older, his mother seemed even less interested in his development. During his early teenage years their interactions were limited and perfunctory. The day he left to join the army, she did not even say goodbye. He wondered privately whether this was why he felt so little for his own children.

This was what occupied the thoughts of Ruben Miles as the Bentley thundered north through the dusk evening light towards Holy Island. Sir Benedict had opted not to come along for the ride.

'No need, Jones, you will be in excellent hands with Armstrong, my driver.'

Armstrong was the monosyllabic, cartoon-like villain who had met him at the railway station and drove him to Longhirst Hall that very morning, which felt like a week ago.

'He will take you to the boat and even row for you. It will be a piece of cake. I can't see there being any local bobbies getting in the way. However, one must always take precautions.'

Benedict handed him a Browning automatic pistol.

'I don't need to ask whether you can use this, I can always tell when a man has killed others. It is in their eyes. You have eyes made of ice, Jones.'

He sounded like a posh version of the Fixer.

'I have my own, thanks,' replied Ruben Miles, patting the left side of his jacket where he had his old but reliable Webley tucked out of sight.

The journey was uneventful and silent. Neither Armstrong nor Ruben Miles offering any conversation. Ruben Miles had his childhood and mother for company, not the most comforting of companions.

Holy Island is a tidal island off the Northumberland coast north of Bamburgh. It is linked to the mainland by a causeway that is twice daily submerged under incoming tides. This means that there are safe crossing times and well, unwise crossing times.

'Fuck,' offered Armstrong when the Bentley approached the beginning of the causeway, clearly submerged under a few feet of water. Before Ruben Miles could offer an opinion, Armstrong nudged the Bentley into the water.

'The rowing boat is on the island. If we can't get there, how are you going to get to the U-boat?'

Ruben Miles had not even thought about Holy Island, until it had been mentioned that day, for over thirty years. And with or without hyperthymesia he believed that he would have remembered that the island was only accessible from the mainland for a limited part of any day. He had actually assumed that the boat was on the mainland and they would have rowed out to the U-boat from there.

'Fuck,' offered Armstrong again as the Bentley found itself in even deeper water. They were only several feet onto the causeway.

'I think we may need a plan B. Did Benedict not check the tides?'

Armstrong gave a 'What do you fucking think?' look. Clearly, his face offered a good deal more conversation than his mouth.

Armstrong managed to reverse the car out of the seawater. They both got out of the car and strained their eyes in the fading light to see if there was anything nearby that could be used as a plan B.

'We need to go to the harbour at Seahouses and find an alternative mode of transport that floats.'

Armstrong agreed.

They drove in silence. As they got nearer the harbour it was clear that there was some, albeit rudimentary, security. A lone copper on the beat, his bowlegs ambling along the sea wall. He appeared to be whistling a Vera Lynn tune badly.

There was a small boat that looked eminently stealable bobbing gently in the light swell about a hundred yards from their position.

Armstrong gestured to a torch he had produced.

'This should take care of him,' he said, his right hand mimicking a downward thrust toward the policeman.

'That shouldn't be necessary.'

Ruben Miles thought about his options. A successful operation was probably not in his best interests. That being said, failure would have to be justified. He knew he could shoot Armstrong if he had to. In fact, he concluded quickly that he would not mind that outcome in any way. He certainly did not want to have to murder a policeman, especially not for a cause he was trying to subvert. Not that he liked policemen. As far as Ruben Miles was concerned there was not a one you could trust or even rely on. This view would be vindicated later in his life.

There was also the nagging concern that the Nazis knew he was a spy and planned to take him with them after the data handover. His memories of the Russian's methods of interrogation made him in no hurry to experience the Nazi version.

On balance, a successful operation would potentially give the enemy some benefit. But Ruben Miles was rather sceptical of the quality of the data being supplied by the Northumberland fifth columnists. Would a few photographs of some concrete anti-tank defences on Druridge Bay have any impact on a possible incoming invasion? It seemed highly improbable. Especially when the RAF was still very much in business and in control of the skies. Quickly, and with the certainty that he wanted sufficient evidence to have Armstrong, Benedict, Hawley-Banks, Lyle and possibly his own mother locked up for treachery, Ruben Miles decided on his course of action.

He produced a small bottle of chloroform and a cloth from his inside jacket pocket. Cavendish had given it to him before his departure, claiming its universal usage by field operatives.

'You know what this is?'

Armstrong reached for the bottle and cloth without replying.

'Don't use more than a little of the bottle on the cloth, we only need him to be out for a couple of hours. How far is the rendezvous point from here?'

'It depends how quick you can row... no more than fifteen minutes, I would say.'

'I thought you were rowing?'

'Change of plans.'

The pair watched the policeman continue on his circular route around the small marina.

'We could put him in the Bentley.'

Ruben Miles scanned the nearby warehouses used for small boat maintenance. There were a couple of rustic looking doors that could be useful. He motioned to Armstrong to keep watching the copper. The first door he approached was firm, locked and unyielding. The second was more promising: although there was a small and unconvincing lock, the door was badly fitted and looked as if it could be forced with a modicum of effort. He reported his findings to Armstrong.

The way they agreed on a plan silently proved to Ruben Miles that Armstrong was either ex-military, always the most likely scenario for men his age, or he was a villain, which is what he looked like. He was of course both.

The night was light because of a clear sky and a full moon. It was what Londoners were already calling a 'bomber's night'. The old bobby was approaching now, still whistling out of tune. With an efficiency that impressed even Ruben Miles, Armstrong waited for the best moment and had knocked out the policeman using the chloroform and bundled him up in his arms on the floor without so much as a peep. They double checked that no one else was in the vicinity before easily forcing the warehouse door, placing the prone body carefully on some discarded rags in a corner and went back out into the night.

The little boat was not well tied and, in short order, Ruben Miles gingerly climbed aboard. He was very much an infantryman. To his surprise, Armstrong clambered in after him.

'To show you the way,' he said, sitting in the stern of the boat, away from the oars.

After a fumbling false start, Ruben Miles quickly found a sustainable rhythm and the little boat made for the harbour exit. Within five minutes they were in open water. They were both more than grateful for the relative flat calm that awaited them.

'OK, you can stop rowing now, Jones.'

Ruben Miles found himself squinting in the moonlight at a clearly amused Armstrong.

'You don't actually think there is a U-boat out here, do you?'

'What are you talking about? Is this some kind of joke?'

'Let's just say that we wanted to see how committed you were to our little project.'

Ruben Miles joined the dots quite quickly from there, relieved that he was not about to become a plaything for a Nazi torture expert.

'I think I'll be able to tell Benedict that you passed with flying colours. I think it's time we headed for home, don't you?'

A little over an hour later, they were back at Longhirst Hall and Ruben Miles found himself ushered into a darkened room at the back of the building. Sitting at the table were Sir Benedict and Hawley-Banks, both looking more self-satisfied than usual. No mean feat.

'No hard feelings, Jones? We have to be sure we can just trust new chaps. I mean you could have been anybody, even a government stooge.'

Ruben Miles supposed he could have worked this out. A U-boat surfacing riskily for such a scant reward did, with the benefit of hindsight, seem at the very least unlikely.

'We have some things we would like you to do for us when you return to London tomorrow. Firstly, you can deliver the data we have collected to an associate. I will supply you with the details later, suffice to say it is just a handover, nothing complicated. However, the second task may require a little more... finesse.'

Hawley-Banks now interrupted his fellow conspirator.

'We need you to find a way to get a message into Mosley. He and his wife are being kept in a little house in the grounds of Holloway prison.'

It would seem that Ruben Miles would have quite a lot to brief Cavendish on after all.

'You will find we have placed your luggage in the guest bedroom on the first floor. There is a sign saying 'trust and honour' in a small frame. Rather apt, what?'

Ruben Miles smiled and nodded, imagining which of these two aristocrats he would have liked to pistol-whip in the face first.

DALKEITH IS NOT
THE NEW PARIS

If you want romance, so they say, head for Paris. Under no circumstances should you pitch up in Dalkeith, Midlothian. Once described, albeit rather harshly, as the 'arsehole of the world'. Clearly said by someone who has never been to Galashiels. Dalkeith lies to the southeast of the Scottish capital and its most attractive feature is a one-way road system.

Luke Miles and JoJo Bartlett had abandoned their attempts to find a hotel room in central Edinburgh during the festival. At least this would be a life lesson they both heeded as they never went anywhere again without an online booking confirmation printed out.

By chance (they took the wrong exit from the large roundabout just off the city bypass), they found themselves in Dalkeith. Tiredness and general irritability led them to knock on the door of a rather austere looking B & B on Eskbank Road, near to a little Italian restaurant they had both spotted as they drove past.

They worried about whether they would be able to get a room together. This proved to be wasted emotion as the landlady was as interested in their circumstances as she was in the recent Bromley and Chislehurst by-election.

It would be an exaggeration to say that they were 'shown' to their room. Vaguely pointed at would be a closer definition. The décor inside was as warm as their welcome. JoJo silently thanked a God she did not believe in that it was August because if it had been February she may well have burst into tears.

They put their little cases on the double bed. They were as pitiful as the surroundings. JoJo felt an emotion she had not experienced before: regret.

'Pizza?' offered Luke.

Did he mean a takeaway from the Domino's down the street?

'The little Italian place looked alright.'

JoJo offered forth her second theological thanksgiving in short order.

Twenty minutes later they were ensconced in a corner table of an Italian restaurant that was as authentic as you would expect from an Italian restaurant in Dalkeith in 2006. The waiter was called Jock, and he recommended a couple of 'voddie chasers' as an aperitif. On the wall was a poster of Pope Benedict XVI.

JoJo looked at the laminated menu and smiled at Luke with as much enthusiasm as she could manage (the vodka had not arrived yet – Jock was more efficient at suggestions than doing his actual job).

'It's not been exactly what we planned, has it?'

Luke Miles conceded that his expectations for their trip had, as yet, not materialised.

JoJo scanned his comment for teenage male sexual innuendo and the jackpot buzzer was ringing in her head. She had to shake her head to make it stop.

'We can still have a memorable night, though.'

She was beginning to think that things could actually get worse.

Earlier in the day, nearly two hundred miles southwest of the Italian restaurant in Dalkeith, Ruben Miles was wondering how he had managed to get himself into his current situation. Mrs Hazel Wharton was sitting next to him on a sofa in Lytham St Annes in the home of a retired detective of the Lancashire constabulary. He was sipping warm, sweet tea. Former Detective Weston was trying, without a great deal of success, to pour cold water on the line of questioning being offered by Mrs Hazel Wharton.

'I can accept that your son...'

'Adopted son.'

'I can accept that your adopted son lived in the area at the time of the disappearance, but there is no other, even vaguely circumstantial, evidence.'

'Detective Weston, here is a list of missing persons, the last known location sighting and the known address of my adopted son at the very time the poor unfortunates went missing.'

She handed over the list. Former Detective Weston looked at the neatly written addresses, the coloured in maps and highlighted areas. There were five names on the list. He could not deny that this was certainly coincidental.

'Has he ever been questioned?'

'I don't think so, but I would not know – even if we spoke, it is not the sort of conversation he was ever likely to volunteer, is it?'

Ruben Miles felt he was doing his bit by being physically there. He certainly was not keen to say anything.

'All that I am asking, is that you share this information with some of your ex-colleagues and see if someone will do the right thing. By the right thing I mean someone actually make an effort to find the person who is responsible for these women disappearing off the face of the universe.'

The list had been edited since it was first shown to Ruben Miles. There had been incorrect information and clarification that a number of incidents had occurred in places that her adopted son used to live, but in fact he had vacated the area in the weeks leading up to the disappearance. Even this fact raised further unanswered questions. But at the behest of Ruben Miles, Mrs Hazel Wharton was concentrating on the five remaining names on the list.

Aside from their seeming proximity to the adopted son of Mrs Hazel Wharton, there were other traits that the five women shared. They all disappeared without a trace in broad daylight and only the body of poor Lisa Pendleton was ever discovered subsequently. They were aged between eighteen and twenty-three. They all had boyfriends that had been questioned by the police at length but never charged with any crime. There had been no contact with their families ever since their disappearances. The cases all happened in consecutive years from 1996.

Detective Weston agreed to see what he could do.

'But I want you to leave this to the professionals, Mrs Wharton, can I have your word that you are not going to take your enquiries further?'

Mrs Hazel Wharton happily lied to Detective Weston and thanked him for the untouched tea she placed carefully back on the adjacent coffee table. It took Ruben Miles three attempts to get out of the soft sofa chair and follow Mrs Hazel Wharton out of the hall doorway, offering silent thanks to Detective Weston as they left.

DOCTOR JOSEPH

Cavendish seemed more irritated than grateful for the details in Ruben Miles's oral report of his trip to Northumberland. He looked thoughtfully at Ruben Miles and said,

'A U-boat? Seriously, Miles, you thought that was likely?'

'With the benefit of hindsight, I can see your point. But they were quite convincing. What choice did I have?'

'I suppose that's true. I bloody knew Oswald would come back to haunt us, even after he has been interned with that mad wife of his.'

Cavendish was not even a moderate swearer, unlike most of the residents of London that Ruben Miles had encountered. Most of the inhabitants of Du Cane Court seemed to use the f-word as a form of punctuation.

'I went to school with the Baronet, Winchester College. He was both a bully and a coward.'

Ruben Miles had been thinking of the task given to him by Benedict and Hawley-Banks. In essence, he could see no significant danger in giving Mosley a message from a bunch of fellow crackpots. After all, unless there was a successful invasion, Mosley was not going to be having much influence any time soon. He said as much to Cavendish.

'Have you been given the message?'

'No, but as I say, how is it going to be significant? For all I know it could just be another pointless test of my fascist credentials.'

Cavendish seemed to mull on this point for a while.

'Without air superiority the Nazis can't invade. As long as this Blitz goes on then the RAF airfields are secure and those damaged can be repaired and remain operational. Do you think it is possible that Hitler doesn't know he may have lost the Battle of Britain already?'

'And without an invasion, Mosley is, at best, a busted flush.

So, what harm can be done by giving him a message?'

'The harm it can do is tell these damn idiots that you work for us. How else would you be able to get access to see the man?'

This had not occurred to Ruben Miles. He had been concentrating on whether he should give the message or what would be in the message, not how it could be done convincingly enough to satisfy the fifth columnists.

'Should I tell them that it is not possible to get in to see him?'

'Not yet. First, you have to try and get in to see him as an ordinary citizen. When that fails, which I assume it will, then you tell them that it was not possible because of the security. Unless they expect you to try and break him out or something?'

They both laughed at this suggestion.

The following day, Ruben Miles delivered the data package to a new contact at the agreed meeting point, a bus stop on Baker Street. As the man disappeared quickly, Ruben Miles realised that a small scrap of paper had been placed in his jacket pocket, a telephone number scrawled on it.

He called it from a nearby phone box. He was given an address in Marylebone. The woman on the telephone said a time and then hung up.

Ruben Miles was now sensing that, with the elongated cloak and dagger methodology now employed by the fifth columnists, they may deserve more respect. He headed for the Harley Street address he had been given, at the allotted time, making sure as always that he would not be late. Ruben Miles was becoming quite fastidious about punctuality as he embraced early middle age.

He found number one hundred and seven and pressed the buzzer for number four. The little name tag said Dr Benjamin Joseph. With a click the door unlocked and Ruben Miles went inside.

Dr Benjamin Joseph was a short, wiry, middle-aged man with a shaven head and a handlebar moustache, rather a Lenin look for a fascist. He spoke in an aristocratic tone but with a faint hint of a Cornish burr. He was very much a bottom line person for a psychiatrist.

'Here is the message for Mosley. They tell me you are an interesting character, Mr Jones. I believe you served at the Somme, is that correct?'

Ruben Miles pocketed the proffered envelope without examining its contents. This clearly surprised Dr Joseph, although Ruben Miles had correctly surmised that any message would be coded and therefore there was little point examining its content.

'Are you not curious as to the content of the message?'

'Curiosity is not a trait that I appear to have.'

'And yet you are here to assist our worthy cause.'

'I am here to pick up a message. A message that I shall then attempt to get to Mr Mosley. But as I am sure you and your colleagues are aware, getting that message to the man may be less than straightforward.'

Dr Joseph motioned for Ruben Miles to take a seat on the couch of his profession. As he sat, he said, 'I presume the easiest method would be to conceal the message within a gift of some sort. You should be able to get to see him quite easily with a little preparation. One of the factors in selecting you for this role is your uncanny similarity to his cousin, one Brendan Curzon, from the Irish side of his family. I take it you can manage a little accent mimicry?'

Ruben Miles conceded he may be able to manage such a feat.

'You simply need to slip him the message because you will not be given any privacy by the guards. Do you have a wife who can bake a cake? I understand they are allowing small treats like that in.'

Ruben Miles suggested that he may be capable of such a domestic chore himself. Satisfied that they had concluded the real purpose of their meeting, he was about to leave when the Doctor said, 'Do you remember much about the war? A lot of my patients suffer from shell shock and other related traumas that have hugely impeded their memories. Many cannot recollect a single episode.'

'Actually, I have an excellent memory. I can remember almost every moment in detail.'

'Every moment? What do you mean by that?'

'I just seem to be able to remember all days clearly in my mind.'

Dr Joseph looked sceptical. But his interest in the capacity of the human memory was long-held and therefore required further enquiries.

Ruben Miles had not discussed his memory with any person before that day in the autumn of 1940. The vagaries of fate that had brought him to Dr Joseph's consulting surgery were to be cogitated upon at a later date. As a person, one only ever lives within themselves, they often assume that any special gifts they have are actually nothing of the sort. Ruben Miles was still of the belief that there must be many people who could remember the contents of their life in such incredible detail. It was something that he gave very little reflection to.

'Are you suggesting that you can recall entire days of your war experience?'

'Actually, I can remember every day of my life since I was about eleven. It is a little less clear before then.'

Dr Joseph looked incredulous.

'But that is preposterous! The human mind does not have the capacity to remember so much detail over such an elongated period of time. Surely, you are exaggerating.'

'Pick a date, any date you like and I will be able to tell you what I did on that day.'

It seemed as if Ruben Miles himself invented his own parlour game.

This did not get much credence from the good doctor.

'Any convincing liar can come up with a good yarn.'

Ruben Miles consented that this was indeed true but as he was not in a hurry, he was happy to answer any questions he might have about his memory and its capabilities. His own interest had been piqued by Doctor Joseph's assertion that most people certainly did not have the ability to remember their lives in such detail.

'Are you saying that my memory is special in some way? Is it not common to remember so much of one's life?'

'I have certainly not read or heard of anyone claiming to be able to do what you say you can do. If true, it would be fascinating to try and understand the processes involved.'

'Pick a date.'

Doctor Joseph's expression had gone from dismissive to intrigued.

As I do not have any further appointments this afternoon, I think I will indulge myself for a few moments. Let's try the 22nd of June 1917.'

'Friday 22nd June 1917. I was in a prisoner of war camp in Germany, I had been since July 5th 1916. The only thing of consequence that happened that day was I was able go to the toilet for the first time in a week, as I had been terribly constipated.'

Dr Joseph was trained to detect obvious lies and falsehoods. He could detect neither in the words, demeanour or actions of the man he knew as Mr Jones. He also was thinking how he could check whether the date was actually a Friday.

'So, your war experience was relatively short, and presumably monotonous from the point of capture and yet you claim you can still observe tiny differences?'

'That's right. Why don't you try the 1920s or 1930s, my days were a little more interesting then.'

By chance of an extraordinary nature, Doctor Joseph chose the very date that Ruben Miles had killed the two gangsters outside the speakeasy in Brooklyn to save the young woman who would become a movie star. Thus, creating for him something of a dilemma.

'Could you perhaps pick another date?'

Of course, Doctor Joseph presumed the incorrect assertion from this request.

'Stumped you already, have I?' He said somewhat triumphantly.

His attitude must have irked Ruben Miles as he replied, 'Don't be foolish, Doctor Joseph. It's just that if I tell you the real events of my life on that day, you will think I am lying as the odds of you picking that actual day were, shall we say, rather large to say the least.'

The doctor chewed on this for a few moments.

'Explain yourself more.'

'The events of that day are some of the most memorable of my entire life and if I tell you, you will be convinced that I am making this all up and for some reason that I cannot really explain, I do not want that to happen.'

More quiet reflection.

'Very well. But if I pick another date, you can tell me about the other more memorable day later perhaps?'

The turn of Ruben Miles to ponder.

'That seems equitable.'

The Doctor selected a less exceptional date from the late 1920s. He seemed accepting of the rather brief description of the routine chores of replacing the solid, liquid and fleshy daily essentials of the Babe. Ruben Miles decided to tell the Doctor the name of his old boss.

'The baseball player?'

It seemed the good Doctor was a rare breed himself.

'He wasn't just a baseball player. He was *the* baseball player. The Babe was more famous than the President.'

Trying to convince the average Englishman on the importance of baseball to the twentieth century American was a futile business. After all, how could anybody be so invested in a glorified game of rounders? Trying to explain the importance and status of an overweight baseball player was literally a waste of time.

'And you were sort of a personal butler figure?'

'Let's just say I had to cater for his rather extensive personal requirements, and on a daily basis.'

It still made Ruben Miles smile to think of the daily consumption of all the commodities required by the Babe.

'And what about that date I picked before, May 19th 1928.'

Ruben Miles made a quick decision.

'That was too easy a day to remember. I got engaged to a

324 | Mark Newies

beautiful women called Barbara on that day. We had a picnic in central park – chicken salad and white wine for her, corn beef and root beer for me. We made love three times in the evening, at her apartment for the first time, on the Upper East Side.'

Ruben Miles had suddenly felt that confessing to a double murder, despite the years and huge ocean between them, was at best a dubious action. And something about the good doctor told him that telling him something so combustible was a poor idea.

The doctor seemed pacified.

'I can see how that day was so easily remembered.'

As a latent homosexual, Doctor Joseph could see no reason to boast about multiple acts of sexual intercourse with a woman.

'I can see that you are not taking my memory very seriously, Doctor Joseph. Perhaps I should leave and go about delivering the message.'

'On the contrary. I am intrigued, if a little sceptical, sir. Perhaps you could visit me another time? After I have been able to conduct some research? I have a colleague more specialised in the most recent work on the human mind.'

Ruben Miles was at least a little flattered that his memory might be something worth a little scientific research and agreed that a future appointment would be possible, but clearly on a complimentary basis, as he had no need of the Doctor's professional abilities.

NOT LIKE ON THE INTERNET

JoJo Bartlett was in the shower the morning after the night before. Luke Miles was still in bed, lightly but persistently snoring. It had woken her at about six-thirty and she could not get back to sleep. It was only good manners and a desire not to communicate that had prevented her from digging him purposefully in the ribs. As she completed her morning routine, washing her hair laboriously twice and then conditioning once, naturally she reflected on the events of the evening before. She concluded that she felt somewhere between relieved and disappointed. It had not been the most pleasant experience. It had been clumsy, unfulfilling, slightly uncomfortable and ultimately rather messy, but at least the deed was done.

Most of the girls at school had lost their virginity in Year Ten or Eleven, so waiting until the end of Year Twelve had made JoJo feel something akin to an old maid. She had of course viewed pornography, but everything about that had felt somewhat deceitful. She could not talk to her parents about sex, obviously. I mean, don't you have to be very suspicious of those parents that say they are comfortable talking about sex with their kids? JoJo certainly thought so. Then, of course, there had been the whole *catastrophe* episode, which still felt like more of a scene from *Shameless* than her own life.

The girls at school had been as educational and helpful as a Daily Mail editorial. In other words, they lied about pretty much everything to do with the subject that did not fit in with their own very narrow and prejudiced world view. Most described athletic sessions with slightly older, handsome and skilled swordsmen, and recounted tales of simultaneous orgasms. In many ways more deluded than even politicians. So, like she presumed a great many young teenage women before her did, JoJo dealt with losing her virginity alone. And don't even get her started on the sex ed at school. I mean, condoms on a carrot? About as relevant as algebra.

She assumed that it would get better with practice, like revising for exams or manipulating a friend to do what you wanted them to do. She still liked being with Luke. He made her laugh and she found him handsome in a boyish kind of way. As she towelled her shoulder length hair dry, she was disturbed to admit to herself that she was missing speaking to the old man about his life. Like her, he had gone away for the weekend on a secret mission with the lady that he was friends with. JoJo did not know what to make of Mrs Hazel Wharton. She seemed nice enough.

Ruben Miles had described it as a 'dirty weekend without the good parts'.

What does this say about me? she thought. I spend the night with a boy for the first time and I'm thinking about a very elderly man and his rather tall tales. Just then, she heard a very loud three-note crescendo fart from the bedroom. It was like a small brass band tuning up in the corner of the room. This romance thing was already proving to be something of a challenge.

Mrs Hazel Wharton had also been reflecting on the nature of physical relationships, but from a slightly different perspective. She knew that Ruben Miles was not interested in such things anymore. He had told her as much, bluntly, over tea and scones when they first got to know each other. Apparently, when he hit ninety his penis had decided to retire, undefeated. At least that is what he had said with a warm smile.

It was her late husband Brian she was thinking about. She found herself doing this more regularly these days. If she was being truthful to herself, which was not a consistent feature of her thinking, she would conclude that she did not really miss him as such. It had felt strange and certainly different after he died, on a confusing wet and windy day several years ago. She had found him on the kitchen floor one morning unresponsive after a massive stroke. He was dead before he got to the hospital.

It was why she moved into The Apple Orchard Retirement Community at the trend-bucking age of seventy-one. Every day she stayed in the matrimonial home reminded her that she did not grieve for her husband the way other widows seemed to. She actually needed to move to stop feeling guilty. She had been proven right when she dismissed the option to buy somewhere new for herself, but instead moved into a ready-made retirement community. The guilt seemed to melt away.

It was only now (she assumed because of the appearance of some form of male relationship in her life), that she was once again dwelling on her marriage and her late husband. The old cliché is true. Every marriage is unique and no one on the outside has much of a clue how it works. Frankly, she was now beginning to question her own understanding of her marriage.

His lack of interest in her physically had been a source of relief during their marriage. Mrs Hazel Wharton decided in her early twenties that if she was going to be denied the ability to have children, she was not going to waste much time with the activity that was supposed to lead to it. She had been a virgin when they married, like many in the early 1950s, and her knowledge was in keeping with her generation. What limited experience she had in her marriage had been to produce two further children, after they had adopted the boy on the incorrect assertion that they could not conceive. Their limited couplings had been uncomfortable and mildly mortifying in equal measure. After their second daughter was born, she told Brian that there would be no more intimacy. He had been uncomplaining and there was not even a need for further discussion. She remembered that he looked almost relieved. They simply shared a bed to sleep in and no more. It was only now, much too late for change, that she had begun to question this almost silent development.

Of course, she never discussed this with anyone and she was not about to start with Ruben Miles. He may be one hundred and six years old, but Mrs Hazel Wharton was very much of the view that men, however old, do not change their spots. Ruben Miles had clearly been something of a ladies' man. He was still careful about his appearance and he did not seem to be bothered about cultivating friendships with his own gender. He spoke to other men, of course, especially in the TV lounge of The Apple Orchard Retirement Community, but you could tell his heart was not really in it.

Overall, Mrs Hazel Wharton was pleased with the progress they had made on their little trip. The retired detective, although a little patronising at first, had seemed sincere in his agreement to look into the matter further with some ex-colleagues. The attempt to talk to the missing woman's family had been less successful. Neither the mother (the father was deceased), or the two siblings were prepared to talk. In fact, they had been rude and even a little aggressive during the brief interaction they shared.

'Probably had too much media hassle over the years.'

Mrs Hazel Wharton conceded that Ruben Miles may well have been right. The poor mother had the look of the hunted, like an elderly Princess Diana. Still, you would have thought they would have been even a little interested.

Ruben Miles had encouraged her to delay any further investigations until after former Detective Weston had reported back. The retired policeman said it would only be a few weeks. Mrs Hazel Wharton was always a little impressed with how blasé Ruben Miles appeared to be about time. I mean, surely at one hundred and six years old you must be pretty much ready to go at any minute. And yet he did not seem to be. He gave the impression that he fully expected to be around for many more birthdays to come. Maybe that was the secret?

They made it back to The Apple Orchard Retirement Community early on Sunday evening. They had not talked much on the return journey as Ruben Miles pretended to be asleep. She could tell he was faking it because he was still slowly tapping his left foot, a habit that he had started in his youth and had never gotten rid of.

The question was why? Why was Ruben Miles feigning sleep to avoid talking to her? She could not suspect that it had nothing to do with her.

One of the side effects of his condition was the stubbornness of his subconscious mind. At any given time, and without any prior warning, it could assume complete control over his mental functions and almost make his conscious mind shut down. It would then show mental images of the events of a day that it wanted to be the focus. Ruben Miles was feigning sleep in the two-seater Smart Car because he was having one of these episodes, the first in several months. As a younger man they were much more regular. He had therefore been surprised when he felt it coming on. As was the norm, it had been preceded by a dull headache, a condition that he had in no other circumstances. Somehow, he knew that reliving the events of 1940 with JoJo Bartlett had made this episode inevitable. He was not thinking about Oswald Mosley. He was thinking about Eleanor de Villiers and her birthday.

THE SCIENCE OF RANDOM

Ruben Miles was more concerned about what to get Eleanor de Villiers for a birthday gift than he was about taking a message to Oswald Mosley. Like many men, Ruben Miles was poor at choosing gifts for anyone, never mind a potential long-term partner. He knew that jewellery was a safe bet, but he knew himself that he lacked even modest taste in this area. The lady in the posh shop on Regent Street had urged him to stick to the classics, perhaps a pearl necklace or diamond earrings? Ruben Miles had money. His adventures in the States had ensured he lived a much more comfortable lifestyle than most in 1940. However, his relationship with money was ambiguous. He easily oscillated between profligate and careful. On the 14th of October 1940 he chose the former and purchased the pearl necklace. He had buyer's regret on the bus back to Balham. It was surely too extravagant a gift for so new a friendship.

He was on safer ground with the meal. Ruben Miles had taught himself to cook as a hobby since returning from the Spanish Civil War. He had been intrigued by the love the Spanish had for food, many without the wherewithal for anything but the most basic of ingredients. They could conjure up a great deal with a simple potato, herbs and some sun-dried tomatoes. He read a surprising book on the subject in the library and spent many hours preparing quite elaborate dishes for a single man dining alone in a south London flat, however modern it was.

The last time he had spoken to Eleanor de Villiers she had agreed, after procrastinating at some length, to come to his flat for a birthday meal. She had assumed that his motive was obvious and while she was at least partially correct on that, he also was keen to showcase his culinary skills that he had so patiently acquired. She had been most insistent regarding the sleeping arrangements. Eleanor de Villiers was clearly nothing like her sister, the Specialist.

He had decided on something simple. He was going to serve roast quail, cream potatoes and seasonal vegetables for the main course. Eleanor de Villiers had expressed her fondness for all game birds, something that she had acquired in her childhood. He had to pay considerably over the odds to persuade the local butcher to supply the quails and the price of the plentiful butter and cream for the potatoes would have made a poorer man wince.

She was expected at 7.30 p.m., as she could not leave Bletchley until her shift ended at 5 p.m. The unpredictability of the railway timetable was something that most Londoners had acclimatised to early on in the blitz. Ruben Miles was aware that they could be eating dinner at any time from the arranged hour until midnight, even with a run of mere modest misfortune. As quail are small and require little cooking, he had decided to cook them on her arrival. He contented himself with firstly preparing the side dishes and chilling the stout and champagne that he knew were her favourite indulgences.

He had bought some fine pâté from Harrods food hall to start and was making a Baked Alaska to ensure further overuse of dairy as a conclusion. He had discovered this dessert during his travels in the States and it was almost unknown in the UK at the time, although it would become very fashionable in the 1950s.

By 7.35 p.m. all the prep had been done and he was already becoming a little anxious, which heightened considerably when the air raid siren sounded moments later. Ruben Miles did not head toward the nearby tube station for shelter. In fact, none of the residents of Du Cane Court did. Who knew how either rumour started, but started they most certainly were and all the residents were waging their lives on there being some accuracy to their content. Ruben Miles heard this firstly from the obese porter who worked the night shifts at the weekend; the Luftwaffe were using the building as a guide for their bombers as they headed to the docks or the West End. Thus, because the building was so visible, despite the blackout and because of its size, the planes were not wanting to drop any bombs on it. Secondly, Hitler admired the modern art deco design of the building and wanted the SS to have it as its base after the inevitably successful invasion. Most chose to believe both rumours. It made them feel a little more secure.

Eleanor de Villiers was having a disappointing day. Firstly, she had fallen out with one of her hut mates over a missing hairbrush and a clumsy allegation. Then, she had been forced to work an extra half hour of her shift at the behest of her permanently sullen line manager, presumably as some petty payback for some perceived slight. He was a very touchy man in more ways than one. Then, she had ran all the way to Bletchley station to find the London bound train at platform one exiting at a slow, almost mocking pace. She tore her stockings on the station railings for good measure.

She had to wait nearly an hour for the next train and when she boarded found it full to bursting with WAAFs and servicemen. She had to stand all the way. When they got into Euston (thankfully without meaningful delay), rather than head for the underground like the majority of travellers, she headed for the bus stops immediately outside.

Eleanor de Villiers had a touch of claustrophobia and a real dread of being trapped for hours on end in an underground station during a bombing raid, although pragmatically she knew she was safer underground than crawling along pitch black roads in exposed buses. Consequently, she sometimes procrastinated between both options of transport. As she was running late, she had surprised herself by opting for the slower method of transport. She had calculated that the underground would get her there by 7.45 p.m. at the very latest, whereas the bus would be about 8 p.m. She did not analyse the reasons for her decision.

As she sat on the damp smelling bus, she thought about her attraction to Ruben Miles. Her sister had been correct. She did have a slight weakness for handsome and slightly older men. She also liked his accent, a seeming rough blend of educated northern England and American. She had only one reservation, that he was teetotal. Her father had been quite vociferous on the subject many times.

'Never trust a man who doesn't drink.'

Hitler was the trite evidence usually trotted out as conclusive proof. But Eleanor de Villiers, without even fully acknowledging it herself, always deferred to her father's views on the world and everything in it. This noticeably jarred with her rather radical for the times view on the role of women in society.

The driver made steady enough progress and Eleanor de Villiers attention moved to what to buy her sister for her upcoming birthday.

At just before 8 p.m., Ruben Miles decided to head downstairs and get a little fresh air outside the main reception area. During a blackout, movement was a slow process of running hands along walls and stair railings and shuffling laboriously forward. For whatever reason, he deemed the effort worthwhile. He made it outside and listened to the anti-aircraft guns sending their near futile shells into the mild October night. He could see fires burning to the north and northwest. At least the docks appeared to be getting a night off. Incendiaries could be seen almost marking the route of the Thames. The roar of the bombers was deafening as some appeared to be almost directly overhead. And then he was blown off his feet.

The bomb landed on the Balham High Road directly outside the entrance to the underground and mainline station. One hundred yards to the south, Ruben Miles had landed headfirst in shrubbery in the communal gardens of Du Cane Court. He was unharmed, although his clothes were badly torn. He looked like an extra from a Charlie Chaplin film. His first thought was for Eleanor de Villiers.

She had sat at the front of the bus as it made getting on and off much easier in the pitch black. The bus had traversed Clapham Common as the air raid sirens had started. Progress was slow along the A24 toward Clapham South Station. The bus came to a complete stop next to a hat shop with an incendiary bomb nestled in the roof guttering. The driver mumbled curses under his breath. None of the dozen or so other passengers on the bottom deck spoke. Eleanor de Villiers realised she was clutching her handbag with enough force to draw a little blood. After several minutes the journey restarted as the bus was able to get past a broken-down bakery van. Moments later, the driver drove headfirst into the crater that suddenly appeared in the road adjacent to the tube station as the bomb hit. There was not even time to scream as the bus plunged into the fifteen-metre abyss.

Ruben Miles was running in the dark toward the burning

station, yet even the light of the flames could not reveal every obstruction and he tripped over a large piece of smouldering shrapnel. This time he had hurt himself; he had broken his right ankle.

Eleanor de Villiers picked the wrong mode of transport and the wrong seat that night. If she had taken the tube from Euston instead of the bus, she would have been through Balham Station and sipping Champagne in Ruben Miles's well decorated flat a full twenty-five minutes before the bomb hit. If she had sat in any other seat, she would not have fallen headfirst through the front glass of the windscreen next to the driver, severing both her carotid arteries with the precision of a surgeon's knife. She had to endure a few seconds of startled panic and then nothing.

Eleanor de Villiers was the only fatality on the bus that infamously fell into the bomb crater during the Balham Station disaster. The driver and other passengers escaped mostly with minor injuries. The death count in the flooded station was more complicated. The final mortality figure reaching nearly seventy, mostly by drowning in the chaos as water flooded down on to the underground platforms via a shattered water mains some ten metres below ground. It was not the last bomb that would directly hit an underground station being used by many for shelter.

In the hours, days, weeks and several months remaining of the 1940-41 Blitz, it was the sheer randomness of the results that Londoners came to hate the most. No right or wrong, no good nor evil, no just or unjust, just the utter fucking randomness of it all. It would come back to haunt them again in 1944 with Hitler's revenge weapon, the doodlebugs.

Ruben Miles was physically fit again within a few short weeks, although he did walk with a cane for a little while longer. However, his mental health was a different story and at a time when it was felt that being told to 'pull yourself together' should be enough of a cure. Unlike other incidents and tragedies that he had experienced in his life, he felt a wholly personal guilt and responsibility for the death of Eleanor de Villiers. For over a week, he slept rarely and fitfully, replaying the telephone conversation that he made to Eleanor de Villiers persuading her to come to Balham that night. He could remember every word of course. He could remember every time she had demurred, giving him the option to acquiesce. He could hear her reluctance and he had to endure his own tenacity again and again. Ultimately, he could not forgive himself and the only way he could get his mind to stop replaying the telephone conversation on a permanent loop was to have a mental breakdown. It lasted several months.

TEST TUBE BABIES

L ike most people under the age of thirty, JoJo Bartlett did not spend time thinking about her own death, never mind anyone else's. She watched TV shows and films full of it, played video games that almost glorified it, but none of the content produced much in the way of personal reflection on human mortality.

Ruben Miles had clearly seen and been personally involved in a significant amount of death and tragedy and he had described it fully to JoJo Bartlett. Yet it was the story of Eleanor de Villiers that got to JoJo the most. As for the old man, he could barely get the words out. In keeping with previous sessions, he shed copious tears for a woman he had met on only a handful of occasions. Despite her sympathy, JoJo Bartlett once again thought about the lack of emotion displayed by Ruben Miles when he talked of the fate of his wife and young children, either burnt alive or abandoned. She managed to shake off those thoughts momentarily.

'I can see why you don't believe in any God.'

Perhaps the most unusual, unique, or most suspicious aspect of Ruben Miles's hyperthymesia, was that he claimed he could not recall any of the days he spent recovering from his breakdown after the Balham tube station disaster in October 1940. One hundred and twenty-seven days that his mind could not or would not recall. The only gap in his personal chronology.

He explained this to JoJo Bartlett.

'None of it? Surely that is impossible with your... condition.'

'All I know is they put me in some kind of mental hospital. I remember I was released on 1st March 1941 to a very different London. Cavendish came to see me and updated me on what I had missed.'

It *was* a very different London. The cumulative damage of the nightly bombing was evident everywhere. By March 1941, the

Luftwaffe had shifted their attention from the capital and instead were targeting ports in the north and west of the island in support of their Atlantic war efforts. Londoners at last had some much-needed respite.

Ruben Miles believed that he could not remember even a single day of his treatment for the comprehensive mental breakdown he suffered as a result of the death of Eleanor de Villiers. He did, however, claim that he had some knowledge of where he was and what he was like during the period in question, as a result of what visitors later told him. Both Cavendish and the Specialist had visited on a few occasions.

The fifth column investigation in which Ruben Miles had played an active role had led to the arrest of most of the ringleaders, with one notable exception. Ruben Miles had kept his mother out of his reports submitted pre-breakdown, for reasons he could not accurately articulate. Whatever the content of the message for Mosley was, he never received it. The only information he obtained was of a further tightening on his security and visitation privileges.

At their meeting on Ruben Miles's release, at an unblemished Du Cane Court, Cavendish had been effusive in his praise for the role he played in the fifth column investigation. But this was probably because it made it easier for him to tell what he had really come to say.

'I'm afraid that we have rather a strict policy on this sort of thing. I am sure that you have made a full recovery, you seem back to your old self to me, it's just that the service won't take any chances. I suppose there could be a desk job of some description, if you wanted that sort of thing. But actual field work is out of the question, I'm afraid, at least for now.'

Cavendish clearly thought this would be a disappointment. Ruben Miles was strangely ambivalent about the whole thing. Besides, he had the oddest sensation that he was not quite through with British intelligence.

'You need to make sure that you don't have a relapse, old man. Cut yourself some slack. If you survived the trenches then you should know just about everything there is to know about the science of random.'

This was not a phrase that Ruben Miles had heard of. His puzzled expression prompted an explanation.

'It's something our boffins say all the time. Simplistically, it means do not look for meaning or understanding in any natural act or event. Some people believe in Gods, others in fate or destiny. But everything in this life, and I mean everything, is random. Normal people would call it luck. Never underestimate the importance of luck. Just accept that and you can move on. It's become a bit of a mantra in intelligence.'

Ruben Miles agreed that any veteran of the Western Front could understand this simple premise. However, it was quite another thing to accept it as truth.

'But if she had not been coming to visit me here that night she would have been safe.'

'Possibly, but you have no certainty that is correct. There are no alternative realities for us to check.'

Another truism.

Cavendish agreed to keep in touch and he made good on his word. Indeed, one could say that he was most diligent in this regard. Ruben Miles's other notable visitor after his release was the Specialist. But Ruben Miles did not want to get to that just yet, as he could see that JoJo Bartlett had something to say.

'The science of random? That's a bit nihilistic, isn't it?'

JoJo was at a point in her development where she still used words she was not completely sure she understood.

'I am not a particularly clever man or for that matter an overly thoughtful man. But all of the things that I have lived through – the wars, the deaths, the accidents – the science of random makes about as much sense to me as anything else. Luck seems to me a more tangible commodity than some celestial creator or pre-ordained destiny.'

'I like the test tube theory myself.'

This required further explanation.

'It's the idea that the world and everything that has happened in it is one big science experiment – some extra-terrestrial beings created the earth in some celestial test tube.'

'I have never heard of that. Who came up with that?'

'Not sure, but I heard it from the Physics teacher at our school. It was the only interesting thing he said in two years. I liked it – E.T. gets bored with the dim dinosaurs and so comes up with a meteor. They probably just chucked a stone into the test tube.'

Ruben Miles digested this slowly.

'It's as likely as any of the religions.'

This pleased JoJo Bartlett enormously. She may just be seventeen and she may be wrong about a lot of things (although she personally doubted this), but she was sure that religions were all a crock of shite to fool the idiots. OK, so your life is shit, but the afterlife is going to be great.

BOYFRIENDS?

L uke Miles seemed very keen to discuss the meaning of the night in Dalkeith. JoJo Bartlett was having none of it.

'Meaning? We had sex. That is an act, not a meaning.'

Luke Miles had to concede the truth in this statement. They were walking along the old railway line in the Tyne Valley, just outside Wylam. They had stopped on the bridge that crossed the river; it was like a miniature version of the more famous bridge in the city centre. They looked for signs of fish twenty feet below them and listened to the red kites soaring to roost overhead. They spent a lot of time out of the city now, mostly due to JoJo's access to her mother's car. Mrs Bartlett did not like driving and avoided doing so whenever possible. Although they did not discuss their mutual need to be away from their respective family abodes, their actions made their motives quite obvious.

'If you ask me whether I'm your girlfriend, I may actually hit you.'

Luke noted that he was just about to ask that question. But then again, that was a recurring theme of their time spent together. JoJo always seemed to have a good idea what he was thinking.

'And yes, we will do *that* again. I am assuming it gets better with practice, like riding a bike or algebra.'

Luke had definitely been thinking about *that*.

'So, does that mean…?'

'Seriously, I will punch you so hard in the face.'

This kept Luke from asking for at least half an hour.

At The Apple Orchard Retirement Community there were less threats to commit domestic violence, but there were lingering ambiguities about the nature of the developing friendship between Ruben Miles and Mrs Hazel Wharton. She had again been thinking a lot about her deceased husband Brian and specifically the nature of their marriage. She was now able to accept that, while a sexless marriage may be by no means unique, especially from their time period, it was certainly on the more unusual side of the spectrum. She concluded that it was not as if their physical activity had reduced to nothing over many years, they had probably only tried the activity on a handful of dispiriting occasions. At times like these, Mrs Hazel Wharton was glad that she did not have hyperthymesia. She gave another of her shudders at the very thought of it.

She liked Ruben Miles and was all too aware of his longevity, but she still felt something for the old man that she never did for her husband.

'And me an old lady,' she said out loud.

'I have told you a thousand times, you are not old, Hazel.'

Ruben Miles had the reputation within The Apple Orchard Retirement Community of being able to seemingly appear out of nowhere, like an ancient ninja. Mrs Hazel Wharton attributed this alleged skill to his penchant for Hush Puppies and the failing senses of the other inmates.

'I am beginning to think my marriage may not have been as normal as I used to believe.' She surprised herself by volunteering this as they made their way to the canteen for the early bird dinner serving; it was 5.30 p.m.

The old man took her by the arm gently.

'Now listen to me, Mrs Hazel Wharton. You will not make yourself happy by raking over the past. I recommend that you let it go, it's not going to change now. What good does it do?'

Mrs Hazel Wharton thought about this for just a moment.

'Ruben Miles, that may be the most hypocritical thing I have ever heard. And this coming from a man who spends half his remaining precious time telling a young girl all the stories of his long life. You are not exactly practising what you preach.'

'I can understand why you say that. But my stories, as you call them, are about events, not personal relationships. You are talking about feelings and emotions. Those are very different kettles of fish. I stick to events with JoJo, much safer ground.'

They both chose the chicken Kiev. They sat down at their

usual table by the patio doors facing the walled garden.

'Is this why you won't talk about your past relationships?'

This prompted one of Ruben Miles's patented trademarks, a weary sigh.

'I find events easier to talk about than people.'

In some notable ways, the pair were unsuitable mealtime companions. Ruben Miles was the slowest eater Mrs Hazel Wharton had ever encountered, often taking up to half an hour to finish a medium sized plate of food. For her part, Mrs Hazel Wharton ate as if she was the youngest child in a poverty-stricken family of eight during the industrial revolution; she was like a bulldozer. Secondly, she was also a committed carnivore and actually tutted when Ruben Miles, as he was prone to do, selected the vegetarian, or God forbid, vegan option.

'I think I've finally realised that not being unhappy isn't the same as being happy.'

Ruben Miles did not have a reply for this.

'I mean we certainly did not dislike each other. I suppose the boy just made things worse.'

The boy, of course, is whom she suspects is a murderer.

It had been three weeks since they had met with retired detective Weston and they had still not heard anything.

'Give him a little more time before you start badgering him.'

'He said a couple of weeks.'

'And that's all it has been.'

Mrs Hazel Wharton was growing increasingly impatient and not just because Ruben Miles had barely started his Kiev.

THE CALM BEFORE
THE NAVAL STORM

After his release following his breakdown, Ruben Miles accepted the offer of a desk job with British intelligence. Most of the men he worked with kept themselves to themselves and the few women that were employed in his sector were clerical and middle aged, not his favourite combination. The task of the small team he worked with was to produce misleading information about the Blitz damage and send it down the chain. They were not aware of the process, but understood that this information was forwarded onto the Nazis via several successfully turned double-agents. The work was mostly dull, but there was one man who could certainly brighten up the most menial of duties, his personality was such that he was literally impossible to ignore. His name was Guy Burgess. Ruben Miles knew him as a humorous oddity. History would remember him quite differently.

Burgess was a literal mess. He was a loud, drunken, promiscuous slob and that was just his friends' description of him. He polluted the office with his ubiquitous body odour, blended with alcohol and stale cigarettes. He reputedly had a perfunctory ablution only once a week. But at least he wasn't dull and, as most of the job was, Ruben Miles found that he could put up with the smell for a little bit of distraction. The two started having the occasional lunch together in a nearby hostelry.

'Have you heard of Guy Burgess?'

Ruben Miles was pleased to be out in the fresh air with JoJo Bartlett. They had come down to the Quayside, across the water from the Baltic. They had sat down on a bench to enjoy the view on a pleasant sunny afternoon. JoJo had still fetched the old man a blanket. They watched people crossing the nearby Millennium Bridge.

'No, should I have?'

'I did not think he would be part of your history classes. Guy Burgess was a notorious Russian spy. He even defected to Moscow in 1951. You would never have suspected he was capable of such a thing.'

JoJo was often surprised by how much of the last century she did not know a thing about. The Cambridge spy circle and indeed the whole of the Cold War were solid examples of her ignorance. There was only so much the exam boards seemed interested in, apart from the Tudors and the Stuarts obviously.

'I think British intelligence were slow to realise that anyone would want to spy for the Russians. And even when that penny dropped, they had a predetermined view as to the profile any mole would have. And it certainly was not Burgess.'

'Was he your friend?'

As we have seen, Ruben Miles did not really do friends.

'No, but he was fun to be around. I just mentioned him because he was about the only interesting thing that happened to me between the end of the Blitz in '41 and the spring of 1944. When I found out years later what he had done, I was gobsmacked.'

'Nothing for three years? That does not sound like you.'

'True. Nevertheless. In the spring of 1944, I met my third wife, Betty. We had been courting for six weeks when Cavendish turned up at Du Cane Court. I had not seen him in two years. It was a Monday afternoon. I was in bed with a head cold when he arrived.'

Ruben Miles had male hypochondria, a condition a good deal more common than hyperthymesia. At the slightest sniffle he would dose himself with tablets and assume his imminent death. That spring day was no exception. He reluctantly propelled himself into a vertical position with the appropriate accompanying male groans, then shuffled pathetically slowly toward the front door.

Cavendish was not impressed.

'I hope you have been practising your German, Miles,' he said by way of an introduction. No pleasantries, no questions about his health, mental or otherwise.

Even though it had also been a couple of years since Ruben Miles had seen Herr Muller, he was able to confirm that he had indeed kept up with his German practice. He read German books in the library. He swore the librarian thought he was a German spy.

'Would you be interested in a transfer out of your desk job for something a little more stimulating?'

'Exactly how stimulating are we talking?'

'More stimulating than a couple of pints with Guy Burgess.'

This sounded like an interesting career direction. In truth, Ruben Miles had been bored with his mundane, mostly clerical duties, and if an hour in the pub with a funny, if malodorous, man was the best your working life was offering, then clearly it was time for a change. He was even beginning to think that his romantic pursuit of Betty James was more about purpose than it was about love. But more of that later.

'Tell me more.'

'For reasons that are obvious, we may be in need of more German speakers shortly. I understand yours is impeccable.'

Again, this was information that had not come from Ruben Miles.

It was April 1944, and for the people of London, as well as the wider nation, all conversations inevitably pivoted around the opening up of the second front that Stalin had been banging on about for eighteen months. Everyone, including the Nazis, knew it was coming, but very few knew the when and the where.

'The invasion is imminent then?'

'I think even my grandmother knows that Miles... and she's been dead for twelve years.'

The job spec sounded unfeasibly like long-term planning for British intelligence. He was not, as he anticipated, going to be used to communicate with captured Wehrmacht officers as the invasion force went from the landing beaches, marching across France and the low countries and into Nazi Germany. This meant that Ruben Miles would be a long way from the frontlines and this

346 | Mark Newies

sounded very encouraging.

'When this thing is finally done, there are a lot of Nazis that will go to ground. We need German speakers with fieldwork experience to facilitate their capture. You are going to be part of a team to help us flush the buggers out and make sure they get what's coming to them. The powers that be are very keen that it's not all left to the Yanks or, God forbid, the Soviets.'

Ruben Miles did not need time to think about the offer. Capturing runaway Nazis sounded a lot more life affirming and rewarding than making up fake newspaper stories.

With the benefit of hindsight, perhaps Ruben Miles should have given a little more thought to his decision to ask Betty James to marry him. They had been stepping out for less than two months when Ruben Miles had popped the question to Betty over a cup of hot, sweet tea in Betty's mother's kitchen in Teddington. In truth, Betty James had just informed Ruben Miles that she was pregnant. Another wife and child he would subsequently abandon. He had no desire to share this additional damaging information with JoJo.

'It was different back then. If the girl got pregnant, you got married, end of story. Although, as we had done it just the once, I did feel rightly aggrieved.'

JoJo felt her cheeks slightly flush. It was bad enough having sex with a boy, but talking about it with a very old man was even more uncomfortable. She could not stop herself from offering the following conventional viewpoint.

'So, you didn't love her but married her? How is that the honourable thing to do, but abandoning your children from your second marriage is somehow acceptable?'

Ruben Miles used the distraction of the Millennium Bridge showcasing its blinking eye feature to avoid this most troublesome question. After a while, JoJo herself was prepared to pretend that she had not asked the question itself. JoJo was slow to realise that silence was the method the old man used to not answer difficult questions. It was certainly effective on JoJo.

The training for the new distraction was surprisingly militaristic. Ruben Miles found himself knee deep in swampland in the fens one week and, the following week, on bracing route marches through the remote Scottish Highlands. It was like old times. After witnessing the relentless bullying bestowed on the one bespeckled, but surprisingly brave, Scouser who foolishly questioned the methods of preparation, Ruben Miles kept his usual counsel, for now.

Cavendish had been uncharacteristically brief when describing both the role and the training. Surely, the only real prerequisite was language proficiency?

'It may not be quite so straightforward,' he conceded when they met up in early June.

'For starters, we have no way of knowing just how much of Nazi infrastructure will still be operational. Who will get there first, the Russians? Let us just say there is a feeling that those that go should be physically as well as mentally prepared. It's not just about speaking the lingo.'

'When are we talking?'

'That is impossible to say. I mean, what if our chaps don't even get off the beaches? That is what Churchill fears, another bloody Dieppe debacle.'

'Well the Nazis never even tried.'

'Precisely. My guess is that you could be needed in anything from three to six months from now. We will get you ready and then stand you down, just keeping you ticking over until you are needed.'

They concluded their discussion promptly, it was the afternoon of Monday 5th of June 1944. The radio was abuzz with the news of the occupation of Rome by US forces. It did not last long on the newspaper front pages.

PAPERWORK

'We have some news,' said Luke's father, standing awkwardly at his bedroom door, his mother partially obscured by the door frame.

'Can we come in?'

It was the first time that the three of them had ever shared this space. Luke's father was wondering whether it was normal for a teenage boy's room to smell better than the rest of the house. His mother tapped her foot nervously, a recent development.

'We took a DNA test last week. We want you to know that your mother and I are NOT blood relations.'

Luke had heard about people feeling extremes of relief as a physical entity but had not experienced it before.

'Thank fuck for that!'

His father proffered a sheet of paper at him instead of reprimanding his son for swearing which had been his first predictable thought.

Luke scanned the sheet quickly. He had a question but failed to ask it. If his parents were not related, why did they look so nervous and pissed off?

Mrs Hazel Wharton was not nervous, but she was definitely pissed off, not that she would have used that phrase herself. She thrust the letter she had received from retired Detective Weston at Ruben Miles. They were sitting in the garden of The Apple Orchard Retirement Community. The letter was polite but unequivocal. After what was described as 'significant enquiries', Detective Weston made it clear that Barry Wharton was not a suspect, or even a person of interest, in any of the unsolved cases written on the list.

'Well at least you have clarity,' said Ruben Miles. Once again, he had chosen his words... poorly.

'Clarity? The only clarity here is that the man is a fool.'

Ruben Miles sighed.

'It's clearly a cover-up.'

It occurred to Ruben Miles that, so far as he could tell, the twenty-first century appeared to consist of people refusing to believe in facts if they contradicted their own narrow viewpoint. In other words, the same as his experiences of the twentieth century.

Luke Miles did not possess a coherent viewpoint, apart from the almost compulsory teenage predilection for not believing anything his parents told him. Consequently, as he relayed the news of his genealogy to JoJo Bartlett over a couple of liveners in the Lonsdale, which was fast becoming their not very local, local, he barely kept his cynicism in check. JoJo offered little comfort.

'Did the document look genuine? I mean did it have logos, an official stamp or signatures, that sort of thing?'

'I think so.'

'It was not just a badly aligned typed document in one font?'

Luke was not an observant individual. As JoJo asked him the question, he could barely recall the document. In fact, he had hardly looked at it. As an auditory learner, Luke had focused on what he was being told, not what he was being shown. The document could have been an A4 picture of a smiling nude clown with a large dildo up his arse and he still would not have taken it in.

'You don't remember the document do you, Luke? Did they give you a copy?'

His expression confirmed her judgement.

'I could just ask to see it again?'

'And so, basically you say to your parents, I think you have lied to me, you are blood relations and you have faked a document to cover up the family shame.'

Luke conceded that this was a possible conclusion.

'I think we might need a better plan.'

HISTORICAL ACCURACY

By mid-February 1945, the American, Canadian and British forces were approaching the Rhine. To the East, the Red Army had already marched through Poland and was about to enter Nazi Germany. Ruben Miles, like the vast majority of the nation, had followed the allied advances from the Normandy beaches onwards via the BBC news on his trusty radio. It at least counterbalanced the casualty figures for the V2 bombing raids which the capital and its inhabitants had endured since the previous September. Hitler's revenge weapon had a much more sinister impact on the public's morale than the aeroplane Blitz of 1940 and 1941.

The Doodlebugs, as they were commonly called, were responsible for the death or injury of nearly ten thousand Londoners during their six-month campaign. Ruben Miles heard plenty of them giving their tell-tale rasping sound as they sped overhead. But his part of south London came off relatively unscathed, with single rockets hitting nearby Clapham, Brixton and Streatham with only a handful of fatalities. Southeast London, the East End and north London fared much worse. It became clear after those first few weeks of September 1944 that London was facing a new and serious threat, but the government covered up the rocket attacks until Churchill finally conceded their existence in the House of Commons on the 10th of November 1944.

In the months leading up to his departure for Normandy in late February 1945, Ruben Miles had been assisting in a minor capacity on the British intelligence campaign that successfully convinced the Germans that the majority of V2 rockets were overshooting the capital. This resulted in more than half of all V2 rocket attacks aimed at London landing in rural Kent. Thus, reducing significantly the casualty figures. British intelligence had come a long way from the amateurish bumbling of the late 1930s.

Ruben Miles's role was simple. He and others wrote many

spurious reports outlining the horrific casualty figures for rocket attacks that in reality had devastated the flower and fauna of the North Weald. The reports would then be transmitted by turned Nazi agents and bought hook line and sinker by the Abwehr. Unknowingly, Ruben Miles's reports were sent to agent Zigzag, one of the many double agents unquestioned by the Nazis. He fed the information back to the outmanoeuvred Germans. It was the same double-cross system that had fooled the Nazis into thinking the Normandy landings had been a feint and the real invasion would come in Pas-de-Calais.

'You must have helped save loads of lives!'

JoJo Bartlett was glad to eventually put something meaningful on the positive side of Ruben Miles's life ledger. The negative side of the ledger spoke clearly and more frequently.

Ruben Miles modestly and correctly outlined again how minor his contribution was.

'Anyone could have written the casualty reports. I just contributed to the pile. I think the others, especially the double-agents, get all the credit, and rightly so. They were the ones who convinced the Germans of their authenticity.'

'Still, you played a part in a campaign that must have saved hundreds of lives. You must be proud of that, at least?'

Ruben Miles conceded that he had wondered over the years how many potential lives and families had been saved by the double-cross team's work on the V2 disinformation campaign.

'If the deception had not been so effective, then hundreds more rockets would have landed in London – it's almost as if you stuck two fingers up at the science of random.'

Cavendish informed Ruben Miles of his imminent departure for France during the last days of a damp February 1945.

'I'm a bit jealous of you, Miles, at least in one regard. You will not only get to see the Normandy beaches, but you will disembark at Mulberry B, one of the marvels of the whole blasted show.'

Mulberry B was one of the two portable and temporary harbours that the allies put in place off Omaha Beach and Gold Beach after successfully landing and establishing beachheads. Mulberry A had been off Omaha Beach but was destroyed by a sudden storm in late June of the previous year.

'I was one of the last of almost three million men to disembark there. It was quite a sight.'

Ruben Miles gave JoJo a potted history of the Normandy invasion and the construction and use of the temporary man-made harbours.

'Why do I not know about this? In Year Nine, I got a sanitised version of the Blitz and was told literally nothing about D-Day.'

'And I would imagine your history books totally missed out that it was really the Russians that defeated the Nazis – over twenty million Russian troops were killed in World War Two. Guess how many from Britain?'

'A couple of million?'

'About 400,000.'

'Wow.'

'There were only 300,000 Americans killed.'

'Why do I not know this?'

'The Cold War.'

'Of course, let the democratic allies take the credit. Not those nasty Communists.'

'That's right – why would you teach your children that it was really the evil enemy that won World War Two? So, they didn't.'

JoJo was beginning to understand the magnitude of the often-told platitude, history is written by the winners, or at least told from the winner's perspective. How could capitalism and the West claim to be superior to the East if they acknowledged just who had actually won the war?

'Instead, it is all Blitz spirit and other such hokum.'

'You are not much of a patriot, then.'

'I have nothing against this country or it's people. I'm quite fond of both. I just despise all forms of nationalism. If the twentieth century teaches just one thing, it should be that. The destructiveness of nationalism.'

'What's worse, religion or nationalism do you think?

'Good question. I suppose the obvious answer is both. If you take the two things out, what else causes mankind to kill each other in huge numbers over the centuries?'

JoJo was tempted to say men, but resisted the temptation.

MULBERRY B AND BEYOND

The beach was still strewn with debris. Mulberry B harbour was deployed off Gold Beach, where British and Canadian troops landed on June 6th 1944. The beach was still cluttered with the last remnants of the invading force. It was easy for Ruben Miles to grasp the scale of the landings by what was still in evidence several months later. The length and depth of the beaches surprised him, as they were much greater than the Northumberland beaches that he had grown up visiting on chilly summer days with his mother. The German defences were much lighter here than on neighbouring Omaha Beach, where the invading US troop casualties had been much greater. But even on Gold Beach, Ruben Miles was able to observe the large distance the soldiers had to traverse to reach the German defences. It was a long way to run with just a rifle and good fortune to protect you.

He was travelling with six others who he had got to know during their intensive training course. The others had formed a seemingly effortless bond during the process and although they were always scrupulously polite to him, Ruben Miles's rather natural aloofness meant that he was not a fully paid-up member of their club. Suffice to say, they were all men.

'I still don't get why we had to come via the beach. Surely flying would have been much quicker.'

Deller was the youngest of the men, in his late twenties and he was also the most vocal.

It was an obvious question without an obvious answer.

Colonel Edwards then emerged from behind a wooden hut with a corrugated iron roof to introduce himself and answer the question. He was a tall man with a narrow, angular face.

'Gentlemen, it was felt that you should experience a taste of what the allied troops had to face during Overlord. That is why you came in by the beach and that is why you will be taking the long and scenic route through the Normandy bocage. On just about every hedgerow, you will see the dangers faced, and evidence of the carnage. We want you to be very aware of the sacrifices that have been made. It was felt by the brass that it may sharpen your focus a little. I am Colonel Edwards and I will be overseeing this important project.'

Ruben Miles felt it was as good an answer as they were going to get. Twenty minutes into the uncomfortable journey by slow-moving army truck and the seven men were already questioning the need for such a process. But Colonel Edwards was right about the scenery. Wooden crosses cluttered roadsides. Overhanging tunnels of trees and bushes gave them an eerie framing. Burnt out tanks and destroyed machine gun nests littered the landscape sporadically. It was impossible not to grasp how difficult progress must have been for the advancing allied soldiers, especially for a Somme veteran like Ruben Miles.

After a bone-shaking couple of hours, they eventually stopped in Caen. The city was a ruin. Nearly seven weeks of intense fighting had seen to that. The Germans deployed most of their Panzer divisions to the defence of the strategically important port immediately in response to the invasion.

Ruben Miles was not a stranger to the destruction of towns and villages during warfare. He had seen his share in other parts of northern France in 1916. However, even he could see how important Caen must have been to both sides. There was barely a building left unscathed.

Colonel Edwards gave a briefing after an adequate, although tasteless dinner. The men huddled around a large kitchen table in a farm that had been taken over by British troops after the local inhabitants had been wiped out by a vengeful retreating German unit several months previously. The Colonel had been eager to share the details of what had happened that day.

'Waffen SS. Rest assured, gentlemen, every one of those men that committed this and other nearby atrocities will be quick to destroy their uniform, don civvies and pretend that they were never here. It is our job to ensure that we catch every last one of them and see they get the justice they deserve.'

It was now obvious to the men. The reasoning behind their convoluted journey to Germany. Each remained quiet and thoughtful.

'Of course, it is not going to be easy. These men are skilled and committed. If they make it into Germany, I am sure many of their friends and family will be happy to cover for them. However, we have some help of our own. When we get near to Germany we will be joining forces with the Avengers.'

Ruben Miles wanted to give JoJo some wider context.

'That was the night that we found out a little about the Holocaust. Colonel Edwards described what British intelligence had gleaned about the death camps – you must remember, at this stage none had been liberated and there was no newspaper coverage either.'

JoJo Bartlett listened intently as Ruben Miles described the RAF aerial photographs of Auschwitz. He mentioned the surveillance reports sent back by agents; many having paid with their lives for informing the allies about the true meaning of Nazi rule of Eastern Europe.

'If the allies knew about the death camps and had photographs of where some of them were, why did they not bomb them or try to get there quicker?'

'That's a question that has never been answered to anyone's satisfaction. But of course, I can remember exactly what Colonel Edwards said to us that evening and it does not compute with what the people were told after the war, that much I am sure of.'

Colonel Edwards had indeed been quite effusive in his description of what had been discovered by the allies in east Europe by early 1945. As an ardent Francophile, he was also indignant about what had happened to Caen and its population. He shared his feelings with his small group as they departed the ruined city the morning after their arrival.

'Caen was supposed to be captured on D-Day. But Monty, the arrogant buffoon, stalled and it took seven weeks of aerial bombardment to get rid of the SS Panzer divisions. They had arrived in Caen two days *after* D-Day.'

The men could see that the town was literally a ruin. Deller asked the obvious question and the Colonel answered swiftly.

'We think about 3,000 killed and 35,000 left homeless.'

One of the men called McLeish was from Clydebank and had witnessed the impact of the two-day apocalyptic Luftwaffe Blitz there in March 1941. That had only killed 528 unfortunate random victims.

'Christ,' he said.

They continued east across a land widely ravaged. The populace were clearly gorging on liberation, but with little else in the way of sustenance. The men distributed a significant amount of their rations to the begging children that seemed to magically appear whenever their slow-moving convoy came to a complete halt. Some of the men were more generous than others.

Colonel Edwards was a man who quickly gained the respect of all of the assembled squad. He was direct and honest in all of his communication. He certainly did not sugarcoat the nature of the upcoming project or of what had been happening in Hitler's name.

'There is an added complication, gentleman,' he said as the squad made a routine stop to refill their water bottles by an eerily untouched and seemingly nameless village, somewhere east of Rouen.

'The Avengers are highly motivated of course and that is why we must be wary. We are getting reports that, how shall we say, they are not making much of an effort to gather solid evidence before they take retribution. I needn't remind you gentlemen that we are after committed Nazis who have been directly involved in a long list of attributable atrocities, not every Hanz, Fritz or Franz in the Wehrmacht.'

The task was becoming more complex and challenging.

'We want you to ensure there is at least a semblance of fair play. We need some proof or corroborated evidence from sources and eyewitnesses. The Avengers are our friends and allies of course and they have a great deal to be angry about, but unjustified retribution is not what we stand for. We shall leave that to the Russians.'

The men listened to the Colonel in respectful silence.

'I'm afraid the evidence is clear, gentlemen. The Nazis have built numerous death camps on the eastern fringes of their empire and have turned the massacre of Jews and other enemies of the Nazi regime into an industrial operation. I have seen the ariel photographs and read the reports. The Avengers do not have this knowledge. But they are fully aware that a huge proportion of the Jewish population of Nazi occupied Europe has been herded up and sent east to an unknown fate. It goes without saying that you are not to share this information.'

'Who are these Avengers then?'

'English speaking eastern European Jews who have been working for us for a couple of years on the resistance front. They are organised, effective and highly motivated. The plan is we work with them to put as many SS criminals behind bars as possible. They are to be tried after the war in largescale war trials, but we have one very pertinent point of disagreement.'

'They want them all dead as soon as possible and preferably without bothersome legality?'

'Exactly.'

THE NECESSARY CONTEXT

R uben Miles was still very much the outsider of the small troop heading east towards the German border in the last throes of winter. Colonel Edwards had completed his final briefing as they headed toward the last intact bridge across the Rhine at Remagen. The Allied forces were now seventy miles further into the Fatherland and the Colonel was keen to stress the importance of his little team meeting up with the Avengers ASAP.

'From what I'm hearing, the Russians are going to be in Berlin in weeks rather than months, which means we need to get you further up the line.'

To the surprise of the whole group, the Colonel then handed Ruben Miles an A4 file.

'Here are all the contacts you will need, meeting points etc. This is as far as I am to take you. Miles, you are in charge from here.'

This drew mutterings of quiet dissent.

'Gentlemen, Miles was selected by my superiors to lead this operation before even my involvement. I strongly recommend that you get on board... quickly.'

'I was as surprised as anyone,' Ruben Miles explained to JoJo, as they sipped their milky coffees in the café of The Apple Orchard Retirement Community. Around them, the staff were taking down all the old signage with the initial branding. The community was being rebranded with a new logo and new name, that clearly had been the result of incompetent management. The new signs were strewn on the pavement. The Apple Orchard *Luxury* Retirement Community. The logo was of a smiling, wrinkle-free couple. The inmates were unimpressed. It seemed a lot of effort and cost for a word and logo that was not totally in keeping with their surroundings.

In northern France in late February 1945, the rest of the team *did* get on board quickly. They met up with their initial contact the following evening after a fast-moving motorised convoy took them within hearing distance of the allied spearhead. He was a fidgety, pale looking Pole, with a hook nose like the ones in all the Nazi textbooks they had used to brainwash their kids into virulent antisemitism.

'You can call me Abe, it's as good a name as any.'

The man did not offer his hand or a salute.

Ruben Miles introduced the troop earnestly.

'I don't want to know your names.'

The Pole was clearly not one for making a good first impression.

'The group you are looking for are hiding in the mountains to the north of Frankfurt. They are responsible for most of the atrocities in the Ardennes region.

'What evidence do you have?'

A shrug of hunched shoulders.

'We know it was them. Besides, why hide in the mountains if you are not guilty of something? I would imagine your file has the most relevant information.'

Ruben Miles glanced at the folder in his hand. It certainly did appear to have all the evidence any court would need.

'We need to take them alive, if possible, especially Obersturmbannführer Peiper. Those are our orders.'

A small sneer.

Some of the other Avengers were less taciturn. They told tales of barbarity that normal mortals never heard. They had commandeered a captured Panzer that was being driven by a huge man with an even bigger beard; he called himself Byk and nobody argued. He drove the tank pretty well, if slightly exuberantly and led the small convoy of vehicles. Ruben Miles and the rest of his troops travelled together in an American half-track that Colonel Edwards had requisitioned on their behalf. They reached the foothills by early evening.

Ruben Miles reread the report given to him by Colonel

Edwards and summarised the salient points for the rest of the group en route. The report confirmed that the group they were targeting were Waffen SS responsible for the slaughter of Belgian civilians and US prisoners of war during the failure of Hitler's Ardennes offensive. They were responsible for what became known as the Malmedy Massacre.

'It is not a pretty story, but then it is a story that pretty much any soldier from either German war would have heard about.'

Ruben Miles shifted in his chair, as was becoming a regular habit. He had lost a little weight lately and his backside was not providing as much comfort as it once did on the wooden benches. JoJo changed the tape in her recorder. She had the feeling that this was going to be a story she was going to need to keep.

'The Germans had counterattacked through the Ardennes Forest in December 1944, it was Hitler's last throw of the dice. He had ordered his Waffen SS units, the most fanatical of all Nazis, to take no prisoners and to treat Belgian civilians as potential enemy soldiers.'

JoJo felt her stomach tighten a little; when the old man started to look this serious, then the stories tended to become even darker.

'About a hundred US troops had surrendered at a crossroads after they had been attacked by overwhelming superior SS numbers and fire power. The commander gave the order to round the Americans up in a farmer's field. They then opened fire with machine guns, killing most of the men. Then a handful of Germans were ordered into the field to finish off any Americans still alive with a shot to the back of the head.'

JoJo felt a bit embarrassed, as she thought the events seemed in keeping with her admittedly limited knowledge of twentieth century warfare.

'Prisoners of war should not be executed, it says so in the Geneva convention – but both sides did it – I know for a fact that in the same campaign, the US killed hundreds of German prisoners of war in retaliation. I am not saying it is right, but it happens. War brings out the worst in most men. Soldiers know what they are there to do and sometimes the rules get blurred. But it was what happened to the local Belgian population that was a whole lot worse.'

The local population had not shown nearly as much deference to their superiors as Obersturmbannführer Joachim Peiper, the commanding officer of the unit that bore his name, thought. In Büllingen, his frustrations about the stalling of the Nazi advance and his sociopathic nature collided with the little village of 111 Belgians.

Firstly, he separated the entire village population by age and gender. He then spoke to the mayor of the village and asked him a simple question in his mechanical French.

'Où sont les Américains?'

When he did not get a quick enough response, he shot Antoine Arnaud in the head. He was five years old. A little slow, but immensely happy little boy who was the most popular child in the whole village. His mother's torment gave her away. One of the SS men grabbed her and slapped her hard across the face. She fell down and started sobbing hysterically; one of her neighbours doing her best to silence her anguish as Peiper looked at the mayor once again.

'Je vais vous le demander à nouveau. Où sont les Américains?'

The mayor pleaded that he had no knowledge of where the American soldiers were now. But he spoke too quickly and unwisely for Peiper, who showed his displeasure by shooting six-year-old Simone Courtois in the forehead. As her mother was hiding in her grubby basement less than a hundred yards away and the rest of the village were already in a state of shock, there was little audible reaction to her murder.

The mayor realised his error and spoke very slowly and reiterated that he had no knowledge of American positions.

'Nein! Nein!'

The mayor told him that he thought they might be in some woodland several kilometres from the village.

This time Peiper shot the mayor in the heart.

He then got his French speaking Gefrieter, Hans Frankel, to speak to the villagers. In his perfect French, he told the village that Obersturmbannführer Peiper would shoot the entire village if necessary. He told them twice to make sure they understood. He told them that they knew the Americans were not where the mayor had said because the Germans had just come from there.

As no villager said anything for several moments, Obersturmbannführer Peiper shot the tallest women, thirty-six-year-old Lucette Martin, in the neck. Blood sprayed like a geyser from her shattered artery. Her boyfriend, thirty-three-year-old Luke Dumas, the village baker and great grandson of the writer Alexandre Dumas, attempted to attack the Obersturmbannführer but was shot down before he could lay a hand on him.

Obersturmbannführer Peiper was not known by his men for demonstrating any signs of patience or mercy. Another of his men pleaded with the villagers to tell them what they knew.

The villagers tried to explain that they did not know where the American troops were. They had left the village several hours earlier. This information was explained to the Obersturmbannführer. He pointed to the nearby village church and ordered his men to put all the women and children inside and lock the doors. As none of the villagers spoke enough German to understand, they were slow to realise what was happening.

JoJo paused the tape.

'You don't have to tell me everything.'

She was surprised by her own plea and apparent sudden squeamishness; it was not as if the old man had not already told her a legion of harrowing tales.

Ruben Miles gave this request some thought.

'But if we do not record what happened it perhaps does not give the necessary context for later developments.'

JoJo steeled herself and told the old man to go on.

Peiper gave the order and then lit a cigar.

The cold and damp weather meant the soldiers had to douse

the church in petrol to achieve their goal. The shortage of the fuel did not change the order or lead to any questioning of the order. The Frenchmen that moved or called out were executed with a hail of bullets.

The Obersturmbannführer tried his French again.

'Où sont les Américains?'

This time he got a response. Yves Chapelle was forty-six years-old and was the village drunk. But he had not consumed a single beverage for over twenty-four hours and his hands were shaking, but not from fear. He was despised by most of his fellow villagers for his sexuality, fecklessness and lack of sobriety. To the surprise of all, he spoke in perfect, if harshly accented English. His reasoning was that even an evil German cunt would understand some basic English.

The Obersturmbannführer listened to the slowly spoken words.

'The Americans are moving west to regroup at Rocroi… you murdering Nazi fuck. And if you stop murdering innocent civilians, I will even tell you why.'

Yves Chapelle had settled in the East End of London after the last war. It was there that he developed his taste for alcohol, buggery and disdain for his own well-being. After what he witnessed at Verdun, he thought it was a reasonable exchange.

One of the SS troops who understood not only English, but the extreme cockney version that Yves Chapelle mastered in the bedsits and opium dens of Mile End, motioned for the other soldiers to hold their fire and spoke to his leader. He told him the mad Frenchman might just know where the Americans were.

'How do you know they have gone to Rocroi?'

'Because the GI whose cock I spent most of last night sucking told me so before they left.'

The sergeant translated this for the benefit of the Obersturmbannführer.

His expression registered little surprise.

'Why?'

Yves Chapelle looked at the Obersturmbannführer with contempt and said,

'Why did I suck his cock or why did they go to Rocroi?'

This made the Obersturmbannführer laugh. His men had never seen this before. He then surprised them more by ordering the fire to be put out.

'The answer to both questions is the same. It was the sensible thing to do. The Americans are waiting at Rocroi to regroup with Patton's advance from the southeast. They will then drive you Nazi scum back to the fucking fatherland...'

The Obersturmbannführer was now almost hysterical, huge tears running down his Junker cheekbones.

'Did I not tell you the Americans were all faggots!'

The village women and children emerged in understandable hysteria from the church. None appeared to have any serious burns, but most were coughing wretchedly due to acute agitation. Slowly at first, the men went to their families. The Obersturmbannführer watched this all impassively. He ushered his most reliable pitbull, Feldwebel Klein, to his side and whispered in his ear. He then spoke to Chapelle in his stuttering English.

'You think this Patton will defeat the Wehrmacht?'

Yves Chapelle looked blankly at the Obersturmbannführer.

'From what I hear, even Hitler thinks Patton will defeat the mighty Wehrmacht.'

At the later war crime tribunal in the summer of 1946, there was a lack of certainty as to whether this was what inspired Obersturmbannführer Peiper to give the order or whether in fact the order had already been whispered into the ear of Feldwebel Klein. In any event, Klein instructed his troops to machine gun to death all of the villagers except Yves Chapelle.

'My God, what an evil man!'

JoJo Bartlett heard the pointlessness of her own words.

'Why did they spare the Frenchman?'

Ruben Miles did not shift his gaze.

'They didn't. They crucified him on the smouldering church

steeple.'

HUBRIS

I t was all in the report given to Ruben Miles by Colonel Edwards. Whatever information the Avengers had, it did not come from British intelligence. Ruben Miles of course did not witness the atrocity in the Ardennes, but he had total recall of the report that he shared with his fellow operatives. It's fair to say that the content of the report had hardened their resolve more than some mechanical debris on Normandy beaches and hedgerows.

'How do you know that those responsible are hiding where you say?'

Abe seemed unconcerned by the question.

'You have your reports and we have ours,' he said, tapping the side of his head in universal signage.

'And Obersturmbannführer Peiper?'

'He is with them, although he has dispensed with his uniform and medals.'

The Avengers suggested a plan. It was not a complicated plan. They were to remain as two separate groups. The main group would initiate a frontal attack on the hamlet where the remains of the SS unit were apparently hiding. The British forces would then hide in the rear to ambush the fleeing Nazis. It would seem that the Germans were unaware that their location had been compromised.

'Like ferrets chasing rabbits into the sack,' was how Ferris, the uncomplicated soul from Somerset, concluded.

Ruben Miles was not totally convinced. He did not think the Waffen SS understood what a retreat was.

'How many?'

'No more than twenty, probably fifteen.'

That seemed more than enough Waffen SS for Ruben Miles's liking.

'Weapons?'

'Nothing big, sidearms and grenades.'

Ruben Miles perused the assorted men at their disposal. Half a dozen British soldiers of varied combat experience and a couple of truckloads of no doubt motivated, but unquantifiable Jewish renegades, albeit armed to the teeth. As well as the Sherman tank, they had mounted Browning M2s on the trucks and assorted mortars and machine guns.

Abe seemed to read his thoughts.

'We outgun anything the Nazis have to offer.'

As the Waffen SS were considered by friend and foe alike to be amongst the finest troops ever put into combat, this did not necessarily assure victory.

'My men will flush them out, the Nazis have no idea we are coming.'

Ruben Miles would have loved to have known the source of such confidence.

'You can round up what's left as they run.'

To Ruben Miles, the British contingent looked understandably a little fidgety and with due cause. They were a special team put together by British intelligence to help root out Nazis guilty of war crimes and prevent them from disappearing into the ether. Their skill set contained language and investigative practices. Taking on a Waffen SS unit in a gunfight had not been part of the pitch. Ferris was the only one seemingly gung-ho, but then he was by some distance the least pragmatic of the group. He was also the only one who had not experienced combat in any form.

Ruben Miles decided a conference with the men was in order.

'Give us a minute,' he said to Abe.

'Well? The way I see it we have two choices,' Ruben Miles explained to the men as they huddled out of earshot of the now amused Avengers.

'We can either go along with the plan or suggest an alternative.'

'I'm for the plan,' Ferris offered unnecessarily.

The others took their time in speaking.

Donnelly was an upper-class maverick from west London who, because of his background, seemed to hold sway over the working class members of the group. The British working class have always liked a toff. It was the middle class, here represented by Ruben Miles, that they had less trust and fondness in.

'These chaps seem quite sure of themselves.'

The others mumbled tentative agreement.

'Besides, they are taking on the frontal assault. We seem to have the safer position. They seem sure that the Nazis cannot match their firepower.'

The other men agreed with Donnelly. Although nominally in charge, Ruben Miles decided that dissenting was not the most viable option.

'OK,' he said, 'so we give it a go.'

Ruben Miles told Abe that his men were on board with the plan.

'We move into position by nightfall and go in at first light.'

The British were given one of the trucks and its accompanying Browning M2 to give more substance to their firepower. Ferris volunteered to use it. Via a meandering route around the lowlands surrounding the hilltop village, Ruben Miles's entourage moved into position in the last of the morning darkness.

The Avengers had assured them that they would neither be visible amongst the hedgerows nor audible as long as they maintained discipline. Even smoking was banned, as any veteran of the Western Front would appreciate. It was a long hour until they took their agreed position in a copse that gave excellent camouflage. They were able to signal to the Avengers via radio that they were in position, several minutes ahead of schedule. There was neither sound nor movement identifiable in the Nazi held village.

'Now we wait for the fireworks,' said Ruben Miles.

There had been no sign of any sentries or outlying defences.

The Avengers' plan had assumed that the Sherman tank and

accompanying Browning M2 would have demonstrated such overwhelming superiority of firepower that it would lead to a swift downing of arms via the remaining SS soldiers. However, the Avengers, to a man, hoped that this was not going to be the case and that the Germans would fight and die rather than surrender.

Every one of the Avengers had lost multiple members of their extended families at Auschwitz, Treblinka, Sobibor and the other infamous names of the holocaust death camps. They may not have known the true fates of their relatives, but they had enough suspicions to prompt very itchy trigger fingers.

As it transpired, a Panzer carefully concealed in a hay barn took out the Avengers' Sherman tank before they had got within three hundred yards of the Nazi position. The truck with the accompanying Browning M2 blew up in the minefield brilliantly concealed in a semi-circle guarding the only road that led directly into the heart of the village. A dozen of the Avengers were dead on the ground before they had so much as seen an SS insignia.

Ruben Miles and his twitchy colleagues heard all this, of course, but had no idea what it was that they were hearing. Ferris predictably took his false conclusions and ran with them. He fired up the truck and lurched out of his concealed position, Ruben Miles cursing futilely behind him. The truck lumbered up the hill noisily toward the carnage. The others inexplicably assumed that this was the signal for them to follow. Ruben Miles stood his ground.

On the other side of the village, the Avengers' truck may have exploded beneath him, but their leader Abe Edelman came to on the ground seemingly uninjured. The same could not be said for the other occupants. He crawled into a nearby roadside ditch and tried to make sense of what was happening. A massacre was what was happening. The Waffen SS knew who, when and what was coming. Obersturmbannführer Peiper and his men were in position half an hour before the Avengers began their misguided assault. They took out the Avengers like aristocrats potting pheasants.

Abe may have been an arrogant son of a bitch, but he was not a stupid son of a bitch. Methodically, he began to edge a retreat from the village road, his chin never further than an inch from the ground. None of his men made it out.

Ferris was still chugging up the hill on the far side of the village at barely ten miles an hour. He had not appreciated that he could not drive the truck and man the machine gun at the same time. His exuberance had clouded his decision making. Colonel Edwards always thought Ferris was a bad choice, but his impeccable German and the good word of a distant wealthy relative had unsurprisingly worked its usual magic inside British intelligence. It would take years, plus the Cambridge spy ring, before British intelligence realised that being given the nod by a member of the ruling elite did not necessarily mean you were either up to the task or even on the correct side.

It was a well-positioned flamethrower that literally burned the ignorance from Ferris; the cold and silent machine gun beside him taunting his foolishness as he burned.

Donnelly was the next to pay for a lack of respect for the skills of the Waffen SS. A bullet moving his stiff upper lip several metres to the southwest of the rest of his face. He collapsed to his knees and was dead before he went half-headfirst to the ground. The rest of the group were shot in the back as they tried to flee.

It had taken Obersturmbannführer Peiper's men less than three minutes to end the Avengers attempt at justice. Only the retreating Edelman and the prudent Ruben Miles had escaped the bloodbath.

Both men escaped on foot. Forty-eight hours later they were put in the same room by Colonel Edwards for a debrief.

'They knew we were coming,' said the Avenger.

Ruben Miles agreed that this was a very likely scenario.

'Apart from the people in this room and your dead comrades, there are only two Yanks who knew about the operation and they were who tipped us off about the Nazi's location.'

Ruben Miles inexplicably and instantly grew another pit in his already deeply unhappy stomach.

THE RETURN OF THE FIXER

R uben Miles had not had contact with the Fixer since the autumn of 1939, when he had seemingly scurried over the Atlantic to safety. When Colonel Edwards led the debrief into the Avengers massacre he had vouched for the reliability and loyalty of the two Yanks who had put the plan together.

'Was either man about six-two, blonde hair and blue eyes – looks more like a Nazi than any Nazi you've ever seen?'

Colonel Edwards nodded quickly that one of the men did indeed look as described.

'Did he refer to himself in the third person?'

'I don't recall that... but one of them had an unusual name.'

The Fixer had scurried across the Atlantic in the autumn of 1939 before the long-predicted Blitz had gotten underway. He spent the next year in Washington. As he had tried to explain to Ruben Miles during their last meeting in Du Cane Court, there had been quite a crossover between American intelligence and the underworld ever since J. Edgar got his foot in the door of the Bureau of Investigation in 1924. Hoover may have infamously denied organised crime existed, but it did not stop him from employing some of their fraternity.

By 1944, the Fixer had been involved in running American spies in the Iberian Peninsula. He was also in the loop regarding American support for Resistance movements in Holland and Belgium. This involved trying to coordinate the disparate Jewish groups that were hungry for revenge in Nazi-occupied Europe. He had even used his old friend Meyer Lansky to facilitate various meetings. He had gotten to know the Avengers pretty well. He had a good idea of what they were actually trying to achieve, which was a lot more ambitious than the more naïve British intelligence believed.

The Avengers did not merely envisage killing Nazi war

criminals. They had far grander aspirations for revenge on the Aryan perpetrators of genocide. Edelman and his fellow Avenger zealots had discussed and facilitated in-depth planning for the large-scale poisoning of the German population. They were going to poison the water supply of entire cities in a simultaneous assault to celebrate the defeat of Nazism in Europe. They had the method and the team to implement such a plan.

The Fixer had come across the Avengers initially as he coordinated resistance in the Netherlands post D-Day. One of the leaders, Ethan Weiss, was furnishing American intelligence with known collaborators of the Dutch holocaust. Over 100,000 Dutch Jews were murdered during World War Two, many in the death camps in the east and many by Waffen SS murder squads working in the low countries after the invasion in May 1940. Weiss was a committed Avenger and arguably the principal architect of the civilian poisoning plan. But as far as the Fixer and his colleagues were aware in the Netherlands in early 1945, he was merely helping them capture actual war criminals and their facilitators.

The Fixer used his uncanny skills for knowledge gathering. After several weeks of profitable collaboration with the Avengers in successfully 'mopping-up' both Nazi war criminals and their willing local enablers, he had also uncovered their more ambitious long-term plans for wider revenge. He shared his findings with the less illegitimate members of American intelligence in northern Europe.

Suitably horrified, it was quickly established that a deception was to be hatched so that the major Avengers involved in the civilian poisoning plan, be 'taken care off'. It seemed that the Fixer had invented 'black ops' before the Agency was even created by President Truman in 1946.

None of this adequately explained how the Waffen SS led by Obersturmbannführer Peiper knew of the imminent attack on their hillside location by the Avengers and their British accomplices.

The Fixer was once again sharing a room with Ruben Miles. The others in the meeting were Colonel Edwards, Abe Edelman and the Fixer's sidekick in American intelligence, the right-wing moral vacuum that was Isaac Taylor. He was a square-jawed descendant of old money and Ivy League superiority complexes, both of fellow Americans and lesser species. He attempted to dispel the feelings of betrayal felt by Ruben Miles and Abe Edelman. They had opened the meeting by bluntly stating that someone must have tipped the Nazis off.

'Absolutely not, only the people in this room knew of the plan. They were just ready. You know the Waffen SS do have a reputation to uphold.'

Taylor even looked like a stuck-up jackass.

The Fixer tried to wave off his colleague, but with no success.

'Besides,' Taylor continued, 'from what I've been hearing, both of you guys had members of your group who were not above suspicion.'

Abe looked at the crew-cutted Taylor with disgust.

'I don't need some all-American boy questioning the morals of my fallen comrades. Surely, if any of the men on either team had betrayed us, they would be alive... unless you have forgotten, we were the only two who made it out.'

'We don't know that for certain...'

'Gentlemen,' Colonel Edwards said, well aware that his role in the meeting was conciliation.

Ruben Miles was quick to offer his view.

'I'm not sure about anything. But judging from the information we have, I would conclude that the Germans not only knew that we were coming, but were aware of just who and what was coming.'

This brought a snort of approval from the Avenger.

Colonel Edwards was determined to achieve his objective.

'I don't think unhelpful speculation is going to achieve anything. We need to move on. We understand from locals that Peiper and his men have vacated the area. They seem to have disappeared without a trace.'

The Fixer had been unusually reticent for the duration of the meeting. He now chose to speak.

'We are of course sorry for your losses. But instead of dwelling on this almighty fuck-up, I suggest we come up with a plan to get these Nazis. Rather than cast unprovable assertions against dead guys. We should move on.'

Of course he did. After all, it was the Fixer that had been wholly responsible for Obersturmbannführer Peiper and his men knowing exactly where, when and by who they were to be attacked.

Would it have made any difference if he had known his old acquaintance Ruben Miles had been part of the British participants?

Unlikely.

THE LAST STAND

Hitler had ordered the Wehrmacht to fight to the last. There was to be no surrender, no negotiated peace. For his part, Hitler believed his people deserved to lose the war, so why should any Germans be spared their deserved fate? There was no ambiguity to his 'survival of the fittest' theory that he'd bastardised from Darwin.

Obersturmbannführer Peiper and his men were, like all remaining Nazi units and divisions, withdrawing nearer and nearer to Berlin for the last stand. Pursued feverishly by the war-loving General Patton and his marauding US 7th army in the west and by the raping red hordes from the east, the race for Berlin was on.

In the aftermath of the Avenger debacle, Ruben Miles grew an initially grudging admiration for Abe Edelman. The two men saw something of themselves in each other. For a man who had never formed close male friendships, Ruben Miles felt a genuine warmth for the senior figure in the Avengers. For Abe Edelman's part, he found the reserved Englishman something of an enigma, but one that he enjoyed trying to solve. They spent many hours in quiet conversation. Ruben Miles surprising himself by describing the wonders of New York in the 1920s. Abe Edelman's eyes would widen with incredulity at the hedonism and new age innovations that were detailed to him. Ruben Miles initially did not even question why he was acting in this singularly out-of-character way.

Preparations had begun for another crack at Obersturmbannführer Peiper and his men, now believed to be on the outskirts of Wittenberg, nearly sixty miles southwest of Berlin. Ruben Miles and Abe Edelman were once again given a plan seemingly of British provenance, but in reality, a concoction solely of US origin.

'Your name is Jewish.'

Ruben Miles acknowledged that his Christian name was of

Jewish origin.

'But you are not Jewish?'

The two men were eating dinner alone, something that had become routine. Ruben Miles's first encounter with a vegetarian, Abe Edelman was thin, but fit, a positive advertisement for his digestive decision making. Ruben Miles had surprisingly little prejudice for a man from the 1940s, especially considering that everybody knew that Hitler was a vegetarian. Not such a good ambassador.

'Not to the best of my knowledge. But then I never really got to know my father. He died when I was quite young and we never discussed much when he was alive. My mother isn't religious at all, well unless you consider her newfound Nazi sympathies a religion.'

'Your mother is a Nazi?'

'Certainly the last time we encountered each other she gave that distinct impression.'

Abe considered this, and the last of his rice with vegetables.

'You believe what the Americans said?'

Abe Edelman was a man who changed conversational direction fluidly.

'I think we have a right to be a little sceptical.'

'What is this sceptical?'

'It means we are right not to completely trust what they have said.'

'I think they lie,' Abe concluded, finishing the last of his supper.

For his part, Ruben Miles was trying hard not to think about the re-emergence of the Fixer as compulsively as he had in the past. A difficult, if not impossible, task. The Fixer's symmetry with major events of his life was beyond coincidental and fully into the realms of the freakish. It now seemed to Ruben Miles that even his mere presence in Germany may have been orchestrated by this malevolent man. And yet there was no real evidence for that. Nor was there evidence that the Fixer had been anything other than a positive influence on his life. Had he not extricated him from the clutches of British gangsters before he fled to New York?

Had he not facilitated a rare adventure in Manhattan with the Babe? Had he not secured his escape form the Spanish Civil War? And yet. There was something about the man that naturally bred suspicion.

The Fixer's emergence in pre-Blitz London had been a shock, albeit of a, by now, semi-predictable nature. But the man being unveiled as the face of American intelligence, along with the deeply nauseating Isaac Taylor, in Germany to facilitate the hunting of fugitive Nazi war criminals was a horse of a very different safari. The fact that he had not even attempted to have a private conversation with Ruben Miles deepened his sense of foreboding.

As his friendship with Abe Edelman developed with unexpected haste, Ruben Miles began to dabble in introspection, a hobby or perversion that he had never countenanced before. Why did he not form close bonds with male friends? Not a question he had ever bothered to ask himself. Now it seemed to bounce around his brain like a hurled ball bearing.

The new plan was another simple affair and once more of historical provenance. This time Obersturmbannführer Peiper and his men were to be betrayed by someone they trusted unconditionally, one hundred percent. Someone they would never consider questioning.

Gottlob Berger was an SS-Obergruppenführer and General der Waffen-SS and a trusted underling of Himmler himself. He also happened to despise Obersturmbannführer Peiper, a fact that he never acknowledged nor made public. He had nourished this hatred for many years The reason for his loathing was a doomed love affair in his youth. For his part, Obersturmbannführer Peiper could not even recall the name of the Fräulein he fucked up against a tree in the garden of her family home while Gottlob Berger knocked patiently and unsuccessfully at the front door, a posy of fresh pansies in his sweaty hands.

Peiper was betrayed by a common friend who shared the

knowledge with a distraught Gottlob Berger. But Berger's response was unique. He neither confronted Peiper, nor even spoke again to Fräulein Schneider. Instead, he waited, entirely convinced that at some undefined point in the future he would have his ultimate revenge.

By early 1945, Obergruppenführer Berger was in charge of all the retreating Waffen SS units in his role as Chief of Staff of the Volkssturm, the entity created by Hitler for Borman to command in the autumn of 1944. The Volkssturm was a militia created to protect communities in the Reich in the last months of the war.

It took Berger twenty-four years, but in March 1945 he finally planned his revenge on Obersturmbannführer Peiper.

Ruben Miles never told Abe Edelman about his previous dealings with the Fixer. He would not have known exactly how or where to begin. Instead, he encouraged the Avenger to have a healthy mistrust of the plans for Obersturmbannführer Peiper and his remaining men. The fact that the odious and clearly disingenuous Isaac Taylor did most of the communicating was reason enough for a lack of confidence.

But of course, they knew nothing of the role and motivations of Obergruppenführer Berger. The career Nazi had waited nearly a quarter of a century to have his revenge on the man who literally fucked his adolescent dreams up against a tree. He left nothing to chance. He ensured the orders came from the very top. His relationship with Borman ensured that the Führer himself had scribbled his scrawny signature with his now noticeably shaky right hand.

For his part, Isaac Taylor did not know initially how to deal with the information that came to him from the opposition. Like all descendants of the first white arrivals to Newfoundland since the Vikings, he had sufficient antipathy for anyone not as American as he perceived himself to be. And he hated Nazis, or at least he told anyone who would listen that he did. Something of an irony, as his post-war career would make him a willing accomplice to a certain Senator Joseph McCarthy.

But the information stacked up quickly, as did the positive identification of Obersturmbannführer Peiper. The material even included more details of the massacre of American troops at Malmedy than the Americans themselves possessed. As the Fixer's default setting was disbelief, he took a little more time to come around to the plan. But even he could see that although the reasons for the betrayal were unknowable, the treachery itself was watertight.

The irony of being dressed as Nazis was not lost on the men that were organised to swoop for Obersturmbannführer Peiper and his remaining men. As well as the Malmedy massacre, Peiper's unit were also the chief suspects for the infamous episode of the wearing of US uniforms during the Ardennes campaign. There was a certain Karma about the sartorial arrangements.

Ruben Miles could not have cared less what he was wearing. He and Abe Edelman had convinced themselves the plan was nothing more than another Yankee stitch-up. The Fixer was a no-show for the final briefing. Isaac Taylor made no reference to his absence. Instead, he sketched a straightforward scenario and even attempted to reel in his usual pomposity. It almost worked.

'I would not envisage any problems this time. We are 100% sure about our information, although I'm afraid the source is classified. You are just going to have to trust your allies, gentlemen.'

Abe Edelman did not trust his own brother, so an American Major with previous and a brush up his arse was more than a stretch.

'What is with the uniforms?'

'We have been assured that this is the way to go. Mr Miles? I understand you have the most convincing German accent of the group, so you will be doing the talking.'

The Fixer may not have been in the room, but Ruben Miles could almost smell his expensive French cologne.

Remarkably and gratifyingly, the operation went as smoothly as the last had failed desperately.

Obersturmbannführer Peiper and his men had welcomed their apparent comrades and why wouldn't they? They had been vouchsafed by none other than Obergruppenführer Berger, subordinate to only Martin Borman amongst the ranks of the Volkssturm.

It was Ruben Miles who handed the written orders to Obersturmbannführer Peiper and told him in his perfect German, with just a hint of Bavarian Junker, that his men were to leave all their major weapons and hardware for another unit to utilise and at once follow his convoy north, to help defend Berlin from the ever encroaching Red Army.

'The Führer himself has requested that your men lead the resistance against the communist vermin.'

Ruben Miles had learnt his lines like the lead in a school play.

Once safely in the back of the truck, Obersturmbannführer Peiper and his remaining fifteen men were fed and watered with additional horse tranquilisers. They slept like dribbling babies during the slow, long trek.

They travelled in convoy for over eight hours until they arrived at their destination. Obersturmbannführer Peiper and his men disembarked when they were told; each man groggy and bad-tempered. They had no idea where they were. They had presumed in the general vicinity of Berlin. They were wrong.

The church steeple was no longer smouldering and the rotting, crucified corpse of Yves Chapelle had thankfully been buried, but otherwise the village of Bullingen looked much the same as the last time Obersturmbannführer Peiper and his men had been there.

Obersturmbannführer Peiper was the first of the Nazis to recognise his new surroundings, when they were offloaded from the truck several hours later.

He asked why they were back in Bullingen.

Isaac Taylor motioned to Ruben Miles to explain. He did so in perfect German, informing Peiper that they were back in Belgium at the request of the Americans.

As Ruben Miles spoke, Abe Edelman emerged from behind a vehicle with a machine gun in either hand. Locked and loaded.

Isaac Taylor looked as if he was about to shit.

'What the fuck!'

For his part, Obersturmbannführer Peiper appeared to be more amused than anything else.

And then appearing in his customary way, The Fixer stood in front of Abe Edelman.

'Now just a minute, chief. I wouldn't recommend doing anything hasty here. You may want to speak with our mutual friend here.' The Fixer said this pointing at Ruben Miles and breaking into his smuggest grin.

'Abe, wait.'

The Avenger looked at Ruben Miles as if expecting a full explanation.

'Just wait.'

The Nazis were surrounded by armed American GIs, but it was the guns in Abe Edelman's hands that got their full attention.

The Fixer focused again on the now noticeably twitchy Avenger.

'Now, ordinarily I could not care less of a fuck if you mow down a dozen or so unarmed Nazis. But I have my orders and he,' the Fixer now pointed to Obersturmbannführer Peiper, 'has to go in front of a judge when all this shit is done. I have my orders and they need to be obeyed.'

Abe Edelman took a few moments to digest this information.

'What about the others?'

It was Ruben Miles who asked the question of the Fixer.

'Let's just say my position on the others is more flexible.'

Abe Edelman looked unconvinced by the change in emphasis.

'Abe, wait. You do not want to make an enemy of this man.'

'Abe, I advise you to listen to Ruben Miles, he is a man…'

'This time you can save the platitudes, give me a minute to speak with him, OK?'

The Fixer nodded his consent.

The two newfound friends held a whispered conversation. It

was short and conclusive. Ruben Miles had got through to his younger friend.

As they did so, the Fixer brought out a young woman from behind the village water pump in the middle of the road. Her eyes never strayed from those of Obersturmbannführer Peiper.

The Fixer spoke again.

'Ask Peiper if he recognises this young lady?'

'Nein.' Replied Obersturmbannführer Peiper, not waiting for a translation.

He was the only person who knew for sure that he was lying. The appearance of the woman had a clear impact on the rest of the Germans; some began murmured conversations. She was vaguely familiar in an uncomfortable way.

The Fixer took the young lady gently by the arm and walked over to Abe Edelman and Ruben Miles.

'Gentlemen, this is Yvette Dupont. She has lived in this village since the age of five when she moved here from Marseille. She was here when Obersturmbannführer Peiper and his comrades had their fun. She saw most everything. She was the only villager who survived the massacre. She played dead and got very, very lucky.'

The men greeted her formally as if meeting at a party.

'I need to take Obersturmbannführer Peiper. Those are my orders. Yvette is going to identify the two men that she saw carrying out his orders. Now, Mr Edelman, you are not going to deprive this brave woman of her village's justice are you?'

Yvette spoke neither English nor German and Ruben Miles had only rudimentary French. But she looked a little Basque to Ruben Miles.

'Hablas Españyol?'

'Un poquito.'

And so, Ruben Miles stood in a deserted village in Belgium and had a conversation with a young French lady in Spanish about a massacre committed by the Nazis standing in front of them, with the Fixer seemingly coordinating the madness.

Yvette Dupont agreed to identify the guilty men but politely and firmly declined the opportunity to take the revenge for her village. Instead, she asked Abe Edelman if he would oblige.

Abe Edelman readily agreed to go along with the plan, something Ruben Miles thought could only have happened because of the appearance of Yvette Dupont. He appeared to be a little smitten.

They made Obersturmbannführer Peiper watch.

But first, the Fixer made Ruben Miles describe in detail to Obersturmbannführer Peiper and his men just who had betrayed them and why.

'You will die, Obersturmbannführer Peiper, and at our hand, but not on this day. As for the men that carried out your orders, they will go to their graves knowing that they were betrayed by Obergruppenführer Berger, because you fucked his childhood sweetheart against a beech tree nearly twenty five years ago.'

How could anyone make sense of luck like that.

Obersturmbannführer Peiper looked unmoved and unsurprised.

Yvette Dupont walked along the line of the Nazis who stood rigidly to attention. Twice she stopped in front of a man and tapped gently on their right shoulder. Neither of the men responded in any way.

She was asked if she was sure. She simply nodded her response. When she had furtively watched the men kill her fellow villagers, her mind had taken mental pictures that would never be erased or forgotten.

Abe Edelman delivered the justice to the back of each of the men's heads. He used Obersturmbannführer Peiper's confiscated Luger to despatch those that had carried out his orders unquestioningly. The man himself watched impassively.

'Sie folgten meinen Befehlen.'

Ruben Miles translated.

'And we are following ours,' he replied curtly.

A shaking Yvette Dupont was led away by Isaac Taylor.

The Fixer slapped Ruben Miles and Abe Edelman firmly on the back and said, 'We have some more turkey to talk boys,' leaving both men confused for very different reasons.

Obersturmbannführer Peiper and his depleted men were led away in handcuffs.

ABE EDELMAN

Abe Edelman felt little when he pulled the trigger on the two Nazis in Bullingen in March 1945. He had killed plenty of Nazis before. However, there was something about Yvette Dupont that seemed to have settled in his body like an invasive infection. For all of his outer confidence, Abe Edelman was a twenty-eight-year-old virgin. His experience of women was almost nil. He had rarely been interested before and the times he had were infrequent and led to swift disappointment. Not that this was something he had shared with anyone before.

Ruben Miles was not someone that people usually confided in. In many ways he was the polar opposite of Abe Edelman. He had zero male friends but plenty of ex-girlfriends and more than the occasional ex-wife. These two very different men with little recognisably in common, had formed an unusual alliance and bond. Therefore, Abe Edelman was not unduly surprised when Ruben Miles said to him twenty minutes after he had executed the Nazis, 'What is it about that girl that has got to you so much?'

'You do not feel sorry for what she saw?'

'Of course I do, but I know that look in your eye and it isn't pity.'

'I do not know what you say.'

Abe Edelman's mastery of English always wavered when it suited him. He decided on his usual diversionary tactics.

'Tell me of you and this Fixer.'

'That is a long and confusing story. Let's say that he has appeared regularly in my life and usually with a big impact.'

'He is criminal, yes?'

'Yes, as well as being in American intelligence.'

'Do you trust him?'

'No, but he has helped me out of a few bad situations in my life. He helped me back in England, America and also during the Spanish War.'

'He told me he knew about our big plans. But how is that possible? I have not said a word, even to you Ruben Miles. And the others, they would never betray our plans.'

Ruben Miles never did work out why so many people in his life addressed him by his full name.

'What big plans?'

'Revenge.'

Abe Edelman told his friend about his plans for revenge, surprising both men in the process.

The Fixer was not always a slavish follower of orders, but with regard to Obersturmbannführer Peiper, he had been happy to comply. His superiors had pitched the need for as many war criminals as possible to be made an example of after the end of the conflict. The Allies were convinced that show trials were needed for not just the ringleaders, but also the mere facilitators of Nazi tyranny in Europe. Not just for overt justice, but also to allow the survivors of occupied countries to receive some form of official closure, albeit one that would not end the night tremors that would never truly dissipate.

However, his superiors were also keen to shield the world from their intended hypocrisy. For they also had lists of Nazis that were not going to get prosecuted. Instead, these names would be welcomed with, if not open arms, then certainly back-alley handshakes. Scientists, of course, to assist in projects that were already underway. But also military men, who would no doubt be handy when it came to fighting the inevitable future enemy, the Soviets. The lessons of Stalingrad, if you will.

An uncomfortable truth was that many in American intelligence thought that they were fighting the wrong enemy. Hitler may be a naughty boy and grudgingly they would concede that he needed to be stopped, but it was communism that was the perceived ideological threat to Uncle Sam. Unfortunately, as far as these committed capitalists were concerned, President Roosevelt had cozied up to Uncle Joe like some kind of closet red. In the same way as every future Democratic President would be viewed by the same CIA cabal. The Isaac Taylors of this world were destined for post-war careers in future CIA black ops. Maybe some day someone will ask Isaac Taylor where he was on November 22nd 1963. They would get an interesting reply: he was in Dallas, with several of his black ops colleagues.

The Fixer had infiltrated the Avengers originally in the low countries in late 1943, immediately after his transfer from Iberian Peninsula activities. He heard the whispers of revenge schemes early and consistently. He had an easy and uncanny knack of gathering unwilling informers. Of course, in those days, liberation was a far-off dream and so what plans they had were mere sketches of outlandish ambition. But from D-Day onwards, especially after the beach heads were secure, the Avengers' leadership began to assimilate some more detailed planning for what they had in mind.

Abe Edelman was one of the true brains of the organisation. He shared his thirst for revenge with a keen mind and a full address book of wealthy Jews in the States. He was also a big picture man and it was his grandiose idea that went before a counsel of their leadership in the late Autumn of 1944. It would seem that they had the financial backing and the organisation to carry out the plan.

But more immediate revenge had superseded the plans. For Abe Edelman and others, they had to be on the ground killing as many Nazis as possible. Only after victory had been secured on the battlefields of northern Europe, could the revenge coup de grâce be delivered.

That victory was now not just undeniable, but imminent.

The capture of Obersturmbannführer Peiper may have been anticlimactic for Ruben Miles, but his reunion with the Fixer was anything but. After letting him dangle for a couple of days, the two men finally had a private conversation. The Fixer cutting straight to his usual chase.

'Once again, I find myself needing a man with your undoubted skills, Ruben Miles. It would seem that Abe Edelman has taken a shine to your reserved English ways.'

Ruben Miles conceded that the two had struck up an unlikely camaraderie.

'I would imagine he has confided in you his organisation's wider plans?'

Ruben Miles played dumb, although he was not at all sure why.

'Your acting skills are effective on most men, Ruben Miles, but not the Fixer. I know that you know exactly what they intend to do. And may I say, you have a humanitarian right to assist in preventing these evil plans.'

'I have no idea what you're getting at. They just want to kill Nazis, which is why we are all here, right?'

The Fixer looked sceptical.

'Let's just say their definition of a Nazi has widened... considerably.'

Ruben Miles was stalling for time. Time to get his head around what he had recently learnt from his newfound friend. It was not often the Fixer appeared to have secured the moral high ground. But, despite the abhorrent crimes of the holocaust, which unlike many men at that time, Ruben Miles had been briefed about by British intelligence in the run up to his current posting, there could be no justification for what Abe Edelman had confessed was his organisation's primary goal.

The plan was so simple it might even have worked. If history teaches us anything, it is that wealth will find a way. The backers of the Avengers had deep pockets and deeper motivation; always a potent combination. But the world is full of dreamers, schemers and mindless optimists. They are usually politicians and incompetent line managers. What gets things done are... the organisers, the implementers. And this is where the Avengers were going to have problems. Coming up with an ideological plan is very far from coming up with a successful implementation.

Ruben Miles could see the vision behind the plan, he could even understand the why. But of course, the plan could not succeed. Two wrongs and all that. The Fixer made it clear that he expected Ruben Miles to use his position of confidante of Abe Edelman, to ensure the plan never got lift off, never mind a chance at success. In retrospect, it was one of the more honest Fixer instructions.

HORST BAUER

Yvette Dupont would never forget, nor would she ever truly forgive. What she had witnessed on that grey Belgian afternoon would occupy her thoughts not just every day of the rest of her life, but most hours, like a parent who loses a child.

Her survival was another extreme example of the vagaries of chance. Every other villager received an execution shot to the back of the head. But as she lay face down in the blood-streaked cobbled main street in Bullingen, she had no influence over the actions of others. The momentary distraction of one man led to her surviving that day and living for another fifty-three years.

Horst Bauer took inordinate pride in the fact that he shared the same first name as a Nazi martyr, Horst Wessel, murdered by communists in February 1930. That he came from Hitler's hometown of Linz deepened his popularity both in the Nazi youth and then onto the Waffen SS. A dyed-in-the-wool Nazi, he even informed on one of his teachers for making fun of the Führer one day in class when he was fifteen years old. The bewildered, middle-aged spinster ended up dead in Dachau within three months. Young Horst never doubted his actions for a second, even when he remembered that she was a good teacher and that she had always treated him with kindness.

He was not a soldier that was easily distracted, especially when he was following important orders from Obersturmbannführer Peiper. But as he and his partner in crime, Gerhard Kohler, despatched prone villagers without conscience, he suddenly found himself thinking about his little sister Elke.

Elke Bauer had been born with a clubfoot and undiagnosed severe autism. She never learnt to speak properly. Instead she communicated via several indistinct guttural noises. It was only her elder brother Horst who could comprehend what she wished to communicate. Three years her elder, Horst was protective of his little sister, aware that she was so different from all the other little girls who skipped and played in the nearby streets. He had been heartbroken when, aged fourteen, his parents had sat him down and told him that poor Elke had died. He cried for nearly a week in his room.

He rarely thought of her as he grew older and became a hardened soldier. Toughened up first by the never-ending route marches and camping trips in the Nazi youth and then later with the intense and exhausting training to make the grade in the Waffen SS. His parents, both unassuming but supportive Nazis, never made reference to their only other child.

He found out by chance on his first leave home after passing out aged nineteen; some fool in the local hostelry asking him if he ever visited his loony little sister. It had ended in a one-sided fistfight, but not before Horst Bauer had been given the address of the place where his little sister had been sent.

The day before he was due to report back for embarkation, Horst Bauer took a bus ride to Lichtenberg, a small town several miles from his hometown. He found the address by following the little map book he borrowed from his father's desk drawer. Someone, presumably his father, had already circled the address of the home. There was no signage out front and when he eventually located a door to the rear of the building and knocked and rang the bell, he was beginning to doubt that there was anyone inside.

The door was answered by a bald, bespectacled middle-aged man who looked anything but threatening.

Horst Bauer explained who he was and why he was there. The man replied that he did not care and closed the door firmly in his face. So much for his deceptive demeanour. Despite his strength and determination, Horst Bauer could not force entry and after several minutes of anguished trying and verbal taunts directed at the man inside, he gave up.

When he returned home, his parents somehow knew of his visit. His father sat him down at the kitchen table and, completely out of character, placed a cold beer in front of him. He then told his son the truth, or at least a version of it.

As a good Nazi, Horst Bauer had learnt first in school and then in other organisations not to question the actions of any Nazi administrator. His father patiently explained that it had been in Elke's best interests to be taken from the family home and placed in state care. She had lived there happily for six years, but the family had been forbidden to tell of her fate or visit her, as this would only make matters worse for his little sister. Sadly, Horst's father then told him that she had died that year from tuberculosis.

He had accepted this at the time. His beliefs and the respect for his parents and authority had ensured this. But over time, and hearing the views of many Nazis on the need for purification of the gene pool, not just on a racial basis of course, but also to irradicate other 'imperfections', meant that he had belatedly worked out the fate of poor Elke and thousands like her. Put to death by lethal injection by competent administrators merely fulfilling their quotas and following secret directives.

For reasons that he could not fathom, it was memories of his little sister playing in front of the fire in the sitting room of the family home that had suddenly demanded his attention as he and Gerhard Kohler were despatching the villagers in Bullingen several years later. It had only been for a few moments, but in the time that it took for Horst Bauer to banish the thoughts about his little sister Elke and how she had been one of the many thousands of young Germans murdered by the Nazis' own euthanasia program, initiated by Hitler himself in October 1939, he had missed the prone and silent body of Yvette Dupont and had instead pulled his trigger on the next in his line of vision. His partner in crime, Gerhard Kohler, was enjoying himself too much to even notice his colleague's error.

YVETTE DUPONT

Yvette Dupont would never understand her reprieve. Somehow, she managed to keep her breathing low, despite the wound she had received to her leg during the initial shootings. It was a flesh wound and although bloody, it was almost painless. She stole the quickest of sideways glances and saw the side profiles of the two executioners. Her brain took a snapshot that she would never forget. After a period of time that she found impossible to estimate, she could hear that the soldiers had departed the village.

Yvette Dupont shared this with Abe Edelman and Ruben Miles after Bauer and Kohler had been shot.

'I could never forget their faces, one of them was even laughing.'

She spoke in French and Ruben Miles was surprised when Abe answered in the same language.

'They will never laugh again.'

Yvette Dupont squeezed the hand of Abe Edelman.

Yvette Dupont and Abe Edelman fell hard and quickly, presumably inspired by the recent traumatic events. Abe Edelman's ability to speak French had only been exposed by his feelings for Yvette. He was never happy when he gave anything about himself away so cheaply. For her part, Yvette Dupont was aware that her feelings for Abe Edelman would always be intrinsically linked to the events in her childhood village.

'You don't really do love stories. Mayhem, death and destruction are your more common staples.'

JoJo Bartlett was enjoying herself. She was wheeling Ruben Miles around the quarry garden of Belsay Hall, a dozen or so miles north of The Apple Orchard Retirement Community. Ruben Miles made a poor patient, but he had hurt his left leg in a small altercation in the TV room over the remote control, the banality of Deal or No Deal and whether he and Mrs Hazel Wharton were indeed a romantic item. It was the first time that he had lost his temper in many years. Although the old man himself had withheld the reasons for his injury from JoJo, the aforementioned Mrs Hazel Wharton had informed her of the events of the evening before with a certain glee. She had never had men scuffling over her before.

'Mind you, maybe after yesterday's event we can say that you have your own little love story developing...'

JoJo was quite pleased that she had lasted nearly an hour in the old man's company before she revealed her knowledge.

Ruben Miles, not averse to playing the age card when it suited, chose to pretend he had not heard her.

'I know you heard me.'

They wheeled in silence for a few minutes, taking in the grandeur of the magical micro-climate of the gardens and the impressive array of exotic plants. Not what you expect in Northumberland, even in the last days of spring.

'I've never been here before.'

This was his signal that he had forgiven her indiscretion and he was ready to move forward, both literally and figuratively. JoJo Bartlett released the brake and pushed him toward the more rare of the abundant Rhododendron species seemingly devouring the rocks behind them.

'I have never seen a pair fall so quickly in love. My God, look at the colours!'

JoJo conceded that the gardens were quite spectacular, even if, like most eighteen-year-olds (her birthday had been the week before and really, don't even mention it), she found the concept of gardens and specifically gardening, one of the more pointless of human pastimes. How much this was to do with the hours her parents spent knee deep in topsoil, compost and uneasy silences was unclear.

'So, what happened to them?'

In the weeks following the revenge at Bullingen, Ruben Miles spent most of the daylight hours with Abe Edelman and

Yvette Dupont. She had been given special dispensation by the Fixer to accompany the men on their next mission, another investigation into rogue Nazi soldiers holing up in the Bavarian highlands. They stayed in roadside guest houses with indignant and rude Germans, each to a man or women proclaiming that they were not and had never been Nazi supporters. Anecdotally, it seemed the Nazis had zero support in the very area that had facilitated their rise.

It became something of a joke amongst the men. Before they were even shown to their humble quarters, they would listen to variations on the same story. They were not Nazis, their family were not Nazis, they did not know any Nazis, repeat to fade.

The last days and weeks of the war were quiet for the entourage as each time they located some Nazis in hiding, whether it be in remote huts in woodlands or in tiny basements of town houses, they gave in quietly and peacefully. Most seemed relieved that it was all over. The Fixer was keen to point out that there were plenty of renegades who had not given in so easily, but there were none on his watch.

By the time that it became common knowledge that Hitler had taken the coward's way out in his bunker in Berlin on 30th April 1945, the Fixer informed the men that their work was done. There were still plenty of Nazis in hiding and the Americans would of course do their share of the looking, but the services of Abe Edelman and Ruben Miles were no longer required. Neither man thought to ask why. The reality was that the Fixer had been ordered to secure the services and special passage west for as many useful Nazis as the US military could lay their hands on. Avengers with itchy trigger fingers were not part of the new plan.

Ruben Miles was heading home, but not before a final summons from the Fixer.

'Use the woman,' he said, offering Ruben Miles a drink he knew that he would not accept. Like most men, the Fixer did not understand or tolerate Ruben Miles's abstinence.

Ruben Miles clearly needed a little embellishment.

'You know what his group is attempting and no matter how

seemingly far-fetched, we need to take it seriously. Don't play dumb, Ruben, I know he told you of their plans.'

Ruben Miles was aware enough to know that the use of his Christian name alone was significant, but he did not know why.

'She will talk him out of being involved and, from what I gather, he is by far the most able, so use the woman to stop your friend from attempting his plan and I will ensure that it is dead in the water.'

Ruben Miles found himself nodding, for once a scheme of the Fixer's that he could be fully on board with without apparent misgivings.

The most difficult part of the task was trying to speak to Yvette Dupont out of the earshot of Abe Edelman; they were almost inseparable. A dicky stomach after a questionable bread soup that contained a fish stock of dubious origin, was the surprising solution. Ruben Miles pounced and told the disbelieving Yvette Dupont of her lover's plans.

The Fixer had of course been right, and within twenty-four hours, Yvette Dupont had convinced Abe Edelman that the Avenger's plans to poison hundreds of thousands of German citizens in several of the major cities via their water supply was beyond even a mortal sin and if he was to be even remotely involved, she would never even speak to him again.

Whether because of his love for Yvette Dupont or the realisation of the injustice of the scheme, Abe Edelman turned his back on industrial scale mass murder and his brothers. He chose love.

They were married the following week, with Ruben Miles as the best man.

'A real love story, at last. I knew you had at least one in you. Admittedly, one not featuring you.'

They had adjourned to the Belsay Hall tea rooms.

'And of course the Avengers didn't try the plan? Or at the very least it must have failed?'

'They never tried, at least not to the best of my knowledge.'

'Do you think their love story prevented some great crime?'

'That is unknowable, don't you think? Once one course of action has begun, other avenues are closed off and will never come to pass, is that not the essence of life?'

'Your science of random stuff again.'

The old man looked thoughtful and a little hurt. JoJo threw him a bone.

'Well, it's still a pretty good way to end their story.'

'Except it was not the end of their story, the sequel happened many years later.'

VE DAYS

R uben Miles was back in London on the eve of V.E. Day, May 7th 1945. It took a little adjusting to. Although the city itself looked much the same as it had on his departure ten weeks previously, the mood of the people had been miraculously transformed. Six years of long and haggard faces seemed to have disappeared overnight, with strangers grinning at each other in the debris-cluttered streets. The spike in the birth rate in exactly nine months was not coincidental.

The man himself was back in Du Cane Court the evening before the announcement of the unconditional surrender of all German forces, making himself a light supper of pickled herring, one of the few things he approved of about his limited time in Germany. When his doorbell rang, he gave a little start and his first instinct was that he would find the Russian and or the Fixer grinning manically on his doormat. However, it was a bigger and much more welcome surprise that stood at his door.

He had not seen Carolyn de Villiers, AKA the Specialist, since before his breakdown. Although she had apparently visited him during his hospitalisation, he had no memory of these visits. This was a disconcerting scenario for a man with hyperthymesia. For her part, despite the countless honeytraps that she had successfully pulled off for her country in the intervening years, none had diminished her beauty in any way. She was, even to a man like Ruben Miles, almost impossible to truly take in.

'I heard you were home,' she said simply.

The pickled herring went in the bin.

The Specialist insisted on the Ritz first, before a proposed Soho club for late night dancing. The basement bar of the Ritz was not what Ruben Miles expected and the Specialist seemed to enjoy his apparent discomfort. She knocked back her usual quota of gin cocktails whilst Ruben Miles felt out of place in the bohemian atmosphere and not just because of the lack of alcohol in his blood.

'It's a bar with a slightly unusual clientele for the Ritz, mostly lesbians,' explained the Specialist.

Ruben Miles took in a scene that was more Berlin in the late 1920s than any London he had ever known. But he guessed why she had brought him here. Being part of a seemingly heterosexual couple, the Specialist received no unwelcome attention from any reveller, something that she had to accept as the norm wherever else she went in the city. Lewd comments from bottom line GIs, stray hands on the underground and being propositioned by strangers on the street were all part of her everyday life. She explained this to Ruben Miles without rancour.

'I'm not complaining, you understand. The way I look has made me what I am and enabled me to do what I have done for my country. It's just that sometimes I like a night off and so as long as I bring a boyfriend-looking bloke here, I can just enjoy myself.'

She still received the admiring glances, but from a non-contact distance. It was the Specialist who brought up the obvious elephant in the room.

'*She* loved it here too, although I never really understood why. She was very straitlaced, my sister.'

Ruben Miles dealt with his mental breakdown by not thinking about his mental breakdown. But standing in the basement bar of the Ritz, with the beautiful Specialist talking in his ear about her sister, made that impossible.

Ruben Miles spent his last day with her sister, Eleanor de Villiers, at the very hotel they were now drinking in. Albeit in the upstairs, more conservative bar area. It had been the day the papers were full of the Nazi invasion of the low countries. It seemed like someone else's lifetime ago, even if he could remember *most* of the days in between.

Ruben Miles did not receive any official diagnosis of his incredibly rare condition, but he knew now his memory was different to other people's. However, no matter how hard he tried, he could not recall a single day of the several months he spent in hospital after the death of Eleanor de Villiers. It was as if it had not happened; the only missing link to his extraordinary mental archives.

'You look a whole lot better than the last couple of times I saw you... in the hospital.'

It was Cavendish that had told him of her visits.

'I'm sorry, I have no memory of your visits. But it was nice of you to come.'

'I'm not surprised. What they filled you full of in there would have floored a horse.'

As one of the many pharmaceuticals that they had used to experiment on him was a horse tranquilizer, this was freakishly accurate.

'They wouldn't have let me in if it wasn't for Cavendish.'

'What can you tell me of that place and what they did to me?'

'Not much, I'm afraid. They said you needed the drugs to stop you from killing yourself. They said that you kept saying you would kill yourself because of... you know.'

This mention of Eleanor made them both quietly reflective.

'It was just one of those war things, Ruben. She was in the wrong place at the wrong time. If this war teaches us anything, it is the importance of good luck. Or rather the importance of *not* having bad luck.'

'But I made her come to Balham that night. She didn't really want to, I know.'

'My sister never did anything she did not want to do.'

'I blame myself. I always will.'

'I understand. But I don't and she wouldn't, she was a scientist, a mathematician. She occasionally talked about the mathematics of luck, I never understood a bloody word she was on about, she said it was...'

'The science of random?'

'No, what's that?'

'I don't really know, but Cavendish kept mentioning it. I thought it was some kind of intelligence mantra.'

'I've never heard of that before and Eleanor never

mentioned it. She just said luck was incalculable and she was clearly fascinated by it. I think it must have been something to do with what she did at Bletchley you know?'

'Did you ever find out what she was working on?'

'Not in any great detail obviously, but something to do with German code breaking. She mentioned the odd small thing from time to time.'

Ruben Miles was relieved when they moved on; he had felt vaguely claustrophobic in the basement bar and the trapped cigarette smoke was making him gag. They walked up Piccadilly to Soho. It was a mild spring evening and it took less than fifteen minutes at a casual pace. The streets were heaving, as if the news coming the next day was already unofficial public knowledge. They continued their conversation more easily than in the cramped basement bar.

'What did Cavendish tell you about me?'

'Just that you had a breakdown after Eleanor's death, nothing else really.'

'And you saw me a couple of times in the hospital, how far apart?'

'A couple of months at least, I had been busy with a job in Paris.'

The Official Secrets Act was written for people like the Specialist.

'Was I the same both times?'

'I'd say yes, totally out of it really. You just talked a load of gibberish about seeing things. Many very strange things I seem to recall.'

Ruben Miles had one of his feelings.

'Was there anyone else there, anyone that stood out? Maybe not a doctor, but someone else taking quite an interest in my condition.'

The Specialist gave this some thought.

'There were a couple of Americans there both times I saw you. They definitely were not doctors. American intelligence chaps by the look of them. They hardly spoke, but I remember one of them was a tall, good-looking guy, not my type, but a lot of girls' type…'

He already knew of course, but he asked the obvious question anyway.

'Blonde crew-cut, square jaw?'

'That's right and the other one…'

'Sour looking, like he was sucking on a lemon. A face you would never tire of slapping?'

This made the Specialist laugh, somehow this made her look even more beautiful.

'How do you know that?'

That was the easy bit. Everyone he met wanted to slap Isaac Taylor. Even the Fixer.

Ruben Miles was not a dancer. But being with the Specialist meant he had little choice. They went to the 400 Club on Leicester Square and Ruben Miles did his best to keep up. Luckily, such a crowded and exuberant dance floor was able to conceal many of his less then rhythmic efforts. The Specialist did not seem to mind. She had a blast. Her dancing, it seemed to Ruben Miles, noticeably improved with each additional gin fizz. They stayed until they were thrown out.

Eventually, the alcohol did seem to have some detrimental impact on the Specialist. Ruben Miles detected if not a slurring, then a slight slowing of her, by now, whispered conversation.

'And now you get to take me home. I think I owe it to my little sister somehow. After all, she never got to take you home, did she?'

And no one would ever argue about that with the Specialist.

KISS AND TELL

JoJo found herself more interested in the Specialist than she cared to admit.

'So, did the two of you become some hot secret service item?'

It took Ruben Miles a few moments to work out exactly what he was being asked.

'No, it was just one night.'

He neglected to say that his detailed reminiscences of that particular night were right at the top of his favourite all time memories, and boy did that girl deserve her nickname. Ruben Miles did not want to sound like some horrid, old pervert, so he wisely chose not to share his thoughts with JoJo.

'Did you ever see her again?'

'We were both in Germany in late '45 and '46, but we saw little of each other as we were on different projects. The next time I spent any real time with her was in 1953 in Washington DC. I understand she was quite friendly with Eisenhower. She was certainly an upgrade on Kay Summersby.'

'General Eisenhower?'

'Eisenhower was the President by then, but he was the Commander-in-chief of the allied forces during the war and Summersby was his very personal English assistant. Quite the scandal at the time because, of course, he was married. But it was all hushed up of course... everything like that was then, not like now.'

JoJo did not ask Ruben Miles what he was doing in Washington in 1953.

'Did the Specialist help you, you know, get over Eleanor?'

'Not in the slightest. But we did keep in touch over the years, although not for a long while now. I'm not sure if she is even still alive, but she was quite a bit younger than me.'

Ruben Miles was not an unaware person. He was aware of the over sentimentality of his feelings for Eleanor de Villiers. After all, the couple barely knew each other and had not even been lovers. But her tragic, unfortunate and ultimately all-too-common death during the Blitz, meant that he had put her memory on an undeserved pedestal his entire life. He thought JoJo was too young to see this. He was wrong.

'You do seem to have been affected by her sad death a lot. I mean, I am not being critical, but you lost a wife and child in even more tragic circumstances and then you kind of abandoned the other two kids...'

Ruben Miles was aware of his hypocrisy; he just had no defence or explanation for it. He may have felt guilt for dumping his remaining children on the future Nazi sympathiser that was his mother, but he spent very little time dwelling on that. He supposed, plausibly, that as he had not been responsible for the fire that killed his wife and favourite child, it was therefore the guilt of his culpability regarding Eleanor de Villiers that was the driving force behind his disproportionate feelings.

'I'm sorry, I don't think you're a bad person, but I have real difficulty with how little that seems to figure in your story.'

She surprised herself with her bluntness.

She had made a resolution since becoming a legal adult. She was going to tell people what she really thought. Although giving her a real sense of liberation, it had already accrued some push back in the several days since it had been in operation. Her mother was not speaking to her again after JoJo told her mother what she thought of UKIP, her new hobby. The biology teacher at school had burst into tears when she told him that he wasn't a very good teacher and she would really appreciate it if he stopped staring at her breasts when he spoke to her. The headteacher had been almost sympathetic, after a fashion.

And then there was Luke. That had gone cataclysmically badly, and on her actual birthday night out. She reflected that she could have chosen her words more carefully. The irony was almost funny. She wanted Luke to be more like the teenager she had first met, not the rather needy newer version. Therefore, she supposed she should be kind of gratified when he decided to grow a pair and dump her loudly in the restaurant in Jesmond where they were supposed to be celebrating her birthday. He had not spoken to her or acknowledged her existence in the days since. Welcome to the complexities of relationships.

The old man was seldom on the backfoot; indeed his default position was always squarely facing the front. But he knew JoJo was right; had he really spent decades mourning the wrong events? It certainly seemed so. JoJo seemed to read his thoughts.

'I'm sure you could contact them somehow. I've heard of this thing on the internet called Facebook. Apparently, it's a way of getting in touch with people you have lost contact with. We could try that or some other website.'

Ruben Miles did not mention the letters he kept in a box in a lockup in Tynemouth. Mind you, he had not told her about any of the stuff in the lockup in Tynemouth. He knew that this was remiss of him, after all, he had to die at some point, didn't he? He should give her a key with instructions that it be opened only in the event of his death before they had finished his memoirs.

'She was a remarkable woman, the Specialist, and no one has ever written a book about her, now *that* would be a story.'

The old man still knew how best to distract JoJo.

'You could become a writer and explore more about some of the people and events I have told you about. Mind you, we still have a lot to get through.'

Another successful deployment. JoJo *was* thinking about becoming a writer. She liked writing essays, and she liked finding out about things she knew nothing about. What else was there to it?

'I've written up everything you have told me so far. Do you want to read the notes?'

'I trust you will have done a good job. You also record everything on tape, don't you?'

JoJo confirmed that this was true. The old man was always clear and concise in what he told her.

'Maybe another time,' he said and told himself that he would need Mrs Hazel Wharton to get a spare key cut for the lockup in Tynemouth. But how was he to organise that without raising her infamously strong sense of suspicion?

THE QUIET MAN

L ike many who lived through it, Ruben Miles suffered a significant bout of anti-climax at the end of the Second World War. One night with the Specialist was not going to change that. The readjustment to peacetime was slow and more than a shade tedious. It was during this period that Ruben Miles finally accepted that he seemed to be predisposed to danger. The evidence was overwhelming. Because of this, he found the next two years to be the most difficult of his by now early middle-aged life. His comfortable financial position did put him at a significant advantage over many of his peers, but his chances of more excitement were curtailed by a conversation he had with Cavendish just a week after the VE Day celebrations. They met, courtesy of Cavendish's rather odd request, at the National Portrait Gallery in St Martin's Place. It was a beautiful, sunny day. Ruben Miles felt that being indoors on such a day was almost a crime.

'You did a sterling job out there, Miles, the Yanks were impressed. The one with the odd name was particularly effusive. Strange chap.'

Ruben Miles did *not* want a conversation with Cavendish about the Fixer.

'Our sources have confirmed that the Avengers are now neutralised as a serious threat. That odd friend of yours was clearly the brains behind the operation. The Belgian girl came up trumps.'

Cavendish seemed remarkably well-informed about recent events in Belgium and Germany.

'Was it really a serious concern?'

'The Yanks were taking it very seriously. Apart from getting their hands on Nazi scientists, this seemed a priority operation for them.'

'So, what now for Abe Edelman?'

'He will be kept under surveillance for now. But that little Belgian girl certainly seems to have done the trick.'

'She was French, actually.'

They strolled around a section of the gallery that appeared to be given over to portraits of aristocratic Victorians with comedic facial hair. Gladstone was ironically one of the more conservative of those on show.

'What's your plan now, Miles, now that the big show is over?'

'Does that mean you have nothing for me?'

Cavendish took a seat directly facing Prince Albert Victor, one of Queen Victoria's grandchildren and the first son of Edward VII.

'Appearances can be deceiving, don't you think? Do you recognise this young prince?'

Ruben Miles conformed that he was aware of the King that never was,

'If I told you that he was knee deep in the Jack the Ripper case, would you believe me?'

'I'm not altogether sure that anything would surprise me now.'

'Indeed. Not that it will ever become public knowledge. Some things never will. We will not be requiring your immediate services, Miles. However, we would like to call on your skills at a later date, perhaps on a more informal basis.'

'By informal, I suppose you mean unpaid?'

'I would've thought a man of your not inconsiderable means would have little concern in that area.'

Ruben Miles had of course not discussed his financial wellbeing with anyone.

'Your skills are held in high regard by both us and the Americans.'

'And just what exactly are these skills that the Fixer in particular seems to so admire?'

'Let's just say that you have a little moral flexibility, Miles and that, in our line of business, can be a real asset. And then of course there is that memory of yours. We all have our roles to play. I believe you have just reacquainted yourself with Miss de Villiers. A very fine case in point.'

Ruben Miles had never discussed his memory with Cavendish.

'Until we reach a point of need, we will melt into your background and leave you in peace.'

A trademark snort from Ruben Miles.

'Your cynicism is one of your less attractive features, Miles. I'm presuming it comes from your years living in New York?'

'What makes you think I want to remain in service?'

'Let's just say we recognise your need for a little, what should we call it, stimulation?'

And that, for the next few months, was the sum of his interaction with his former colleagues. In the weeks that followed, Ruben Miles gave considerable thought to his next actions. At one stage he had almost convinced himself to move back to the States permanently. He had heard that the climate in California was like the Mediterranean all year round. The one thing he hated about Britain was the interminably lengthy gloom of winter. He also considered travelling further afield and seeing what Australia had to offer. But he liked his apartment in Balham and, although the city had taken one hell of a battering during the war, his fondness for London was not diminished.

Having settled on a location, he now needed a focus. And that, like a great deal of what preceded it, was decided by what can only be defined as fortune.

THE EDELMAN FINALE

Ruben Miles was usually a stickler for chronology. It was an issue that had frustrated JoJo Bartlett sporadically throughout their project. Therefore, when he announced over a pair of frothy lattes in the tearoom at Wallington Hall that he wanted to 'tie up a few loose ends' from earlier recollections, JoJo was taken a little by surprise. Once again, the pair had taken advantage of the warm weather to escape The Apple Orchard Retirement Community for the delights of another National Trust offering. Ruben Miles found that he liked his days out and, although he never said as much to JoJo, there was certainly a feeling that he was going on a farewell tour of his favourite places from his homeland. Despite his voluble distaste for the landed gentry and inherited wealth, he certainly liked to visit where they had lived.

'Abe Edelman and Yvette Dupont did live a version of happy ever after. Up to a certain point,' he said, by way of a preamble.

JoJo was distracted by the last slice of ginger cake. She was also feeling self-conscious that she may be one of the only teenagers in Britain who enjoyed National Trust tearooms as much as pubs and nightclubs.

'I told you that they were married?'

'That was the last thing you said about them.'

'After the war they settled in the south of France...'

Abe Edelman became an engineer after the war. His wife, although periodically suffering 'difficult moments' as a result of her experiences in Bullingen, seemed to settle easily into the suburb of Toulouse that they chose, specifically because they both knew no one from the area. Neither wanted to answer questions about their recent past. She opened a little patisserie and prepared herself for the children that sadly never came. Despite their cultural differences and genealogical disappointments, they remained devoted to each other for the remainder of their marriage.

They managed to shake off the personal sadness of a lack of progeny and doted on one another in compensation. The little patisserie thrived and Abe Edelman made a comfortable living advising local town councils on small scale planning projects, specialising in particular on raised tourist walkways in the nearby national parks.

'You must have seen them again then, after the war.'

'We exchanged the occasional letter for several years and then out of the blue in the summer of 1957 I got an invitation to come and visit them at the little gite they had built for themselves on the outskirts of Carcassonne.'

Ruben Miles found himself in a position to take advantage of the kind offer. In fact, the invitation came at a very suitable time for him. It was a good time to get out of London and the stifling demands of another imperfect wife and family. The additional prospects of catching up with Abe Edelman and getting a suntan had made his decision very straightforward.

He took the train, a journey that reminded him of twenty years earlier and his passage to Spain to fight in the Civil War. For most people, a gap of twenty years would produce incomplete, incoherent memories at best, peering through the gloomy depths of over two decades. Not so for Ruben Miles of course, and he spent most of the journey revisiting in full technicolour those weeks and months after he escaped from London following the house fire that killed his second wife and favourite son. As was his way, he did not judge his younger self.

Abe Edelman had aged prematurely. Despite being only forty-five, he had lost almost all of his hair and had weather-beaten wrinkles strewn across his over tanned face.

'How can you look the same?'

If Abe Edelman had known that Ruben Miles was nearer his sixties than his forties he would have had him tried as a witch.

Yvette Dupont had endured childlessness by consuming a little too much of her own produce. However, she was refreshingly lacking in self-consciousness about her weight gain.

The reason for the invitation was less clear than changing appearances. Ruben Miles, being a man not prone to curiosity, had not spent a second pondering the possible reasons for the invitation. However, its source was perhaps unsurprising.

'Age has made me thoughtful, Ruben Miles. Look at me, I look like an old man already! I wish I could take whatever you do to keep cheating time.'

Ruben Miles had long since took the precaution of lying about his age. He had by this point even found an East End forger to give him a forged passport and driving license, both proclaiming him to be nearly twenty years younger than he actually was. He deemed it a harmless and rewarding deception.

'Yvette may have changed me and certainly my path, but some of the old Abe Edelman has remained. *He* will pay for what he did, if it is the last thing I do. I may need the assistance of my old English friend and how did that American say… your special skills?'

It seemed like most of these old roads led inextricably to the Fixer.

'I take it you mean Obersturmbannführer Peiper?'

A simple nod.

'Yvette has made me swear that my killing days are behind me. She is determined to give me a fighting chance of getting into her heaven, despite the obvious difficulties. She is a good woman.' He paused.

'Do you know where he is?'

Another nod.

'Let's just say that he is under observation.'

'Did he not go to South America like most of those cowards did?'

'When did Obersturmbannführer Peiper do what was expected of him?'

Abe Edelman outlined his plans calmly. He finished just moments before Yvette returned from her patisserie with something to go with the fresh coffee.

'You will help me, for old times' sake?' he whispered, out of earshot of his slightly out of breath wife.

This time it was Ruben Miles who did the nodding.

'Obersturmbannführer Peiper settled in France, would you believe.'

Ruben Miles's latest request was to attend a football match at St. James' Park. This unusual request seemed rather in-keeping with his increasingly unpredictable behaviour. First, he was breaking his own rules on chronological storytelling and now he was paying good money to watch overpaid haircuts show off their tattoo collections in front of 50,000 fellow citizens. OK, so this was a bit of editorialising by JoJo Bartlett, but the old man had never expressed any fondness for association football or indeed any other organised sport before.

They were sat in the main stand as the crowd, dressed in short sleeves despite a late spring nip in the air, happily burped their way through the first half of the game. The endless walk up the many flights of stairs after a few rushed pints in the local hostelries taking their inevitable toll.

'He settled with his wife in a place called Traves, in the east of the country. Only a man like Peiper could have thought that living in France was a sane idea. Mind you, the bloody French gave him residency, even though they knew who he was and what he had done!'

Ruben Miles had thus far managed to hide his fairly well-advanced dislike of all things French. JoJo was distracted as someone sat evidently nearby had decided that oral flatulence was not nearly gross enough and had progressed effortlessly to a satanic level of arse emissions. She thought for a moment that she might actually pass out.

Ruben Miles seemed not to notice, apparently another advantage of old age.

'Abe Edelman had died in May 1976. I got a letter from his wife. Stomach Cancer. Terrible business.'

Despite his marriages and frequent travels, Ruben Miles had kept the flat in Du Cane Court in Balham. He mostly rented it out, but it was also a worthwhile point of contact. Various important communications had come his way via the letterbox of his old place. The letter from Yvette Dupont was a case in point.

'Apart from bringing me the news of my old comrade, she also said that another old friend wanted to get in touch with me and gave me his details.'

'Have I heard of him?'

'I very much doubt it. As it happens, *I* had never heard of the man in question, at least that was my immediate reaction.'

The volume of the crowd peaked as the small inflatable object bounced unscientifically between some seemingly random placed wooden posts, at least this was JoJo's instant assessment on the 'entertainment' on offer.

'Even with my memory, for a few minutes I could not place the name in the letter, then it came to me. The last time I was with Abe Edelman, in the summer of '57, he mentioned this acquaintance of his and that, should his name be mentioned, then he would be eternally grateful if I would put his plans in place. He was therefore not a real person but more a codeword.'

JoJo was getting one of her stomach feelings and although it could have been the lingering pungent aroma around them, she felt it was more likely to be her instinct that the old man was going to become morally flexible again.

At their meeting in the summer of 1957, between the charcoal-grilled sardines and freshly baked bread, Abe Edelman had outlined his wishes. He sipped his brandy while Ruben Miles settled for black coffee.

'I gave her my word that my days of violence and vengeance are over.'

Yvette Dupont had gone to the kitchen to check on her cakes in the oven.

'As you can see, I will be keeping my word, if you agree to the arrangements. Of course, in the highly unlikely event that my wife dies first, then I would no longer require this... favour. I will happily take care of it myself.'

The conversation lasted only long enough to allow a spousal check on some delicate pastries.

Back at the football match, JoJo was able to breathe fresh air again.

'So, the name was actually a signal not a person?'

'Exactly. It had been nearly twenty years since I had heard it and it took a few seconds to join the dots with the letter and its contents.'

'But once you realised, did you go through with the agreement?'

'Of course. I had promised Abe Edelman that and I was not going to let him down, even in death. Besides, some men deserve what they get.'

JoJo decided not to pass any comment on this one-sided statement.

Obersturmbannführer Peiper and his wife had moved to Traves in 1971 and, for the first few years, lived in harmony with the nearly 250 locals that populated the village. The Peipers lived in a humble, three-bedroom cottage nearly half a kilometre from the centre of the village and, although they mostly kept to themselves, they received no hostility during the first years of their residency. In fairness, despite his appearance and accent making his nationality obvious, there was a surprising lack of animosity toward the Germans living on the outskirts of their village. But then the war never really made it to the backwater of Traves.

Things changed at the beginning of June 1976, a week after Abe Edelman had died, suffering acutely with cancer of the stomach, which had spread mercilessly whilst in a hospital in Toulouse; his devoted and distraught wife Yvette by his side.

A hate campaign was launched by persons unknown. Leaflets had been sent through the letterbox of all of the villagers, outlining in graphic detail just who lived in their midst and what he had done a mere couple of hundred miles to the north over three decades ago. The road leading to the Peiper's house was daubed with the insignia of the SS. The leaflet detailed events at Malmedy and Bullingen; the front page showed Obersturmbannführer Peiper in his Waffen SS uniform during his trial in Italy in 1968 for additional crimes committed there in 1943.

The story was taken up by both local and national newspapers. The locals became openly hostile. Obersturmbannführer Peiper went to the local police who, perhaps surprisingly given the circumstances, offered a guard for his protection, but only during daylight hours.

The man himself gave his cause no assistance by giving a newspaper interview in which he claimed he should be left in peace.

When asked about his Nazi past, he had simply said, 'That is a ridiculous question. I was young and idealistic against Bolshevism. I do not understand why people keep dragging up history. As the Italians say, 'The coffee is cold'. Today, it is time for reconciliation in Europe.'

But the villagers were by now openly talking about Malmedy and Bullingen. The newspapers had thrown events in Italy into the mix. A death threat was received. Obersturmbannführer Peiper sent his wife, Sigurd, on a family trip to Strasbourg.

On the evening of the 14th of July, once darkness had fallen, an angry mob turned up on mass at the Peiper residence, the only thing missing were the pitchforks. Obersturmbannführer Peiper fired shots from his bedroom window in an attempt to disperse the crowd. It was a partial success. Those that remained set the grounds on fire, the land was already parched and as dry as tinder. Within minutes, the house was ablaze.

JoJo Bartlett raised her eyebrows at the old man. It was half time in the football match and she could hear him more clearly than in the previous forty-five minutes.

'You got a hate mob to burn his house down, presumably with him inside?'

'You are making two and two make twelve, again.'

'So, you didn't?'

'I never asked anyone to burn the house down. It would have been an odd request with me already inside.'

JoJo took a few moments to digest this.

'I don't know whose idea it was to set the grounds on fire, nor whether they meant the house to go up too.'

'But you were responsible for the campaign against Peiper in the first instance.'

'Actually no, that was all coordinated by the remnants of the Avengers movement, Abe's old comrades.'

They were drinking Bovril in plastic cups. JoJo looked at hers disapprovingly.

'Is this not just watery gravy?'

'Pretty much. It's the same recipe as the last time I was here in 1951. I saw Jackie Milburn score a hat-trick. I was taking a short break from further adventures in America. This place has changed a lot more than I have over the years.'

As far as JoJo was concerned, the old man may as well have been talking in Esperanto. So, she concentrated on the little she did understand.

'1951?'

Before the old man could confirm the date, the man sitting directly behind JoJo said, 'He doesn't look that old.'

The man was in his early twenties and had spent the first half of the match inhaling three Greggs' steak bakes and two cans of diet coke for dessert. JoJo often forgot how young the old man looked to most people.

'He's a lot older than he looks.'

'But that was like eighty years ago.'

JoJo thought it was necessary to politely point out the inaccuracy of the young man's mathematics.

'Stuck-up bitch,' he replied, by way of thanks.

This telling the truth at all time thing was beginning to get right on JoJo's tits.

Ruben Miles turned to face the sallow-looking man and demonstrated something that he had never shown JoJo before... his efficient use of controlled intimidation and violence.

'I may be a foolish old man. But if you do not apologise to this fine young lady for the crime of pointing out your monumental ignorance, I may have to come out of retirement and show you the error of your ways.'

'Mad old tosser!'

Ruben Miles had his hand around his opponent's windpipe before he could say another word.

'You have a simple choice. Either apologise or you won't be around to give Greggs any more of your parents' money...'

The boy nodded vigorously. He suddenly looked much younger.

'I'm sorry,' he said to JoJo, once he had got some oxygen back in his windpipe.

'That's OK,' she replied.

'I think it's time to go. I have seen young master Shearer with my own eyes and can concur, with typical old man's bias, that he could not hold a candle to Jackie Milburn, never mind the mighty Hughie Gallacher.'

JoJo wondered if they had a dictionary for Esperanto at the WH Smith on Gosforth High Street.

The boy actually waved at them as they left.

'You didn't want to stay until the end?'

'I think it best we make ourselves scarce, I may have left a mark on that kid's neck.'

'I've never seen that side of you before, but I suppose I should not be surprised.'

'I am old fashioned, JoJo. I do not like men being disrespectful to women, that has always brought the worst out of me.'

JoJo decided that honesty was not the best policy here. I mean, how does that statement tally with some of the tragedies of his own life? Like dumping bereaved children with a grandmother who can best be described charitably as 'unmaternal'?

She let it go.

They made their way slowly to the car park; the old man was finally beginning to walk like an old person. Maybe acts of random violence made him tired.

When they got back to The Apple Orchard Retirement Community, Mrs Hazel Wharton was waiting for them in the car park with a face like thunder and what appeared to be a rolling pin in her right hand.

The conclusion to the Edelman tale was clearly going to have to wait.

JoJo rolled her mum's Fiesta into the solitary available parking space at The Apple Orchard Retirement Community. Regulars at the pub over the road used the retirement community as an overspill car park. Very thoughtful. JoJo was already a little wary of Mrs Hazel Wharton. Although she was outwardly friendly, there was an undercurrent of something that she could not put her finger on. She seemed a little on the intense side of the spectrum, JoJo thought.

'While you were wasting your time at the football match, I have had *him* on the phone. Apparently, he's coming tomorrow, he would not take no for an answer.'

Ruben Miles was not following any of this. He had dozed off in the car and was still in splendid, befuddled mode. He had only managed to calculate that Mrs Hazel Wharton was not impressed that he had been to a football match with JoJo. But then she never liked him doing anything with JoJo. She never said as much, but her entire body language screamed disapproval.

'Who are you talking about?'

'*Him*, who exactly else could *him* be?'

The penny dropped.

'Your son?'

'Adopted son,' she corrected.

JoJo felt like she should say something just to reassure herself that the angry looking woman with the rolling pin knew she was there.

'Right, well, I will let you get on then. You clearly have things to discuss.'

JoJo helped the old man out of the passenger seat as she said this and made to exit, stage left.

'But we haven't finished the Edelmans yet.'

'That can wait until tomorrow, don't you think? I mean, it's not as if you're likely to forget.'

Mrs Hazel Wharton was now tapping the rolling pin into the palm of her hand.

Ruben Miles nodded his agreement and his heart sank a little. He was tired, but he correctly observed that he would not be resting until he had been given a stiff talking to.

He was right. Mrs Hazel Wharton had made coffee, a sure sign that their normally rigid bedtime had been delayed indefinitely.

The recap lasted twenty minutes. The missing schoolgirl, the murdered garden bird, *the list* and the clearly incompetent investigation by the ex-policeman. Ruben Miles stifled his exhausted yawns and strapped his big boy pants on.

'He's getting the train tomorrow afternoon. Apparently, he lives in Dorset now. I did not even know he knew where I lived...'

She spoke almost without punctuation for a further twenty minutes.

As she eventually paused for breath, Ruben Miles asked the only question he had.

'And the rolling pin?'

'I'm making a cake, a chocolate cake.'

Raised eyebrows prompted no further response.

'For him?'

'Well, of course, don't be so stupid.'

FÜHRER, DESTINY, GOD, CHANCE

You pay your money and take your choice. It would appear that homo sapiens need to hitch their wagons to something, however absurd. Obersturmbannführer Peiper seemed most clear on this as he sat on a rickety piano stool in his snug sitting room, handcuffs on his broad wrists, leather straps binding his ankles tightly. Ruben Miles took the safety catch off the pistol he was holding firmly in his right hand.

Obersturmbannführer Peiper was still a huge, powerful man and Ruben Miles was acutely aware that without taking him completely by surprise, he would have lost any kind of fair fistfight conclusively. As it was, his normally healthy resting heart rate was thumping worryingly in his own ears.

Abe Edelman had been most insistent concerning the methodology. Obersturmbannführer Peiper had to be in a position to hear clearly what the former Avenger was going to tell him prior to his execution, albeit via the afterlife and through a willing conduit.

'My wife believes in God,' Obersturmbannführer Peiper said.

Ruben Miles was not looking for an extended conversation, although he had given some thought as to what he might add to Abe Edelman's instructions before he carried out the sentence.

'Can you believe that a Nazi could be happily married to a good Christian?'

Ruben Miles choose not to answer.

'Most of my men chose the Führer as their faith over any religion, but some with a side-dish of destiny. We were big on destiny in the SS.'

Ruben Miles knew that the authorities would not appear anytime soon. The mob had already sabotaged the village fire response unit, their pump subtly but effectively crippled. This to ensure that the cause of death would be, if not conclusive, then with enough reason not to facilitate further investigation.

He spoke in his precise German.

'Und woran glauben sie, Obersturmbannführer Peiper?'

The Nazi insisted on speaking in his heavily accented English.

'Life is luck, nothing more, nothing less.'

Ruben Miles told him in his native language that his luck had ran out.

'Du hast keine mehr.'

He actually laughed.

'Many had a great deal less luck. I was at Stalingrad.'

He said this with a shrug.

Ruben Miles explained briefly why and, most importantly, who had brought Ruben Miles to his door in June 1976, thirty-one years after events at Bullingen.

'I remember you, but not the *Jude*.'

He spat out the last word.

'Das Mädchen?'

Another shrug.

'There were a lot of peasant girls.'

Ruben Miles asked if he remembered *the* Belgian girl that his men had failed to silence. The one survivor had been the wife of the Jew.

'Is that luck or destiny?'

Ruben Miles had switched to English as a mark of disrespect. It brought a sneer from Obersturmbannführer Peiper.

'You English talk a lot of destiny. Is that why you are here? To fulfil your destiny?'

'I am here because a decent man asked one last favour of me.'

'My bad fortune.'

He was smiling again.

'I think you have had more than enough luck,

Obersturmbannführer Peiper. Abe Edelman, for that was his name, and he wanted you to hear it. He wanted you to know that you have only lived this long because of Yvette Dupont, his wife and the sole survivor of the atrocity you ordered at Bullingen. She is a woman too good to seek bloody revenge, no matter how justified. She used to say that even murdering Nazis needed to be shown compassion and forgiveness for their sins.'

The Nazi said nothing, his eyes now to the floor.

'Abe Edelman foreswore any revenge during his wife's lifetime. But if he was to die before you, he asked me to finish his task. He died, riddled with cancer, two weeks ago. And with his death, your luck has finally run out.'

Ruben Miles had given little thought to what response he might get from Obersturmbannführer Peiper. His preoccupation had been his physical restraint, not his verbal utterances.

'Every man must die.'

Both men remained silent for a minute, the light sounds of the burning foliage creeping ever nearer.

'You don't have much time, English.'

'More than you might hope.'

Another shrug.

'We are all animals. We are born and we must die. Some get no choice about the when or how. Others, well they get to choose for them. You are a soldier. You know these things.'

'And you got to choose for so many.'

'I did not keep count. War is not a fair place, just like life. You have a face that says you have killed your share.'

'I never killed defenceless civilians.'

'They were my orders, from the Führer.'

'That excuse was not good enough then, nor is it now.'

Another shrug.

It was clear that Obersturmbannführer Peiper felt not a shred of shame or remorse for his actions. His only regret was his doomed cause. He pitied his dead Führer, not the millions that were murdered in his name. Ruben Miles had suspected as much. Nazis were not known for their contrition.

'Is there nobody in your life that would stop you from killing a defenceless man?'

'None of your business.'

'How did the Jew die?'

'I told you, cancer.'

'You see. All life is luck, especially death,' he nodded at the gun. 'Some ways are better than others.'

'I saw a lot of death on the Somme. Good, clean ways and slow, agonising ways. It's all we ever thought about. That is something all survivors remember.'

'You don't look old enough for the Somme.'

'I'm older than I look.'

A sudden doubt now etched on the Nazi's face.

'I am not going to waste any more words on you. Your time has finally come to an end. Whatever you chose to believe in, think of it now. It will be one of your last thoughts.'

Obersturmbannführer Peiper watched quizzically as Ruben Miles lowered his aim and pulled the trigger of his pistol pointing at the Nazi's still trim stomach.

HIM

He was not what she expected. But what had she ever expected? Not to see him again for one. But having her entire life narrative ripped to pieces and by *him*, was quite another.

He had insisted on speaking to her alone. He said she would thank him for this later. Reluctantly, she informed Ruben Miles that he should wait for them to finish in his rooms. It was a mild, bright day and so they talked in the garden, empty as the inmates were all hunkered around the TV in the lounge, eyes glued to a Strictly rerun.

'I understand you went to the police and told them I was a murderer.'

She didn't answer.

He told her everything. He was clear and concise throughout. Nothing he said was ambiguous.

Barry Wharton was one of the founding members of a most unusual and secret charitable organisation. Its remit was to remove individuals from dangerous domestic situations. His professional training as a lawyer and then a barrister had given him some of the skills that had facilitated a harmonious and successful relationship with most of the police forces of England and Scotland. The Welsh, for reasons never openly expressed, refused to cooperate in any way with the agency, as it was euphemistically referred to by the few that knew of its existence and purpose.

Every man and women who worked for the agency had been a victim of domestic abuse of some kind. Simplistically, they operated like the Samaritans. They could be contacted via an advertised helpline. But they did a great deal more than offer helpful advice. Sir Richard Dorchester, the Conservative Party peer and donor, was the driving force behind both its creation and its toleration by successive governments. He had been physically and sexually abused by a maternal uncle.

Barry Wharton had joined the agency part-time in its

infancy, shortly after he passed the bar exam. As well as his own traumatic experiences, he had also been profoundly moved by the disappearance and murder of a little girl that lived in the next street from his childhood home. The murderer was never caught.

Like most organisations, the agency had grown organically. Barry Wharton had been the radical member who came up with the idea of doing more than giving mere advice and counselling. Was it not possible to remove individuals from whatever hell they existed in?

The pitch had been relatively straightforward. Crown prosecution witnesses and even supergrasses can be given new identities, so surely those in desperate domestic situations, who can see no positive outcome in their predicament, could be treated in an identical fashion? Taken out of danger and given the opportunity to lead a completely new life, away from their tormentors. It was easier than most domestic crime prosecutions.

It helped that the first two cases were so successful and, pre the internet, had been relatively easy to facilitate and camouflage. It was a good deal more complicated now. But the agency still existed. It just had a much narrower breadth of scope to rescue individuals. The victim also had to understand and accept that they would be permanently removed from their previous life, only a small proportion were able to go through the extensive vetting procedures.

'That is why I can be traced to areas where people disappeared from.'

'It sounds absolutely ridiculous.'

'I suppose it does, but it explains why, when you went to that retired detective and he checked me out, his superiors were able to, if not explain why and what I was involved in, they could confirm that I was not a suspect in any of the cases on your list. All the names on your list have never been found, but not for the reason that you assumed. It's because they all have new identities.'

'Why didn't they tell me?'

'Not allowed. I should not be telling you this now. But my

time with the agency is coming to an end and I'm getting married. I finally decided that you needed to hear the truth.'

His last point was the only dubious one he made. Mrs Hazel Wharton felt that ignorance would have been much the better option.

'You need to know why I did what I did. I mean why I joined the agency after I heard about it through a colleague. We need to talk about your husband.'

Mrs Hazel Wharton felt that, at least on some level, she already had an inkling about what the boy was going to say. Not that she had ever *seen* anything. Her husband may have been mild mannered and polite, but there was always something that did not quite add up. She wanted not to believe. She wanted to be angry. Instead, she had to listen.

'It started when I was seven. He would come and say goodnight, but he started staying until after you had gone to sleep.'

She knew this was true. Their lack of intimacy was more than just sexual, they never even touched. Never a cuddle, a perfunctory hug, or even a handshake. She therefore did not think that there was anything unusual about him not coming to bed until after she had fallen asleep.

'He started to touch me after a few weeks, and this was just the beginning.'

Mrs Hazel Wharton thought that she would throw up. She wanted to run, but her son placed a firm hand on her knee.

'You need to hear this and I need to say it. It's taken a lot of therapy to get to this point. It's taken me years to finally not blame myself and you...'

She would of course blame herself for the rest of her life. How could she not?

'He told me if I said anything to anyone, he would kill me *and you*. He started raping me when I was ten.'

The first time was the day before he had killed the beloved pet bird by throwing it at a tree.

She had seen *that.*

HADES

Obersturmbannführer Peiper made little noise. He lay on his side in an ever-increasing pool of his pure Aryan blood. Ruben Miles watched on with indifference.

'I saw a friend of mine in the trenches die of a bullet to the spleen, it took six hours. Our sergeant would not let us put him out of his misery. He said that we should wait for a medic. Well, Obersturmbannführer Peiper, no one is coming to finish you off. You will still be alive when the flames come through these walls. There may not be an actual hell, I agree with you on that. But I have created a version just for you. You will burn. I have chosen your destiny.'

And with that he left, not looking back. Obersturmbannführer Peiper to his meagre credit offered nothing.

JoJo watched the old man's eyes carefully. As far as she was concerned, he was telling the truth.

'It's all true, isn't it?'

She had never asked him quite so bluntly.

'You shot the Nazi and left him to burn to death. Because you promised Abe Edelman that you would and you kept your word. And everything else. The Burgess brothers, The Babe, Maria Delores, Cavendish, The Fixer, your family, your father, mother... it's all true, isn't it?'

He nodded.

'I had not planned to do it that way and Abe did not give me instructions on the method. It's just that what he said to me during our brief conversation really got to me. The unfairness of it all, the randomness of it all. That probably does not mean anything to you, you are so young and that is not a criticism. I am glad that is difficult to understand. It should all be difficult to understand.'

'I think killing the Nazi is perhaps the easiest thing to understand. I mean I'm normally against capital punishment, but his crimes are difficult to get past.'

'It is not one of the things that come to me regularly in the middle of a sleepless night.'

'I'm figuring you may have quite a few of those.'

'Not so many now, in the past, yes. But I seem to have made peace with a lot of the things that I have done, good and bad. Telling you my story has helped me a lot. But there is still much more that I need to tell you about.'

'I think one of the things I have the most difficulty with is the memory gap when you were in the hospital in London during the war. Your recall of everything else is very convincing, so I don't understand why you know nothing of that period.'

'Me and you both.'

'Unless, for some reason, you don't want to remember.'

'It's not that, I have tried so hard over the years and yet I have come up with nothing. It's like there is a whole missing file.'

'Did you try and find out from the Fixer or anyone else?'

'He denied all knowledge of being there. He said he was in the States, and that fits in with his story.'

'But when you spoke to the Specialist, she told you that a man fitting his description was at the hospital when she visited.'

'Hardly conclusive.'

'Any other clues later? I mean, I presume you tried to find out more, perhaps from intelligence? Did you speak to Cavendish?'

'I drew a lot of blanks. It's not the only mystery I didn't solve though. We are only about halfway through my story. That's why I gave you that envelope, remember? You haven't lost it?'

'Of course not.'

'I have to be realistic, at our current rate and again, that's not a criticism, it's taking longer than I thought. Good job I have back-up.'

'What do you mean?'

'Just keep the key safe and don't use it until, you know…'

JoJo did know.

'I would love to know what happened in the hospital.'

'Maybe you could solve that mystery for me, you have more brains than I ever had.'

Like many people, JoJo really did not know how to handle such a strong compliment.

She chose diversion.

'How is Mrs Wharton?'

'Pretty bad I'm afraid and with due cause. In fact, I need to go and see how she is doing, do you mind?'

WARM HAND LUKE

Luke Miles was having plenty of reservations about his rash and uncharacteristically firm decision to end things with JoJo Bartlett. Having reached the teenage promised land, going back to the old five knuckle shuffle was just not cutting it. His unenthusiastic attempts to replace JoJo had no traction. He tried to flirt with a couple of girls in his form class, but they simply looked at him as if he was Simon Cowell in a onesie.

Besides, he knew he cared about JoJo. It wasn't just the naked fumbling. She was smart, funny and was not a liar or a bullshitter. He tried to remember why he thought dumping her was a good idea. Wasn't it the old man's fault? Had Ruben Miles put him up to it?

Luke Miles was already well versed in blaming family members, most notably his parents, for his own poor decision making. This was a tactic he would utilise with little self-awareness for the rest of his adult life.

He sent JoJo a three-word text with surprising honesty: I miss you

He remembered after he sent it that JoJo hated texts without punctuation. He remembered a recent monologue on the subject.

'If you can't be bothered to put a full stop, what does that say about you as a person?'

She had been adamant to the point of indignation.

Much to his joy and surprise, she messaged back instantly.

Me too. That's a full stop btw. They end sentences. :)

He actually guffawed.

Can we meet later?

He thought about leaving off the question mark before common sense kicked in.

Yeah, I wanted to talk to you about Ruben anyway.

They met later in the afternoon at The Lonsdale; neutral ground for a peace conference. Luke apologised for being a total twat. JoJo let him.

'I don't know what I was thinking.'

'You had your reasons. I wasn't making things easy for you. I promise not to criticise when you're being a bit needy.'

'And I will forgive your obsession with correct punctuation.'

She punched him on the shoulder. They were going to be OK.

'Ruben is not great. He looks really tired. He was talking as if he thinks he is finally going to, you know, die.'

'He is ludicrously old. I mean, I sometimes forget that, just because he looks so much younger than he is.'

'You haven't seen him for two weeks, he's changed noticeably. I think whatever is going on with that odd woman he knocks about with is taking its toll. I never mentioned this to you because he asked me not to. But he gave me this a few weeks ago.'

She dropped an envelope on the table in front of their pint glasses.

'What is it?'

'Duh! I haven't opened it, he told me not to.'

Luke was going to ask why she brought it then, but decided against.

'Do you want me to? I mean then, at least technically, you've not gone against his wishes.'

'I need another drink. I'll get them.'

She knew he would have no money.

When she returned from the bar ten minutes later (it always took her a while to get served as she was overly polite amongst the impolite regulars) Luke was fingering the envelope like an incompetent bomb disposal expert.

'There is a small key in here, I think.'

He handed her the envelope.

'What do you think it is?'

'A key to something.'

'Have you started on a course of moron pills or something?'

So much for the dial back on criticisms.

Luke opened the envelope and pulled out some folded, lined paper and a little leather pouch, which did indeed have a small key inside. It looked like a padlock key.

JoJo communicated only by raising her eyebrows.

The paper had an address in Tynemouth written on it and a crude, but clear hand drawn map.

'He is only going to know you opened it if you tell him.'

'What do you think it's for?'

'It's pretty obvious, isn't it? Must be some kind of lockup storage place. We have the address and a key, what else could it be?'

'I suppose so.'

'Do you want to go?'

'Yes, but we're not going to. He was very clear that it was for after he… wasn't around anymore.'

'He would only know if we let on.'

'Luke, both of us are very poor liars. We may as well have the word 'lying' tattooed on our foreheads whenever we try to. Besides, I feel like it's the right thing to do, you know, follow his wishes.'

They drank their pints quietly.

'I'm not sure we have the patience to wait.'

'*You* don't have the patience to wait, but I do.'

And with that she put the contents back in the envelope and zipped it back into her small handbag.

Then her phone rang. It was The Apple Orchard Retirement Community.

REVELATION

It should have been her, she told herself repeatedly. She made it happen. She was a dreadful human being.

She *had* kept him awake all night. Crying and screaming in equal measure. She told him everything that *he* had said. She left out nothing. During a rare moment of respite, she had gone to the kitchen to get them both a glass of water. When she returned, he was lying face down on the floor, seemingly having pitched forward out of his armchair. He was still breathing.

At least she did the right things. She managed to manoeuvre him into the recovery position and hit the nearest panic button, located next to the sitting room light switch. The inmates often wondered in awe which level of idiot had been responsible for this design flaw.

But assistance came quickly nevertheless and an ambulance took Ruben Miles to the Royal Victoria Infirmary as the morning was breaking. They let Mrs Hazel Wharton go with him.

He had suffered a stroke. The first tangible failure of his body, at the age of one hundred and six years old. The medical staff who treated him did not believe his age. This was compounded because he was still carrying bogus identification, a habit not discarded from his more dubious past entanglements.

But this wasn't America, so they treated him anyway.

JoJo got the call from The Apple Orchard Retirement Community later that afternoon. She was such a regular visitor that even the incompetent duty manager felt the need to let her know. She immediately felt a greater level of anxiety than before any exam, even her driving test, before which she was convinced that she was going to hyperventilate. All she knew was that he had collapsed and been taken to hospital.

Luke took the news with less emotion.

'He is a hundred and three or something.'

This was seemingly meant to be comforting, but JoJo had no notion of how.

'He is a hundred and six actually, that's what he says.'

This made Luke ponder whether his reinstated girlfriend should know a great deal more about his great grandfather than he did.

They took the bus to the RVI in the city centre. It took them twenty minutes to find the right ward, only to then be informed that visiting was only permitted between 5 and 7.30 p.m. The only exceptions were for next of kin. They decamped to the nearby Trent House to sit out the hour long wait.

'Even though he has done some pretty bad things, like abandoning his children with his Nazi mother and being personally responsible for the death of at least several people, I do think he is a decent person at heart.'

JoJo knew she was trying to convince herself as much as Luke. For his part, Luke did not say or really think anything. Disconcertingly, he was beginning to conclude that his parents might be right about the morals of Ruben Miles.

'Most of the people that he killed undoubtedly deserved it, especially the Nazi war criminal.'

As Luke did not know what JoJo was referring to, he defaulted to thinking about the devil again. Shouldn't he be past that stage by now?

Mrs Hazel Wharton was sitting in the reception area when they returned to the ward.

'They told me that you were coming and he's not allowed more than two visitors at a time. I can go in when you're finished. He is still unconscious, but they think he will come around soon. They can't believe how strong his heart is and they simply refuse to accept how old he is. Did you know his identification says he is only eighty-three?'

'Yes, he has told me about that. He said he was sick of people not believing his age and so he got a dodgy passport and driving licence. He said it was easier than you think.'

JoJo had another prickle of doubt. Was he really only eighty-three and a world class bullshitter? Suddenly, waiting in a hospital waiting room, it did seem an awful lot more plausible than his stories.

The doctor on call did little to ease JoJo's concerns about the old man's sincerity, but he also gave a slightly confusing prognosis of his medical condition.

'For a man of his age, he is very strong. The stroke he suffered is on the mild side of the spectrum. But he is clearly confused. He regained consciousness about half an hour ago. He has been given a mild sedative because he became quite distressed. Some of the things he was saying were upsetting the nursing staff. He clearly has had a previous bad experience in a hospital and he was taking that out on our nurses, I think. We do not know yet what, if any, damage the brain has suffered.'

'What was he saying about being in hospital?'

JoJo had picked up on this immediately.

'He was screaming some bizarre nonsense about experiments and American intelligence. Pretty disturbing and rather *graphic* stuff.'

JoJo's stomach actually flipped, but she had another issue to address first.

'Doctor, this may sound like a weird question, but do you think it possible that he is well over a hundred years old?'

'His friend asked something similar, but his identification says...'

'I know, but he told me months ago that they are fake.'

'I find it highly, and I mean very highly unlikely, that someone that old could be in the condition that he presents in, even after a stroke.'

'Even my parents have no idea how old he is.'

Luke had definitely not mentioned that before.

They went in together.

Ruben Miles had propped himself up in his bed. He was a shadow of the man that JoJo was used to seeing. She saw something in his eyes that was entirely new: fear.

At least he seemed to recognise them both.

'I hope you two are going to cheer me up,' he said uncharacteristically.

JoJo had never seen the old man looking so down. In all the time they had spent together, Ruben Miles's spirits were consistent and upbeat. The version that presented itself now required a period of readjustment.

'How are you feeling?' JoJo asked nervously.

'How do you think I look?' The old man threw this question out like a challenge.

'Grumpy,' offered his young relative. Luke Miles was not known for his perception or empathy.

These exchanges led to an uncomfortable silence.

JoJo whispered in Luke's ear, and he took no further persuading and backed quickly out of the small room. Luke said his goodbyes before the old man had time to respond.

JoJo turned back to face Ruben Miles.

'Why don't you and I pick up your story from where we left off? That might cheer you up a bit, you always enjoy telling me your stories. I even brought the tape recorder.'

'What stories?'

JoJo felt another twinge of unease.

'Don't you remember? For the last six months you have been telling me the story of your life. I have recorded all our conversations on this tape recorder.'

His face said it all.

'I think so,' he said unconvincingly.

'I've got an idea, why don't I play you a bit from our last session and that might help you... get back up to speed.'

The old man concurred.

JoJo rewound the tape and pressed play.

It was the demise of Obersturmbannführer Peiper.

He sat in silence and listened to the voices. He had no difficulty in recognising his own. Like many people, he had always disliked the sound of his own voice when played back to him.

'I don't remember this,' he said after a few minutes.

The ambiguity of his comment hung heavy on JoJo. It took her a minute to ask the needed question.

'Do you mean making the recording or…?'

'The whole thing,' he replied, before she had a chance to finish.

'You don't remember anything about Obersturmbannführer Peiper?'

'Who and the what?'

JoJo was crestfallen. But the doctor had said that he may have short-term issues with his memory and this offered her some comfort. The doctor said that this would often rectify itself. There was still hope that she could finish the rest of Ruben Miles's life story.

'I fucking hate hospitals.'

The old man had never used such high-level profanities in front of JoJo before, ever.

'Did I ever tell you about what they did to me in the hospital during the war?'

JoJo nearly had a stroke, but she still had the wherewithal to put a new tape in the machine and press record.

MIND GAMES

He never saw their faces. But he could hear two distinct voices. Always throaty whispers as he struggled to catch their words through the head restraint. Both were male. The first an even-toned, public school voice with more timbre than Cavendish's. The other, more parochial and with a hint of rural northwest. Like many who served, Ruben Miles had been accustomed to the many nuances of British dialects and accents. Indeed, he had become quite a successful mimic in both the trenches and, later, in the German prisoner of war camp. It had helped to pass the time.

On the first occasion they made him take the pill, he giggled in wonder at what he could see. The colours and shapes were almost overwhelming.

The second time they gave it to him, he thought he would lose his mind. The unholy visions tormenting his fractured mind. When they took off the head restraint and he could see what was in the room, he soiled himself. There were devils everywhere.

It wasn't just the Nazis and Japanese who conducted human experiments during World War Two. The Americans had come across a Swiss scientist at a conference in Paris in 1938 who had discovered lysergic acid diethylamide while experimenting with a fungus growing on various types of grain. When the US entered the war in the last month of 1941, their scientists were tasked with putting forward any global research that could assist military victory. There were more games afoot than the Manhattan Project.

The remit had been simple sounding.

To engage and develop with any research that could '*assist with mind control, information gathering and other purposes that could be used for wartime advantage'.*

That the Fixer had been allocated to the team in London was predictable, given his deserved reputation for effortless information gathering and ethical flexibility within the murky world of American intelligence. The fact that the German doctor who had stumbled on the potential of Ruben Miles's memory had fallen in their lap after he had been arrested as part of the fifth column investigation was more fortuitous.

But it also explained the Fixer's seeming awareness of Ruben Miles's condition. And so, after the death of Eleanor de Villiers in Balham and the overdue moral meltdown suffered by his English disciple, the Fixer was informed by British intelligence of where Ruben Miles had found himself and just what sort of condition he was in.

It would seem that the scientific community of any nation will produce those ready to push boundaries where others might hesitate. The two British scientists came from Christ's College, Cambridge. Their alumni may have included Darwin, but Robert Groves and George Edwards were looking to evolve a whole different kind of ball game. Latching on to the discoveries of the Swiss scientist Albert Hofmann at the Paris convention, the pair had been experimenting on rats before moving on to chimpanzees. Ruben Miles was the obvious next link in the evolutionary chain.

It was the baby steps of the project that would evolve into MK-Ultra in the early 1950s, when Korea and McCarthy had sent the Cold War into the stratosphere. A lot of the batshit schemes that began during the war reached their dubious conclusions during the era of Mutually Assured Destruction. The CIA were not formally constructed until 1947, but its genesis was The Office of Strategic Service, set up by Roosevelt in 1942; a direct result of finding out just what British intelligence was already up to. The Fixer was there from the get go.

They wanted to know what he saw. They wanted to know how he felt. His entire being told him to tell them nothing. His eyes were blood red and the size of dinner plates. Although they had removed his head restraint, he was clamped fiercely into an office-like chair, unable to move his arms or legs. His head kept facing forward by a neck harness.

He saw the Russian first, knife in one hand, a fistful of testicles in the other, a severed cock on the blood spattered floor. His screams nearly ruptured his vocal chords. Then he saw the

Burgess brothers, beseeching him to follow the instructions of their pact. Somehow it was the sheepish Babe that tormented him the most, failing to give an apology of any flavour for fucking his wife. It felt like a lifetime, but as the initial dosages were low it was more like seven hours.

He could not see them watching him. They, of course, saw nothing, which is why they fired questions at him via a two-way radio. He knew not to reply.

Then he saw his mother handing Celia the nanny a tartan green scarf.

He lost consciousness when he felt a sharp prick in his right arm. This time it was an injection, not a pill to swallow.

JoJo recorded it all faithfully. Once the old man started, he could not seem to stop. Detailed descriptions of both his treatment and his accompanying hallucinations during his wartime hospitalisation. The old man appeared not to be aware that they were depictions of some of the more notable events of his many stories, told in such detail, over the last several months. To Ruben Miles, post-stroke, the wartime LSD-fuelled images were of a dark fantasy world, not simply the many ghosts of his infamous past. They were lengthy nightmares; nothing else.

JoJo was as fascinated by the reappearance of the Specialist as she was about her newfound knowledge of the missing period in the life of Ruben Miles. In her mind, she had reshaped Carolyn de Villiers into a wartime feminist, making a telling contribution in a patriarchal world using her intelligence and her more obvious charms. But here she was appearing as either a benevolent visitor offering compassion, or perhaps a more sinister co-conspirator in crude, mind-altering experiments.

Ruben Miles had now remembered her clearly talking to the two Americans in huddled whispers as he pretended to be asleep.

'The memory experts tell us that he claims he can remember every day of his life, in detail, from the age of eleven.'

'Surely that is a lie.' The Specialist, arms folded, was displeased by her orders to check in with what the Americans were up to. She had presumed that her personal interactions with Ruben Miles would have removed her as a viable option. It had seemed to do the opposite.

'The doctor claims that, at the very least, Miles was convincing. Graves and Edwards say their experimental drugs may be able to help ascertain the validity of some of his more far-fetched stories.'

'What are they?'

'Sodium pentothal and lysergic acid diethylamide.'

'I don't do science, especially chemistry.'

'A truth serum and some kind of mind altering substance. Taken individually at first, but yesterday together with quite interesting results.'

This time it was the taller American who spoke.

'At one point yesterday he talked about his time in a German prison of war camp during the Great War and I was able to confirm that what he said was true.'

'How so?'

'That is where we first met, over twenty years ago. He reminded me of events that I had almost forgotten. It was extraordinary, the detail that he was able to recount.'

The other American piped up again.

'You might not approve of the ethics, but what these doctors are discovering seems like it might have a good deal of potential in our particular line of business.'

'Namely?'

'Surely it's obvious? It seems that these drugs compel a person to bare their very soul, and in his case, in outstanding detail.'

'Surely there are older and cruder means of achieving that?'

'True, but those methods are not as reliable as you would think. Some spies can withstand just about everything. There are also other more infinite and interesting possibilities. For instance, what if we had a spy who was able to memorise huge amounts of complex information without the need for the collection of damaging evidence?'

'Surely that's not possible.'

'Not if this odd doctor mixed up with those fifth columnists is right, and we have every reason to believe he at least thinks Miles is telling the truth.'

The Specialist was at heart a healthy cynic. She did not trust science or technology. Somehow her experiences of the Blitz had cemented these views. She told the Americans of her doubts.

'Besides,' she said, 'he is one of our own, he is almost a friend of mine, for God's sake.'

The Fixer seemed unimpressed with appeals to his conscience.

'I have known this man since 1918 and I believe he has more resilience than ten men. If anyone can take this stuff and prosper, it is he.'

'I think that is what you Americans call bullshit.'

'I don't know how well you know Ruben Miles, or indeed in what capacity, but I'm betting I know more about his capabilities than you and your plummy-mouthed colleagues.'

'Can we speak with the doctors?'

'I don't think that's a good idea. They have their own language, those guys.'

At least the Specialist had not played an active part in the experiments and subsequent deceptions.

When Ruben Miles finished explaining his experiences at the 3rd London General Hospital in Wandsworth in 1941 to JoJo, he looked an exhausted and beaten man.

JoJo Bartlett's mind was rotating wildly on the bus back home. Beside her, Luke kept up a flow of one-sided chitchat on Saddam Hussain's ongoing war crimes trial. She found herself reflecting on the hours and hours of listening to the confessions of Ruben Miles. The gap in his memory, a frustration to them both in unequal measure, now had been unplugged. The Americans had experimented on him with new drugs. The British were either in on it or at least acquiesced to the experimentation. They were both trying to fathom just what his memory was capable of. Were they trying to make some sort of super spy? Did this not prove his story was real?

Or was the stroke another fine work of fiction? The question that seemed to boomerang regularly with uncanny timing. It did not seem plausible. She craved corroboration from another source that she could trust. Was Carolyn de Villiers still alive? She was, after all, much younger than the old man. Unless of course his age was the biggest lie of all.

Was she traceable? It seemed the sort of thing that the internet could solve. But that evening, as she cogitated at her father's desk and surfed as far and wide as she could muster, there did not appear to be a trace of Carolyn de Villiers to be found anywhere. She spent a frustrated night failing to turn her mind off the reoccurring questions, sleep eluding her until seemingly minutes before her alarm went off at 8.00 a.m. She was so tired she could not remember why she set it on a non-school day.

She was having her breakfast when someone knocked on the front door. Hers was not the sort of house where people routinely knocked on the front door. Her father's aloofness and mother's unpopularity saw to that. She could see the spiky top of Luke's hair through the glazed window in the door. Why had he not just texted? She knew before he opened his mouth. His eyes were bloodshot and there was a small trail of mucus from his left nostril that made him look about seven years old.

INEVITABILITY, SURPRISE
AND THE NEW ORTHODOXY

Her father cracked the old gag about death and taxes. He thought it might help. It didn't. JoJo had never encountered bereavement before. She understood why people said they felt numb, she could not seem to access any other form of response. Her father seemed more concerned about the loss of a potential bestselling crime book rather than his daughter's feelings. This resulted in timeless platitudes.

'He lived a very long life, it had to happen sooner rather than later. I'm sorry.'

Luke was almost catatonic. A surprising development. JoJo called the hospital and they confirmed the news. Ruben Miles had passed away peacefully in his sleep. It appeared to be the only factual information that JoJo possessed.

She was surprised by her own emotions. Eight months ago, she did not even know Ruben Miles. That seemed like a long time ago. He was not kin, but she had clearly found something in her connection with Ruben Miles and his life stories. But what caused her the most hurt was the knowledge that his story was to be incomplete. She felt guilty about caring more about the story than the death of the man. She kept these feelings to herself for now. Maybe she *would* make a proper journalist.

Helping make the arrangements for the funeral was another challenge. Mrs Hazel Wharton, capsized in her own private grief about the crimes she may not have committed, but certainly was complicit in, was not capable of helping The Apple Orchard Retirement Community liaise with the local funeral directors. JoJo offered to step in.

The first surprise was the detailed instructions left by Ruben Miles in an envelope prominently positioned on his writing desk, next to his collection of early twentieth century fountain pens. JoJo had noticed neither before, despite conducting several of their conversations at that very location. His handwriting was incredibly neat and legible. A handwriting expert would have deduced the author was an optimist and devoid of any feelings of regret. But who listens to experts?

The second surprise was the level of antipathy directed toward Ruben Miles by his former inmates. Their words said they would attend, but their eyes told a different story. JoJo thought at least it would get them out into the fresh air for an hour or so and this became her pitch after she realised the man himself was not an attractive selling point to this reluctant group.

Luke was the only family member who agreed to attend. His parents declined, almost politely. JoJo's dad wanted to come, as he claimed to have grown fond of the deceased after they had met several times to discuss the alleged involvement in the 1970s bank job. JoJo reminded herself that she really did need to speak to her father about this at some point, but maybe not for a few weeks. JoJo wanted to tell her father she would prefer it if he did not attend the funeral. But she didn't. She seemed to be getting over her desire to tell the truth all the time.

The third surprise was the offer, made most earnestly by Mr Sykes junior of Sykes and Son, funeral directors of West Jesmond, to display Ruben Miles in an open casket the day before the service was due to be held. JoJo said she would think about it. But the reality was that she had no idea what to think about *that*. In the end, she decided that inaction to this offer was perhaps the best plan of action.

She tried to have a conversation with Mrs Hazel Wharton, but she came away from the process not sure if the clearly distressed woman had understood anything of what was said. The woman looked almost completely hollowed out. Her previously buoyant cheeks having seemingly shrunken onto her now protruding bones. JoJo wondered what level of grief could have such a physical response. Of course, she possessed none of the most pertinent facts.

Then she remembered the key.

Luke had bounced back quite quickly after the news. In fact, as far as JoJo could ascertain, twenty four hours after the death of Ruben Miles, his great grandson seemed to have taken the news quite calmly. He did not share his thoughts with JoJo, but Luke tended to agree with his parents that the old man had been not just lucky to live so long, but also lucky to die in the easiest way of all, in his sleep. They made many comments about the unfairness of this in particular. His mother had even said that the old bugger should have been 'burnt at the stake' for what he had done, although declining to pass further comment when probed.

Luke had stopped talking to JoJo about his parents. It seemed the only viable solution.

'I think they should come, for your sake as much as anything. I mean he's dead now, what difference does it make? Whatever they think of him, he was family.'

Luke pretended to agree but was internally shocked by the fact that, as a teenager, he had started the debilitating early adult process of agreeing with at least a little of what his parents said.

They agreed to try to find the location for whatever the key fitted the following morning.

They took the metro, as JoJo's mother had pranged the car at Sainsbury's in Heaton that week. She blamed the working class specifically for any personal misfortune, but then she was an avid Daily Mail reader. Apparently, the car she drove into was to blame. Mrs Bartlett said the girl had a tattoo on her neck, as if this was somehow the primary reason for her own inability to drive safely and correctly.

JoJo liked the metro. It was a method of public transport that did not make you feel that you needed a good shower afterwards. It was a warm, sunny day and there were mothers with young children clearly heading to the beach for the day. Beach balls, buckets and spades spilling from overflowing carrier bags. The sun, that rarest of UK birds, making a comedy guest appearance for the day. The forecast for the rest of the week was bleak, which did not bode well for the funeral generally and for the attendance especially. JoJo already found herself worrying about how many would come to say goodbye to Ruben Miles. She also felt some of the inmates from The Apple Orchard Retirement Community may come along just to boo. A truly dispiriting thought.

For his part, Luke was at best slightly inquisitive as to what they may discover in Tynemouth. He was a young man, after all, and therefore only capable of a finite amount of imagination and most of that concerned itself with attractive older women and logic-defying circumstances.

They were halfway to Tynemouth before JoJo realised she had left the all-important envelope, with the key safely inside, back on her bedroom dresser.

'We need to get off,' she said, taking several minutes to decide the best course of action.

She was apparently *not* going to admit to such an out-of-character mistake.

Luke did not question, he merely stood up as if he knew why there was a change in plan.

'I need to make a call and I've somehow left my phone at home.'

As she said this she pushed her mobile deeper into the pocket of her jacket.

'You can use mine.'

'I don't know the number, it's on my phone.'

When they got back to JoJo's house she plonked Luke in front of the TV in the kitchen and went to her room to make the fictional call. Luckily for all concerned, Mrs Bartlett was out. She was probably canvassing for UKIP, her new hobby. She had recently become obsessed with Nigel Farage, who had just become their leader. JoJo thought his pasty face and untrustworthy, hooded eyes were reason enough to be cynical. Luckily, nobody listens to racist nutters like that, she said over dinner the night before. In response Mrs Bartlett made what sounded like an impromptu speech on the evils of EU membership. In reality, it was the entire comment section, verbatim, from that morning's Daily Mail.

When she came downstairs Luke was reading a flyer with the aforementioned nutter grinning from the front cover.

'Don't,' she said.

She double checked that she had the key for whatever awaited them in Tynemouth and then her heart sank as her mother drove the newly-repaired Ford Fiesta onto the front drive.

She had a quick idea. She told Luke of her plan. He looked

confused.

'Don't,' she said.

Reoccurring themes of his existence.

At least the plan worked. As Mrs Bartlett entered the kitchen and took in the presence of Luke Miles with an unconscious lip curl, Luke pointed to the UKIP flyer in his hand and said to Mrs Bartlett with a commendably straight face,

'This all seems very sensible, Mrs Bartlett. JoJo tells me you are quite the fan.'

It is always surprising what one can get away with when one deliberately plays into the narrowness of someone else's ideological world view.

Mrs Bartlett scanned Luke's face for signs of sarcasm and found none.

'It is *very* sensible. It's Luke, isn't it? I hope you don't pay any attention to JoJo and her opinions, I'm afraid she has been brainwashed by the lefty teachers at her school.'

Whatever the origin of this theory, JoJo was particularly grateful that at least her mother had chosen not to air this view at her recent parents' evening.

'Great, the car's fixed. Can I borrow it for a couple of hours? We have to go to Tynemouth.'

'Yes, of course, but be careful. It will be very busy there as the sun has come out, which invariably unleashes the hoi polloi. Avoid the fish and chip shops, they will be mobbed.'

JoJo managed to extricate them both before Mrs Bartlett could pontificate further on the vacuous nature of the English working class at leisure, blissfully unaware that, in time, she would be most grateful to this particular, rather predictable cohort.

THE LOCKUP

I t took them over an hour to find the right street. Map reading was clearly not a life skill taught during the tedious hour a week Luke had to endure in the Year Eleven Citizenship class; the graveyard shift on a Monday afternoon, where he learnt scintillating facts about current affairs, the British constitution and the one unavoidable truth for later life: never, under any circumstances, become a teacher in a UK secondary school. He even shuddered at the very thought.

Luke's practical skills were worse. At one point, he clearly had the drawn map upside down in his hand. But being both male and middle class, he refused to see the error of his ways. The inanimate object was clearly at fault.

The garage was situated in a quiet back street, three hundred yards from the sea front. As Mrs Bartlett had been correct about the crowds, it took a while for JoJo to find somewhere to park; it did not help that she needed a space the size of an aircraft hangar.

The grey garage door had not been painted for decades. The padlock was the size of a boxer's fist. But the key worked on the first try. JoJo entered first and instantly gave an hysterical shriek. Luke thought the old man may have been capable of booby trapping the entrance, but there was a much more ordinary explanation, a cobweb of chilling proportions for any arachnophobe, had engulfed JoJo's entire head.

'Get it fucking off!'

Luke was not keen to assist as he was a fellow sufferer, but ultimately grasped the seriousness of his position and gingerly at first began to clear the webbing. Thankfully, neither of them saw the huge, giant house spider that fell to the floor and scuttled for the nearest drain.

It took a few minutes for either to feel brave enough to go inside. Luke was nudged into leading the way.

He found the light switch and turned it on. JoJo regained her composure and, seeing no further cobwebs, eased Luke aside.

The first thing she noticed was the writing desk, identical to the one in Ruben Miles's quarters at The Apple Orchard Retirement Community. On top of it was a large, old-fashioned leatherbound ledger. Next to that were four identical shoeboxes, stacked neatly. JoJo scanned the rest of the garage and found it almost empty. The only exception was a dark wood wardrobe opposite the writing desk.

Luke had picked up the ledger, requiring both hands.

'It's really heavy.'

There was nothing on the cover to suggest its contents.

JoJo opened up the ledger and instantly recognised the red, looping calligraphy. She read the words quickly.

To whom it may concern

'My name is Ruben Miles and I have lived a very long life. Some would say too long a life, and I am not sure that I can disagree with that.
However, it has been an interesting life, some may say an extraordinary one. I have lived through and even participated in some of the most historic and tragic events of the last century. The twentieth century was no ordinary century. The following is an account of my part in it.
This is my confession, I will leave it for others to judge me.'

'Fuck me, he's already written an autobiography!'

'Are you sure?'

JoJo was flicking through the many pages.

'Pretty fucking sure!'

They both came to the obvious question simultaneously.

'So, why did he want you to record his story?'

'Exactly. That is now *the* question. The only question.'

Neither came up with an immediate answer.

Luke opened the shoebox on top of the pile. It was full of black and white photographs. The first one depicted a very young man, really just a boy, in army uniform. On the back was written in black ink:

Army training camp April 12th 1916

John Burgess.

Luke passed it to JoJo. She put down the ledger carefully. Like most Millennials, JoJo preferred visual learning to written learning.

'It's him. It is recognisably him.'

Luke was scanning through the large collection.

'Who's the guy with the rounders bat? He is way too fat to be Ruben.'

JoJo had done some googling when Ruben Miles first mentioned his name and knew instantly who the picture would be of.

'That's Babe Ruth. Believe it or not, probably the most famous person in America at that time.' The writing on the back said:

The Sultan of Swat doing his second favourite thing! June 12th 1927

RM

Based on what the old man said, JoJo knew what the Babe's *favourite* thing was. The initials on the back suggesting who the photographer was.

There were over a hundred photographs in the first box. On the lid was written:

1916 – 1929

The second box said, *1929 -1945*.

The other two boxes covered the second half of the century.

'Hey, look at these.'

Luke had opened the desk drawer and took out a stack of faded envelopes.

'Don't open any, I need to take all this in.'

JoJo sat on the writing chair, still searching through the photographs. There was only one photo that she had seen before.

Even in black and white, the ladies were striking and clearly sisters.

On the back it said simply:

The de Villiers Sisters – August 25th 1939

RM

It was the only evidence the old man had ever proffered forward during their conversations for corroboration purposes. The Specialist and her doomed sister Eleanor, smiling in Hyde Park several months before national and personal catastrophe. Why had he not shared more?

'I don't understand,' she said, as she flicked through more pictures. The one of Abe Edelman and his wife smiling in their garden in the south of France being particularly poignant.

'Why didn't he show me more of these?'

Luke was too busy flicking through a pile of letters to answer.

'Look at this letter, it's from one of his kids.'

'I told you not to.'

It was from Rose, the eldest of the children abandoned by Ruben Miles when he took them to his mother's house after the fire that killed his wife and youngest child before he fled to Spain. It was written in 1953, on the day she turned twenty-one. It was addressed to Du Cane Court. She explained that his mother had given her the address.

JoJo read it with incredulity. It was a straightforward plea not to be excluded from his life. She told her father that, although her brother wanted nothing to do with him, she wanted reconciliation. She did not ask for money. She just wanted to know her father and have him in her life. She was getting married and she asked if he would meet her fiancé. She enclosed a photograph of the handsome fiancé, clad in his navy uniform.

Of course there was no evidence of any reply. More unanswered questions, at least for now. Maybe if she read all the many letters, as well as the hefty manuscript, she would have all the answers that she now agitated for.

Luke was now looking through the wardrobe. He emerged, holding gingerly the gun that executed Obersturmbannführer Peiper. Not that there was any mention of that.

'Put it down!'

Luke was dangerous enough with a stapler.

There was a uniform and other miscellaneous possessions.

JoJo was having difficulty processing it all. And then she found some letters from the Specialist and her heart missed a beat.

Q AND A

JoJo had never been to a funeral, never mind help to organise one. But Mrs Hazel Wharton was still incapacitated with whatever private shitshow she was dealing with, and so JoJo continued to liaise with the funeral directors. Of course, she was merely confirming the instructions that the old man had left on his writing desk.

One task she was happy to take on was trying to contact Carolyn de Villiers. JoJo was sure that, if she was still alive, she would want to attend the funeral. The letters she had sent Ruben Miles were interesting, although unsettling, almost as if some aspects of them were written in a kind of code. They were dated from the mid-1960s and the last one appeared to be from 1997, although the date on the envelope postcode was smudged and no date was written on the letter. The letter had mentioned the recent funeral of Princess Diana and so JoJo was able to conclude that the letter was written in the late summer or early autumn of 1997.

There were seven letters in total and two had her address written on them, the latest one from 1993. It was a longish shot. Would she be alive? If she was, did she live at the same address? Would she still have all her marbles? JoJo made a quick calculation that as she was perhaps up to twenty years younger than the old man, at least according to him. This would place her in her in mid to late eighties.

She tried and failed to track down a telephone number. She resorted to an act she had never done before. She wrote and posted a letter. Did people really communicate in such a primitive fashion? She asked her smirking father this question later in the afternoon and got a twenty minute monologue on how spoilt her Millennial generation were as a response.

Her phone rang two days later as she was trying and failing to concentrate on an essay about the expansion of the Cold War into Asia in the 1950s.

'Is that Miss Bartlett?'

The voice was refined, but clearly not that of a very old woman. JoJo concurred that she was Miss Bartlett, although had never previously been addressed in this manner. She quite liked it.

'My name is Eleanor De Villiers, you sent my mother a letter.'

'I see your mum named you after her sister.'

The lady seemed taken aback by JoJo's knowledge of the family.

'How did you know about my name?'

'That is a long story. Is your mother no longer with us?'

Her dad had told her that this was the most polite way of asking that question, if she needed to.

'No, she is still with us, but her memory is not always what it was. She lives in a retirement home now as she isn't very mobile and did not want to be a burden to my brother or I. She can still be rather formidable when she wants to be.'

JoJo outlined the reasons for reaching out to her mother.

'She has never mentioned him, but then my mother has never shared too much about her career. She says she was a civil servant, but over the years she has hinted at a few things that make that harder to believe...'

'Well, Ruben Miles certainly had a few interesting stories about your mother.'

'And he knew my mother professionally?'

'Yes, but he also knew her socially, he went out with your mother's sister, just before she died.'

'You seem more informed about my family history than I am.'

But she sounded more intrigued than annoyed.

'The funeral is next week, in Newcastle. Do you think she would like to come? I would love to meet your mother. Because of the stories I have been told, I would so much like to meet her.'

This was a calculated gambit and it paid off.

'I think she might, but I will need to check with her, of course. I will go and see her this afternoon. I should be able to take time off work to take her.'

JoJo had a feeling that Eleanor de Villiers might have some questions for her about her own mother.

JoJo was thrilled the following day as she got a polite but short text message confirming that Eleanor de Villiers was bringing her mother, AKA the Specialist, to the funeral.

Luke was clearly underwhelmed.

'You said that the lady said her mother's memory had gone.'

'Not in those exact words, she said it was in and out. I want to see how *in* she might be.'

'What are you hoping to find out?'

'What she knows about the memory experiments for one thing. And of course anything that she can shed a light on after World War Two. I mean, he crammed a lot into the first half of the twentieth century, I am sure he would have kept, you know, busy.'

'But you've got his book. Surely, that is all you need.'

JoJo had barely glanced at it yet. She had been too busy trying to track down the Specialist and persuade the inmates of The Apple Orchard Retirement Community to do the right thing.

'Yes, but I also think Carolyn de Villiers may have some interesting stories of her own.'

'So, you are already thinking about your next project, right?'

Luke had been joking.

'Well, I want to finish off Ruben's story first.'

But she was excited. Perhaps once she had finished the story of Ruben Miles, she could move on to the enigmatic and captivating Carolyn de Villiers. There was definitely another story to be told there.

A LONG TIME IN COMING

Queen Victoria had still been on the throne when Ruben Miles was brought home screaming by his mother from the Cottage hospital in Morpeth in 1899. When he studied at the Royal Grammar School in Newcastle, Edward the Caresser was still fondling the wives of his best friends with abandon. Ruben Miles had been a boy who turned into a man in the trenches of northern France. He had marvelled at the brave new modern world that was New York in the 1920s, and he was able to contrast that with the misery, confusion and inevitability of what the depression and subsequent wartorn era had sown. He has seen the very worst that mankind could conjure for his own species.

He had lived soberly through it all, perhaps for his age one of the more unexpected of scenarios. His memory appeared to be extraordinary. JoJo Bartlett had researched hyperthymesia extensively on the internet. It is an *extremely* rare condition. Experts felt that in the entire last century, there was evidence for approximately fifty cases of the syndrome. There was no explanation as to how or why the condition had developed. However, there was research that was robust and difficult to challenge. Some people really did have the ability to remember in extreme detail all the days of their lives, usually from mid to late childhood. Most individuals felt that they had been cursed.

Even the anecdotal, circumstantial evidence was favourable. All known men with the condition had been left-handed. They all could effortlessly recall the events from many years before with perfect clarity, as if they were watching a film of their own life. But none of them had lived a life quite like Ruben Miles. It is not as if he commuted to the same office for forty dreary years.

These were thoughts occupying the mind of JoJo Bartlett as she stood in the cemetery in West Jesmond with a small gathering of mourners. Predictably, only a handful of the inmates of The Apple Orchard Retirement Community had made it to the service. Mrs Hazel Wharton was still ashen and speechless.

The service was short and secular, at the old man's firm insistence. He had held no regard for religion, organised or otherwise, of whatever flavour. He had been vociferous on the subject with JoJo on several occasions.

'One of man's greatest follies,' he said, 'alongside bloody nationalism.'

Surprisingly, the brief words spoken had been quite moving. The poem the old man chose as a reading was *Sailing to Byzantium* by William Butler Yeats.

> *That is no country for old men. The young*
> *In one another's arms, birds in the trees*
> *—Those dying generations—at their song,*
> *The salmon-falls, the mackerel-crowded seas,*
> *Fish, flesh, or fowl, commend all summer long*
> *Whatever is begotten, born, and dies.*
> *Caught in that sensual music all neglect*
> *Monuments of unageing intellect.*

JoJo didn't like poetry; it all seemed a bit pointless. And yet somehow, she felt the words were appropriate, even if she could not articulate why.

Luke had seemed quite affected by the service, gripping her hand quite tightly. If JoJo had known that Luke was waiting for the appearance of the devil at the graveside, she may have come to a less flattering conclusion regarding his emotions.

Carolyn de Villiers was not the only invited guest from the past. Via the fledgling UK Facebook website, JoJo had managed to connect with a granddaughter that Ruben Miles had never met. She was the daughter of Rose, the abandoned daughter that had wrote to her father in the 1950s wanting a blessing for her marriage. JoJo tried to imagine why she had wanted to come. But come she had.

'I know nothing of my mother's family, nothing.'

'So, your mother never reconciled with her father?'

'He never even answered her letters.'

JoJo was often aghast that she could feel empathy and even sympathy for an old man who had committed such heartless and inexplicable acts, even if there were things that he had done that she approved of.

The granddaughter was called Olivia, and JoJo agreed that they should have a more meaningful exchange of information in less formal surroundings. The two would become friends, despite their near twenty-year age difference.

Carolyn de Villiers more than lived up to her billing, but only when her daughter was out of earshot. It would appear that her subterfuge skills were still functioning intact.

'I have as many questions for you as you seem to have for me,' she said, as JoJo handed her a generous dry sherry. Although wheelchair-bound and a little hard of hearing, her eyes told you that she was still as smart as a whip; her memory only faltering when her daughter hovered with a plate of dubious looking vol-au-vents. The Apple Orchard Retirement Community had been most forceful in their desire to cater for the wake. Most of the inmates managed to make an effort to attend *that.*

'I can't believe he lived so long, although I suppose a lifetime of not drinking or smoking had one tangible benefit.'

'I've been recording his life story, he told me a lot about you and your sister. You both meant a lot to him.'

JoJo did not add that he seemed to have cared more for the de Villiers sisters than his own wives and children.

'He also wrote an autobiography. I'm going to start reading it now. I found your letters to him, that was how I tracked you down.'

'I had not seen him for nearly forty years, but we kept in contact occasionally, usually when someone we worked with had died.'

This was at least partially true.

'Does anyone still know you as the Specialist?'

JoJo had been dying to ask and as there was no fitting time that was appropriate for such a question, she simply blurted it out at the first opportunity.

Carolyn de Villiers laughed as loudly as a wheelchair-bound old lady can.

'My God, it must be over thirty years since anyone has

called me that.'

She looked at JoJo with a keen gaze.

'I'm beginning to think that Ruben Miles may have told you an awful lot about my past, Miss Bartlett.'

'Call me JoJo, please.'

'And perhaps what he did not tell you might be in the autobiography you mentioned.'

JoJo conceded that she hoped so.

'I am happy to answer your questions. But can we do it when my daughter is not around, she would make such a fuss. And another thing, you have heard of the Official Secrets Act?'

'Yes, he mentioned it a few times.'

'Good, because whatever I tell you could get us both into trouble. Unless you are as sensible as you look and tell no one until after I fall off my perch.'

JoJo had hoped the questions could start immediately, but the return of her daughter led Carolyn de Villiers to seamlessly metamorphose into her previous incarnation of doddering old lady.

She was going to have to wait a little longer.

PENDING PROJECTS

With the burial of Ruben Miles and the accompanying traditions and customs completed, JoJo Bartlett realised that any remaining answers to the numerous unanswered questions about his life were going to come from just two remaining sources. The first would be the unread memoir discovered in the dusty Tynemouth lockup. The question of the accuracy of the old man's words and of course the truth regarding the diagnosis of hyperthymesia were other factors to ponder. Secondly, the re-entrance of the Specialist into the life story of Ruben Miles offered both the chance of more corroboration of what JoJo had already learnt and the tantalising prospect of more knowledge of the old man's post-war years. As Ruben Miles had said memorably into her tape recorder on their last pre-hospital meeting,

'We are going to have to speed up, we are only up to the end of the Second World War and that is not even *half* of my story.'

JoJo had been listening to all the tapes again in chronological order. She felt that was an important step before she started reading the manuscript. To the best of her knowledge, Ruben Miles had never contradicted himself or given differing versions of any of his life episodes during their many conversations. Would it be the same with the written words?

She was also excited about arranging to visit Carolyn de Villiers at the beginning of the school summer holidays, an alluring five weeks into the future. She hoped to have read all the manuscript by then with of course plenty of notes in her neat shorthand. The Specialist had been most accommodating and promised to tell JoJo everything she knew about Ruben Miles and, as she said before she left for home, 'It's fair to say that there are some events worthy of a wider audience. Why don't I send you a letter when I have had time to gather my thoughts on the subject?'

JoJo felt that at least some of these stories *must* shed some illumination on what actually happened to Ruben Miles in that

London hospital in 1941 and what impact it had on his future actions.

She shared these thoughts with Luke Miles three days after the funeral. Luke's mood had improved considerably after the failure of the devil to pitch up at either the non-religious ceremony or the below average buffet.

'At least I can come with you. I will have finished my GCSEs by then.'

JoJo may have conceded that this was true, but hardly the most important aspect of the upcoming adventure.

'There are many things that I hope the book and the Specialist can help answer, although I am aware that this may not be the case. I mean, what happened to his mother and of course his abandoned children? I mean, it was good to meet Olivia at the funeral, but I'm not sure she is going to be able to help too much with that. Then there is the whole wider family dynamic, the bank job, time in prison, was he a super spy?'

'I don't get it.'

This was not an uncommon statement from the mouth of Luke Miles.

'What?'

'I don't get why you care so much about an old dead man that you are not even related to.'

'I think you should read the book.'

'I don't read books.'

'OK, well then listen to the tapes. Your relative had one extraordinary life, and I only know half of it. I mean, he could have been literally involved in anything based on the first half of the story.'

Luke Miles seemed to have forgotten that, without his elderly deceased relative, his role in JoJo Bartlett's life would have been restricted to being the odd boy from next door who was not very good at washing cars.

JoJo's expression seemed to confer this.

'Besides, I might want to be a writer one day and it could make a good book.'

'Are you going to try and get his life story published?'

'Maybe, I don't know. I would imagine that is a very difficult thing to do. I just know I want to find out as much as I can. I think I owe him that. It's why he talked to me in the first place, isn't it? To get his story out there.'

'But he had already written his story.'

'Another question I would like an answer to.'

Luke Miles agreed to listen to the tapes. To his utter surprise, not only did he listen to them all *twice*, but his conversion to the project was almost a religious experience.

HALF-TIME COMPLICATIONS

'**Y**ou have got to be kidding me!'

JoJo was in the family bathroom, the same disappointing shade of yellow that it had been since she was seven years old. Interior design taste and redecorating were not staple skills of the Bartlett household.

No matter how many times she looked at the damn thing in her hands it told her the same disastrous story.

JoJo was a serial pragmatist and so she went to her bedroom and googled a few quick questions. The answers were far from reassuring. The chance of better news was only 9%. Not a lot to hang your future on.

Disappointingly, she found herself thinking more about her parents' reactions than the consequences for her own future. I mean, proving your mother right, is there anything more depressing? She literally gave her head a shake.

Luke Miles had sat the last of his GCSE exams three weeks after the funeral. With JoJo's considerable help, he managed to scrape six passes; not that he would know this for nearly three months. He knew that they had gone better than his mock exams, but that was not really something to shout about, as he had failed them all. He thought he would spend the summer worrying about his exam results. He was wrong.

When he got her text message, he predictably misread the tone. He thought he might be about to get dumped. Instead, he felt he got dumped *on*. Not the kind of response JoJo could use.

'The number of times we have done it is not the key point,' she said patiently when Luke rambled on about statistics, probability and the unfairness of it all.

When he made another factually incorrect observation, JoJo lost her temper.

'Well, I think we can safely assume you fucking failed biology.'

She was not wrong.

'But we used a condom.'

'And it clearly did not work.'

JoJo Bartlett remembered distinctly the old man telling her that the reason he married his third wife, Katy, in London during the war, was because she had fallen pregnant the first time that they slept together. She failed to appreciate the irony of now having at least something remotely in common with him.

JoJo had a sudden premonition of Luke getting down on one knee.

'Don't,' she said out loud.

'What?'

'Just don't get too weird on me, OK? As you can see, I am having enough problems trying to process this.'

'What are you going to do?'

She gave him a withering look.

'You mean what are *we* going to do?'

He suddenly looked even younger than he was.

'That's what I meant.'

Except it wasn't.

'Well, by my reckoning, once again based on the sub-standard quality of secondary school sex education, I can either have the foetus killed, give it away to some random stranger... or I could ruin my entire life.'

Luke took a few minutes to *not* process these options.

'Unless of course you are not pregnant and the test is wrong.'

This was the first time he had mentioned the word out loud.

'On the basis of probability, I think I have more chance of bumping into the Queen at the chip shop.'

'There is less than a 9% chance that the test is wrong, according to the internet.'

'When will we know?'

'Depressingly quickly, I should think.'

She was right.

EPILOGUE

Ms Carolyn De Villiers
Ascot House
23/9/06

Dear JoJo,

It was very nice to meet you last week, although of course it could have been under nicer circumstances.

As we discussed, I do have more information that I can share with you regarding some aspects of Ruben's life. In particular, his relationship with both British and American intelligence dating from his hospitalisation during the war after the tragic death of my sister Eleanor.

From that point our paths continued to cross for more than two decades as we both found ourselves working in the US, usually for the same side! Most of my information refers to Ruben's activities with the CIA, either officially or not...

I have been rereading my old diaries and other documents and there is a lot that I can share with you that I think will help you with finishing his story.

As I am sure you are aware, some of these activities come under the realm of the Official Secrets Act, something I seem to be less concerned about as I contemplate my own mortality.

I would appreciate you respecting my desire not to share any of our discussions with my family for personal reasons. After I have gone, I have no issue with you publishing any of the material I share with you.

Kind regards,
Carolyn de Villiers

Printed in Dunstable, United Kingdom